The Dungeon

Rob Horner

ISBN 978-1-64471-982-4 (Paperback)
ISBN 978-1-64471-983-1 (Digital)

Copyright © 2019 Rob Horner
All rights reserved
First Edition

All rights reserved. No part of this publication may be reproduced, distributed, or transmitted in any form or by any means, including photocopying, recording, or other electronic or mechanical methods without the prior written permission of the publisher. For permission requests, solicit the publisher via the address below.

Covenant Books, Inc.
11661 Hwy 707
Murrells Inlet, SC 29576
www.covenantbooks.com

For Jill, who always believes.

Part 1

The Dungeon

CHAPTER 1

Zachary

Zachary awoke to pain.

Before opening his eyes, before registering any sounds or smells, he felt pain. Every muscle in his body ached with a dull fire, like he'd participated in a marathon exercise regimen the day before, or as if he'd suffered a fall, or a beating. Nothing felt sharp, which seemed a good thing. He groaned as he felt hard earth beneath his side, drawing his sore arms and legs in close in order to rise. Muscles protested, but everything worked.

He opened his eyes.

He was in a cavern, or a cave, of some kind. Dim light, diffuse and with a slightly gray tint, like cloudy sunlight seen through dirty glass, illuminated the area. There were others here with him, four in front, and what sounded like several more behind. The cavern wanted to spin when he tried to raise his head, so he looked down at his feet, waiting for the vertigo to stop. The floor really was of hard-packed dirt, with a loose film of grit that probably wouldn't hold a footprint.

Zachary saw that he wore a brown leather vest over a dingy, once-white shirt. The shirt appeared and felt like it was made of some thin material, spun cotton or silk. It was tucked into leather breeches and bloused above the waistband like a poet shirt. Raising his arms, he noticed the full sleeves, though thankfully no frills at the cuffs. No matter what had happened, at least he hadn't woken up dressed like a pirate. The breeches were tucked into the tops of calf-high, black, leather boots. He wiggled his toes, finding the fit acceptable, though firmer in the sole than he was used to.

"God, I feel drunk," one of the others, a woman, mumbled, drawing Zack's attention.

He slowly raised his head, thankful when the room stayed still. He felt a dull ache behind his eyes, though nothing he couldn't tune out. Stretching his arms out as he took his first good look around, he felt pops in his shoulders as tension released, which removed a good measure of his discomfort. Craning his head first left, then right, he worked a few kinks out of his neck as well, almost ridding himself of his headache.

The woman was just a few inches shorter than him, maybe 5'9" or 5'10". She wore the exact same clothing he did, leather vest over blouse, breeches and boots, though he could clearly see the faint outlines of tattoos beneath her sleeves. She had dark red hair that ended at her shoulders, with a single thick strand at the front, like a forelock, that had been dyed purple. The forelock caught the eyes, focusing the attention on her face, which was narrow and vulpine. Brown eyes squinted in discomfort looked back at him, under brown eyebrows; red wasn't her natural color. Her nose was small and sharp, her mouth wide with thin lips. She had a good body, long and lean, but there was something about her that prevented him from categorizing her based on her appearance.

"What're you lookin' at?" she demanded. "And what the hell happened to me?"

He didn't answer, just let his eyes rove the room, a tactic ingrained in him after long years of experience first as a patrol officer, then as a detective with the Virginia Beach Police Department: Look first, listen always, act with discretion.

The cavern appeared to be natural: earthen floor, rock walls a slightly lighter shade of brown, bulbous ceiling above. Perhaps sixteen feet across and roughly square, there were few features that one might call distinguishing. There was certainly no visible light source, no opening to sky that could account for his ability to see.

He pressed down a momentary feeling of panic, of being trapped. More sounds reached his ears from the others in the room; more of them were waking up. Soon, he knew, the questions would start, for which no one would have any answers. Better to determine what he could from the two things he could see that looked different, before everyone started talking. Off in one corner was a small pile of wood, like a carpenter's leftovers. First, though, he wanted to check out the door.

Moving helped him focus, brought his thoughts back to clarity. Whatever had been done to him, whatever drug had been used to render him unconscious, was clearing his system. What had he been doing? The last thing he could remember clearly was leaving the police station at the end of a fourteen-hour day.

He'd entered his quiet townhouse and then... nothing.

Four steps brought him from where he'd risen to the far wall, which featured a wooden door made of thick, dark planks banded together by iron straps. The door didn't completely fill the opening; there were gaps all around, but whatever lay on the other side was shrouded in darkness. There was a crude iron bolt running from inside the wood of the door on the left side, disappearing into the wall, holding it closed. There didn't seem to be a bolt handle, or any way to unlock the door. There were no hinges visible on this side.

A nail had been driven into the center of the door, and suspended from it on a crude yarn string was a small wooden placard. The placard might be a foot tall, maybe twice that in width. Words were etched into the wood of the placard. No, not etched, these looked carved, rough at the edges, almost like the letters were formed by hand. But who did that in this day and age of laser cutters and Dremel tools?

Welcome to the Dungeon.
Make it to the end and live.
Watch out for traps.

CHAPTER 2

Zachary

"What the hell?" the tall redhead said, coming up behind him. "What do they mean, dungeon? I didn't sign up for this shit."

Zachary turned, noticing again a small pile of wood off in one corner, before focusing on the group of people behind him. Everyone was on their feet now, a ragtag group of men and women, dressed alike but as different as possible in every other way. Tall and short, young and old, eight other faces were turned toward him and the woman. They had a few seconds before the questions started, and then maybe a few more before the questions turned to shouting.

Zachary didn't think of himself as a leader. He was the solid cop, the by-the-book follower of leads. It was the brash guys, balls forward, who took the risks and got the accolades, when they didn't end up in the hospital or the morgue. At six feet tall and just over two hundred pounds, with features a little too thick to be called refined, and thinning, light brown, brush-cut hair, he cultivated the image of "not the sharpest tool in the shed." No one would ever accuse Zachary Pavese of being a coward, but they also wouldn't look to him to take charge.

The redhead next to him apparently had no such compunctions.

"This is some serious bullshit," she said, her voice sharp, with a hint of a New England accent that sharpened her vowels but stopped just shy of irritating. "'Just sign this paper, Liz,' they said, 'and we'll get the charges dropped. You just gotta do this one thing, like, complete a small test.' Is this what they meant?"

She didn't seem to expect an answer. Or if she did, she was too impatient to wait for one. Her hands came together in front of her, clasping, fingers twisting around themselves nervously. She started to say something else, then gave her head a quick shake, short red hair flying. Her lips moved soundlessly, almost like she was arguing with herself.

Some of the others were coming up now. Zack took notice of a few, cataloged features and mannerisms by habit, classifying them based on years of experience. Two of the men were about the same height as Zack, both white, but the similarities ended there. One had broad shoulders on a lean frame. He wore expensive wire-rimmed glasses over intelligent brown eyes. Stepping up to the door, he gave the sign a brief glance, dismissed the redhead with a practiced disinterest that spoke to arrogance, then approached.

"I'm Matt," he said, offering a hand. Zack took it automatically, gave his first name in return, noting manicured fingernails and a smooth palm, though the fingertips bore the calluses of hard use. He was probably a lawyer or an accountant, someone who spent a lot of time clacking away at a keyboard. "A dungeon, huh? So this is what they meant."

Before Zack could ask him to explain, the other man reached the door. Though they were all dressed alike, the clothing looked slovenly on his fat frame. Extra jowls quivered as he stuck a meaty hand into the gap between door and frame, giving it an experimental tug, then several quick jerks in and out. The door didn't budge, didn't even so much as rattle. There was more to that bolt than a simple lock.

Jerking his hand back with a grunt, then rubbing it over his pig-bald head, he turned beady eyes on Zachary and Matt. The paper-pusher looked down, but Zachary met the fat man's gaze. This man was a bully, easy to recognize, easy to deal with. He'd probably lived his whole life with people giving in to him because of his size and aggressive attitude. "Skank's right," he muttered, "this is some bullshit!"

"What the hell did you call me?" the redhead sneered. "I heard that. I heard you say that." Suddenly she was in front of the fat man, her brown eyes glaring a challenge. There was something else in that gaze, Zack realized. This woman wasn't completely sane. He'd seen that kind of stare before, on a homeless man he and his partner stopped in the street, right before the guy jumped on him. It was a look that disregarded every learned instinct—size didn't matter, physical strength didn't matter. *Nothing mattered*. It said, *I will hurt you, and you can't stop me.*

Before Zack could step in to try to defuse the situation, before he was even sure he wanted to—a person with *that* stare could turn on anyone—the tallest man in the room stepped up between them. The guy had to be 6'4", at least, with shoulders like a professional football player. He placed one large black hand on the fat man's chest, and turned deep brown eyes on the redhead. "Ma'am, please," he said, his voice a rumbling, gravelly bass that Al Green would envy, but quiet and articulate, "let's not do anything rash."

The redhead didn't back down, though her eyes lost some of their heat. "You heard what he called me! Why should I let him call me that?"

Speaking to her, but now looking at the other man, Smooth Voice said, "I'm sure he didn't mean anything by it. Isn't that right, sir? He's just as confused as we all are. I'm sure he's sorry for it, aren't you?"

There wasn't a moment's hesitation. "Yeah, sure, I'm sorry. Just nervous, is all," the big man said, looking down as he answered.

The redhead somehow seemed to stare through the football player for a moment before backing away, once again shaking her head. Zack caught something about "how many days" and "when will they start again?" Then, "I don't know if I can handle it if they start again," before her words faded away completely.

"Something's not right about this," the only other woman said. Short and a little thick-bodied, she had a mop of greasy, dirty blond hair and intelligent green eyes. Those weren't laugh lines around them, however. Zack recognized this type as well, and suddenly something clicked for him. "Something's not right about you all," she said, pointing a dirty finger at the redhead, then the piggy guy, then the black tight end, and finally at Matt and Zachary. "You all seem to know what's going on here. But I don't have a clue where we are, or why I'm here. Last thing I remember I was leaving the library."

This earned a snicker from Matt, but before she could say something about his laugh, and before Zack could say anything to separate himself from the others she'd named, one of the other young black men spoke up. "Yeah, what she said. I ain't supposed to be here, you know? I was in da library, too, a'ight. Lookin' at some porn, then bam! Here I am witchew people."

Though he was the shortest guy in the room, nothing about him could be called scrawny. His dark skin was visible through the white poet shirt, mainly because it was as tight on him as it was on Piggy-Man, but where the larger man's clothes bulged from fat, his stretched over a well-developed chest and arms.

THE DUNGEON

Seeing everyone's attention on him, he shrugged muscular shoulders and said, "I'm DeShaun, by the way, but most people jes call me Li'l Bit, 'cause, you know." He indicated his height with one hand held horizontally over his head. "All 'cept for da ladies, you know?" he chuckled.

"So you didn't ask to be here?" a much thinner, maybe a little older, black man asked. He spoke fast, words almost tripping over themselves. His clothes hung on him like his shoulders were a coat hanger, all bone and no meat. His teeth looked like blackened nubs, what few there were, and small scars surrounded his light-skinned mouth, like old, healed burns. It all spoke of a drug addiction, probably methamphetamines or crack-cocaine. But his eyes were arresting. Zack wasn't sure he'd ever seen tan eyes before. "Like, the men didn't come to you and tell you about this test? They didn't offer to get you off?"

"The hell you think I am?" Li'l Bit shouted back. "I wouldn't let no guys get me off! Now if some thick-ass hottie was to offer, well, heh, you know. But no, man, I ain't got no idea whachew talkin' 'bout."

A small kid, no taller than Li'l Bit and probably weighing about as much as Skinny Guy, raised his right hand, as if asking permission to speak. "I was in the shelter, and now I'm here." His voice was soft, almost feminine. When he looked up, Zack could see the story of loss in his eyes, almost identical to those of the shorter woman. Another homeless person, maybe even an orphan, with long hair that hadn't seen scissors in probably a year, bangs almost covering bright blue eyes. He had a wispy mustache struggling to life on his upper lip, almost invisible. "I'm scared," he said. "I don't know where we are, or where my friends are. I just...woke up here." Zack placed his age at somewhere between fourteen and eighteen; it was hard to be sure, with those soft features and quiet voice.

The short woman, the one who looked older than she probably was, moved over to the young man. Zack didn't catch everything she said to him, just her name as she offered it, Tory, and his in return, Eddie. The young man seemed reassured by her presence.

Before he'd been taken...wherever he was... Zachary had been working a string of disappearances among the homeless of Virginia Beach. It was a sad case, full of a lot of bad information, dead-end leads, and reluctant witnesses. Homeless people avoided police as a matter of course. Many of them had mental issues, quite often involving paranoia about government conspiracies and wanted nothing to do with Big Brother.

Most of his best information came from the benevolent souls who volunteered at the food kitchens, or who offered bedding for the night. They'd talk about a young girl who hadn't shown up in days, hoping she was all right, or the middle-aged man who had finally gotten off the sauce and was about to start a new job. They'd talk about them like they were already dead and buried, not just missing for a few days.

Neither this Tory nor Eddie fit any of the descriptions of those whose disappearances he'd been looking into, however. He wondered how many he hadn't known about.

"I didn't ask to be here," the last man, of medium height with brown hair over green eyes, said, "but I know where here is." Zack pegged him as middle-aged, somewhere in his forties. He didn't look overweight, though there was a softness about him that spoke of a less than physically demanding profession. Maybe a teacher?

THE DUNGEON

His words, though not loud, drew the attention of everyone. If he was bothered by it, he didn't let it show. Probably a teacher, then maybe even a professor.

"Okay then, spill it," the fat guy said, already moving away from the door and toward the teacher.

"Yeah, where is this?" the skinny guy added.

"We're in the labyrinth," he said, but something about how he said it sounded off.

"Okay, brainy boy, we know it's a labyrinth. It says so right there on the sign," the short woman said, stepping away from Eddie. "Dungeon, labyrinth, what's the difference?"

But the man shook his head. "Not just any labyrinth. This is *the labyrinth*, as in the famous dungeon built for King Minos."

"What the—" the fat man started to ask.

"I remember reading about that," Matt, the tall guy with glasses, said. "Didn't some archaeologist find it a couple of years ago?"

The shorter man nodded. "Magellan Enterprises funded the dig. They found Daedalus's labyrinth just south of Knossos, near the center of the island of Crete."

"Okay," Matt said, drawing out the syllables. "But that doesn't explain why we're here, or how we got here."

Li'l Bit shook his head, moving closer to the teacher. "It don't tell me shit, bro. I don' care nothin' 'bout no Crete or no No-Sus. I wanna know how the hell I got up in this place."

As he got closer, Zack noticed several tattoos on the well-built man's arms. Though the artwork was good, the thick lines and uneven pigment told him more than the designs. Those were prison tattoos.

Some of the others were moving closer as well. It looked like an almost classic case of the scared mob attacking the man with answers, rather than listening to his explanation. Zack moved for the first time since approaching the door, intent upon protecting the teacher. But even as the other seven—Eddie still hung back—crowded closer, a new voice filled the room, amplified and projected from the very walls.

"Ladies and gentlemen, welcome to *The Dungeon.*"

CHAPTER 3

Zachary

To a person, they all jumped. From hardened criminal to overweight bully, from the tall, aggressive woman to the shy and frightened young man, they jumped away from the walls, spinning to face all different directions, unconsciously backing toward the center of the room. Zack was no different, craning his neck, twisting, trying to identify a source. Was one side louder than the other? Did it only seem like it came from all directions because of the nature of the room, the walls?

"I know you have a lot of questions, but please hold them until I'm done. We have a lot of ground to cover before the live feed starts."

Zack thought the voice was familiar. An almost-remembered name tickled the back of his mind.

"Is that Mike Callahan?" the accountant, Matt, asked softly.

Zack nodded. That was the name. Mike Callahan was the host of innumerable game shows dating back some thirty years, most often heard now on the radio, touting one back pain cream or another.

"For those who don't know, I am Mike Callahan. And you are all about to compete in a brand-new reality game show. The ultimate reality game show. *The Dungeon.*"

A swell of orchestral music sounded, complete with tympani and cymbal. It sounded perversely similar to the *America's Got Talent* mini theme, probably written by the same composer.

"Hey, man, I didn't sign up for a game show!" the tall, skinny, black man said.

"Neither did I," both the redhead and the fat man said simultaneously.

"Well, let's address that first then, shall we?"

The redhead and the fat guy looked at each other, then nodded, as if agreeing to listen before saying anything else.

"Some of you were approached with an opportunity. A chance to wipe the slate clean of past sins, start over with a new identity. You weren't given a lot of details, but that was intentional. This is your briefing. Elizabeth, Matthew, Zippy, Daniel, and Richard—"

"Call me 'Big Rich,'" the tight-end sized man shouted.

"Very well, Big Rich. You five all signed the waivers. Survive, and be reborn."

"What about the rest of us?" Zack shouted, unsure where to aim his voice.

"For the other half, you didn't volunteer, but the opportunity is being given you nonetheless. For Eddie and Tory, a chance to get off the streets. For DeShaun, a way to escape a life sentence for a crime of passion."

"You won't get away with this," the teacher said. "I work for this company."

"This is kidnapping, plain and simple," Zachary yelled.

"Brian, Brian, Brian," the voice chided, a parent talking to a recalcitrant child. **"You *used* to work here. You threatened the interests of the company. Now, you don't exist, at least as far as any national registry will show."**

THE DUNGEON

"You can't do this! My family—" the teacher, Brian, trailed off. His eyes closed, hands fisted at his sides. He looked like a man coming to a hard decision or accepting a harsh reality.

"And you, Zachary. Weren't you warned to back off of your investigation? Weren't there hints that you were getting dangerously close to something too big for you to handle? You have also been erased from your digital existence. Like the others, should you survive, you'll be given a new identity. But be warned, should you try to reestablish your old life, you will find that Zachary Pavese has been a very bad cop."

Zachary didn't say anything. He schooled his features to stillness and held his anger in check. The ability to maintain a stony facade often worked in his favor. Far better to let them think him beaten. More opportunities might present themselves if they thought he was sufficiently cowed.

And there *had* been hints, some subtle, little questions from the captain, wondering why he cared so much, asking if he really thought "those people" were worth so much effort.

"Man, that's cold," Li'l Bit said.

"Are there no more questions then?" Zack had the distinct impression of a lecturer looking around the hall, making sure no one else wanted to raise a hand.

He looked up and met Matt's eyes, who indicated the nearest corner of the room with a quick tilt of the head. Looking closely, Zack was able to see a slight discoloration in the stone of the wall. Nothing so obvious as a reflection, but certainly an anomaly that could represent a camera lens. Scanning around, he noted similar small discolorations in all four corners, all high up, providing a complete view of the room.

"**Good. Let's get down to business,**" Mike Callahan said. "**As Brian already alluded to, this set is a fairly faithful recreation of a portion of Daedalus's labyrinth, with a few modern alterations. It has a set beginning and ending for one thing. Your goal is to get from one end to the other. It's as simple as that. Like our men promised when you met them, all you have to do is survive. But there is something special about almost every room that makes this a dangerous proposition.**"

"You talkin' 'bout dem traps?" Li'l Bit asked.

"**Give the man a prize! Yes, traps. Some are classics, painstakingly remade just as they existed thousands of years ago. Others are brand-new. Survive the traps, survive The Dungeon, and win your freedom.**"

"What about the Minotaur?" Tory asked.

"**You don't have to worry about him. We're saving that for season two.**" The voice issued a short laugh. "**The audience will be able to see everything you do, hear every word you say, though on a slight delay, of course. The only time you will hear my voice again will be when I introduce the show and give occasional updates. This is your last chance to ask questions.**"

Tory started to speak, then apparently thought better of it and remained quiet. Brian, the former employee, glared at one of the corners. He'd figured out where the cameras were. Or he'd always known.

It was the tall redhead, Elizabeth, who asked the question he hadn't thought of, but one which should have occurred to him. "You keep saying we just have to survive. But this is just a game show, right? People will be watching. You can't just kill us. That's not legal. So what does that mean?"

"Excellent. Straight to the heart of the matter. This is a reality game show. The traps are real. Your lives are in danger in every room, from every room. It's legal, because we have signatures saying you waive your rights to hold us responsible. It's legal, because for the moment, none of you exist. And it's legal because, for right now at least, the audience is made up of those who routinely pay money to watch people fight to the death, those who have no interest in attracting the attention of any country's authorities.

"No one will mourn your deaths, Elizabeth. On the contrary, they will cheer for them. Live or die, it's about the entertainment. The struggle. So make it a good one."

The tight end, Big Rich, shook his head and muttered, "I'm really starting to hate that guy."

"Join the club," Matt said.

"And now, I'll bid you all good luck, and happy running."

The room fell silent after the amplified voice disappeared. For several long moments, the ten strangers looked at each other, at the walls. Most of them cast quick glances at the barred wooden door, perhaps wondering what lay beyond it.

That's what Zack thought about. For maybe five seconds. Then he raised his hand and said into the silence, "I'm the cop. Well, if what that guy said is true, the ex-cop. I'm Zack."

For a second, no one said anything, and Zack felt a spike of fear. He knew, with the surety of instinct honed by years on the force, that they couldn't survive this alone.

Then the accountant raised his hand. "I'm Matt. I volunteered because I tried to embezzle from my company, and I didn't want to go to prison."

Surprisingly, the shy, young man, lanky hair hanging over his eyes, spoke next. His voice was firmer now, though it broke back into a near sob as he spoke. "I'm Eddie, and I'm only nineteen. I don't want to die in here."

"Tory," the stocky woman said. "Off the grid and proud of it."

That opened the flood gate, and most of the others offered their names and reasons for being in The Dungeon. Zack was thankful for the opportunity to put names and faces together. The redhead was Elizabeth, though she didn't say anything other than she set fire to a dumpster. Big Rich, or Big Dick, as Li'l Bit jokingly called him, before being glared to silence by the massive man, actually was a high school football star, before a shoulder injury ended one career and started him on another as a heroin addict. Both he and the redhead had willingly signed the waiver papers.

Li'l Bit just confirmed his name again and offered no details on his incarceration. "I don't know if it's better back in jail or in here, but I guess at least in here I gots a chance to get out."

The skinny black man was Zippy Brown, another volunteer. "I ain't quite right in the head anymore, ya know? I can't remember if I was right before I started smokin' da pipe, but I can sure as hell tell you it don't feel right bein' clean, neither. I'm gonna get higher than a mountain once we get through this."

The only holdout was the fat man with the bad attitude. Zack didn't remember what other name had been recited by the announcer. He resolved to try to find out, see if he could cool off that attitude, or at least try to keep it from aggravating too many of the others.

The last member of their group, Brian, didn't offer any other information. He did keep glancing at Zack, a

THE DUNGEON

look that projected a need to discuss something. Every police officer knew that look.

Before he could, the speakers in the walls once again blared to life, filling the large room with a much longer version of the orchestral fanfare they'd heard earlier. Once again Zack thought he could detect similarities to that variety show, the only reality television he'd ever looked forward to watching.

The group of ten tensed. He could see it like a ripple through the room, shoulders tightening, fists clenching. They looked like runners setting their feet at the starting line of a track meet. No one's gaze wandered the walls. Their eyes were drawn to the wooden door like iron filings to a magnet. Zack noticed Matt and Brian both stepping a little away from the center of the room, though whether it was to avoid something on the other side of the door or to avoid the rush to reach it, he wasn't sure.

As the music swelled to a crescendo, the announcer's voice came back, louder now, a slightly higher pitch, shouting over the music but also pumped up, infused with adrenaline. Zack had no doubt that if Mike Callahan wasn't being paid to MC the show, he'd have been among those paying to watch it.

"Welcome, ladies! Welcome, gentlemen! Welcome to *The Dungeon*!" As before, there was a fanfare blast when Mike yelled out the title of the show. **"Dungeons have existed since time out of mind. The word used to be synonymous with prison, as in "Throw him in the dungeon!" But then, sometime in the twelfth or thirteenth century BCE, a man named Daedalus constructed a massive labyrinth, filled with traps and monsters. Flash forward to more modern times, where pencil and paper warriors battle through similar circumstances to achieve fame and glory. We call**

these underground constructs dungeons, and that's what we have created for our players.

"We have ten contestants for you, ten people who have never met before today. Ten individuals who will have to come together as a team, or fall to the perils of The Dungeon." The music swelled again. There were other sounds, some easily recognizable to ears trained to the Hollywood special effects of the last twenty or thirty years—bright "ching" sounds like long blades sheathing and crisscrossing, whooshes of air that brought to mind billows of fire, deep rumbling/grating noises like stone sliding across stone. The viewers were most likely seeing an example of the traps in action, or a CGI representation of them. They heard no sounds from the audience, not even a pre-recorded ooh/aah track.

"The dangers are real, ladies and gentlemen. But so are the rewards. Freedom from any and all trouble in their previous lives, enough money to live in luxury wherever they choose. In exactly sixty seconds, the locked door will open and the game will begin. Every room is different, but one rule applies to them all.

"Five minutes. From the moment the first contestant sets foot in a new room, a five-minute timer will start. Leaving the room does not stop the timer. After five minutes, the room will be sealed and"—there was another loud whooshing sound—"**anyone left behind will die.**

"So once again I bid you all welcome to The Dungeon. Good luck to our contestants."

Mike Callahan's voice faded away with the music, and a new voice, female but obviously computerized, announced, *"Thirty seconds."*

Now the tension was palpable. Everyone but Matt and Brian grouped up a few feet from the door. Even shy Eddie moved forward, keeping close to Tory, who didn't seem to mind the company. Old-seeming and young-appearing, they were a mismatched pair, drawn to each other by shared circumstance. Zack noted this, noted also the glint in the short woman's eyes. Though his hands felt slick with nervous sweat, his heart pounding in his chest, sounding in his ears like a drum beating underwater, she stood firm and ready. Life had been hard on her, and it looked like she'd learned how to fight back.

"Fifteen seconds."

No one said a word. All eyes focused on the wooden door. Zack realized he'd been holding his breath and let it out.

Whatever the others were expecting, a gunshot as if to start a race, a horn, maybe another of those corny fanfares, they were disappointed. The only thing that happened to indicate the start of their trial was the sound of the iron bolt retracting into the wooden door.

The computerized voice said, **"Five minutes until room lockdown."**

CHAPTER 4

Zachary

"Well, that was anticlimactic," the tall accountant, Matt, said with a chuckle, pushing his glasses up on the bridge of his nose with a long finger. With the same finger, he flicked an imaginary strand of hair up off his forehead. The move looked habitual.

For a moment, no one moved. Heads turned left and right, faces scanning faces to see who would move first.

"Screw this," the fat man said, stepping through the grouped-up people. He didn't push people away so much as he expects them to move for him. He was a man assured his place because of his size, probably because he'd always been bigger than everyone around him. Maybe he'd once been in better shape too. "I signed up for this," he said, stepping up to the door. "I ain't gonna go back to jail, nuh-uh. Not for what they got me for."

He didn't seem to realize he was still talking, offering justifications. He reached for the door with its carved warning sign.

"You don' think they really gonna kill us, do ya?" the short, black man, Li'l Bit, asked. "I mean, they can't just kill us."

"Yeah, mebbe we should just, like, you know, sit tight," Zippy said. Zack had no problem remembering his name. His jerky movements and rapid-fire speech

THE DUNGEON

made him a poster child for Ritalin. Zippy just fit, as a name. "No way, no way they can just kill us for not playin'."

"Put it this way," Matt said, once again adjusting his glasses, "it makes great television to put us in danger, or at least make it appear that way, like that *Fear Factor* show. They probably won't kill us for waiting, but I'm betting they can make it so uncomfortable to stay that we have to move on."

The football player, Big Rich, answered, "I don't know about that." He spoke slowly, his deep voice thoughtful. "They've already broken a lot of laws just bringing some of you here. And I've been offered money before to fight, like underground. I went to see what it was all about, and those were some of the meanest, nastiest SOBs you've ever seen. If you can imagine the devil in a power suit, but like a hundred of them all in the same room, that's what these dudes looked like. There were women and men, black and white and Asian. Man, it didn't matter. Not a one of them would flinch if one of us fighters got killed. I think some of them would get off on it."

Li'l Bit nudged Zippy, "I take me a horny rich bitch and get her off, no problem."

Zippy ignored him.

Big Rich looked at Zack. "You're the cop in the room. You ever see anything like that? Tell 'em, man." He moved closer to the door.

These were the situations Zack hated. Put him in the middle of a mess, and his instincts would guide him through it, without thought. But if he needed to think about something, he preferred some time to weigh all the options. Too many bad decisions were made hastily. He agreed with Big Rich, however, that the people who had brought him here had already committed at least two felonies. Multiply that by five, since five of them were here against their will. How could he ignore that trend?

Before he could answer, Screw This said, "Yeah, well, I ain't planning on sitting here and waiting."

"Be careful," Brian, the ex-employee, said. His face was worried. He watched the fat man at the door with a sort of…what…anticipation?

"Four minutes."

"What do you know?" Zack asked before he could stop himself. Four years with his partner had ingrained the phrase into his lexicon, though he'd spent hours trying to get Mike to quit saying it. It sounded unprofessional.

But Brian answered, "I don't know what's beyond that door, not specifically. They had us design over a hundred different traps for this place. I—"

"What?" Elizabeth, the wild-eyed redhead said. "You designed this place? That's what you did for them?" Her shout drew everyone's eyes. Even Screw This looked back from his place near the door.

Brian shrank down. "Look, I was an engineer, all right? At first, they hired us to examine the old ruins, try to reverse engineer the traps, see how they worked. Then they wanted us to improve them, modernize them, see what else we could come up with." He looked down. "It was the coolest thing I'd ever been asked to do." His voice grew quieter. "None of us knew what they were going to use our designs for. When I found out, I left. I was going to expose them. Then—" He spread his hands, a gesture which summed up where his morality had gotten him.

The redhead turned away, her anger gone as fast as it appeared. She moved over to the small pile of wood stacked in the corner of the room. He looked away for a second, but felt his eyes drawn back to her. She'd turned away from the wood, apparently watching everyone else, though her gaze looked unfocused, like she was once again conducting an inner monologue.

"Screw this," Screw This said again, sticking a fat hand between the door and the door frame and giving it a yank.

The door didn't move.

"So it's still locked?" Zippy asked, starting forward.

The large man removed his hand from the edge of the door, placed it palm-forward against the wood, and gave a push. The door swung in easily, revealing nothing. The room beyond was absolutely dark, as though a curtain or some other kind of barrier yet remained between that room and this one, preventing the steady glow from penetrating even to the other side of the doorway.

"Can you see anything?" Tory asked, turning from her quiet conversation with Eddie and edging toward the door.

"Dark as the devil's ass," Screw This said, edging forward, thrusting his thick-jowled head into the doorway. "Can't see nuthin'."

"Maybe there's a light switch," Li'l Bit said.

"Because that totally fits with the setting?" Tory asked, her voice dripping with sarcasm.

Li'l Bit shrugged. "Just sayin'. Could be."

The fat man reached through the doorway, his arm invisible in the blackness. "Nuthin' on the wall. Feels like more rock, just like on this side."

"Everything is going to feel like rock and wood, at least on the surface," Brian said. Zack wondered if the man knew how to talk about something without sounding like a teacher. In these circumstances, with these characters, appearing to be a know-it-all might be the worst thing he could do.

The big tight end moved over to Brian, who seemed to wilt again. Apparently realizing how intimidating he looked, especially to someone so much shorter, the younger man held his hands up. "Look, man, if you know what's over there, just tell us."

Before the engineer could answer, a scream sounded from the doorway. The big guy, Screw This, appeared locked to the door frame, the right side of his body swallowed by darkness, the left hand clinging desperately, struggling to keep himself from being pulled the rest of the way into the room. He screamed again.

Zack stepped forward, reaching the door, joining Zippy, who was already grabbing at the fat guy's clothes, trying to pull him back. Zack forced himself to reach around the big man's waist, his arms not quite long enough to meet in the middle of the large gut. He pulled but felt a strong resistance. Between his effort and Zippy's, he thought they could pull the man back.

Then suddenly the resistance was gone, and the fat guy was laughing.

"What the hell, man?" Elizabeth asked.

The fat guy pulled his right arm, unscathed, back into the light. He wiggled his fingers to show they were all still attached.

"Dat's messed up!" Zippy said, backing away.

"Just screwin' with ya," the fat man said, still laughing.

"Three minutes."

"So are we moving or not?" Tory asked.

"I am," the fat man said. "Always better to move when someone says you'll die if you don't." And he stepped through the doorway.

Light blossomed in the room beyond the door, revealing another rough-hewn space carved out of the rock, almost identical to the room they stood in, though a good bit larger. Standing a pace beyond the door, Screw This looked around, said, "Huh, lights must

THE DUNGEON

be motion activated," then the floor opened beneath his feet and he disappeared with a surprisingly high-pitched shriek of surprise, cut off almost immediately by the wet, slapping sound of raw hamburger hitting a butcher's block.

CHAPTER 5

Matt

Watching the big man step into the next room, Matt shook his head. This was all so stupid. They were safer staying right here. No way they were in any real danger. No, the real risk lay in pushing blindly ahead. Then three things happened at once. Light filled the next room. The big guy disappeared through the floor with a girlish shriek. And that computer voice, which sounded so much like his Amazon Alexa that they had to be the same chick, announced, **"Five minutes until room lockdown,"** but the voice only sounded in the next room.

The big cop and the skinny black guy leaned in and looked down.

The shorter black guy with the chip on his shoulder about women said, "What da hell happened to 'im?" at the same instant that the huge football player started moving to the door. The skinny dude, Zippy, said something like "Oh my god!" then turned around and hurled all over the floor, which made the big man stop and dance back like he was avoiding a tackle.

"Gross," the redhead said, then turned back to her study of the pile of two by fours in the corner.

Matt moved up behind the throng, nose already wrinkling from the pungent smell of the crack head's vomit. The engineer moved with him, leaving only the short, homely chick and the slow kid in the middle of the room. Stepping up beside the cop, Matt took the spot just vacated by Zippy.

The room beyond the door, now as brightly lit as their current room, which wasn't saying much, appeared to be about twice as long, though not much wider. Maybe forty feet across, the far wall also sported a door, presumably leading further into the dungeon. There was a hole in the floor just on the other side of this door. It wasn't really deep, no more than ten feet or so, but the bottom featured rows of gleaming, metallic spikes, four or five feet long, at least, and all pointed up. A good number of those spikes were covered in thick, wet blood in two different shades of red.

The fat man must have leaned back as he fell, because no less than five or six spikes had impaled him. He had one through each leg. The right leg was pierced from the back of the thigh, and the left through the knee. There were others coming out at various points on his arms and torso. It was the one through his chest that probably killed him instantly, though. It looked like he'd taken it right where God split the tail to make the legs, driving up through his pelvis and gut until it emerged from the center of his chest.

"Jeez," he whispered, sickened and suddenly afraid. This was serious. Just like that, one of them was dead.

The fat guy's head had escaped impalement. Unseeing eyes stared up at them, a warning to get moving, but be careful.

"*Two minutes*," sounded from the walls around him, and suddenly everyone was moving, everyone was talking. They were panicking.

"Is he dead?" Tory asked.

When Zippy nodded, wiping his mouth but still leaning forward, left hand posted on left thigh like he wasn't sure he was done puking, she said, "They really did it." The kid next to her moaned.

The pit looked to be about ten feet across, extending far enough into the room that Matt knew he couldn't just broad jump it, but would need a bit of a running start.

"Let's take a moment," the announcer voice said, again coming from everywhere, reverberating through both rooms, **"to say goodbye to Daniel Kirkland, age forty-nine."**

"We don't have a moment," the cop said.

Matt could feel the press of time like a knife to his throat. Two minutes ago, he was certain this was all a bluff. Now, he couldn't wait to get out of this room, just as certain that it was suicide to stay.

"Hey, Rick," the cop, Zachary, said, turning to the big man.

"Richard or Big Rich," the big guy responded, coming up behind them. "Shit, what a sorry ass way to go," he said, looking over their shoulders.

"Daniel was a man obsessed with staying out of prison. His crime? Child prostitution."

"Think we can get across that?" Zack asked.

The big man studied it for a second. "Some guys probably could, but not me. I got a decent vertical, but to get across that I'd need a runnin' start, and this doorway is too short to allow that."

"Oh shit, so da shawt man is up, huh?" Matt hadn't noticed Li'l Bit coming up behind them.

Big Rich moved back, and the weird little man squeezed up beside them. "Yeah, I can make dat. But why?"

"Yeah, why?" Tory demanded. "Just because he can doesn't mean the rest of us can."

THE DUNGEON

Matt kept himself from saying anything about every man for himself. One look at the cop told him that wouldn't be appreciated.

"He was apprehended crossing the southern border, his eighteen-wheeler full of underage Mexican girls. There were more than fifty of them, destined for a short life of sexual servitude. He'd already raped a dozen of them."

"Those boards," Zack said, and Matt looked over at the pile, grasping the idea immediately.

Moving away from the door, he stepped up beside the tall redhead. She turned her icy glare on him as he approached but said nothing. What was her deal, anyway? She was just standing there, hadn't said a word since Zippy puked, and hadn't said much before that. She'd been so full of piss and vinegar when this all started. Matt would never have figured her for the give-up type.

He quickly scanned the collected wood. They were indeed two by fours, cut into two different lengths. There were some about five or six feet long, maybe four of them, and a larger number of longer pieces, these easily twelve feet long, which should be more than sufficient to bridge the pit preventing them from entering the next room.

"Four minutes," sounded from the other room.

"As I said, Daniel was terrified of prison, because he knew what happens to pedophiles. Looks like he got what was coming to him in the end." The announcer's voice trailed off with a dry chuckle.

Something's not right, Matt thought, but couldn't quite figure out what. There were more than enough long boards to get them across, but it felt wrong. He was an accountant, not an engineer. Give him a list of credits and debits, and he could spot an inconsistency right away. Give him a ten-key, and he could figure out the problem in a matter of minutes. But this kind of spatial math was beyond him.

"Brian," he called. "Which ones do we use?"

"Okay, I'm goin' for it," Li'l Bit announced. Matt turned just in time to see the squat black man take a two-step running start into the doorway. He couldn't see the jump, but he heard the clump as he landed.

"He made it," Big Rich said.

"Oh yeah, he did!" Li'l Bit yelled. "Now whachew want me to do?"

Zack looked from the door to Matt, then back. Brian came up beside him, glanced at the wood, and said, "Gotta be the short ones. The long ones will bow in the middle. The ends will come up, then slide down into the pit. If they don't just break."

"Go to the side," Zack said to Li'l Bit. "I'm going to hand you some wood, build a little bridge."

"Help me grab them," Matt said, as he bent down to collect two of the shorter pieces of wood.

"One minute," the computer voice announced.

"Shit!" Zippy said. "Shit! Shit! Shit!"

Brian grabbed two more pieces of wood, handing them one at a time to Zack, who passed them through the doorway and off to the right. As each piece was pushed out and caught by Li'l Bit, the cop would kneel down, placing his side on the floor.

Everyone was grouped around the door now, everyone but the redhead, who still stood staring at the wall, or maybe at the pile of longer wood pieces. Matt doubted she was actually looking at anything in the room. She seemed to have wandered off into her own little happy place.

"Three minutes," came from the second room.

Big Rich passed into the next chamber, followed by Zippy, Tory, and Eddie.

A new sound filled the room, a hiss that sounded like a thousand snakes giving warning, but which could only be an air valve opening.

"*Thirty seconds,*" said the voice, and a countdown began in Matt's head.

Matt took a tentative sniff and was rewarded with the pungent not-quite rotting egg smell of natural gas. He knew the gas had no real smell but was treated with isopropyl mercaptan to make it detectable by the human nose, giving it that weird sulfurous tinge.

Brian passed through the door next, and then it was his turn. Stopping in the doorway, his internal clock crossing the twenty-second mark, he saw Zack, the cop, walk up to the redhead.

Fifteen seconds. The cop leaned in close to her, his head next to hers.

Ten seconds. Now they were coming, running. Matt backed up across the makeshift bridge, giving them room.

Five seconds. The redhead came through the door, angled immediately to the right, crossing the bridge in two fast, shuffling steps.

And there was the cop, using his right arm as a fulcrum as he swung to the right.

And the room they'd just vacated bloomed with brilliant orange-red light as the air filled with the whoosh of a fireball. Matt watched it, captivated, as flame rushed into the room as if it were surrounded by a platoon of World War II soldiers carrying flame throwers. There was no way that expanding mass of fire would stay confined to the one room. It would billow in on them, maybe not fast enough to flash fry them where they stood, but more than sufficient to end their lives.

Someone screamed behind him, one of the women, joined a second later by one of the men. Matt had eyes only for the fire, as enraptured as any since Prometheus first gifted man with the life-saving light and heat.

Then a sheet of metal, like one of those instant blast doors on a science fiction movie, shot across from one side of the doorway, sealing them off from the blaze.

But Zack was still there, and he was shouting and for just a moment Matt thought, *Oh god, his arm got stuck in the door. It's stuck and his hand is frying on the other side.*

Then he realized it was only the cop's sleeve that was stuck, one of those ridiculously loose sleeves on these ridiculous shirts. Zack tore his arm free, leaving a generous expanse of white linen sticking out of the steel door, like a flag of surrender.

He crossed the bridge to join them, took a quick look around the room, and said, "Where's Li'l Bit?"

Chapter 6

Elizabeth

Liz took pride in having a refined vocabulary acquired from thousands of hours of reading an eclectic variety of books, both historical and modern, fiction and non-fiction. She grew up surrounded by them, with a writer father and a mother who devoured every book she could get her hands on. Everything except what her husband wrote.

The discovery of that divide, revealed during an interview—one of his books was being developed into a movie, Oprah was doing a "women behind the men" program, and her mother had one too many mimosas prior to going on air—and touted by a salacious and sensationalist media, drove a wedge into their family dynamic. The movie project was pulled, and sales of his books dried up; after all, what good could he possibly be if his own wife didn't like his writing?

The logic of that argument never made sense to her. His books were good. They sold well. Three had hit the top ten on the New York Times Bestseller list, and one was chosen as the basis for a movie. None of that had changed. He became no good because society deemed him so based on one bad interview with a half-sloshed spouse. It proved the old adage: society loves a hero, but they love watching one fall even more.

It was around this time, when she was sixteen, that the characters in her books began speaking their lines in her head. Each had its own voice, its own diction. At first it was strange but felt like a natural outgrowth of her love of reading. Already alive for her, the books took on new dimensions. If the text described a person as having a dirty British accent, she heard that gutter-trash when he spoke, the prominent F's that came through despite everything else being marble-gargled.

Then the divorce, the months in rehab for her alcoholic mother, the abrupt shift as her father won custody. The voices no longer stopped when she put the book down, but would continue conversing with each other, arguing over points of view. It didn't take long for her to realize they were discussing aspects of what she was thinking about or deciding to do. Now for every dress she tried on, she might hear, *Lordy, have mercy. Dear, that cut just doesn't flatter your figure*, in a genteel Southern Belle voice. Even worse were the comments about food: *Damn, girl, if you eat that, you gonna bust outta them jeans.* She stopped eating, lost weight, and started falling behind in school.

It was the grades that alerted her dad something was wrong, not the weight loss or the circles under her eyes, not the brittle hair or the sudden withdrawal into herself. He thought she was doing drugs, hanging out with the wrong crowd. He took her to an emergency room for a drug test.

That was her first exposure to the ugly side of mental health problems. A sympathetic doctor listened to her, but didn't have the resources to keep her, since she wasn't acutely suicidal. He told her father she wasn't on drugs, but she needed help, and recommended an outpatient mental health center. When he refused to take her, she flew into a rage. And she discovered something amazing. When she yelled at the voices to stop, they got louder. But if she directed her anger outward, at another person or at a thing, they went away.

That got her admitted, then committed. It also got her medicated, and that, finally, pushed the voices away.

Now she lived like a junkie, desperate for her next dose of medicine, not to get high, but to stay sane and alone within her own mind.

She kept track of the time when each dose was due more carefully than a chef watched the food on the stove. She never took a dose early and never missed a dose. For seven years she was so careful, so in control. She got her life back.

And then her father died, and her insurance was gone. The voices came back with a vengeance. She screamed at strangers, set fires in trashcans, and finally got herself committed again. That was why she signed the deal. Come do this one thing, play this one game, and if you win, you'll have a lifetime supply of your medications.

When was her last dose? In the hospital, certainly. She remembered some pills and a couple of shots. But she was pretty out of it, lost in her rage, beating back the voices with anger and destruction. The shots might have been just to calm her. Already, the voices were returning, taking on aspects of the people around her, total strangers yet already inside her head, telling her how worthless she was, asking what she could possibly contribute to their efforts to survive.

You're no use to us, said by the fat slob.

Dead weight best left behind, said by the short woman, who had no right talking about weight.

Do us all a favor and stay here, said by the guy who helped build the dungeon.

Stupid skank, in the voice of the short black man.

Then the cop was beside her. She knew he was real because he touched her shoulder. She felt his short hair tickle the side of her face as he leaned in and whispered in her ear. "If you don't come with us now, you'll die. And if you die with voices in your head, they'll be with you forever."

How did he know?

It didn't matter. She sensed that what he said was the truth, even if there was no logical way he could know it. She knew he only said it to get her to move, to face another few minutes of life. But it was enough. It was the first time a man had shown such kindness to her since she was a child, before the schizophrenia took over her life.

Well, there was that doctor, but he was only nice to her for as long as it took to get her strapped into the chair.

She felt an anger building, the kind of anger that enabled her to suppress the voices for a time. She couldn't get angry at the people around her, however. That much was clear. As Zachary towed her to the door, then pushed her through first, she resolved to focus her anger on the people who'd tricked her into coming here.

Then she was through, and that other tall white guy, the one with the glasses, helped her across the bridge. Everyone else was already there. Well, everyone but the fat slob who'd looked at her like a piece of meat. That's all he was now, a load of meat already rotting before it was dead, if that announcer voice was right.

She stumbled to a stop just past the accountant—Matt, that was his name—and looked around, amazed at the size of the underground chamber.

Easily twice as long and just as wide as the first room, it appeared to be carved out of the living rock, a hollowed-out space, an untold distance below the surface. She could feel the age of the place despite the modern lighting contrivances. This was no elaborate set designed for a game show. It was as the engineer said, this was the labyrinth modernized.

Everyone stood bunched up, not spreading out like they had in the first room. All except the little black guy with the foul mouth, who stood staring back the way she'd come. She felt a gust of warm air blow against her back, saw the short man take a step back, then another, then suddenly the floor...unfolded... under his feet, and she let out a small scream as he dropped. She expected another of those wet meat sounds, but instead heard him shout out in surprise. Then...nothing.

She turned back to see if anyone else had noticed and saw Zachary rip his shirt to free himself from a metal door. Where had that come from? Then he strode across the wooden planks and asked, "Where's Li'l Bit?"

"Two minutes."

She ran up to the edge of the second pit, which lay directly across the room from the first. It seemed to have approximately the same dimensions as well so that the boards they had brought from the first room would be too short to bridge directly but should work well on the oblique. "He fell into here," she said, looking down hesitantly.

Surprisingly, there were no spikes, no blood, no dead black guy with blood pooling out of his smart mouth. Instead she saw what looked like a drop of about five feet, followed by a sharp slope, which angled to the left. The walls of the sloped area still looked like stone, but the bottom resembled nothing so much as the dark gray metal you see in the movies, when the super-hot actor playing a spy goes crawling through the ventilation system of some maniac's skyscraper. It was a slide.

She sensed the rest of the group coming up behind her.

"Wonder what's at the bottom," Matt said, "and if it's safer than going through the door."

Brian shook his head. "This wasn't my area of expertise." He looked around and seemed surprised at the hostile glares. His cheeks turned red, his green eyes blazed, his chest puffed out, and he yelled, "Look, let's get this shit straightened out. Yes, I worked for them. Yes, I helped design some of the things we're probably going to have to deal with. But I didn't know what they were going to be used for. Do you hear me? I. Didn't. Know. And when I found out, I tried to expose them.

"So quit looking at me like the rabid dog in the room and just listen to what I have to say. I promise we have a much better chance of surviving if you let me help."

Both the black guys looked down, maybe a little ashamed. She felt embarrassed as well. She knew what it was like to have people look at you strange because of something you might do or might say. She should have been a little more perceptive to their similarities once they learned who he was, but her voices had started tormenting her, taking all her attention.

"Brian, right?" Zack asked. "I can respect you wanting to do the right thing, but you've got to understand that, for now at least, you're the only face we can put on the people who did this to us. Now that's not fair to you, and I know that. So how about if we try to remember that it's not your fault, and you try to remember that we need someone to blame, and we'll all try to work together?"

So not just a brick block of a cop, not just a guy who somehow knew exactly what to say to get through to her, but also a peacemaker. He looked a little slow, but she could see now that it was just a facade.

Brian's cheeks took on a different shade, fading from red to pink. He cleared his throat. "Sorry. I'm sorry for yelling. I'm just…scared. My family—"

"We're all scared," Big Rich said, putting a hand the size of a baseball glove on the smaller man's shoulder. "I got a family too. I'm sure we all do. So let's get back to them." Liz closed her eyes for a second, letting that gravelly bass sweep through her. She didn't have any particular desire for a man his size, but damn! That voice was so sexy.

"One minute."

"Okay, all right," Matt said, as he and Zack started pulling up the boards. "Kumbaya, and all that. Now, while we set up the boards, can you please tell us if we should move through the door or take the express elevator to hell?"

Liz moved over by Tory, Eddie, Big Rich, and Zippy, who'd been pretty quiet so far.

Brian peered down at the pit where Li'l Bit had vanished. "From everything I learned after I figured out what our designs were going to be used for, the dungeon is built to promote a linear exploration. Any deviation is either deadly, in the case of that disgusting pig in the first pit or leads to something worse."

"What the hell could be worse than a big ass metal spike up your ass?" Zippy asked.

Brian thought for a moment while Matt and Zack placed the final boards. "The first guy died instantly, I'm sure. Who knows what Little Bit will have to face?" He seemed to stumble over the nickname, enunciating it fully, which drew a chuckle from Big Rich.

They lined up to cross the second pit, Zack and Matt taking the lead, which no one argued with.

"It's a damned shame, s'all I'm sayin'," Big Rich said quietly.

"What is?" Zippy asked.

"It's just like a horror movie. Either the brother dies first, one of those horrible ways that tell the half-naked, drunk, white kids that this shit is serious, or they try to make it funny, let him see it coming. They always drag that part out too, you know."

"Thirty seconds."

Zippy added, "Yeah, there'd be a loud mouth guy running, screaming, making the audience laugh. Then he'd stop, and the bad guy wouldn't be behind him, and he'd start shoutin', 'Yeah, lookit dat, I got away!' That's when the bad guy would cut him up! He'd just appear, stepping out from behind a skinny tree way too small for him to really hide behind."

"I saw that one!" both Liz and Eddie said at the same time, which made the young kid flush and look down.

"I must have missed that one," Brian said.

Carefully, Zack pushed the next door open. He stepped inside, and the lights turned on, revealing another rectangular room, no wider than the second but the longest one yet. No pit opened beneath him, for which Liz felt a shudder of relief.

The rest of the group filed past.

There was no sudden blossoming of fire. No metal door came crashing across this time as time expired. Instead, every floor surface in the large chamber dropped away, revealing hundreds of rows of wicked, gleaming spikes, except for that one place with the chute.

"Jesus," Brian breathed. "I had no idea."

Liz shivered. The rooms weren't just filled with traps for the unwary.

At any time, the masters of this game could kill any or all of them, probably with just a push of a button.

Chapter 7

Zachary

"Five minutes until room lockdown."
As light filled the room, Zachary took a careful look around.

He and the others stood on a solid area of floor that extended five feet from the door and ran left and right to either side of the room, about ten feet in both directions. The room stretched away perhaps another thirty feet, and he could see an identical solid platform in the center of the floor on the far side, with another iron-banded, wooden-plank door.

In between the two solid spans of flooring were what looked like floor tiles, though most of them were at least two feet long on a side, and they were fit together in a haphazard fashion, like one of those multi-hued tile backsplashes some people glued behind their kitchen sinks. Each tile had a single stylized capital letter in its center, one of those weird document fonts, like Algerian or Edwardian. Squares, rectangles, and other less common shapes somehow formed a cohesive net of connected letter tiles that spanned the room from side to side and extended its length from one door platform to the other.

"I've seen this movie," Matt said, a laugh in his voice. "We've just gotta spell out Jehovah, right?"

"Don't forget it starts with an 'I' in some forgotten language," Tory added.

"Right on," Matt said.

"Okay," Zack said, "so anyone got any idea what we're supposed to be spelling here?"

Zippy looked to Big Rich. "Do you have any idea what they're talking about?"

The bigger man laughed. "No clue, but I'm guessin' it was a boring movie, since only the white people know about it." He stepped up next to Zack, looking out over the linked tiles. "So we're gonna have to spell something to get across? Like, step on just the right letters?"

"I think so," Zack answered.

"And if we're wrong, something bad'll happen?"

"Probably," Matt said.

The football player just nodded. "Got it."

"In the movie, only the right letters would support weight," Matt added. "Every other letter crumbled and broke, and it was a very long fall."

"Somehow, I don't think this is something as nice as a fall," Elizabeth said.

"Check the floor, I guess," Zack said, scanning the ground, sweeping dust and grit aside with his boots.

"That won't be necessary," Brian said. "Look."

Zack turned around, noticed the engineer pointing at the wall behind them. To the right of the doorway leading back to the previous room, four lines of prose were etched into a placard like the one which had hung on the door leading from the initial chamber.

> **I am the cause of a mad king's ire.**
> **Mine is the curse of a bull's desire.**
> **My daughter proved a spider true,**
> **Who gave the Athenian his clew.**

Zack read the lines once, then again. Nothing in them rang any bells, and so he began reading them a

THE DUNGEON

third time, not hoping for any insight, but rather hoping someone else would say something to give them a clue. Did it mean anything that clue was spelled incorrectly in the passage? He didn't think it was a mistake. The people who could plan all this weren't the type to make simple mistakes.

"Man, I hope one of you white people has seen this movie," Big Rich said. "'Cause about the only thing I remember about the Greeks was that snake-headed chick and the dude with the flying horse."

"Perseus," Eddie whispered.

"That was a Pegasus," Matt said, "and wasn't he a half-god, half-human? Like Hercules?"

"He was a demigod," Tory said. "That's what they call the children the gods had with humans, but I'm not sure that helps us here."

"Four minutes."

"Okay," Brian said. "Let's try to reason this out. It starts with the word 'I.' So the name of that person would be the name we have to spell out."

"Makes sense," Matt said. "Which means all four of these lines are clues to who this person was."

"I can live with that," Big Rich said. "So who's the pissed off king? And who pissed him off?"

"Are we sure it means pissed off?" Tory asked. "Wasn't there a Mad King in Greek mythology?"

Elizabeth said, "From what little I remember, all those kings did a lot of crazy stuff, started wars, sacrificed kids—"

"Built wooden horses," Tory added.

"Sent people on wacko quests," Zippy added. "What? I watched that Sorbo guy in Hercules too."

"Exactly," Elizabeth continued, "so maybe they were all a bit touched in the head, and the line really means pissed off. It does use the word 'ire' at the end, which means anger. So the line is claiming to be the person who made the king angry."

"But isn't that like a double negative?" the football player asked. "I'm the person who made the mad king mad?"

"King Minos was mad," Eddie said.

"Or just a statement of fact. If it weren't for this person, then the mad king wouldn't be mad," Elizabeth said.

"Hold on," Zack said, peering through the group. While most of them had moved out onto the platform, either studying the scattered letters, or turned back to the wall to look at the verse, Eddie remained near the door. The skinny kid, with his lanky hair falling over his eyes, didn't even seem to be paying attention to their surroundings. He'd looked like that every time Zack had thought to check on him. And yet, every time they needed to move, the kid was ready to go.

He appears to be checked out of the situation, so as not to be caught up in the situation, Zack realized. What had he said before? He was picked up in a flop house, just trying to find a place to sleep. Several of the others continued discussing the first line, but Zack focused on Eddie, watching him twitch his head, turning an ear to whoever was speaking.

"Eddie," he said. "What was the name of the guy who killed Medusa?"

Eddie shook his head. Zack didn't think it was an indication that he didn't know.

Tory picked up on Zack's attitude, turning to look at the young man. "It's okay, Eddie. If you know the answer, you can tell us."

"Three minutes."

CHAPTER 8

Eddie

Edward "Eddie" Artios never wanted to be the center of attention. Even before the…accident…he'd been quiet and reserved, more inclined to pick up a book than a video game, preferring the company of his family to the companionship of friends. He had a little sister to look out for and parents who worked too much and barely had time to take care of either of them.

After the thing happened that made him a ward of the state, he found his natural inclination to be still and quiet within himself a blessing that kept him safe. The bullies left him alone, because he didn't rise to their bait. He chose to avoid rather than to confront, a strategy which engendered in kind-hearted people a desire to protect him, rather than to abuse or misuse him. His passivity had gotten him robbed numerous times on the street, but never beaten.

He hadn't moved out to look at the letters. He didn't take a turn to look at the riddle. There were always others, louder, more experienced, who would know what to do. He just needed to listen and be ready, and he'd be okay, if only because those others would do the right thing to save themselves. No one was ever upset if their actions in the name of self-preservation also helped him. If anything, it gave them justification that they had done something good, even if they hadn't cared before.

These people didn't seem like bad people. Well, the big, fat guy wasn't a nice guy, not at all. But none of the others were bad like him. Maybe they'd made some bad decisions, but they were dealing with them. Ms. Tory was definitely nice, like his mother had been. Maybe she was a mom too, and that's why she could be so nice to him.

Mr. Zachary must be a nice guy. He was a police officer, and they were always nice, modern-day knights in shining armor. But good guys like that always want to do more than just protect little people like him. They would do that, but then afterward they wanted to go get the bad guy. Eddie didn't know who the bad guys were, but he knew he didn't want to face them. He wanted to be quiet little Eddie Artios, the kid who survived because others did. He did not want to be the reason they survived, which might make the really bad people mad at him. You didn't survive as long as he had with really bad people mad at you.

So when Mr. Zachary asked him the easy question about Perseus and Medusa, he shook his head. He wished he hadn't mumbled the answer earlier. No one should look to him for answers, that way no one could get mad at him.

"Eddie, please just talk to him," Ms. Tory said, and she sounded scared. The computer voice telling them how long they had until something bad happened really seemed to have scared her. Eddie didn't want Ms. Tory to be scared. She was the nicest person he'd met who didn't either run a soup kitchen or let him sleep on a mattress on their floor in a long time.

Eddie looked up through his hair and saw the other people, the tall, pretty redhead, the big black man, the police officer, everyone else, looking at him. They weren't talking through the problem anymore.

They weren't going to solve the riddle in time.

THE DUNGEON

"I—"

"It's okay, kid," the redhead said, and she smiled at him. Even the police officer seemed to soften a little when she smiled.

"Perseus," Eddie said. "His name was Perseus, and he was a demigod. Zeus was his father."

"I knew it!" the skinny black guy crowed. "Like in that movie, about the Titans."

Eddie flinched at the sudden volume, then realized he wasn't being yelled at. Ms. Tory making soothing noises helped.

"Okay, Eddie," Mr. Zachary said, "what was it you said about the mad king?" The police officer had kind eyes, brown and deep, like his father's. He was big and strong too, someone who could protect people.

"King Minos was known as the Mad King," Eddie said.

"Minos...wasn't he the one who could turn things into gold?" Ms. Elizabeth asked.

"That was King Midas," Ms. Tory corrected.

"Oh yeah...the Midas touch," the skinny black guy, Zippy, said. He hummed a few bars of a television commercial jingle.

"So who was Minos again?" Ms. Elizabeth asked.

"He had this place built, right?" Mr. Zachary said.

"That's right," the engineer guy said. "He had Daedalus build it to hold the Minotaur."

"Who was a half-man, half-bull?" Big Rich said. "Bet that dude could play some defense on a field."

"No doubt," the tall man with glasses said. Eddie didn't particularly like that guy. He felt like someone who always looked out for himself first, like he thought he was smarter than everyone else, more important. "And didn't Daedalus end up in the labyrinth himself? Am I remembering that right?"

"Yeah," Ms. Tory said. "Him and his son, Icarus."

Eddie shook his head but didn't correct them. Daedalus and Icarus had been imprisoned in a tower, not in the labyrinth. King Minos hadn't wanted anyone else to know the way through the labyrinth, so he imprisoned its creator to keep the secret safe.

"Okay, so what did Daedalus do that got him thrown into his own prison?" Matt asked. "Must have been pretty bad. I mean, he'd probably be someone the king wanted to keep around."

"Two minutes."

"Shit!" Big Rich said. "We cuttin' this crap too close. How do you spell Daedalus? I mean, I get it starts with a *D*, but is the next letter an *E* or an *A*?" Eddie could see the big black man scanning the floor tiles, looking at the letters.

"That's not all of it," Ms. Tory said. "It says his child was a spider who helped an Athenian."

"Daedalus only had one child," Eddie said, but Big Rich didn't hear him.

"I'm jumping for the big *D* right there," the big man said.

"Wait!" Ms. Tory shouted, reaching out for the big guy's white shirt. Mr. Zachary reached too, both of them grabbing a hold of the shirt as Big Rich tried to take a big step. The result was that only his right foot went forward, though the force of his lunge pulled both Zachary and Tory a good ways toward the edge. Big Rich's foot landed on an *S*, and the tile immediately fell away. Big Rich would have fallen too, if not for the police officer and Ms. Tory holding onto him.

"Shit! Shit! Shit! Pull me back!" the big man cried.

"What the hell?" Matt asked, running to help, grabbing Big Rich—never call him Richard—by the left arm while the skinny man grabbed his right. Once they got him back onto solid ground, Eddie eased forward, wanting to see.

THE DUNGEON

Under the tile was short drop of only a few feet, and then more rows of those wicked spikes, like in the last room.

"Well, they're nothing if not consistent," Brian said.

Big Rich shuddered, standing at the edge of the platform, looking down at the spikes. "Before I turn around and whip all your asses for almost getting me killed, please tell me why you stopped me."

"Eddie," Ms. Tory said, ignoring the big man. "Eddie, please come read this riddle and tell us what it means."

She reached out for his hand, and he let he take it. She pulled, and he followed, turning away from the maze of letters and looking at the message on the placard.

I am the cause of a mad king's ire.
Mine is the curse of a bull's desire.
My daughter proved a spider true,
Who gave the Athenian his clew.

Remembered stories from a children's book of Greek myths opened in his mind, how Hercules slew the lion, earning himself the fleece, how Echo got her name. Newer stories by Rick Riordan, that juxtaposed the modern world with Greek mythology, also came back to him. Reaching out a tentative hand to touch the sign, feeling the rough edges of the letters burned into the wood, he started talking through the stories.

"Theseus came to Crete to slay the Minotaur. Ariadne, who was the daughter of King Minos, fell in love with the hero and gave him a clew, which is another word for a ball of string or yarn, so he could find his way into the labyrinth, kill the Minotaur, and then find his way back out again."

"Start looking for an *A*," the redhead said.

Shaking his head, Eddie continued, "It's not Ariadne. She's just one of the clues. Ariadne's half-brother was the Minotaur."

"Say what?" Zippy said.

"At the beginning, Poseidon sent a great bull to King Minos for him to sacrifice. The king didn't want to, so Poseidon got mad. He made Minos's wife fall in love with the bull. She begged Daedalus to help her, so the inventor made a cow statue for her to hide in. When she did, the bull got her pregnant, and she gave birth to the Minotaur. That's when Minos had Daedalus build the labyrinth."

"Eddie," Ms. Tory said. "Think carefully now. What was the name of King Minos's wife?"

Eddie smiled. "That's an easy one, Ms. Tory. Her name was Pasiphae."

"Are you sure, Eddie?" Mr. Zachary asked.

"Dude, there's only one *P* near this side, and it's a long step away," Big Rich reported.

"He's right," Matt said. "You gotta commit."

Eddie turned to the nice police officer, met his brown eyes for just a second, and said, "I'm sure. She's one of the tragic people. Bad stuff happens to her because other people don't act right."

"Sounds like you can relate," Mr. Zachary said. He would probably never know how right he was.

"All right, Big Eddie," Big Rich said, and Eddie smiled again. "Spell that name out for me, and let's see if we can do this."

"And hurry," Matt said. "Um...but no pressure...or anything."

"Easy," Eddie said. "P-A-S-I-P-H-A-E. Pasiphae."

The big black man muttered something about Greeks and the funny spelling of their names, which Eddie thought was hilarious, considering the names of some of the black people he'd shared a night's lodging with. He didn't say anything, though.

Big Rich took a long step, out and away from the safe platform, aiming for the only *P* visible. His back foot actually left the platform before his front foot landed. The *P* held him, allowing him to bring his back foot up and settle himself.

"One minute."

"Seriously," Matt said. "We can't keep cutting this crap so close."

"You next, Eddie," Mr. Zachary said, making him smile. No one ever asked him to go before them.

Despite being hesitant about engaging with other people, despite a life spent mostly within the confines of a book, Eddie was not sedentary. His parents had made sure of that, before they died. A year of living off the generosity of others had kept him lean. And running when he had to helped keep him trim. He was the shortest man in the room, so what was just a long step for the others was a jump for him, but he made it safely to the *P* even as Big Rich took a smaller step to a nearby *A*. He tried to look back but got nothing but calls to keep going and hands making shooing motions. As soon as Big Rich moved from the *A* to the *S*, he followed.

Say what you want about big guys who play football, Big Rich wasn't stupid, and he didn't need to be reminded how to spell something. The **"Thirty seconds,"** warning came just as he landed on the far platform, with Eddie only a second behind. Quickly, the two men moved to the door, though neither moved to open it.

"Don't go in yet," Matt yelled unnecessarily.

"Don't start the next timer yet," Elizabeth added, also unnecessarily.

Big Rich looked down at Eddie as Eddie looked up at him, their eyes meeting, and they shared a quiet laugh. Eddie recognized a kindred spirit in the big man. Although probably for different reasons, both found an advantage in allowing others to think less of them. Neither of them raised a response to the shouted instructions.

In short order and with no mishaps, Elizabeth, then Tory, Brian, Matt, and Zippy joined them on the final platform. The police officer came last.

"We got ten seconds," Matt said, reaching for the door.

Eddie also reached for the wooden surface, and Big Rich used his big paw to stop Matt from opening it. "Let Eddie do it," he rumbled.

Still smiling, Eddie pushed the next door open. He stepped inside, and the lights turned on, revealing a long, narrow passage that ran off into the distance with what looked like a curve somewhere at the edge of sight. No pits opened beneath him, which was even better than being the one to open the door.

The rest filed quickly through, and as the timer expired, the floor in the tile room fell away, the tiles daisy-chaining down like rope bridges that were cut free on one side. The platforms disappeared too, swinging down on hidden hinges to bang against the walls below the doors. Like they'd seen when Big Rich stepped on an incorrect letter, beneath the floor was a short drop onto a field of spikes, just enough of a distance to make sure the fall was fatal.

Chapter 9

Zachary

"Five minutes until room lockdown."

"All right, Alexa, stop timer," Matt said, drawing a chuckle from a couple of the others.

"I knew that chick sounded familiar!" Big Rich said.

Still shaken by the disappearance of the floor in the previous room, Zack didn't immediately start moving down the new corridor. He wanted to look around and take stock. The second room had featured two traps, the third a riddle, and their numbers were already reduced by twenty percent. Who knew what could be hiding in the walls or on the floor of this passage.

"We gotta move," Brian said interrupting his thoughts as the engineer broke into a pace that was almost speed walking. When no one followed him, he yelled, "I designed this section. It's a long one, more than a quarter of a mile, and every minute a section will be closed off. If we don't make it to each break in time, we're trapped."

After having just promised to listen to the man, Zack didn't waste time on questions. "Okay, Brian says we gotta move, so let's move!" he said, wincing even as the words left his mouth, hearing the echoes of academy instructors and police captains from every part of his past. Suiting action to word, he quickly moved up to the engineer, the two of them walking rapidly along the corridor.

A loud scuffing/scuttling noise announced that others were catching up.

"You sound like a football coach," Big Rich said, his long stride easily covering ground next to them. "I'm not necessarily saying that's a good thing. I hated my last coach." Zack caught a weird sound in the man's voice and looked up to see him smiling.

A glance back showed everyone keeping up fairly well, though he noted the two homeless people bringing up the rear. Since that meant they were only ten or fifteen feet behind him, he didn't worry too much about it.

"So this corridor was your baby, huh?" Matt asked, coming up behind Brian. "Anything more you can share with us about it?"

Brian took a moment before answering. Zack looked over at the engineer and noted he was already breathing harder than anyone else. That poet shirt must be hiding a little extra girth, the cop thought.

Thinking about it, he was struck by the sheer scope of what had been accomplished here, disregarding for the moment the fact that he was trapped inside of it. For a modern construction, it was impressive. To think that it was all based on an actual construct more than three thousand years old, and he couldn't help but admire the architecture. Though it must have originally been lit by torches, if it was lit at all, the hidden electric lights didn't detract from the grandeur. They actually seemed to be flickering slightly, maintaining the illusion which had begun with them waking up in these old-style clothes. The walls weren't mortared stone, not built from the ground up, but rather carved, excavated like a mine, then reinforced and shaped. The floor was smooth and covered with a fine grit that provided good traction. There were no protrusions to trip the unwary. The ceiling was high enough for Big

THE DUNGEON

Rich to walk upright, and so far there hadn't seemed to be any low spots, where a taller man would have to watch out or get his bell rung.

"I designed this corridor as a way to break up a large party into smaller groups," he answered quietly. "Each division was to lead to a different challenge room. The first leg was the shortest, and you can judge your pace for the second leg by how far past the first division you are when the dividing panel comes down."

"So none of these, um, divisions, is supposed to be deadly?" Matt asked, also keeping his voice low.

Brian shook his head.

"Well, that's a relief."

"That's not what I meant," Brian said. "I was shaking my head because I don't know. I didn't design the corridor to hurt anyone, but that doesn't mean it wasn't altered. For all I know, it won't even divide. Maybe we just need to get to the end, and that's hard enough in five minutes."

Matt nodded. He didn't seem to be having any problem with the pace.

Zack looked around, noting Zippy right behind him and to the left. Big Rich was also close to the front with Matt and Brian. Elizabeth came next, her face grim as death. Was she even aware how close she'd come to being immolated, back in the first room? He wasn't sure. Just as he wasn't sure what had possessed him to go after her. The others probably thought it was just the cop part of him, if they wondered about it at all.

The truth was, he recognized that thousand-mile stare. He'd seen it often enough both as a cop and as a husband. Well, ex-husband. It's hard to stay married to a paranoid schizophrenic who won't take her medication and who thinks she hears his voice saying bad things about her when he's not even in the house. It was during one of her worst times, when the voices were telling her that she'd be better off dead, that she'd confided her worst fear, that they would follow her into death, that her eternity in hell would be spent with nothing but those imaginary voices for company.

After that, she started sticking to her medication schedule, but still filed for divorce. She'd said she could only keep going if she knew, beyond a shadow of a doubt, that he wasn't in the house any longer.

"Right before this curve, we'll pass the first division," Brian said, and Zack saw the curve approaching. The corridor made a gentle left, and he thought he could detect a slight downward slope, which would make keeping a fast pace easier, as long as no one slipped and fell.

They reached the curve and started following it around, Tory and Eddie still bringing up the rear. Zack wanted to chivvy them along, but his own fear kept his toes pointed forward. Brian had started counting Mississippis as soon as they entered the bend, and they heard a solid thump when he reached five Mississippi. The ground trembled beneath their feet.

"Four minutes."

"Five seconds, that's not enough," Brian said worriedly. "We've got to pick it up, try to maintain a jog."

"Yo, people in the back!" Big Rich shouted, his deep voice booming in the narrow corridor. "Engineer dude says we gotta move faster, so let's show some hustle!"

Everyone broke into a light jog, and for a few seconds, Tory and Eddie caught up to the main body. No one spoke now. Matt and Big Rich seemed to have no problems with the increased pace. Zack didn't like running, but he still used his treadmill regularly to stay in shape. Gone were the days when pork-pie police officers were the norm, especially in a place like Virginia Beach, where even the bad guys were health nuts who knew the difference between a Cafe Mocha and a half-caff soy milk latte. Zippy and Elizabeth kept up well too. The redhead's face flushed a little with the exercise, and when he caught her eyes for a second, she flashed a smile at him.

Her smile was transformational. The wide mouth didn't seem so wide; the lips became more full. Even her eyes became engaged, the outside corners tilting up, changing her from plain to exotic. Hers was a face made for smiling, and it was a shame that life seemed to have planted a permanent scowl on her features.

They came out of the bend still jogging, making good time. Zack heard a fast, wheezing sound, and when he looked to his right for the source, he saw Brian, the engineer, puffing like every taste of air would be his last.

"You okay?" he asked, concerned.

The shorter man nodded, though his face had taken on an unhealthy gray tinge. He was shaking his hands as he walked, like Zack sometimes did if he slept wrong and his hands fell asleep. But he wasn't grabbing his chest, wasn't complaining or trying to make anyone stop, so Zack kept jogging.

"Any…second…now," Brian puffed, "then…we…can…slow…down."

The sliding/grating of a mass of rock falling, closing off the corridor behind them, scared Zack and almost sent several of them colliding into each other. The ground bucked.

"Three minutes."

"Too…close," Brian said, already slowing from his jog, though he didn't stop moving. "I hate this blood pressure medicine…it won't let my heart rate increase, so I can't pull enough air to keep everything running smooth. Damn hands and feet are numb."

"We good for a bit now?" Zippy asked.

"Yeah, this stretch is shorter, then there's one more long one."

Zack took a look back, saw Elizabeth still smiling at him, and…nothing, just a blank wall blocking the corridor. He stopped so suddenly that she almost ran into him. "What?" she asked.

Mutely, he pointed at the wall.

The other men got a few steps further along before they realized he had stopped. "What is it?" Big Rich called.

"Tory? Eddie?" he called, ignoring the large black man.

"Aw shit, they get left behind?" Zippy asked.

"Or squished?" Matt asked. "Could they have been squished?"

"Not likely," Brian answered, "the sliding walls are only a few inches thick. Zachary, they're probably fine. Remember, I designed this to separate the group, not hurt them."

"Then why aren't they answering?" he responded, turning and jogging to catch up to the other two men. Brian quick-stepped beside him. The accountant and the football player hung back until they got close, then started moving again.

"Because I also designed each section to be sound-proofed, isolated. It made sense if the goal was to make people feel alone. Now, please. We need to keep moving and hope for the best."

Zack gave another glance at the dividing wall, which looked so much like the rest of the corridor that, if he hadn't just come through this part, he'd have sworn the wall had always been there.

"So we just gonna leave them?" Zippy asked as Zack and Elizabeth caught up to them.

"We don't seem to have a choice," Big Rich answered, tossing a fresh glare at Brian who, thankfully, didn't seem to notice.

"We don't," Brian said. "But like I keep saying, this is my design. The timing is right, the fit of the wall, even the soundproofing. If they incorporated my design whole, there shouldn't be anything dangerous in the hallway itself."

"Yeah, but didn't you say something about some kind of trials?" Matt asked, a slight nasal tinge to his normal tenor. His glasses were down low on his nose again, but he seemed more concerned with moving fast than with fixing them.

"On paper, that was the idea," he replied, his breath again coming in quick gasps. "My corridor would split up a group, and when the timer expired, every section would have a door open, leading into similar but separate rooms. A few of the other engineers were developing tests and traps for those rooms, supposedly stuff that could be handled by a single person, if need be. They called them trial rooms. They—"

His words were cut off as another rock wall slid into place, so close behind them that the wind from its passage blew their clothing away from them.

"That can't have been a minute," Elizabeth said.

"No way," Big Rich agreed.

"Shit, we need to run!" Brian said.

"What? Why?" Matt asked.

"Because that wall came too early, both in distance and timing. Which means we have a very long stretch ahead of us." He smiled grimly, forcing his body into a faster jog than before. Cheeks that had only just regained a measure of healthy color again paled, adopting a ghastly blue-gray tinge. Zachary wasn't sure if the out-of-shape engineer could maintain that pace for very long.

Fifteen seconds after the fall of the third barrier, the computerized voice announced, **"Two minutes."**

"Alexa needs to check her timing," Matt puffed, but no one responded.

The well-lit corridor stretched out in front of them. Putting one foot in front of the other, Zack easily matched the pace set by the bigger and younger tight end, Big Rich. Elizabeth, Matt, and Zippy kept up well, and only Brian seemed in any danger of falling behind. But every time Zack turned to check on him, the engineer was still there, keeping pace, though he looked like a man in the middle of a massive heart attack, one of those "widow-makers" you hear about on the news.

Running near the left side of the corridor, he looked to his right and saw that Elizabeth had increased her pace and was now running beside him. She flashed him another smile that said, *I can go as long as you can.* Smiling back, Zack nodded.

Then, suddenly, Big Rich slowed down. Zack and Elizabeth dodged to either side to avoid colliding with him. Looking up, seeing what he'd noticed first, they slowed to a walk as well.

"What is it?" Matt called.

"A dead end is what it is," Big Rich said, and it was the first time Zack had heard anything approaching anger in the big man's voice.

"Say what?" Zippy asked, stopping beside Brian, who was bent over with his hands on his knees, trying desperately to catch his breath. Matt stopped beside them.

Zack looked back, worried they were going to be separated further, but the trio was only five or six yards behind them and the tunnel ended the same distance in front of them. Surely the last leg of the race couldn't be that short. Quietly, letting his body recover from the jog, he moved up beside Big Rich. Elizabeth joined them.

The corridor dead-ended in another rock wall, identical to the ones which had slid down behind them. Zack didn't know whether this was a permanent wall or if something had gone wrong and it had slid down sooner. Obviously they would have made it. The voice hadn't announced the next minute yet.

As if on cue, another wall dropped, this time between the two groups of three, leaving Matt, Brian, and Zippy on one side and Zachary, Elizabeth, and Big Rich on the other.

"Shit!" the big tight end said.

"One minute."

"You go to hell, you sadistic bitch!" Elizabeth yelled.

They were trapped in a stretch of corridor no more than ten feet long, from unexpected dead end to the recent barrier.

"So we never had a chance at this part of the puzzle, huh?" Big Rich asked.

"Unless it's like Brian said," Zack replied, "the whole point is to separate."

"They probably want to make us scared, make us feel like it's hopeless," Elizabeth added.

"They doing a pretty good job," the tall man admitted.

"But Brian told us that was the plan," Zack said. "So maybe we can hold off on the hopeless and just be scared."

"I'm good with that," Elizabeth said softly.

Zack took another look around the ten-by-five-foot area that remained to them. The walls looked no different. The floor was the same. The ceiling was still high enough that the tall tight end could jump up without fear of hitting his head. And it all looked perfect, a solid tube like a subway tunnel, bored through the rock with no imperfections, no possible means of escape.

"It reminds me of a wormhole," Elizabeth said, watching him as his head worked its way around the confines of their space.

"Like in Star Trek?" Big Rich asked.

She laughed, an honest laugh, and because Zack was already looking at her this time, he watched the dramatic change take place. Somehow, between one smile and the next, his internal description of her had already gone from plain to pretty. The smiles made her beautiful.

Zack shook his head. What the hell was he thinking?

"No, I mean a real wormhole. Haven't you ever read about them?"

"Didn't read much that wasn't a playbook, or something I was assigned to pass a class," Big Rich replied.

"*Thirty seconds.*"

"There was this worm discovered in 2011 called the Mephisto worm, in honor of that Faust guy, and they could burrow holes almost a mile into the soil," she said. "They eat the earth and rock, and excrete it behind them, like a crystal coating, so you get these perfect tunnels deep into the earth."

"Are we gonna run into any of them?" Zack asked, half-jokingly.

She laughed again. "No, those are just little worms. I was only saying this tunnel kind of resembles what they can do, but on a much larger scale."

Zack felt her hand scrabbling for his. He took it, understanding that this was her way of admitting her fear. He gave it a little squeeze and felt her squeeze in return.

"Here we go," Big Rich said.

Zack held his breath.

THE DUNGEON

The lights went out.
A loud, grating sound, more stone sliding on stone, started up.
Elizabeth screamed.

CHAPTER 10

Tory

The stone wall dropped, and Tory heard the sound of a mausoleum door closing her in. She might not be dead yet, but it felt like her tomb had already been sealed, and all she could do not was wait for her air to run out.

"Sorry. I'm so sorry," the kid, Eddie, said.

"It's okay, Eddie," she said. "It's not your fault. You didn't put us in here."

They had a little less than three minutes to live. She couldn't let him spend those last minutes feeling responsible. He needed to perk up and face whatever was coming like a man, not a victim.

It hadn't taken long on the streets to learn that if you thought like a victim, that's how you'd be perceived. Those liberal snow lilies had it all wrong. Acting like a victim didn't get you more stuff from the government. It got you preyed upon by those who either wanted to use you to gain more power or wanted an excuse to exercise their power over you. In the case of most politicians, it was both.

So when her husband depleted their savings and lost their house gambling, when he lost his job and then took his own life rather than face the consequences of his addiction, she went out on the streets with her eyes open. She was thankful they hadn't started a family; she didn't want to think about how hard it would've been taking care of more than just herself. After a thousand days of day labor, soup kitchen meals, and shelter beds, she was no closer to getting back on her feet.

That was the way the world was designed. There were three classes of people: the rich, the poor, and people like her. Oh sure, the president could talk about lowering taxes for the middle class, but the middle class were the poor in today's society. They were the ones living paycheck to paycheck, one crisis away from losing everything. Maybe there were different levels of poor, with the upper levels having some small savings that might prolong their slide into abject poverty, but once the slide began, it was almost impossible to stop. Forget about climbing back up. The only slides you could climb were on the playgrounds, and even the kids eventually figure out it's too much work to try going the wrong way.

Uncountable hours on library computers looking for work had led her to a string of websites promising a deeper insight into corporate America and why people like her were destined to be left behind. Like Eddie too, let's not forget about him. Considering his age, he was one of those the safety net should have caught, a young mind ripe for indoctrination into the political zeitgeist. She wondered if a Hillary campaign person had driven him to a polling place to cast a ballot, after feeding him a healthy breakfast of lies and Kool-Aid.

Not that the "Republicrats" were any better, just the other half of the same coin. The Deep State truly ran the world, she thought, a cabal of people with familiar names and faces who smile for their constituents, snarl at men with a different letter under their pictures, then retire to a secret clubhouse to share hooch and hookers with the same people they argued so vehemently against in public. There, in their special dens of iniquity, they made deals to carve the country up a little finer amongst themselves.

Take their current situation, for example. The idea that whatever corporation wanted to make money to fund continuing projects by building a reality show was laughable. Oh, not that it wouldn't work. There were plenty of brainless idiots in the world who would gladly volunteer for such a thing. Hell, there were already plenty of shows like *Ninja Warrior* where people put themselves through amazing hardship just to make a buck and get their fifteen minutes of fame.

No, what didn't make sense was the need to kidnap homeless people or get convicts and drug addicts to agree to participate. How did you even go about securing permission to remove convicts from a prison? Why go to so much trouble, break so many laws, unless you already knew you were safe from prosecution? Who stood to gain from such a plan?

You just had to be able to see the big picture, step away from the pretty lies told by a trusted voice, and really look to see the truth. That Mike Callahan? Must be one of them.

Homeless didn't mean stupid. If you target a few homeless shelters in one city, pretty soon all the homeless would pack up and leave. One of the few advantages to their situation was the ability to be nomadic. But if you got a politician who promised to clean up a city's homeless problem if only you elect him, some slick-haired district attorney coveting a governorship, start harvesting for him, get him elected, and now you've got a happy state who loves their new governor and a politician who owes you big time. As an added bonus, you've got a state with more money because it's not spending as much on Emergency Room care, food stamps, and disability for the itinerant. Win-win-win.

This same concept of harvesting would work for every other type of undesirable person. City got a drug problem? Round up the addicts, send them to The Dungeon. Cue orchestra. Prisons overcrowded? Send them as well. Oh, the city's emergency departments and mental health facilities can't handle all the mental illness cases? Round them up too. Maybe a few cray-crays would make the show more entertaining.

The only losers were those like her, and Eddie, and all the other down-and-outs, people just trying to survive one more day, every day.

That's what was really going on here. She'd bet on it.

She was also sure there were enough rich and amoral assholes who couldn't find enough reason to get it up without watching someone die a horrible death, gamblers who found no excitement in dice or cards, but who'd gladly wager millions on which one of them would die first. That's who this whole dog and pony show was meant for.

"Two minutes." The ground shook, but the source seemed far away. Just another wall dropping. She wondered if anyone else had been separated yet.

Eddie huddled next to her, and she idly put an arm around him, still thinking furiously.

Something just didn't add up about the numbers.

That detective, Zachary, had gotten too close to something while investigating the disappearance of homeless people in Virginia Beach. How many homeless would need to vanish before a cop got involved? Not that she thought he was a bad person. No, he didn't seem the type to turn a blind eye to a problem. But what would it have taken for his department to get involved, for him to get the assignment? It had to be more than just one or two. Neither she nor Eddie were from Virginia Beach. So where were those who were?

It also didn't make sense to try to minimize any of the population groups she'd determined were the targets by groups of ten. It would take hundreds, if not thousands, of "episodes" just to cull one city. Even if they ran ten or a dozen of them through their dungeon every hour, it would take years to clean up one state. So what were they doing with all the others?

"I'm scared, Ms. Tory," Eddie said.

"Shhh, baby, I know. Me too," she said. "Why don't you tell me what happened to you, Eddie? How did a sweet kid like you end up in a shelter?"

"Car accident," he said simply. He had a soft voice, but it seemed more like an attempt to not be noticed, an intentional softness. He wasn't just scared now. He'd been afraid for a very long time.

"A car accident? As in your parents were killed in a car accident?" she asked.

He nodded. "But not just them. We were…in a van, coming back from a vacation to Disney World. It was dark, late at night. They said it was a drunk driver, but I don't know if that's true. I don't know anything. One minute we were all sleeping, then there's a loud noise, and my body wants to fly into the front seat, but my seat belt holds me back. The van rolls over, and there's crashing sounds, and my mom screaming, and the baby crying, and the ceiling…the ceiling comes in a little. There's suitcases flying around, windows breaking, and we're still rolling, rolling down a bank…an embank—"

"Embankment?" she offers.

"Yeah."

"I remember everything. I never got knocked out. I remember hanging upside down because of the belt across my lap, freaking out, because no one was screaming, or yelling, or talking, by the time we

THE DUNGEON

stopped rolling. It was night, but the lights inside the van still worked. I could see—"

His voice dissolved into wrenching sobs, his thin frame quaking next to her. She wondered at the ferocity of his shaking, wondered if he had ever told anyone about that night. She tried to picture what he must have seen, tried and failed, not because her imagination wasn't up to the task, but because she simply didn't have to courage to make herself do it. Tears swam in her eyes as she tried to tell him it was all right, that he didn't need to keep going.

"I think I do," he said. "I think I need to get it out."

He flinched against her as they heard **"One minute,"** announced, but kept talking.

"If I'm going to die today, I want to get it out. You're the first one who ever asked, and I want to tell you."

She nodded, trying to will herself to stop crying. Whatever happened when the timer stopped, she wanted to see it coming.

"The baby's car seat had come undone. She was still in the seat; the harness worked. But the straps that held it to the car had broken. She was quieter than I've ever seen her. She was only two. My aunt and uncle were in the middle seat when it happened. The roof squished them. I…I couldn't find my mom, even when I got unbuckled. She wasn't in the van, but the windshield was busted. My dad was the worst. His face was all wrong. It wasn't just shadows, either. There was blood everywhere, on the steering wheel, the door, the dashboard. And his face was wrong. I know I said that already, but it's important. His face was wrong, like it was a silly putty blob that someone tried to make into the shape of a head but didn't do a very good job."

"Thirty seconds."

"I didn't have any other family. My grandparents died when I was really little. So I went to a foster home and they were nice, but they stopped being nice when I turned eighteen. I don't think they ever really liked me, you know, because they never asked. Not like you.

"I found out later that foster families get paid money to take in kids like me, until we turn eighteen. I think that's why they let me stay that long, just until the money stopped."

Tory nodded. She'd seen dozens of young men and women in the shelters, still more kid than adult, who could testify to the greed of some foster families. She knew there were far more good people than bad, families whose generous hearts and loving natures blessed the lives of countless children with nowhere to go, but that didn't lessen her feelings of anger and frustration with those who only played the system to make a buck.

The lights went off.

Eddie tightened his grip on her waist even as she clenched him harder. So much for going out eyes wide open.

Then came the sound of stone sliding against stone, and little by little, a small pool of radiance grew in front of them, resolving into a doorway, leading into another room.

CHAPTER 11

Brian

Brian Taxis knew what was expected of him, he just didn't know how to get it done. Tell him you want a section of floor that folds up like an accordion, and he could design it. Ask him to create lighting fixtures so cleverly hidden that no one could find them but still be able to light up a room, and he could make it work. But put him into a group with nine other people and have him somehow influence their decisions, guide them to a particular outcome, and he was at a loss.

Facts and figures don't talk back. Math doesn't have its own opinion. People are just too unpredictable to be dealt with properly by an engineer. At least, by his type of engineer.

But this was his plan, so he had to find a way to make it work. At least two of them needed to make it through. No, it was more than that. Two of them *must* make it through, or it would all be for nothing. It went without saying that he'd like to survive as well.

So far, he'd been able to get away without outright lying to anyone, and that was important to him. He hated what the company was doing with The Dungeon, hated the blatant disregard for the moral character of its employees. He was embarrassed at how naive he'd been when he was scouted for this project. It seemed a dream come true, to get paid a ridiculous salary to design the kinds of things he'd only imagined when he was a teenager, sitting in his parents' basement playing *Dungeons and Dragons* with his friends. Those years were long behind him, but the fantasy and excitement never go away. You only had to look at the faces of the forty-year-olds waiting in line at your local GameSpot to know that.

He'd told the truth when he said he'd been planning to leave the company. He really was going to go public. But a call from a man whose voice he hadn't known changed everything. Oh, don't worry, his wife and kids were fine. They had no idea they were being followed, watched every minute of every day. They knew that dear Daddy was in a crucial part of the project and wouldn't be home for a few days. Wasn't Becky such a wonderful and understanding wife? Did she always sleep in a red nightgown, Brian?

That man was a friend, despite how sinister his phone call had seemed. It was all for effect, and Brian could not deny the effect it had on him. They had a goal, he and this friend and several others, and to make it work, he would need to participate in the inaugural dungeon run. They let a version of the truth slip to the higher-ups, a way to explain Brian's participation without bringing outright suspicion or hostility toward him or his family. The true threat posed by Magellan Enterprises was too far-reaching; what Brian had discovered was merely the tip of the proverbial iceberg.

Don't worry, Brian, we'll make sure you get through it all right.

Easy for them to say. They weren't down here in the dark, heart thumping, hoping that Dan was at the controls, hoping that Mike Callahan would stick to the script.

Brian didn't like to think of himself as a coward, but what else could you call it? He'd planned and prepared for this as much as anyone possibly could.

To use a football metaphor, he was playing with the other teams' signals. But even with the deck stacked in his favor, he was scared. No amount of preparation or planning could dictate what the others would do, and that was at the heart of his fear. What if he died because of someone else's actions? What if no one made it through, or the right people didn't?

What if all of this was a waste of time and Magellan ended up redesigning the world the way they wanted?

"So basically," Matt was saying, "once you guys design something, there's no guarantee it'll stay that way?"

Brian nodded, glad for an excuse to get out of his own thoughts and fears. "In a lot of industries, the engineer has a great deal of control over the final product. His input is constantly required, fine-tuning numbers, reacting to real-time data that can't be predicted on paper, like designing a manufacturing line. But for an exercise like this, it's like designing an elevator or an automatic door. Once you figure out how to make it work, it should work for everyone. So you design it, get whatever patents are appropriate, then it can be reproduced over and over without a lot of oversight by the engineer.

"That's how we were set up. Make a room that does this, make a corridor that does that. We designed it, submitted it, and then moved on to the next project. I can tell you that I personally submitted over a dozen designs for different aspects of this thing, but so far the only one I recognize is this corridor."

"But they changed it, right?" Zippy said. "You were complaining about that when this wall cut us off."

Thirty seconds.

"Damn, I hate that bitch," Matt muttered.

"Timing is a computer issue," Brian said. It wasn't a total lie. Timing could be completely automated.

But for this run, there was a literal finger on a button, Dan's finger, actuating the dividing walls at just the right moment. Only one of the trial rooms could be planned for and practiced. Just thinking about it made his fingers start to tingle again.

He hated taking a beta blocker medication. It did exactly what he'd said, when they were running down the corridor. It prevented his heart rate from increasing as rapidly as it should, so when his body squirted adrenaline, activating the fight-or-flight response, it was like stepping on the gas pedal of a car stuck in neutral. His body wanted to run, but his heart didn't respond, so his tissues starved for oxygen.

"Either they modified my programming when they built the Dungeon, or they changed it on the fly once they knew I was going to be in here. I wouldn't put it past them either way."

"Fifteen seconds," Matt said. "We gonna be okay?"

"I don't know," Brian answered honestly. "It all depends on who built the next room."

"I ain't the fightin' type," Zippy said, "not normally. But this shit has got me wantin' to punch something."

Everything went dark, and a door opened in the left wall, spilling a dim light into the corridor, just enough to show that there was a new doorway, not enough to see far into the room.

A smell wafted out to them, powerful and cloying.

"What the hell is that?" Matt asked, gagging.

The air smelled wild, a musky funk, like the den of a wild animal. Dimly he could hear a chorus of low whirring sounds, like a bunch of small motors humming. There were other sounds as well, more subtle, like a soft cough, a breathy rumble.

It was what he'd been expecting.

It was what he'd been afraid of.

"Ah, crap," Brian said.

CHAPTER 12

DeShaun

DeShaun "Li'l Bit" Bitner felt like a damn fool. Not for doing what the cop wanted. No, he did good there. He jumped the jump that the big ol' brother couldn't do, and he helped make the bridge for everyone else. He saw them all come through too, even that hard-eyed redhead bitch. He was going have to watch it around her. Might have to tone down the come-on, so to speak. Not that he really wanted her. That would suck to get ganked by a chick who only thought he wanted her because he wanted her to think that.

He shook his head, wondering if he'd really just thought himself into some kind of double negative.

No, he was dumb for not standing still and waiting for the others.

As soon as he saw everyone come through, then saw that mess of fire shooting up in the other room, he backed up, moving closer to the other door. He moved two or three steps, and it was cool. But on that fourth step, damn if the floor didn't open up, just like with that big ass white dude. DeShaun knew he was ten kinds of lucky he didn't have a metal stake up his own ass right then. Instead, he'd been dropped onto some kind of metal slide. His ass hitting pulled the rest of him down, and the last thing he remembered was the side of his head hitting the stone wall.

Now here he was.

But where was here?

He was sitting at the base of another damn rock wall, looking down a half-lit corridor of stone, like a tunnel in a *Tomb Raider* videogame. Except there were no torches on the wall, just more of that crazy light that came from nowhere. The passage was about as wide as he could stretch his arms. Wingtip to wingtip, isn't that what they called it? He wasn't a rock expert, so he didn't know if he was surrounded by anything special, anything that could give him a hint how far down he was. There was no opening in the rock behind him either, like the damn slide was a laundry chute, and now that his dirty laundry—with his dirty ass still wearing it—had been deposited at the bottom, the chute had closed up.

If only he'd kept his head from being hit, he might have a way to tell where he was in relation to everyone else. At least he'd have some idea of how long he'd slid. Should have tucked and rolled, like they said in the fire safety commercials.

The tunnel stretched ahead of him a good ways and didn't seem to narrow or widen. Until he started moving, he wouldn't know if there were any changes in elevation. It certainly didn't look like the floor had a major slope to it. Other than the walls and him, the only other thing was a small pile of pebbles on the floor near the base of the wall, right beside him.

Reaching out and hefting one, he found them to be about the size of a shooter marble but made of rock instead of glass. They weren't perfectly round either, but there were enough of them with roughly the same shape, smoothness, and size to make them look man-made. One smooth ass round rock might get spit out by Mother Nature, but not a whole pile of them.

Something tickled his mind, something else the pile of rocks looked like.

Way back before everything went sideways and he ended up in that hellhole of a prison, before he learned that Li'l Bit was synonymous with Bitch, DeShaun Bitner had a real life, a momma who didn't understand him but who loved him regardless, and a baby sister.

Now why was he thinking of Lajuanda right then?

Because she had a rabbit, a big ol' fat thing, and she had it trained to use a litter box like a damned cat. Briefly, he entertained a fantasy of a real cat coming in to use the box, only to find that fat ass rabbit already squatting, and the rabbit saying to the cat, "Wait for your turn on the shitter."

Li'l Bit giggled, something he could do now that no one was watching him, judging him, and took another look at that neat pile of round rocks. Damn if that didn't look like a tidy pile of rabbit shit. Well, a tidy pile of shit from a really big rabbit, anyway.

He talked coarse, and he acted rude around everyone, especially if there were women present, but DeShaun was neither of these. His momma would have his ass if she heard even a tenth of the things he said nowadays. She'd say he was raised better than that. And he was. But she didn't know what it was like being a gay black man in Clinton, South Carolina. Oh, it's all fine and respected, being out of the closet, if you lived in Atlanta, Georgia, or Asheville, North Carolina, one of those places with the Gay Pride Parades. But when you grew up dirt poor, surrounded by tom cats all looking for a pussy, you better walk the walk and talk the talk, or you be dead.

He got away, though. He rose above, as Momma would say. Got a full ride out of Clinton. Almost made it too. Then he went and did the dumbest thing ever. He fell in love.

Shaking his head, trying to banish the memories, Li'l Bit started picking up shit-stones, stuffing them into the pockets of his leather breeches until they bulged like hamster cheeks. Taking a step away from the wall, he noticed something missing. How long he'd been down here he didn't know, but he'd definitely been awake for more than a minute or two. There hadn't been any warnings about time. What did that mean?

He stopped himself before he'd taken more than a few steps.

He'd already fallen into one trap and was damned lucky to still be alive. How stupid would he be to go traipsing down this corridor, skipping and singing, like that Judy Garland with her munchkin friends, dancing down the yellow brick road?

Hefting one of the round rocks, he bent down and rolled it along the floor of the corridor, like he was bowling in the lanes.

Five feet in front of him a set of spikes shot out from the right wall, stopped just shy of the left wall, then retracted.

Ten feet in front of him a big ass blade like from a guillotine dropped from the ceiling, clanged off the rock floor, then rose back up.

The pebble stopped a few feet beyond the blade.

"Damn, they really trying to kill me," he said. He swallowed back an unpleasant burning in the back of his throat, afraid of puking.

He bent down and lobbed one more pebble, harder than the first, just wanting to see if everything happened the same way again.

The pebble passed where the spikes were, and they came out again. Beyond that he watched for the place in the ceiling where the blade came out, and it didn't disappoint. The pebble rolled farther. A deep boom sounded from somewhere down the corridor, followed by a grinding-rumbling noise. A similar noise started up behind him as well, and he turned to look and almost got smacked in the face by the back wall.

Wait, he'd moved away from the wall.

The back wall was moving forward, grinding, ready to push him ahead of it. And from down the corridor that rumbling sound grew louder, a shadow growing, resolving into a mass of rock as tall as he was.

Shit! A boulder was coming at him.

"Why me?" DeShaun asked, then started trying to figure a way to not get dead in the next fifteen seconds.

CHAPTER 13

Tory

Tory didn't want to go into the room that opened off the corridor, but Eddie was pulling forward, more eager to be free of the dark tunnel than he was afraid of what came next. Tory resisted, holding him back. "We don't know what's in there," she whispered to him. There was light coming through the portal, but there was also a small wall a few feet in front of the door, extending left and right, like a Japanese screen, only not silk, and certainly not decorative. It was designed solely to keep the contents of the room hidden from those still in the hallway.

"But we can't stay here," he said back. "The floor could open, or we might get burned." He pulled at her hand again. "Listen, there are voices in there. Maybe it's the others."

He had a point. Just because the floor *hadn't* yet opened up beneath them or pressurized flammable gas wasn't flowing from the walls didn't mean it *couldn't* happen. She cocked her head to listen, and did indeed hear voices, at least two male voices, but talking low enough that their words were incomprehensible. Brushing her lanky hair out of her face, hair which had badly needed a wash before she woke up here, she tried to think through the possibilities. Something wasn't right, and it wasn't just that the room was designed so they could see light, but not see into it.

"I can't stay here, Ms. Tory. I'm sorry," Eddie blurted out in a rush, letting go of her and stepping through the doorway.

"No. Wait!" she whispered fiercely, reaching for him but missing his shirt completely. Heart hammering, she stepped after him, through the doorway and into the soft light. He had already turned left, moving a few feet laterally in the small space between walls. She had the very distinct and extremely unpleasant feeling that they had just stepped into a cattle chute and were being herded from the truck to the slaughterhouse floor. Get the cows bunched up first, then open the gate.

"Five minutes until room lockdown," came the computerized voice.

"What the hell does that mean?" asked a deep male voice.

The door behind them closed, and the dividing wall began to fall into the floor.

"DJ, look, the wall's moving!" said a second voice, also male but higher and with a Southern accent, what Tory's husband had called a *hick-cent* whenever he heard someone like Trey Gowdy speak on C-SPAN.

"It's about damned time, Goob. We been waiting here forever," said the first voice. Both voices sounded rough, uncultured.

The wall descended slowly, revealing a small room maybe fifteen feet square. The walls were of the same gray-brown rock as every other wall and room, with a ceiling perhaps twelve feet overhead. The lighting came from everywhere and nowhere. A small wooden table sat in the center of the room, about eight feet in front of them, with two plain wooden chairs, turned now so that their backs were to the door on the opposite side of the room. In front of each chair stood a man, both white, both dressed in thick, orange coveralls, like prisoners, though without any of the usual black stenciling that should provide the name of the facility at least, perhaps even a prisoner number.

The man closest to Eddie, on her left, was tall and wide, bald, but with enough facial hair to more than make up for it. Starting at the halfway point of each wide, squashed ear, he had thick, bristly, auburn sideburns running along the sides of his face, merging into a beard that twisted and curled and matted but still managed to hang halfway down a broad chest that stretched his coveralls, with an equally wide abdomen below it. His wide-set eyes glinted in the light, and his small mouth twisted into a cruel smile as he said, "Looks like we finally get to earn our freedom." His was the deeper voice they'd heard.

"Mebbe a li'l more, eh, DJ?" the second man said, nodding at Tory. He was as tall as the other man but considerably thinner; his coveralls hung slack at the front and shoulders. His brown hair was cut short on top, but fell to his shoulders in the back, a classic mullet. When he leered, all four of his teeth showed.

Moving quickly to Eddie, Tory tried to push him behind her. He moved sluggishly. Maybe seeing two complete strangers had undone whatever courage he'd managed to build. She didn't know and didn't have time to find out. Whoever these two guys were, they looked like trouble. But that might just be what she was supposed to think. Maybe they could be persuaded to help.

"DJ, right?" she asked. "I'm Tory, and this is Eddie. We thought we were alone. How'd you two get here?"

"Don't care what yer name is," DJ replied. He still hadn't made any threatening moves, but he also hadn't relaxed back into the chair.

"She's sure pretty," the skinny one said. He'd taken a hesitant step toward her, then looked back at the larger man.

Slowly, Tory slid a foot to the left, her hands behind her back, guiding Eddie to keep up with her. Maybe they could edge around to the far door.

"Nah, she ain't, Goob. But for how long I been locked up, I'd do a dead gramma, and she's definitely better than that."

Goob laughed, a donkey bray of sound with more than a little crazy in it. She slipped a little farther to the left. "Come on, guys. Don't tell me you made it this far and all you can think about it causing trouble."

"Made it this far?" DJ asked.

"What's she talkin' 'bout?" Goob asked.

Four minutes.

"That's what I'm talking about," she said, trying not to shout, not wanting to show these animals any fear. What had she been wondering before? How could this weird social engineering work if they only used up ten people at a time?

"First time we've heard anything since we walked down here but our own voices," DJ answered.

"Well, there was them others what showed us the way," Goob offered. Tory took another step, realized she had reached a corner, and quickly shifted herself and Eddie a little more.

"What others?" she asked. Eddie quaked behind her.

"Same ones what told us to sit here and wait, take care of anyone that came by. We do that, we get to go free."

"So you see," DJ said, picking up the thread, "we got no reason to want to talk to you. Then again, we wasn't expecting any women. Might be we could see our way clear to work something out with ya, if you take my meaning." He tried on a smile, which looked worse on him than on the other. She was running out of time.

Time. They didn't know about the timers. Could she use that to frighten them?

"That voice that's counting down. When time runs out, everyone in this room will die!"

The two convicts looked at each other, then back at her. She inched a little farther along the wall. Then they laughed.

"She's mine first!" DJ said, launching himself at her.

Tory couldn't help it. She screamed.

Chapter 14

Zippy

Zippy Brown knew he wasn't that smart. Maybe that's why his momma named him Zippy, instead of some other name. Maybe she'd known what he'd end up like. A little ADD, not quite normal smarts, he really did have the deck stacked against him. But he was good people, he told himself, and he meant it, so it must be true. He'd never hurt anyone, not even when people bothered him. Some nights, when sleep slowed him down and his thoughts cleared a little, he could almost understand the chain of events that had put him in prison.

Momma always watched out for him and never let the other boys take advantage. But then she got the cancer and died, and he had to go live with his brother. Jamal wasn't bad people, but he had a *bidness* to run. He needed runners, and he put Zippy to work. But there was this one guy he delivered to who was in a sharing mood, and Zippy the runner became Zippy the running crack-head. One high ran into another, and soon Zippy was doing whatever his slow brain could think of just to get another hit. He figured his brother might have killed him eventually, to protect the *bidness*, you know, but they got raided. That was Zippy's fault too, since it was him the police followed back to the warehouse.

He'd been clean for over a year now. No crack for a crack-head in prison. Maybe Jamal was out now too. He could do this one little thing, couldn't he? Just get through a little television show and then go home to his brother, who must be worried sick about him. So when the suits asked, he said yes and made his mark on the line.

But this wasn't just a television show. He'd already seen one guy die, saw a brother disappear, and now he was stuck with two white guys in another kind of prison. He didn't know how to spell sucker, but he figured if you wrote the word under his picture instead of Zippy, it'd fit.

He didn't know what was on the other side of the lit-up doorway, but he knew that when the timer ran down, bad shit happened. So what if it smelled like one of those wild animal pens at the Central Park Zoo? While the two white guys waited to get Crispy Crittered, he was gonna go on ahead.

"Ah, crap," Brian said as Zippy stepped through the doorway.

Now this was a total letdown. Nothing here but a little three-foot-wide hallway, running left and right. There wasn't anything at either end either. No turns, nothing. He was about to go back out the door and tell the other guys that this was a dead end, when they came through the door instead. Just like that, the doorway closed and the wall started dropping. Damn if they didn't do some cool shit with this place.

"Five minutes until room lockdown."

In here the noises like a hundred toy robots were louder, and the smell stronger. There were more weird coughing sounds, and then a long, low, snarling sound.

"It's an animal room," Brian said.

"What the hell does that mean?" Matt asked.

THE DUNGEON

Zippy saw them standing on either side of him and drew his shoulders in a little. He didn't have anything against white people in particular. The nice guy who shared his dope had been white. But Jamal used to tease him about being lighter skinned than the rest of the family, said if he rubbed up against too many white people, he'd end up just as white. Zippy was pretty sure that wasn't true, but it never hurt to be safe.

The wall was halfway down, and Zippy's eyes widened in amazement at what he could see in the room beyond. Not a small room, heck, it was probably as big as his momma's whole apartment! It was lined floor, walls, and ceiling with metal grooves, like the kind you jimmied marbles through in those kiddie puzzles at the doctor's office. There were square poles, running from floor to ceiling every three or four feet in every direction, and they had those metal runners on them too, only those were going up and down.

That's not what made Zippy's lips widen in a toothy grin.

"What the absolute hell?" Matt asked. "Are those cougars?"

"Cougar, mountain lion, panther," Brian said, "all different names for the same thing."

There were lots of cages, maybe more than he could count, all with big cats in them, mounted on the tracks, moving up and down the poles, sliding across the ceiling, the floor, motoring along the walls. It looked like there were always two or three moving up a column on one side or coming down another. It was like a light show, only instead of lights, there were big cats in lots of different colors, moving around willy-nilly.

"We have to get through that?" Matt asked, and Zippy thought he'd never heard a man sound so scared before.

"Yup," Brian answered. "And it won't be easy."

"As long as we don't bump into a cage, won't we be okay?"

"The bars are the problem," Brian explained. "I remember Chloe talking about it. She was so excited about doing something with big cats. Not all of the bars are the same distance apart. There's at least one side on every cage where some of the bars are too far apart."

"Too far apart for what?"

A huge, tawny beast, all glaring eyes and smiling teeth, let out a very unfriendly hiss as it came across the floor. Because they hadn't yet gone beyond the boundary set by the disappearing wall, they weren't in any danger. But the great cat still tried to get at them, lunging at the side of the cage, shoulder to the bar, claw-tipped paw reaching out through the bars.

Two of the up and down poles had cages coming in opposite directions, one going up and one coming down. When the cages were about four feet off the ground, giant paws slashed out of them as the agitated cats attacked one another. The paws almost met.

Dozens of cages moving in different directions. You couldn't stand still because eventually one of them would get you.

"Four minutes."

The cages rose and fell, swept across the floor, and trundled along the walls. Forget about the cages on the ceiling; those were too far away to do any harm. It was all about the cages in the middle, how they moved, rotated. There was something there, something he couldn't quite see but could feel. It was the same feeling he got when Jamal would show him a map and say, "Go deliver this package to that corner." No one ever understood how he got places so fast. He could just feel the way the streets were supposed to go.

THE DUNGEON

The cages were cars and the columns were buildings, and the path between them was the streets. Zippy could feel it, could feel how it should work.

"Follow me!" he shouted and stepped out into the room.

CHAPTER 15

Elizabeth

The lights went out, but that was okay, because Zachary was holding her hand. Liz didn't know what she felt for the police officer. She didn't stop to think or worry about anything happening too soon; she had no real basis for comparison. He was this handsome guy who understood. It didn't matter why.

The sliding stone noises started up, and a dim light began to shine from an opening door.

You're no good for him, you know.

The voice, her mother's voice, so close, whispering in her left ear, startled her. That's what made her scream.

"What the hell?" Big Rich asked.

Zachary's grip on her hand tightened. He pulled her back away from the door. "What is it?" he asked.

He'll leave you, just like your daddy did.

She shook her head, denying the voices. Where was her anger? Why had she let her rage go? It worked. It helped. It—

Maybe you want him to be just like Daddy. You'd like that, wouldn't you?

Liz held her breath.

"C'mon, Richard, help me get her into the light."

She felt herself half-lifted, half pulled through the new doorway. She had a vague impression of another hallway, narrow, with no escape.

THE DUNGEON

"Shit, man, the door just closed," Big Rich said.

There was something to her mother's words. Something hidden. Something she needed to know, something she'd once known.

"Five minutes until room lockdown."

From the other side of the corridor wall, there came a tapping, scraping sound. A low sound, like a gasp of air through a desert-parched throat, accompanied the scrapes.

Her father had loved her. He'd fought for her, fought to win custody when her mother turned into a drunk.

Oh, your daddy loved you, all right. That was the voice of Brad, one of the counselors at Mind and Body Wellness. All of the mental institutions had fancy names nowadays. You couldn't call them asylums or state hospitals anymore. They had manicured lawns, shrubbery cut into fanciful shapes, and medical assistants wearing crisp, white scrubs. Visitors were treated to open foyers with soaring glass walls, palm frond ceiling fans maintaining a comfortable seventy-two degrees. They sat on couches while they saw their loved ones or took a walk along meandering garden paths. They saw pristine tennis courts, workout rooms with the latest equipment from Nautilus.

Behind the facade, where visitors never trod, were the puke-green hallways, the doors that locked from the outside, with slots so trays could be passed through into padded rooms, some of which had nothing but a mattress in the center of the floor, with metal eye loops bolted in at the cardinal positions for restraints. Behind the shiny exterior, medical assistants became orderlies again. The pretty girls up front, who smiled for the cameras, never worked in the back. They never had to deal with the unconscious patient, drooling and soaking in his own urine after his latest electroshock therapy, still unable to move from the paralytic drug he'd been given.

Louder noises, like the shrieks of a patient in the midst of a psychotic break, arms flailing at imaginary targets, throwing their own bodies against the padded walls, reached her. There were no words in the screams. There never were words in those kinds of screams, just animal vocalizations that somehow conveyed pain, loss, and need.

"Elizabeth?" Zachary asked, but she shook her head again. She'd never been this close before. She couldn't force the truth, that never worked. She couldn't argue with the words either. That only made things worse. She had to let the voices take her where they wanted. She'd never heard Brad's voice, trying to incite her anger, maybe that meant something too.

"Dude, the whole wall is coming down," Big Rich said.

"I don't like those sounds," Zachary added.

You told me once, what he did to you, right before we shocked you. You forgot afterward, but I didn't.

I didn't forget, she thought, not trying to argue, just trying to center herself. *It never happened to me! That was someone else.*

The room disappeared.

She was on her back but moving somehow. The click-clack of wheels going over floor planks shuddered through her. She could turn her head, could see several large people wearing white lab coats, walking on either side of her. Banks of fluorescent lights seemed to slide along the ceiling, there, then gone, there, then gone. She tried to sit up but could only manage to raise her shoulders an inch before something restrained her. Desperate, panicked, she tried again, with the same results.

THE DUNGEON

One of the people, a man, with caring gray eyes and a soft voice, said, "There now, be at peace, Ms. Ott. We talked about this procedure, remember?"

One of the other men turned and opened his mouth. **"Four minutes,"** he said, which didn't make any sense, since his lips didn't move and the voice wasn't right.

Something made her gurney shift violently to the right. The supporting frame, the wheels, everything underneath her seemed to disappear, and her breath blew out as she fell two or three feet to the ground.

"Liz!" someone screamed at her. She blinked, trying to draw breath, feeling new aches at hips, shoulders, and head, while the hospital corridor disappeared, to be replaced by a small room with walls of rock. Six or seven people weaved and danced around the room, but only two looked familiar.

There was no gurney. Someone had bumped into her, knocking her sideways against a wall, and she'd slid down.

Groaning, she pushed herself up onto an elbow, squinting, trying to focus and understand the scene.

It was Zachary and Big Rich, standing near her, guarding her, and coming at them were a group of... she didn't know what to call them. They were people, obviously, skinny men with blackened and missing teeth, bushy beards, and tattered clothes. They smelled awful, like a group of football players stuffed their sweat-soaked jock straps in a plastic bag, put it on the back window ledge of a black car on a hot summer day, and then opened it in this small room. They were breathing heavily, making a moaning/keening sound as they moved, drool spooling out of their rotting mouths, wide, wild eyes staring, not blinking. And they were attacking the other two men.

As she tried to stand, Big Rich rushed forward, shouting wordlessly. He swung a huge fist at one of the lanky men, connecting solidly. She heard the sound his fist made. The thin, bearded man pivoted away, moved by the force of the blow. But he didn't go down. The punch didn't seem to bother him. He pivoted right back and ran at the football player, dirty hands grabbing.

Zachary fought differently, not attacking, just waiting for one to grab at him. He took hold of the reaching hand, twisted, and threw the man into the hard rock wall. Flesh struck stone, a bone cracked, but the crazy man bounced off the wall, pouncing on Zachary, who had turned his back to face a new attacker, thinking the first one dealt with. A mass of shaggy hair and rotting clothes bore the police officer forward to his knees, and Liz finally found her feet and her voice.

Letting go a scream almost feral in its intensity, frightening because of the fear behind it, not fear for herself but fear for Zachary, Liz rushed to help. She grabbed a lanky arm in one hand and a handful of greasy mane in the other, and she pulled. The crazy man-thing came up off Zachary, but instead of trying to prevent injury, as a normal person would have, it twisted, trying to see. Her left hand came away holding a wad of putrid hair as her right arm was pulled in front of her. She released the arm, dropping the hair, just in time to get her hands up. The crazed man lunged, teeth snapping like a rabid animal, going for her face.

She stepped back, striking the wall with her hips. The man pressed forward, hands grabbing for her shoulders, holding her in place.

She screamed again as his face closed in on hers.

Chapter 16

DeShaun

You had to be able to think quick to hide a secret like his for as long as he had.

"Why ain't you gettin' up widdat chick? She smilin' atchew like yo dick already up in it."

"Yo, Li'l B! Why ain't you got da drippies? I swear Shequa gave it to me, an' I know she ain't got it fixed yet."

A fast lie here, a quick evasion there, and then off to college, where he could choose who he spent his time with, where he could escape those for whom status was measured by the number of girls you'd slept with or the number of kids you'd fathered almost as much as by the drugs you'd sold or the white people you'd robbed. Thankfully, though every kid was in a gang of some kind, murder was still taboo, not because the kids weren't that bad, but because the gang leaders weren't ready to fight the cops. It was South Carolina, and there was still enough racism in the state that if brothers started killing white people, they'd be rounded up and put down pretty quick.

So DeShaun "Li'l Bit" Bitner thought quick, seeing his death coming for him in the rolling, rumbling boulder, ready to turn him into a brown patty flat against the moving wall behind him. Hardly stopping to think, he rolled a third pebble, aiming for where he thought the trip plate or motion sensor was for the wall spikes.

As soon as the pebble was out of his hands, he rushed after it, praying to his momma's baby Jesus that he'd guessed right.

The pebble arced across the ground, skipping like a rock on a lake, and the spikes shot out, crossing the corridor in an instant. No way anyone caught in their path would be able to move out of the way in time. They were almost completely silent in their passage, the only noise a faint ting as one of the spikes, maybe not screwed in as well as it should be, so it hung out just a tiny bit farther, hit the far wall. Immediately after reaching their full extension, they began to retract. Li'l Bit hit the left side of the corridor just as the spikes started to move back. He hugged the wall, moving fast, not knowing if they could reverse without completely resetting, but not intending to find out. The rolling boulder motivated him further, so that when his right shoulder came too close to a spike, he didn't slow, didn't bother trying to ease past. He let it scratch him, let the pain be a reminder that he was still alive, still moving, and pushed on.

His pebble had also tripped the guillotine, which was retracting back up into the ceiling.

Then he was through, and the boulder came on, only a few yards away now, not going any faster but certainly not slowing. Pushing away from the wall, he took two quick steps, getting past the blade, then jumped. It was like that moment with the cop all over again, only this time no one had to ask him to do it. He planted his feet and pushed off harder than ever before, pulling his legs up after him, tucking a little. He had one chance and one chance only. He wasn't trying to clear the rock. That wasn't possible.

He hit the rolling surface, hands and feet finding a quick purchase then pulling with his hands and pushing with his feet again before that purchase could dwindle and disappear. Like a parkour runner he scrambled for the smallest bit of grip, hands pulling, feet pushing, fighting the call of gravity, fighting the motion of the boulder, fighting to reach the top. Scrambling, he pushed off again, gaining another foot, now able to see over the top, gathering himself one last time, driving upward and forward just a little bit more. He felt the boulder start to roll out from under him as he gained the top, felt something incredibly strong tug at his right foot as he toppled over the backside of the rolling rock.

There was a loud clang, a rumbling crash, but he paid no attention to the noises, trying to get his feet under him as he fell the five or six feet back to the gritty stone floor. He managed to avoid face-planting or belly-flopping, getting one foot down and landing on the opposite knee, a classic superhero pose, and then moving forward again, momentum requiring the motion, fear of the guillotine driving him to it. But even as he rose and stepped, his toes caught on the floor and he stumbled, staggering, something not quite right with his right foot, throwing off his balance so that even as he continued forward, he twisted to the right, his face coming dangerously close to the right wall before he could save himself with his hands.

That inadvertent twist saved his life.

A loud popping sound filled his ears just a split second before a rush of searing hot pain raced up his legs, burning his back, setting his ass on fire. Then he caromed off the wall, still twisting, now facing back the way he'd come, feeling that awful burning even as he saw the jets of flame shooting out of the floor in front of him.

DeShaun lost his balance, falling flat on his back and away from the flames. Quickly, driven by instinct honed by a dozen years of fire drills in public schools, he rolled left and right, from one side of the corridor to the other. He batted at his pants legs, at his hair, but felt no remaining flames. His back and butt still felt hot, but no longer like they were actually on fire.

The jets of flame cut off, a few last spurts shooting up before disappearing altogether.

Sitting up, he surveyed the short stretch of corridor he'd somehow survived. Where it had once appeared clear of debris, a death trap for the unwary, it now resembled a war zone. Large chunks of rock covered the floor, some still showing a gently rounded edge here and there. The boulder which had threatened him was gone, reduced to rubble. The moving wall which had driven him to move forward had advanced past the area with the wall spikes and was coming into the area with the dropping blade. He must have cleared the rock just as it hit the sensor to drop the blade. The guillotine apparently shattered the boulder. He shuddered to think what it would have done to him.

Remembering the weird way his right foot felt as he tumbled off the boulder, he examined his boot, finding the thick heel had been sheared of half its thickness. Any slower, and it would have been his whole foot.

He wasn't untouched, not completely. The flame jets had left his back sore and raw. Moving his arms experimentally, he found the pain didn't increase too badly. It certainly wasn't as bad as the way white boys described a sunburn. So either his back was really bad, and he couldn't do anything about it. Or it wasn't, and he didn't need to do anything about it. He could still function, that's what mattered. No crazy death for Li'l Bit Bitner in a death trap tunnel.

The lingering smell of burnt hair reminded him to check his head for burns. There wasn't any real pain up there, but he did make note of the short, stubby feeling of hair nubs at the base of his neck. Only blind luck, the inability to catch his balance because of the cut in his boot heel, had allowed him to escape the worst of the flame jets. If he'd landed square and stepped forward into the center of the corridor... He had a vision of char-broiled Bitner Balls, blacker than marshmallows left on a stick too long in a campfire, before he could force the image away.

The wall was still coming, now pushing chunks of rock in front of it like the world's slowest avalanche, creating a hell of a noise as it swept them along. Struggling to his feet, Li'l Bit turned away from the moving wall, noting that the corridor continued a short distance before ending in what appeared to be a dead end. The floor sloped up slightly, probably what had allowed the boulder to gain momentum. Limping a little due to the uneven boots, he moved up the corridor to the dead end. No doors, no turns, just a wall of rock.

The moving wall behind him kept coming.

CHAPTER 17

Eddie

Eddie Artios might be young, he might be inexperienced in the ways of men and women, but he knew how babies were made. He knew that holding hands led to kissing, which led to sex, often all in the same day. He also knew the difference between consensual sex and rape. So when the two bad men started talking about how surprised they were to see a woman, with that special twist to their voices that meant they had no intention of letting a woman, any woman, get away, Eddie knew they meant to rape Ms. Tory.

The other parts of the conversation helped him understand a few other things. These guys were part of the same program. They had volunteered, unlike Ms. Tory or him, and they thought all they had to do was kill whoever entered the room. They didn't understand the timers, which probably meant that even if they succeeded in killing him and Ms. Tory, they were still going to die. Eddie didn't think the mysterious *they* who created this show and recruited people like these guys would have any qualms about reneging on a promise of freedom.

Which brought to light a serious concern. If volunteers weren't safe, what chance did any of them have, especially the involuntary contestants?

He appreciated Ms. Tory's worry for him, her attempt to shield him as she moved them along the

THE DUNGEON

wall. It wasn't going to be enough, but the gesture was welcomed. This would be one of those very rare times when passivity wouldn't work and running away wasn't possible.

Which left one alternative, something he tried to avoid at all costs, just as he'd been taught. If ever there was a time to fight, it was now. Not for himself, though he had no intention of dying in here, not to two losers like these. He would fight for Ms. Tory, because she certainly deserved better than what they had in mind.

Short for a man but still taller than the woman who wanted to protect him, Eddie saw the bigger man charging. Ms. Tory's hands stopped bracketing him, instead moving in front of her. She screamed, and he ducked out under her arms, his sudden aggression serving to slow the big man's charge. More out of surprise than worry, he was sure.

He scooted to the left, around the big guy, who turned his head slightly, which allowed Tory to choke off her scream and drop down to a squat. Eddie wished DJ would face-plant the wall, but that kind of luck only happened in the movies. A strangled grunt reached his ears as he found himself facing the skinnier of the two men, the one known as Goob, who didn't seem all that alarmed.

Why would he? Eddie thought. He must look like a pretty easy target.

"Eddie, be careful!" Tory warned.

Even Ms. Tory thought he needed to be protected.

"You...bitch," DJ groaned. She must have hit him in the nads somehow. Not many other things could make a guy grunt like that.

But now Goob came at him, arms out and high like Eddie was just gonna stand there and let the meth-head grab him. He ducked instead, again sliding to his left. As Goob passed him, he kicked out with his right leg, toes pointed as he'd been taught, slamming the top of his foot into the taller man's midsection.

The air blew out of Goob in a whoosh as he doubled over, coughing.

"Nice kick, Eddie!" Ms. Tory said. "Where's you learn that?"

"Tae Kwon Do school," he responded. "Tiger Kim's. Dad made me go because he thought, you know, since I was small, I should know how to protect myself."

Both DJ and Goob were regaining their feet, though DJ still hunched forward slightly, one hand guarding his crotch.

"I head-butted him," Tory said. "Pretty sure that's not what he had in mind."

Eddie smiled. Grabbing Ms. Tory's hand, he pulled her to the far door. Maybe they could just get out and hold the door closed, trap the other guys inside.

But the door was locked, an iron bolt clearly visible in the gap between door and frame, holding it closed.

"Three minutes."

"You ain't gettin' away that easy, bitch!" DJ said, coming at them again.

Goob was coming as well. He reached a hand behind his back and pulled out a wickedly serrated, six-inch-long hunting knife. "I'm gonna gut the boy," he said.

Chapter 18

Matt

When an avowed convict and crackhead, who either smoked a few billion brain cells away or was born with that many less than normal, says, "Follow me," you tend to hold back. When that same crackhead then proceeds to jump into an ever-changing maze of moving cages, all filled with angry, screaming, clawing mountain lions, scaring the crap out of everyone, that tendency becomes a terror-fueled necessity.

That was the case for Matt Absher, anyway. The geeky technician, Brian, didn't move either. So they had that in common.

But as the skinny black dude wended his way in a strange sort of back and forth, left then right, series of hops that seemed to cover the whole room, somehow staying a step ahead of the angry felines, never coming close to being touched, Matt started to wonder if he should have followed after all.

Brian started cheering for the crackhead. "Yeah, Zippy! You go! You got this!" which was answered with more snarls and hisses as the caged cats alternated their attention between the moving Zippy and the stationary white men.

The columns that allowed the cages to track up and down were maybe six feet apart. They ran four across and three deep, making the room roughly thirty feet wide and twenty-four feet from one door to the other. Though it was hard to get an accurate count of the moving cages, Matt estimated there were at least thirty of them, with every column having at least one going up and one down at all times. Zippy dodged through them all.

"It's incredible." Brian exhaled. "Somehow, he can see the pattern."

A pattern. There was a pattern!

Of course there was, Matt realized, or else the cages would eventually collide. He was good at patterns, at least those on paper, involving numbers. Credits and debits might look like just so much scribbled data to everyone else, but those rows and columns often provided a pattern that could help him figure out when things weren't quite right or aid him as he sought to hide his own theft. Ironically, it was a distinct lack of a pattern that had tipped the FBI off to his embezzlement. Nothing could be that random by accident, they'd said, so they'd gone looking for the design behind the randomness and caught him in a web.

There was a pattern here as well, the way one column had two cages on perpendicular sides, going opposite directions, while the closest adjacent columns in every direction each had one cage in motion, raising or lowering opposite its neighbor. There were always an equal number of cages on the floor and the ceiling, as well as along the left and right walls. Movement from the far side of the room to the near side was accomplished through a series of column shifts; the cages never traversed the walls for farther than the distance between two columns. Likewise with the floor and ceilings. He could see it, could see how it should work. The random factor was the bars. He couldn't predict which sides of which cages would have bars far enough apart to allow the cats a chance to claw at them.

THE DUNGEON

Zippy didn't seem to be too concerned with that. Maybe his lower IQ was a blessing there. He could see the pattern, so he could follow it. He didn't necessarily understand the random danger of some bars being farther apart than others, so he didn't worry about it. In watching him navigate the room, it seemed his method of dealing with it worked quite well. He was quick enough to stay ahead, taking only thirty seconds or so to reach the far door.

Matt watched him try to open it, thinking if he could get it open and hold it open, he'd be more comfortable making a run for it. Unlike this side of the room, there was no grace boundary on the far side. The cages almost touched the far wall as they moved between columns.

"It's locked!" Zippy shouted over the growls, snarls, and spinning track wheels.

Matt looked a question at Brian, who shrugged. "What the absolute hell, man?" he asked.

"Some of the doors won't open until a condition has been met," the engineer answered, "or until a certain amount of time has passed."

Zippy was moving again, a sort of herky-jerky figure eight that involved actually leaping onto and over a cage as it came by at ground level, all in an effort to stay near the door. He looked back at Brian and Matt, shook his head, and kept up his dance.

"*Three minutes.*"

"Doesn't look too hard, right?" Brian said, with a wry twist to his mouth that loaded the comment with sarcasm. His face had gone pasty again, and he was doing that hand-wringing thing which meant his adrenaline was surging, his heart should be trip-hammering (like Matt's) but wasn't able to speed up properly.

"Whatever, man," Matt said, watching, waiting for the pattern to give him an opening.

"All right, here goes!" Brian said, rushing out.

Matt tried to stop him. The timing wasn't right yet! The pattern hadn't cleared. He darted forward, tried to grab the engineer's billowing white shirt, just as a snarling cat came down the column, hooked claws reaching out, swiping down, fishing for whatever it could reach.

The claws raked across the back of Matt's extended arm, tearing lines in his shirt, drawing a scream of pain and fear. Matt jumped back, already cradling his arm as the cats raised a chorus of hungry feline sounds. They were louder now, more of them adding their voices. They smelled blood.

Shuddering, terrified, Matt checked his arm, seeing the four gouges going horizontally across the back. Thankfully, none seemed to be too deep. There was blood staining the white linen, but only from three of them, and that was just a seeping kind of bleeding. His hand still worked when he flexed and extended his fingers. But crap, the pain! He was going to need a rabies shot, a tetanus shot, and some antibiotics. Assuming he survived, of course.

Brian was now halfway across. The pattern was finally starting over as the computer voice announced, **"Two minutes."**

Matt readied himself, saw the opening, and rushed out between two cages, just as Brian tripped over something, falling forward onto his hands and knees, right by a column with a descending cage. The cage held a massive black beast, eyes locked on the engineer, huge forepaw reaching through the bars, coming closer and closer as it descended.

CHAPTER 19

Richard

Big Richard Cranston, or Big Rich—as the students in the bleachers at his high school shouted whenever he lined up at tight end—was pretty good at pushing people around. He wasn't a violent person—well, maybe he was, but football provided such a natural outlet for his aggression that it was never an issue off the field—-but he understood when a little force would be better appreciated than a soft voice.

He wasn't sure what was wrong with the skinny, filthy, white guys who mindlessly clawed at him with hands blackened by dirt, or blood, or some other substance, which not only caked the grooves and ridges of their knuckles but which also seemed to be embedded in their skin past the elbow. They were crazy or hopped up on something...it didn't matter to Big Rich. They were attacking him, trying to hurt him, so he would hurt them first.

If he could figure out how, that is.

He'd slammed one in the face with a roundhouse punch that sent a stinger of pain jolting up to his shoulder, and the guy had reeled back. But then he came right on in again, snarling and gnashing his rotted teeth like some kind of animal. What the hell?

The second dude came up on his right, trying to get a hold of his arm, reaching out with hands covered with dark brown flakes that might be dried crap.

Rather than let that happen, Rich stepped forward, putting his back to the other crazy man for a moment as he grabbed the second one and twisted, yanking the much smaller and lighter man off the floor, swinging him around to the left, slamming him into the first one.

The two men collided, their grasping fingers latching onto each other's hair and clothes, as they tumbled to the ground. Neither man made so much as a sound of protest or pain. Neither one seemed to be injured from the impact. Their hands groped at each other, pulling at hair, faces lunging as if to bite. Stunned, Big Rich couldn't take his eyes from them, two lost souls who had gone from attackers to objects of pity.

Elizabeth screamed, drawing his attention. Turning back to the side of the room they'd entered—though you couldn't easily see where the door had been—he saw the tall woman with the funny-colored hair rise up from the floor, eyes almost as wild as the weirdos around them. Big Rich shuddered as understanding dawned; that woman walked a very fine line between sane and psychotic, and right now, as one of the *Friends* characters famously said, she was so far past it that the line was just a dot to her.

As he watched, she reached out and grabbed one of the scrawny drugged out zombies off of the big cop's back, tearing out a chunk of hair. Then she was pushed back because, crazy or not, she probably didn't weigh as much as the guy she grabbed. She struck the wall behind her and screamed again.

Whatever had been done to these four guys to put them in this state obviously didn't allow for baths or clean clothes. They didn't seem to feel pain, and they were a lot stronger than they should be.

Big Rich realized he was going to have to be a lot tougher on them.

He saw the cop pressing against one of the others, holding it against a wall with his forearm pressed in on its throat, like he was going to choke it out that way. Those dirty hands with ragged nails were flailing at him, but not able to do much because the cop was in so close.

The two he'd knocked down had apparently figured out they weren't supposed to be fighting each other, because they rose once more to their feet, stumbling back toward him. Rich took a deep breath, then summoned his inner offensive tackle, charging at them, angling between them with his big arms outstretched, catching both men high on the chest, knocking them back down. One landed face down, smacking the rock floor hard enough to make Rich wince, though he immediately began trying to stand again. Rich could make out a stream of blood running from a fractured nose.

They could be injured, he thought with satisfaction. So maybe he could hurt them enough that they stopped getting back up.

Using fists and feet, he went at this goal, punching and kicking, keeping the two hopped-up-out-of-their-minds dopers down. He didn't want to kill them, harbored no real anger or animus toward them. They were just two more people trapped here and might not even be aware of their actions.

By the time the computer voice announced, **"Three minutes,"** the two were down for the count. Their faces were swollen and bloody, and he was pretty sure one had a broken arm, but they were still breathing.

Big Rich was breathing hard, but nothing hurt other than his knuckles. Looking up, he saw that both of the other crazed men were also down. Elizabeth straddled one of them, riding his back like a pretty girl on a placid horse. The man wasn't moving, but that didn't stop her from reaching forward, pulling his head up by his lanky, greasy hair, then slamming it back to the floor.

Zachary stood near her, saying something in a voice too soft for Big Rich to make out the words. He had a tentative hand out, like he wanted to reach out to her, maybe try to stop her, but was afraid of touching her.

Walking over to them, Rich said, "Don't you think he's had enough, Liz?" But he said it slow and soft. He was young, but he knew the lessons of Al and Barry. Women loved his voice and responded better the lower he spoke.

When he said her name, she stopped slamming the dude's head and looked up. Her eyes were still wild but filled with tears, some of which had escaped, leaving lines of cleanliness down her dust-streaked face. When the cop reached out to her this time, she let him pull her up and away from the prone man. Big Rich didn't want to look at the man's face. It had to be messed up. He did watch for a moment to make sure the man was still breathing.

Turning away from the still figure, he saw the form of the fourth attacker, on the floor right where the cop had been choking him, back still propped up against the wall. Turning back, he saw the tall redhead with her face buried in the cop's chest. Was there something going on there? He couldn't be sure, and it really wasn't his business anyway. Clearing his throat, he asked, "Any idea what was up with those guys?"

"Bath salts," the cop answered, "or PCP. Maybe both."

"So they just got all doped up while waiting for us?"

The cop shook his head, but he did it in a strange, gentle fashion, like in slow motion. Maybe there *was* something growing between those two, if the cop was trying so hard not to disturb her. "No, I think this has more to do with what I was investigating. I'll have a better explanation later, I think, after I can stop for a moment, try to put some of these pieces together."

Big Rich nodded. He could respect that. Despite that the man was a cop, he found a lot to like in him. He didn't talk down to anyone, didn't try to act like having a badge made him something special. And he listened. He might be the best cop he'd ever dealt with. Considering he'd been arrested for Possession with Intent to Distribute, that was saying something.

Zachary and Elizabeth separated just as **"*Two minutes*"** came over the hidden speakers.

"Come on, let's get out of here," he said to her.

All too happy to oblige—one of the dopers looked like he might be coming around—Big Rich led the way to the far door, just another of those old-fashioned-looking things, all vertical slats held together by wide iron bands. When he pulled on it, it wouldn't open. Pushing it did nothing either.

The door was still locked.

CHAPTER 20

Tory

Tory didn't like to think she'd ever been naive. That she hadn't seen the oh-so-obvious signs of her husband's spiral into addiction which led to a suicidal depression, or that maybe she had, but then ignored the signs, or glossed over them, or found some strange way to rationalize them into thinking they weren't as bad as they seemed, had been a hard lesson in confronting truth when you see it, accepting truth rather than trying to paint a pretty face onto its ugliness, if only so you felt better while looking at it. Those few people she counted as friends, aged and wise by street standards, helped her understand other truths as well, how a man willing to give cash to a homeless woman rarely is as safe as he appears, or how a young kid who appears helpless could still knife her just so he could claim her meager possessions, or maybe just take over whatever comfortable spot she'd found under an overpass.

    She was a fast learner and had kept herself as safe as possible, under the circumstances, for almost three years. Despite those hard lessons, despite the hardness that she'd discovered within herself, she felt a thrill of surprise mixed with a small surge of disappointment as she watched Eddie. As Goob came forward, swinging his wicked blade, calling out how he would gut the kid, open him from chin to nuts, Eddie

THE DUNGEON

just shrugged his shoulders. He stepped back with his right leg and then he went...loose. Loose was a good word, loose but also somehow tense as a coiled spring, like he could explode into motion at any second, but offering no clue which way he would go.

DJ was standing straighter now, though he seemed content to hang back a little. His heavy brow was still creased and drawn down, eyes tight, showing pain. He urged the skinnier man on. "You get 'im! Cut that li'l cocksucker! Then we can do the bitch!"

Tory sucked in a breath and suppressed the urge to scream as Goob lunged forward. Eddie's body seemed to flow sideways, fast as a snake. His hands did something, too quick to follow. There was a sound like a hammer tenderizing meat, then Goob was falling back, still holding the knife but now waving it drunkenly in front of him, almost defensively. His nose no longer appeared straight, and fresh blood covered his lower face, more of it pouring out of his nose every second, spraying away from his mouth as he cursed, spitting.

"Tha' fuck, Goob?" DJ said, pushing the skinny man away as he backed up. Eyes closed, Goob took a single staggering step forward, arms out to the sides, pin wheeling, propelled not by any urge to continue the fight but by the force of the other man's shove. Eddie moved, spinning in place, letting one leg fly out behind him, catching Goob, who stood a foot taller, on the right side of his head. The blow was fierce, toppling the skinny man. The knife skittered across the floor, spinning away to her right.

As Goob fell away, DJ suddenly looked exposed. He didn't immediately rush forward. Instead, his eyes wide, he looked nothing so much as like a man trying to process the unexpected fact that a little kid just took out his partner in crime and the chunky chick he wanted to rape had given him the worst case of blue balls he'd ever experienced. Maybe what he really saw were two people who were no longer afraid of him, and that alone was enough to hold him back.

Shaking herself, like trying to force herself awake from a heavy sleep, Tory moved to the side, never taking her eyes of the large man. Swiftly, she knelt and retrieved the knife from the floor, feeling a sense of empowerment with the weight of the weapon in her hand. Feeling more in control of the situation than at any time since this whole hell-spawned amusement park maze ride began, she walked back to Eddie's side, the knife held before her like a talisman.

Though still much larger than either of them, DJ no longer appeared such a threat. Like all the bullies she'd encountered in her life, female as well as male—and let no one ever try to tell her than women aren't worse than men—all the blustery wind left their sails as soon as it became obvious they weren't going to win easily, that their larger size and louder mouth couldn't compete with grit and determination. DJ saw himself losing, and that possibility robbed him of his false courage.

"Two minutes."

Still holding the knife with her right hand, its sharp point aimed squarely and steadily at DJ's chest, Tory reached out with her left hand, patting Eddie's right arm and indicating they should move back. Eddie still held his easy stance, though the muscles of his right arm were taut and hard as iron under the poet shirt.

"I wasn't lying to you before," she said to the burly man. "When that countdown ends, something bad is going to happen in this room. It could be fire from the walls—"

"The floor might open up," Eddie added.

"Or who knows what," she finished.

DJ's heavy brow lowered, narrowing his eyes. "Look, I don't know what kind of stupid you think I am. All I know is we supposed to kill anyone what comes into our area. That was our instructions. There's others all set to do the same in other places."

"Others?" she asked, still backing away.

DJ's posture relaxed, even as a measure of his former arrogance returned to his voice. "Yeah, me an' Goob? We wasn't alone. There was over a hundred of us. Me and him? Hell, we looked good in that group. Might be you'll meet some of them and remember ol' DJ and allow as how it would've been better to play with us instead."

"What do you mean?" Eddie asked as Tory's hip struck the wooden door.

"That won't do y'all no good," DJ said. "That door's been locked ever since they put us up in here. Don't you think we checked it every time we heard a noise out there?" He waved a beefy left arm vaguely in the direction Tory and Eddie had come from.

"What did you mean," Eddie asked again, "about you two looking good in your group?"

DJ's leering sneer returned. "Oh, there was some real prize winners moving along with us, doncha doubt it. Real crazy mofos. Some still had arm and leg irons on, clanking like ghosts in chains down the halls. Some didn't seem like they could even talk, just wild-eyed and starin', growlin' at people like animals.

"Me and Goob? We walked down here. But some of them had to be hauled or herded, you know, like sheep, being poked with those 'lectric shock sticks."

The way DJ described these other people, without the slightest indication of understanding that they were of the same species and perhaps deserving of a modicum of sympathy or empathy, sickened Tory. To

DJ, those *were* animals, and as long as someone had it worse than him, he felt all right with himself.

"One minute."

Tory felt more than heard a thunk in the wood behind her, like a brief shudder in the door, noted mainly because her backside was pressed firmly against it.

"Seriously," DJ continued as Goob made a groaning/mewling sound on the floor, his body twisting in slow motion as he fought to regain consciousness, "after seeing some of them, I'm happy to stay in here. I figure me and Goob got the good side of this deal. Not too hot, not too cold. No dicks in uniform screwing with us." He licked his lips, drawing another shudder from her. "You could do a lot worse, babe."

"We're leaving," she said, finding the side of the door and easily pushing it open. She started to admonish the large man not to follow them, but then realized she couldn't be that cruel, couldn't knowingly let another human being die, not even drug-scum-wannabe-rapists like these.

"You two should come with us," she said, and though she meant to be polite about it, she didn't let the knife tip droop a millimeter. Her body language, as tense as she felt, must be screaming, *Come with me if you want to die.* It might be funny if she wasn't so scared.

"Thirty seconds."

"Let's go!" Eddie hissed. He hadn't crossed the threshold yet. Good kid, she thought. He remembered what happened with the big man entered the second room early. God, was that only twenty or twenty-five minutes ago?

DJ moved slowly over to Goob, bending down to reach under his arm and haul him to his feet. "You two go. We'll stay and wait for the next group. Maybe we can get free then."

Tory sucked in a breath to argue again, but then let it out in a sigh. Turning to the door, she saw another corridor made of a darker stone, a deep gray color, with little white specks throughout the matrix that refracted the indirect lighting. The corridor ran to the right and left, though it only went a short way left before hitting a dead end.

Acutely aware of the passage of time, seconds ticking away before the room went into "lockdown," Tory and Eddie stepped through the door and into the corridor. The door remained open behind them, showing DJ helping a still-groggy Goob remain upright. Unsure what to do, unsure what would happen, Tory stood spellbound, looking into the room almost like she was glued to a television set, the open doorway a glass screen showing a dramatic tableau, the scene set for a sudden appearance of a Jason or a Freddie.

Then the door slammed itself shut, swinging back on its hinges with such force that the sound of its closing echoed like a canon blast in the corridor. A half-second later, both of the men in the room began to scream, awful, high-pitched shrieks of the purest anguish. With the view gone, there was no way to know what grisly fate they faced.

Eddie's hand found hers, and she clenched it tightly, glad for the human contact, grateful she was still alive to appreciate it.

The screams faded away and there was only silence.

Silence.

"There's no countdown," Eddie said softly.

"Maybe we've earned a break," Tory said.

Neither of them thought that they had reached the end of the labyrinth.

The corridor stretched away in front of them, monotonous gray sparkly stone, at least ten feet high and three or four feet across, as far as they could see.

"Let's see where this goes," she suggested, and they started walking.

Chapter 21

DeShaun

A desperation unlike any he'd ever known filled Li'l Bit as he scanned the dead end. Three walls of dingy gray-brown rock enclosed him, with not a hint of an opening. He looked back over his shoulder, more to see how much longer he had until he was crushed than out of any belief or hope the moving wall had stopped moving. He could hear it coming, after all, a cacophonous rumbling/grinding noise that was almost deafening in the close confines of the corridor.

The wall hadn't reached the up-sloped floor yet, so he still had maybe fifteen feet of freedom. Looked at another way, he had maybe thirty seconds before they'd have to scrape the black smear off the far wall to even know he'd been there.

The slope might stop it, he thought, though without much enthusiasm. Some of the debris from the crushed boulder had already reached the slope and was happily churning and grinding its way toward him. He'd be dancing soon to keep his feet from being trapped.

Despite the noise of the moving wall, he heard a distinct *chunk* come from wall on the right side of the dead end. Nothing else had changed, but renewed hope flooded him.

"Hey!" he shouted at the wall, scrabbling with thick fingers, looking for a gap, for a handhold, for something. "I'm in here! Get me outta here! The wall is coming! Let me out!" Scrabbling turned to pounding, fists slamming into the wall with about as much effect as could be expected. His hands hurt with each strike, and nothing seemed to change, but blind panic drove him to continue trying.

The wall continued inexorably forward.

Twenty seconds, and it would be over.

*****

Brian

Brian screamed as he fell, unable to hold it in, uncaring that he sounded like a woman in his fear.

It was his feet, his stupid, tingling, half-numb feet, clumsy at the best of times, but worse when he needed to move fast. It might have been that computerized announcement of two minutes left startling him. The boots the producers made everyone wear definitely didn't help. He'd never done this with boots before.

It's all about the presentation, Brian. You, of all people, should appreciate that.

And now, as pain sparked bright and hot in his knees, as the claws of a massive black cat arced out between the bars of its cage, once, then again, closer with each swipe, *now* his stupid heart caught up with the adrenaline flooding his system. Now he went from a calm and steady rhythm to something in the stratosphere, heart trip-hammering in his chest.

And now that it was probably too late, everything started to work.

Even as his knees hit, he drew them in, booted feet scraping and pushing against the stone floor. The growls and snarls, the grinding of the machinery, filled his head. The musky scent of the cats was almost overpowering. For just an instant, as the cat began a final swipe through the bars of its cage, a swipe that would probably open his neck and chest, Brian imagined he could pick out the individual smell of that one mountain lion, could determine its voice amongst all its brethren.

He pushed off against the floor, hoping to get clear of the reaching cat, but then his shoulder slammed into something, hands grabbed at him, halting his momentum. Brian screamed again, thinking it was the cat, and felt himself pushed down, falling backward, ass-over-tea-kettle, as his dad used to say. He went from surging forward to landing on his backside, and he saw the skinny form of Zippy, the crackhead, standing tall with his arms out in front of him. Zippy moved with him, flowing forward, following him, even as Brian fell back, and his mouth with its missing and rotting teeth opened to say something, but all that came out was an anguished scream.

*****

Matt

Matt heard the two minutes warning, and his mind split, operating at two speeds as he stepped into the whirring, snarling, up and down maelstrom of moving cages. One-half watched the pattern of movement in slow motion, coaxing his body forward a little here, step right, step back, step left, surge forward. He felt graceful and wished all dancing could be as organized as this; maybe he wouldn't look like such a fool on the dance floor. Of course, if he was smoother in life, he probably wouldn't be in this mess in the first place. Feeling like maybe his mind was just a tad bit beautiful too, he followed the motions of the pattern almost in slow motion.

A magnificent tawny specimen went from floor to vertical pole on his right, starting to move up just as he got his leg out of its reach, side-stepping left under a descending cage. His six-foot frame too high for full clearance, he ducked and stepped forward, coming in behind another cage moving left to right, walking a tightrope between too early and too late, that fine line that kept him safe.

He couldn't help smiling despite the fear, the near hysteria. Maybe this was the allure of skydiving, the pure adrenaline that made you feel remarkably alive despite the sphincter-tightening knowledge that one misstep could put a panther in line with your head. In the midst of the noisy machinery and the raucous calls of the agitated great cats, Matt laughed and wondered if he shouldn't try to tamp it down a bit.

No reason to let everyone else think he was going crazy.

The second half of his brain, that emotional, reactive right half, was a gibbering mess of panic, catching motion as a blur almost after it happened, unable to process everything he was seeing, unable to focus in the face of danger. Even as he navigated the moving maze of wild animals, a part of him couldn't look away from the looming disaster with the engineer. First on his hands and knees, then dumbly, stupidly lurching *toward* the descending black cat, it was a tragedy in the making, a train wreck in progress. Even though he normally wanted nothing to do with blood, some deep, dark part of his mind looked forward to the coming gory display, anticipating the swipe and spray and splatter. Maybe it was just a "too bad for him, but it would be worse if it was me" kind of *schadenfreude*. Perhaps it stemmed from a desire for misplaced vengeance. Brian wasn't actually responsible for him being there—hell, Matt had volunteered—but the man worked for the company who put them there, he represented the people who sold Matt a bill of goods. His was a reachable face for the pain in Matt's lacerated arm, the fear tightening his gut and filling the back of his throat with burning acid.

But then Zippy was there, cue the magical crackhead, who could dodge mountain lions and figure out a complex mathematical pattern on instinct, but who didn't understand oral hygiene or how to just say no to drugs. Zippy, all hundred and ten pounds of him, somehow stopped Brian's forward lunge, even managed to topple him backward, away from the slashing cat and out of immediate danger.

As Matt stepped and twisted, moving closer and closer to the far wall and its locked door and questionable safety, Zippy lunged forward after Brian, trying to get out of the reach of the great, black cat.

He didn't make it.

With one-part horror and one-part clinical detachment, perhaps a bit of what those mysterious high-roller audience members experienced, Matt saw the massive paw swipe out, curved claws extended and tips pointing down. From his angle, coming in almost between the two, Brian scuttling backward to his left and Zippy falling from right to left, Matt was in the perfect position to see the claws tear into the back of Zippy's shirt at just below the left shoulder blade, where they raked through layers of loose, billowy, white cloth, before catching skin somewhere around the level of the right lower back or right side. Zippy's scream was horrifying, the blood-curdling shriek of an animal mortally wounded, erupting from his skinny frame as his lunge turned to a fall, and the claws of the cat exploded out of his side, throwing a sizable gout of blood and dark flesh.

With that same strange sense of detachment, as Matt shuffled left one more time, then moved forward to stand over the other men, he noted the black cat bring its paw back through the bars of its cage, eyes slightly closed as it licked its claws, savoring the treat.

Now the two sides of his brain came together, both the analyzer and the horrified yet titillated spectator, and time crashed back into his head, slow-motion pattern runner and frantic, gibbering hysteric combining with one thought, one shrieking instinctive fear.

They had no time.

"Get up! Get up! Get up!" Matt screamed as he came up to the downed men.

Brian was already scrambling, bucking backward, while Zippy landed on him, drawing in another breath to scream again. The back of his shirt was a bloody, shredded mess, but still intact enough to hide the damage underneath. Zippy rolled to his right, moving closer to the door, somehow moving in the right direction to avoid the next crossing cat. Whether his mind was still keeping to the pattern or he was responding to something like an instinctive need to move toward the side of the injury to huddle around it, Matt couldn't tell.

It freed Brian, but Matt couldn't afford to wait for the plumper man to struggle to his feet. Reaching down as he moved to follow Zippy, the tall accountant grabbed the engineer's hands, somehow finding the strength to lift and pull, literally hauling him to his feet and towing him along, feeling the man's legs churn and gain balance.

"One minute," sounded from the speaker as Matt juked right, almost toppling Brian again with his sudden motion, feeling the resistance as the shorter man tried to set his feet. Unaccustomed to such exertion, feeling a pain burn along his back and the scratches on his arm flare, Matt somehow kept Brian with him. Zippy pulled his knees in and hopped/stumbled to the right as well, staying just ahead of them.

Behind them the cats were snarling and roaring, but they only needed to step forward one more time.

They made the final step together. Seeing Zippy start to stagger, Matt relinquished Brian's hands and lunged for the skinny black man, catching his left arm and keeping him on his feet. Zippy moved with him, shuffling his feet for the door, hissing in pain with every breath, every movement, his breathing short and fast. Matt's surge of voyeurism had passed; the idea of looking at the wound now was not something he relished. He hoped it wasn't too bad.

Brian reached for the wooden door, shoving his hands forward.

The door opened.

Whaddaya know? Matt mused. Brian was right after all. The door was probably set not to open too early. The bastards watching them needed to get a good show, after all.

The door opened onto a gray corridor, featureless except for the ubiquitous hidden lighting and small white specks ingrained in the stone that served to amplify the ambient lighting a bit. It looked to run left and right of the door, but it was hard to see to the right because the door opened out in that direction.

Stepping out into the corridor, the three men heard shouted exclamations of surprise and relief come from the left.

"Thank God you're all right!" the short, dumpy blond with greasy hair said, emerging from the dimness. Something flashed in her hand for a second, then disappeared behind her back. The skinny, quiet kid was with her, though something about him was different. His shoulders weren't as slumped, for one thing, like he'd found something that made him stand taller.

"Thirty seconds," sounded from inside the mountain lion room.

"What happened to Zippy?" Tory asked. "Oh god, he's hurt!" She rushed forward to do something, but before she could reach them, the kid shouted something about the door and the blond went straight to Brian and pulled him sideways, out of the line of the door. Matt stumbled left as well, with Tory holding his arm and pulling, and no sooner had they cleared the way than the door slammed shut, audible clunks signifying the locks had engaged again.

"What's that smell?" Eddie asked.

"I don't hear any screaming," Tory said.

"Cats," Brian answered. "Big ass cats, a lot of them."

"What's that mean?" Tory asked.

"It's what we faced in our room," Matt explained. "Big mountain lions in cages, moving on tracks. One of them got Zippy."

"Looks like one got you too," she said, starting to examine his arm.

Matt pulled his arm away from her, though not roughly. "Zippy's hurt a lot worse. Mine will wait."

"My fault," Brian mumbled.

"I'm guessing they probably won't burn that room then," Tory said. "Animal rights and all that."

"Still no timer," Eddie said quietly. "We got out of our room before you, and there hasn't been a countdown yet."

"Well, we can use that," Tory said, "to get a good look at Zippy here. Matt, help me get him down to the floor."

THE DUNGEON

Matt moved to change his stance, pivoting sideways to help Zippy get down to the floor, but the skinny black man pushed away from them, hands going to his torn side as his feet staggered to a wide, bracing stance.

"Hey, man, let us help you," Matt urged.

"S'okay," Zippy said. "If I sit down, I might not get back up, you know?" His pattern of speech was slower than at any time since they'd met him. "Doesn't hurt too much, an' ain't much we could do 'bout it if'n it did." He pivoted to the right, looking down the corridor. "So let's just get to walking. You two come from back there, so I guess we go this way." He placed his left arm against the rough wall of the corridor's left side and, holding his right side with his right hand, began to slowly shuffle down the corridor.

*****

That was another click, Li'l Bit thought as he anxiously continued to pound on the side of the corridor. The moving wall was still coming on despite the slope in the floor. Apparently those rich, white boys watching on camera had a real hard-on to see a gay man get pancaked.

He was having a hard time keeping his feet, alternating his gaze from the floor with its rumbling, tumbling leading edge of debris making him shift, shuffle, climb, and hop. He was pretty sure he'd already rolled his right ankle more than once, and only fear and adrenaline was keeping him upright and moving. And still that damn wall kept coming. Another fifteen seconds or so, and it wouldn't matter.

But now that second clunk and his pounding on the wall was rewarded with minute shivers in what must be a cleverly hidden door. It wasn't opening, not yet, but his mind told him it must open soon; his panicked desperation would allow no room for anything but that single hope. Two clunks like two bolts releasing. Someone was enjoying taking their time about this. Someone would have a lot to answer for if he ever got out of here.

If the door opened in time.

Chapter 22

Elizabeth

Liz still wasn't fully in the room with the other two men. Part of her was there, certainly, the part that felt paradoxically safe despite the threat behind the two minutes warning, and despite the fact that she'd literally just pounded a man's face into the hard-stone floor. The reason that part of her felt safe was both easy to understand and impossible to believe. She was leaning on a man, and not only was he not pushing her away or pushing her down, he was helping to hold her up.

That was something wholly new, completely unexpected. Her entire life had been a study in forced independence. First from a broken family, a father who didn't understand her, and a counselor who…no, that's where the other part of her currently lived, back in time, back with the pain.

No one ever understood, not even those who suffered the same affliction, because everyone's experience with schizophrenia was different. The disease itself was one of internal stimulus, so how could you possibly relate to the problems of others? How could you even be sure what you were relating to when half the time your own perceptions were imaginary? How could you allow yourself to be open to empathizing with others, when doing so also meant opening yourself up to your own inner demons?

Liz did things the way Liz did them, for herself. Half of her life was an argument with herself. If the voices said conform or no one will like you, she dyed her hair red. When the voices said red hair that shade made her look like a whore, she added a purple forelock, anything to see if she could push the critical, constantly nagging voice of her mother, the condescending voice of her counselor, or the disappointed voice of her father further away. Long experience taught her that she could never meet their demands, could never comply with them enough to make them go away. Though she had tried, at least for the first few years, like all the other schizophrenics she used to listen to in group therapy.

So now she was an anti-conformist, except perhaps in this. For the first time in as long as she could remember, she actually felt safe. Maybe it wasn't about conforming to her voices' wishes, but just being true to herself. No man ever looked at her with real understanding. Part of her was afraid to ask where that understanding came from; it couldn't be natural. No one was that naturally accepting. But calm Liz refused to poke that bear just yet. Maybe later. For now, just relish the feeling of safety.

The other half was back in time.

Something half-remembered, something Brad alluded to, assuming it wasn't just a hallucination. *You told me once what he did to you, right before we shocked you. You forgot afterward, but I didn't.*

And then she was home, and she was arguing with her father. He was sitting behind his desk, where he always sat, working on a new book, always another book, something that would magically fix the unfair societal rejection of his work based on his ex-wife's drunken interview. None of the books ever fixed anything, no publishers wanted to risk their reputations by trying to fix his. He spent his own money, buying printed copies and delivering them to bookstores, setting up autograph sessions. He still sold well, and the digital copies sold like crazy, but the beauty of the digital copy was that no one had to be seen in public holding a book with his name on the spine. Regardless of his sales numbers, he would never be the up-and-coming writer he once was.

She couldn't remember what started the argument, whether she had approached him with those awful accusations of things barely remembered, if they had even happened. She wasn't certain if they were her memories or just memories of things described by one voice or another. They might even have been suggestions of things, by her counselor, by others in one group therapy or another, that were then internalized and played back until a part of her believed them as if they had happened.

He never molested her. He never raped her. She knew that now.

She only wished she'd believed it then.

He might not have gone into cardiac arrest during the heat of their argument.

She might not have waited to call the paramedics, with what she thought was a righteous anger.

He might not have died believing the little girl he loved so much hated him.

"Yo," the deep voice of Big Rich intruded on her thoughts, bringing the past and the present colliding together. "Those two I put down are starting to move an awful lot."

She felt Zack's left arm reach out and wiggle the door again. "Still locked," he said.

Hastily, she swiped an arm across her face, scouring away the tears brought on by the memory of that awful afternoon.

"You feeling better?" Zack asked, and she nodded, not yet trusting herself to speak. She wasn't sure if her voice would come out quavery, if the effort would rekindle the tears, or if it would come out hoarse and painful. There was a rawness in her throat, obvious when she swallowed, and she had a vague mental image of herself as some kind of psychotic harridan, hair flying wildly while she screamed and slammed that poor man's head into the ground over and over again.

Looking up at the two men through her dyed forelock, she saw what looked like an awareness of that potential in her from Big Rich. Certainly, the large man seemed to be avoiding looking at her. Zachary was solicitous but standing back now. His eyes showed concern but remained focused on the larger danger represented by the strange, hopped up men on the floor. He also seemed to know that giving her her space, allowing her to work through what she could, but being there for her when she needed him, was the best way to deal with her.

How could he know that?

"They're definitely moving more," Zack's deep voice observed. It wasn't as deep as Rich's, but it was still had that good *manly* depth to it. "Let's all get a little closer to the door."

"You said it was locked," she ventured, and though her voice felt raw, it didn't sound any the worse for wear.

"It's gotta open, you know?" Rich said, moving away from the two men on the floor. "Doesn't make any sense to give us a challenge we can't get away from."

"One minute," came from the hidden speakers. In the immediate silence that followed, all three clearly heard the sound of a lock disengaging.

"Let's try it now," Liz said, reaching past the men and giving the door an experimental push. It opened easily, swinging out into a corridor that was made of a lighter color stone than the long passage that led to this room. Hopefully, it was also free of falling dividers.

"Some kind of timer, I guess," Big Rich offered, moving past Liz and Zachary and heading into the corridor. Liz watched him look left, then pull the door back a bit so he could peer right around it. She looked up and caught the cop's eyes for a moment.

"Thanks for," she stammered, breaking eye contact and looking down, "you know. Back there."

Looking down, she couldn't see his face, but she saw his strong hand coming into her field of vision as he reached for hers. Hesitantly, she let him take it, his right hand on her left. He might have started to say something, but it was drowned out by a loud groan from one of the two struggling psychotics on the floor, who suddenly reared and lunged, gaining his feet.

Instantly she was yanked away from him, pulled by Zachary, so that she staggered forward and out the door, where Big Rich arrested her movement, redirecting her and getting her clear of the doorway.

She turned in time to see the skinny doper, all greasy hair and nasty clothes, face bloody and left arm dangling unnaturally, come lurching, roaring meaningless syllables that she supposed expressed pain, or rage. Perhaps he felt driven to attack those he believed placed him here, or he wanted revenge against the one who hurt him.

"Thirty seconds."

Big Rich took a long step back into the room and grabbed Zachary with about the same forceful gentleness with which he'd manhandled her out into the corridor. Giving the cop a quick pull and twist, he forced Zack through the doorway. The crazed man grabbed for Rich's trailing left arm, but Rich was faster, twisting back and driving his large right fist squarely into the middle of man's face. The man's head snapped back, his body reeling in the same direction, feet shuffling, trying to stay upright. The backs of his legs bumped up against the second figure, who was just now starting to rise, and the first toppled backward over the back of the second.

Then Rich was out in the corridor with them, pulling the door shut, preparing to brace it with his back. But the door yanked itself out of his grasp at the last second, slamming shut, almost catching the big tight end's fingers between itself and the edge.

"Sonuva—" Rich swore softly.

There was another loud thunk, then a sound like a roaring rush of air, and suddenly Rich was backing away from the door. From a few feet away, Liz could feel the heat coming off the barrier.

"Did they just?" the tall man said.

"Would have been us, if you hadn't gotten us all out," Zachary said.

"But those guys—" Rich shook his head. "Lord, save 'em. They didn't even know what they were doing."

Liz resisted the urge to express her gratitude at still being alive. All she wanted to feel was relief. Nothing in her life had prepared her to truly consider the well-being of others, and the sudden choking sensation in her throat was uncomfortable, to say the least. That the two strong men with her could so easily express remorse for the lives of the four who had attacked them when she couldn't...did it say something about them, or about her?

Was she somehow permanently damaged by her past? Had she been made differently, less human?

Or was there hope for her, because she *did* feel... something?

Maybe it was just being around decent people for once, despite that one was a criminal and another an experienced law enforcement officer who probably had more right to a jaded soul than just about anyone else she'd ever met. Yet they were working together, sharing ideas, sharing values, helping everyone, maybe even including her.

To take her mind of its musings, which could quickly turn into something much worse, she looked around. This corridor was indeed different than the last. Instead of dingy browns, the walls were gray, with glowing flecks of something that seemed to take the invisible lighting and magnify it, somehow.

They were standing at what appeared to be a large *L*. The corridor marched away to left and straight ahead, though the straight portion was relatively short and ended in a wall of stone that matched the walls and floor of the corridor. With the door behind her, there was another door to their right, at the junction of walls forming the *L*. Mounted on the door was another of those placards, similar to the one that had greeted them in the starting room.

Numbly, already fearing a new riddle they might not be able to solve, she moved toward the placard.

"Hey, back here!" a woman's voice called from behind her.

"It's the homeless chick," Rich said softly.

"Tory," Zachary added.

Turning, Liz saw that it wasn't just Tory. The skinny kid was with her, as was the tall guy with glasses, Matt, and the engineer. And between them, one arm over each of the other men's shoulders, feet almost dragging, was...

"Oh my god, Zippy!" Liz said.

"What the hell happened to him?" Rich shouted, moving down the corridor to help. Even from a dozen yards away, Liz could clearly see that the skinny black guy's shirt was drenched in red, and as they came closer, that fat drops were still falling, dripping from the flaps of shirttail that looks tattered and ragged on his right side.

"He saved me," Brian said softly, drawing closer. Big Rich moved to his side first, but the smaller man refused to give up his support of Zippy. Maybe he felt he owed the skinny man something for saving him.

"Big ass cats," Matt panted, still holding Zippy up on the left. "Moving cages, long claws, cats every-damn-where. One of them got Zippy in the back."

Tory and Eddie were silent as they approached, until Eddie saw the placard on the door.

"Is this another riddle?" he asked. He seemed to be walking a little taller, to Liz, not quite as intent on shrinking into the background.

"We need to take a look at Zippy's side," Zachary said as they grouped up around the door with the placard, "see if we can stop the—"

Then a new sound reached them, coming from the short arm of the *L*.

*****

DeShaun

Oh dear, sweet, baby Jesus on my momma's wall, please let me get out of this, DeShaun prayed, the words tumbling around in his head like the rocks tumbling around his feet and ankles. He was at least three feet off the floor now, his legs aching from the climbing and the bumping, feeling like one of those rodeo clowns you sometimes saw, whipping their legs to stay on top of a rolling barrel. *Crazy ass white people! Oh wait, I take that back, baby Jesus. I'll do better, I promise, just get me out of here.*

He wasn't going to make it.

The moving wall was looming, not enough space separating it and the back wall of the corridor for him to stretch out his arms. And every second brought it that much closer.

"This is such bullshit!" he shouted, barely able to make himself heard over the clattering din. "That fat ass child molester got an instant BAM with a stake up his ass, and you gonna do me like this? All slow and shit?"

It wasn't the dying that scared him the most, not really. Oh, he remembered his momma's warning and imprecations, how God doesn't allow homosexuality, how he had to be right with God if he wanted to go to heaven. That hadn't scared him half as much as hoping the guys in his high school didn't figure out his secret. He'd lived pretty well, didn't do too many drugs, got good grades. Despite his bad mouth and adopted manner of speech, he was nobody's idea of stupid.

So now he was gonna die, and that part was all right. He'd been in danger of dying ever since he figured out he'd rather be with Jack than Jill. So he was used to the threat.

But dying slow and painfully, bones crushed one at a time as they strained and broke under the implacable weight of a moving slab of stone. That was more than he could stomach.

Even though he had less than five feet of space remaining, he pounded on the wall where the clunks came from, where the wall vibrated a little with each strike. He couldn't see a gap, couldn't feel even a wisp of a draft, but he pounded until his fists hurt worse than his burned back, pounded though his arms ached with the effort as badly as his legs ached from straddling the shifting rocks.

Four feet.

The largest chunk of debris, what had to be a sizable chunk of the boulder that wanted to splat him earlier, wound up laying curved side up, flat part down, bridging the gap between wall and wall. The moving wall slowed, the grinding noises quieted. With his feet atop the rock, he could feel that it wasn't over; it had gotten much worse.

"Oh shit, this gonna be bad," he said, as the rock beneath him began to vibrate. Chemistry and physics classes taught him that energy had to be expended. However much force was being placed on that rock by the driving mechanism behind that wall, it would be exciting the atoms in it, charging them, making them vibrate to give off the charge, which would be transmitted to its surface, something he could feel by his contact with it. Sooner rather than later, those vibrations would be enough to break the bonds of cohesion that bound the rocks' molecules one to another, starting a chain reaction that would make it erupt upward from under him, because up was the only way it could explode. The shards of rock shrapnel would cut him in a thousand places, might even take his Li'l Bit off, so that his dying agony would begin even before the moving wall managed to turn him to jelly.

The quivering intensified. A low thrumming sound issued up from the rock, another manifestation of its coming explosion. The thrumming ramped up, rising higher in frequency, becoming almost high-pitched, a sound most people would never hear. *I can always tell the other people in hell that I got to hear a rock screaming.*

Leaning into the wall where he thought the door was, DeShaun felt a third clunk an instant before the wall gave way, plunging him headfirst through the door. Problem was, he was three feet off the ground, and though he wasn't tall by any stretch of the imagination, three feet up still put him a foot or two higher than the upper door frame, so that he smacked his forehead into the rock above the door even as his body tumbled through it.

A god-awful pain erupted in his head, pounding in time to the new lights that were flashing behind his eyes, all winding up in his stomach, so that even as he managed to gain his feet and stumble forward, unseeing, just wanting to get away from the doorway before that big ass rock exploded, he threw up whatever was left of his last meal, drew in a whooshing breath that barely made it into his lungs before he vomited a second time.

At least he had the presence of mind to turn his head sideways as he blew chunks. No way he wanted to smell like puke for eternity.

There was a loud boom from behind him, and he thought, *Here it comes, I'm dead.* But no pain came, and another boom, much louder, like dynamite, sounded, and that must have been the rock, but maybe the door closed first. Still he stumbled forward, the strobing lights behind his eyes slowly receding, allowing him to open them.

"Dude! You look like shit!" was the first thing he heard as hands, big ass black hands, reached out to stop his headlong run.

"S'not what yo momma said last night," DeShaun mumbled, before his legs gave out and he collapsed on the floor.

CHAPTER 23

Zachary

As the accountant, Matt, and the engineer, Brian, deposited Zippy against one wall, easing him down to a sitting position, and as Big Rich, Eddie, and Tory, the homeless woman, tended to the shorter man who had disappeared after jumping the first pit, Zachary Pavese finally found a moment to think. At least, he hoped he had a few moments. So far, he hadn't heard any time warnings since escaping the room with the four drugged-out zombies.

He didn't like the way his thoughts turned, how they kept coming around not to solutions for the problems they'd faced, or to an attempt to reason out the meaning of the next message, which he hadn't yet read. No, his mind wanted to focus on what Mike Callahan had said back in his introduction, and on what he hadn't said.

Zack was neither stupid nor slow. You didn't rise through the ranks of the police force by being either. He kept his light brown and thinning hair cut short in a military manner and liked to round his shoulders when he was on the job, which helped him blend in as much as possible. He hung back in interviews, let his partners do the talking, and just listened, watching mannerisms, picking out the inconsistencies that were always there, if only you took the time to find them.

Now as Li'l Bit tried to wake up and as Zippy tried to stay awake, he gnawed on the inconsistencies in Callahan's presentation, the small things left unsaid, which gave the lie to the whole process.

That a large corporation was behind this went without saying. No single person could have brought this stage to life. The manpower required to build this set alone bespoke a large budget and numerous teams working simultaneously, not to mention the brainpower required to design and implement the various tricks and traps they'd already survived. That there would be those in the world with the money and desire to fund such an operation also didn't surprise him. Morality was a commodity often displaced by wealth, though there were certainly exceptions. Combine excessive wealth with a sense of power and entitlement, a feeling that one was above the laws of man, and the depths of depravity to which one might plunge could be bottomless.

Those feelings weren't wholly tied to wealth, Zack knew. Dog fights, cock fights, even underground blood-sport fighting rings, all existed to provide entertainment to those who had seen it all, had done it all, and who could derive no pleasure from any activity that didn't pose a risk to someone's life.

Would that translate into something the general public could accept as Callahan proposed? Zack wasn't sure. He thought it might, if the audience could be guiled into believing it only *looked* real and that *no actual humans were harmed in the making of this reality show.*

So no, the premise isn't what bothered him, but rather the promise. Wealth and power could accomplish all the things Callahan proposed. It could snatch a cop off a case, drug him, and bring him overseas. It could pay for the technological expertise required to erase a lifetime of service to the law and plant false stories in the digital realm that made sure said police officer could never resume his former life. It could certainly play a part in pulling large numbers of homeless off the streets, as in the case of Tory and Eddie, and could probably find participants both willing and unwilling in the overpopulated and chronically underfunded penal system.

But what it couldn't do was guarantee their cooperation after the fact. His own resolve was testimony to that. Even if everything else Callahan said was true, and there was no way for him to resume his previous life, there was also no way Zachary Pavese could walk away from the injustice of his and others' kidnapping, or from the blatant disregard for their safety and basic humanity in placing them in such life or death situations. He couldn't ignore what amounted to outright murder in how those four others were drugged out of their minds, set up to attack them, then immolated after they escaped.

He had no idea what kind of lies they planted about him, but he knew the hearts and minds of the cops he worked with, good men and women, who would believe him, would believe in him. They might have erased him digitally, but they had no power to remove the organic connections he'd made throughout his life.

Their only method of keeping this under control revolved around never letting him leave this place alive.

Zack looked around at the motley collection of people trapped in this nightmare with him. Some had volunteered for this, supposedly on the promise that old sins would be erased, old debts forgiven. How much had they known going in? Were they truly warned of the risks involved, the threat of imminent death? He assumed they would have signed some legal forms, liability releases, confidentiality agreements...would those stop a media starved for *if it bleeds, it leads* new stories from covering the details of their ordeal in this dungeon? Generally, those forms only provided legal remedies for the industry if someone violates them; they offer no protection from the societal and political backlash the company might suffer if enough of them survived to bring their case to the public.

If any of them survived.

Zack didn't think they were supposed to. Those spectators might think someone lived, or perhaps more than one, because that would allow the public to believe in the show and its purported promise of redemption. He believed that at some point after the cameras shut off, those who survived the dungeon would be killed. There was no other way to protect the company and the people who ran it.

So he needed to start thinking in those terms. Not how do we survive the next room, or how do we make it through the dungeon. No, he needed to think both bigger and smaller.

How do we survive? Period.

Looking over at the engineer, Brian, who stood near Zippy, Zachary thought he knew just how to gain that information.

Turning away from the door with the placard, Zack moved a few feet down the long hallway. His eyes roved as he turned, seeing Tory and Big Rich helping the much smaller black man to his feet, before settling on the tall form of Elizabeth. The redhead certainly had issues, and maybe auditory hallucinations weren't even the worst of it, but she also had grit and toughness. She had proven that in the last room, coming to his defense. She seemed to appreciate him, though he wasn't sure yet how she perceived him.

He shook his head. Those kinds of thoughts, though pleasant, weren't helpful right now. At any moment their brief reprieve could end, and he needed a plan.

"How's it look?" he asked, coming up to Matt and Brian. He heard Liz, turning and coming up behind him.

"Not good, man," Matt answered, idly pushing his glasses up higher on the bridge of his nose, then using the same finger to brush his bangs back. His hair was sweat-greasy, and the right sleeve of his shirt was torn and bloodstained. "Mountain lion raked his back. I"—he made a swallowing sound—"I haven't had the guts to look at it yet."

Kneeling down beside the wounded man, Zack said, "Zippy, can you hear me?"

"I can hear you, all right, big fuzz," Zippy said, his words slow. His face had taken on an ashen shade, and he licked dry lips as he spoke. "Momma used to warn me about girls, but I never thought—" He coughed, and although there wasn't any blood on his lips, which Zack half-expected, the action almost made him pass out as a spasm of pain wracked his body. "I never thought a little pussy could hurt so much."

Zack chuckled as the skinnier man tried on a smile that stretched his lips wide.

"Hurts like hell though. You think I'm gonna make it?"

Zack didn't know what to think, not without looking at the wound. When he said as much, Zippy said, "You go on 'head and look, jes don't expect me to let you hold nothin' and cough."

Zachary nodded, then leaned forward, gingerly taking hold of the frayed ends of Zippy's shirt. The edges were saturated with blood, still fresh enough that although the shirt clung to the injured man's back, it did not adhere to it. Lifting the cloth gently, Zachary exposed four long, deep lacerations that ran almost half the width of Zippy's back. Three of them seemed to begin around his spine but weren't very deep at that point. The outermost edges showed signs of clotting. The fourth began, also shallowly, on the right side of the backbone, quickly going deeper, tracking with the first three, until it became obvious that the great cat had gotten enough of the curved edges of its claws under the skin to be able to pull and tear as it withdrew its paw. Like a hollow point bullet that does ten times as much damage when it leaves the body as it did upon entering, the cat's claw had torn through skin and muscle, leaving a gaping wound on Zippy's right side that resembled a fist-sized opening. Zack could see into the opening, though he didn't want to, could see the inner sheathing of muscle that kept the abdominal contents from spilling out of the opening, could see a glistening mass of shredded, bright red flesh hanging suspended just above the opening.

Something from barely remembered anatomy courses tickled the back of his mind, something about how the kidneys exist outside the abdominal contents, and Zack had to fight back a sudden urge to vomit when he realized that the dangling mass of tissue was probably Zippy's right kidney, torn apart and bleeding. What other substances might it be leaking into his body? Urine, certainly.

Even if immediate surgical intervention was a possibility, Zachary doubted Zippy would survive.

A hiss from behind him, as Liz also got a look at the wound, caused him to turn. She didn't say anything, just met his eyes. He shook his head, and she seemed to understand.

"How bad is it, doc?" Zippy asked sleepily.

Zachary hesitated to answer. He didn't want to lie but couldn't see what good the truth could possibly do.

"Looks like the bleeding has mostly stopped," Liz said firmly, turning to look at Zippy. "But let Zack pack that shirt back down good and tight, so we keep it that way."

"Okay," Zippy said, though he stiffened when Zack followed Liz's advice.

"Damn, you said I was messed up, but dis' brother done got it worse than me," Li'l Bit said from behind them, as he, Big Rich, and Tory came to join them.

"I'm still taller," Zippy said softly.

Zack stood up and backed away, letting Li'l Bit continue to talk with Zippy. He waved an arm at Brian, beckoning him away from the injured man. Brown eyes watching intently, Matt rose and followed.

"This a white boy conference, or can I come too?" Big Rich asked, his deep voice for once pitched low enough not to carry.

Zack nodded, gathered Liz with a gentle hand on her arm, and moved over near the door with the sign hanging on it.

"Watch where you step," Eddie cautioned as they approached. He pointed to the ground in front of the door, where a slight alteration in the stone caught the eye only because it was pointed out to him. "I don't think that's a trap or anything, but I bet it starts a timer back up. It probably also lights up this sign."

Matt made a *harumphing* noise deep in his throat. "I didn't even notice it was blank until you said something."

"So maybe we got a minute to talk," Rich said. "Okay, Mr. Policeman, what's on your mind?"

Unsure if his precautions were even necessary, or effective, Zack motioned the other six to gather around, to huddle up. He indicated his desire by first putting his right arm around Big Rich's shoulders and his left around Elizabeth's. Rich pulled in Matt, who gathered Brian, while Liz reached back and brought in Tory and Eddie.

"Okay, coach, you got us in the huddle," Rich said. "Now what?"

"This might be stupid," Zack whispered, "because we might be bugged, but maybe we're not. The point is, I don't think we're going to be allowed to survive."

"I been thinking the same thing," Rich whispered back, his voice an almost inaudible low hum. "This isn't a game, you know?"

"They never said it would be easy," Matt countered.

"No, they didn't," Liz said softly. "But they also didn't tell us they were going to try to kill us."

"Like sending hopped up whackos to attack us," Rich said.

"Okay, yeah, or big ass, pissed off mountain lions," Matt agreed, sighing.

"And at least you got to choose," Tory added, drawing a nod of agreement from Eddie. "Me and him, we were just, I don't know, collected up like trash, and now we're being recycled for someone else's amusement. Look everyone, let's see if we can get one more use out of these washed-up nobodies before we put them in the landfill."

Tory's voice rose as she spoke, her anger spilling over, earning her a strident *shhhing* from Eddie.

"Whachew guys rappin' 'bout over there?" Li'l Bit called.

"Sorry," she said.

"So...what?" Liz asked. "You thinking we won't be allowed to win?"

Zack shook his head. "I think, for the sake of those watching, we might be allowed to look like we escaped."

"But they'll just finish us when the lights go off. That's what you're saying, isn't it?" Matt sighed. "Shit. I should've known it wouldn't be that easy."

"Looks like you already figured that out," the big man said, nodding at the accountant's arm.

"Yeah, well, I consider myself lucky compared to Zippy."

"Poor guy," Liz said.

"He was saving me," Brian said softly, his first contribution to the huddle.

"Maybe you can return the favor," Zack said.

The engineer looked up and met his eyes. He was the wild card, the one man that Zachary couldn't quite figure out. He should be the most outraged of them all at the way he'd been treated. A former employee who found that his work was going to be used to harm others. Indeed, his initial vehemence when he discovered the understandable but misplaced animosity many of the others felt for him seemed perfectly in line. But then they'd been separated, and something had happened. Now, he just looked guilty, the man who goes willingly into the injection chamber because he knows he deserves to be there.

Would he be willing to stand up with them, help them find a way out of this? Or would he rather put his faith back in the company, hoping they would keep their word? He had to know, with the possible exception of Zachary himself, that he was the most expendable of them all. With his knowledge of the program, he could never be allowed to survive.

Then the engineer's eyes narrowed. His back straightened. "How can I help?" he asked.

Chapter 24

Brian

"Eddie is right, you know," Brian said after Zachary finished explaining his plan. "Once we step on that plate, we start a timer in here. That's all the preparation we have for the next room."

"Do you know what's in the next room?" Matt asked.

Brian shrugged. "I have a pretty good idea, but I won't know for sure until we see the riddle."

"Couldn't we just…you know…*not* step on the plate?" Tory asked.

Zachary and Brian both shook their heads. "I think," the cop answered, "if it became clear that was our plan, they'd just start the timer anyway."

"When will you know if there's a way?" Zachary whispered to Brian, just before the group broke their huddle.

"Once we see the room. It all depends how its set up, if it's even the room I think it is."

The others moved away, leaving Brian to stare at the door with its blank slate of a sign dangling on it. Out of the corner of his eye, he saw the cop and the tall redhead leaning their heads together, still talking. The accountant and the large black man moved off to where Li'l Bit sat next to Zippy, who was now regaling the dying man with an extravagant retelling of his adventure in the trap-filled tunnel.

"You can't say your foot got cut off," Zippy interjected. "You said your boot the first time."

"Jes' checkin' to see if you still checkin'," Li'l Bit responded. He was definitely a lot smarter than he appeared, Brian thought.

"He's a good man."

Brian jumped slightly, surprised by the appearance of the shorter blond on his left side. She also stood facing the door, her words almost as though she was just saying them, but clearly meant for him. "I think a guy like him sees the whole picture and wants to find a way to help as many people as he can."

Brian nodded, not trusting himself to reply.

"I also think it might be easy to, you know, find a way to work against that kind of guy, maybe save yourself."

Brian looked down, his mind racing, but nothing came that he could offer as a reply.

"I would bet, though," she continued, and the change in the sound of her voice meant that she had finally turned to face him. Slowly, he lifted his eyes to hers. "I would bet he's already thought of that too, and figures he knows that here, in your heart, you know his way is the best way." She punctuated the comment by lightly tapping on his chest with a stubby finger. Brian noted her fingernails were rough, chewed, how a person who couldn't lay claim to a nail file or clippers would keep themselves presentable.

She was the second person who'd redefined his understanding of how people communicate in less than five minutes, of how some, regardless of their circumstances, could surprise you with a depth of insight greater than anything he'd ever experienced. Maybe he'd been wrong, thinking he could interject himself into this group of people and fool them into accepting him as a prisoner like them. They had microphones everywhere, but they weren't actually bugged, which Zachary had figured out. Maybe he could tell them.

He shook his head. That might ruin everything. It was the one thing they all agreed on, even those on the other end.

If he screwed this up and really got himself in trouble with leadership, it would be relatively easy for them to dispose of him; he had a personal history of high blood pressure that started young, a gift from his dad's side of the family. That blood pressure caused his father to suffer a stroke before the age of fifty. But his family should be safe enough. A multinational company like Magellan wouldn't want to give the impression that it couldn't care for the families of its employees.

It was his discovery of what Magellan was really after, the true reason behind their so-called public service efforts to help beleaguered cities with their homeless population, to relieve the worldwide strain on overtaxed mental health facilities. It wasn't just about fleshing out a recreation of the labyrinth with a cast of human monsters, the so-called detritus of society, pitting them against each other in such a way that no one would truly care who lived or who died.

It was about power, the kind of power that could literally change the face of the modern world.

This was so much bigger than him, or them, or any of their families.

All it had taken for him to see the truth was one thin piece of bronze and one long discussion with Daniel.

He needed to step up his efforts, reveal a bit more to the principals, or he was going to die with the rest of them.

He'd probably die anyway, if the next room was what he thought it was, but maybe his death could mean something, if it bought the others a chance to escape. The last room was always the weak point in their plan with him.

Taking a deep breath, Brian said, "Okay, let's gather around and see what this next room has to offer."

Turning, he watched Zachary and Big Rich help Zippy to his feet. The kid looked bad, his skin almost ashen white, but he still wore a smile and still traded quips with Little Bit, so maybe it wasn't as bad as it had seemed. An image flashed through his mind, that wonderful man, unthinking in his desire to be helpful, jumping in front of him, saving him from his own panic, pushing him backward and away from the big cat. And then came the awful ripping sound, the scream of anguish, and the blood and gore exploding out Zippy's right side.

Quickly, swallowing his guilt, Brian banished the image. The best thing he could do now was try to help as many as possible, and that meant focusing on the next room, and on the one small chance they might have to survive it.

"Yo, we ready, engineer-man," the teasing voice of Little Bit said behind him.

Brian nodded, then stepped forward toward the door. He knew, with all the experience he had working on specific parts of this project and consulting with others, that this was nothing more than a small plate that would illuminate the sign and signal a short countdown before the group moved into the next room. He knew that. But that knowledge couldn't keep him from squinting his eyes shut, adrenaline dumping into his veins and every muscle fiber in him clenched, expecting some horrible fate to strike.

"Five minutes until room lockdown."

THE DUNGEON

The murmuring voices behind him, as half-a-dozen different speakers began to read the sign aloud, told him he was safe.

He opened his eyes to read the sign.

> **Four plates aslant the compass lay**
> **The keys to four sealed doors.**
> **Behind each door another plate,**
> **To unlock the chamber's core.**
> **The ones without will hold a door,**
> **As long as they're in play.**
> **The ones within must all engage,**
> **For you to get away.**

"There's nothing Greek about this," Eddie said.

"Sounds like a fairly straightforward set of instructions," Matt offered.

"The hell is aslant?" Little Bit shouted. "Stupid people can't just say across, like a normal person."

Zachary held up his hands for silence. "What are we facing, Brian?"

The engineer took in a deep breath. It brought a measure of relief to know what lay ahead, but it also brought its own set of fears, because what if something was changed? What if he made everything worse by presuming to know what to do? If this is what it felt like to be a leader, to have people depend upon you, it's no wonder he was so drawn to a life of working numbers, designing things.

The policeman placed a gentle hand on his shoulder. "Just tell us, Brian."

"It's the Octagon," he said in a rush.

"Isn't that a fighting thing?" Big Rich asked.

Brian shook his head. "No, well, maybe. I don't know. We called it the Octagon because of the shape of the room. It's a huge room, maybe two or three times bigger than any other room we've been in. It's roughly circular, but it has four small rooms placed at the diagonals."

"How can there be diagonals in a circle?" Eddie asked.

"Imagine you're quartering a circle, and you get the idea," Tory said softly.

"Exactly," Brian said. "But you won't be able to see the rooms until the doors open, because they're outside the circle, and the doors look like all the other rock."

"So these plates?" Matt began.

Brian nodded. "There will be four plates near the middle of the room, but they won't be too close together. Each plate will open one of the four outer rooms, but there's supposed to be a randomness to it. Each plate can be programmed to open any of the four other rooms."

"So just because a plate is on your left doesn't mean the door it opens will be," Big Rich said.

"So eyes on a swivel," Zachary said.

"The door the plate opens will only stay open for as long as someone stands on the plate," Brian continued. He'd closed his eyes again, visualizing the way the room was supposed to work. "Inside each of the smaller rooms there's another plate, and each of those is one of the four locks for the final door. We have to put something heavy on those inner plates, because all four of them have to be engaged in order for the escape door to work."

"Four minutes."

"So," Matt said, "someone has to stand on one of the plates in the middle of the room and keep standing there, while someone else runs into whatever room opens up and puts something heavy on the plate in there. Once they come out, it's okay to step off the plate outside the room?"

Brian nodded.

"Will there be things in there that we can use to hold those plates down?" Zachary asked.

Brian shrugged. "There are supposed to be objects lying around the room that approximate the weight of an average body."

"What kinds of things?" the tall redhead asked.

"I don't know, different things, but all in keeping with the theme. Wooden crates, chunks of rock, things like that."

"I begin to see the challenge," the accountant said. "If the room has a five-minute timer like all the others, it might be difficult to maneuver enough loose debris onto four of these plates in time to escape."

Brian nodded.

"Well, nothin' else has been easy, am I right?" the shorter black man said.

Brian turned and looked out at the gathered men and women. He hoped they would listen, hoped they would offer him enough trust, without asking too many questions. It wasn't that he didn't know the answers, but that the answers might make it worse for them. And the cop would know, like cops are supposed to know.

"Three minutes."

"What is it, Brian?" Zachary asked softly.

The others crowded closer.

Quietly, Brian told them about the south wall.

Chapter 25

Zachary

"One minute," sounded from the invisible speakers, and Zachary reached out to grasp the inner edge of the iron-bound wood door. His mind reeled from the whispered revelations Brian provided. Beside him, ready to take the first steps into the next room with him, Elizabeth waited. Feeling a little foolish at allowing himself to be distracted with such an obvious time limit looming, Zachary pushed away the news, forced all the incredibly damning new knowledge to the back of his mind, where it could percolate without interrupting the focus he needed to get through this next trial.

"Do it," Liz urged. "We're ready."

Zachary nodded, took a deep breath, and pushed on the door.

It swung open easily, revealing a vast open space, a hollowed-out bowl deep beneath the earth. As he hurried through the door, making room for the next person to come through, he couldn't help but stare at his surroundings.

The great, circular room opened around him, far larger than he would have thought possible. Though its rounded sides were visible all the way around, the farthest point across the diameter was difficult to see. The ambient light was present as always but didn't seem quite adequate to fully illuminate the area.

Being circular, the chamber was as tall as it was wide, so the upper reaches were also shrouded in shadow. The walls retained their look of mined and cut rock, though someone had added interesting touches, little garnishes, to make the space look more believable as an offshoot of digging, rather than a contrivance. Bracing beams of wood ran along the circumference at regular heights, paralleling the floor and each other, with cross-braces mounted perpendicular to them, appearing to reinforce the sides, giving the impression that only those struts held back the monstrous weight of the earth outside the room.

Directly ahead, in what should roughly be the center of the room, rose a statue. Brian hadn't mentioned that. It looked white but could be some offshoot shade; it was hard to tell from the distance and whatever distortion the unnatural light provided.

Even knowing it was all fake, knowing that there were four smaller rooms attached to this larger chamber, knowing that two of the walls held secrets between the rooms, was not enough to keep him from a sense of wonder. It was those two secret areas that would offer damnation or salvation, according to Brian. One of them held a very modern mechanical door. If they survived the room, it might open to allow them to escape, but it could just as easily be hiding a small troop of armed security personnel ready to put them down.

The second secret was their one true hope. Brian knew it was directly across the large chamber from the mechanical door, but he didn't know where that would be in relation to where they entered the room. All he claimed to have seen was a top-down model of the room. So until they triggered the fourth plate inside the fourth small room, they couldn't find what he'd termed "the southern wall."

Farther into the room, walking over more of the rough stone floor, Zachary moved toward the statue.

"Yo! Dis room is crazy big!" Li'l Bit shouted from behind him. His voice carried across the distance, though there didn't seem to be any echo. Despite the size of the space, he knew that certain building materials absorbed sound sufficiently to eliminate the echo effect. Zack looked over his shoulder and saw the smaller man helping Zippy across the threshold. They would be the last into the room.

"I mean, look at dis' place, Zippy. You could fit my whole apartment complex in here." He started gesticulating with his free arm, making Zack smile. "That corner over there, that would be da Shepard's place. They lived beside us for years. Never saw the daddy, but damn dat momma was hot. And over there—"

Liz and Matt came up on either side of him. He resisted the urge to reach for the redhead's hand. If ever there was a need for a clear head, this was it.

"Notice anything missing?" Matt asked.

Zachary swore softly. Stopping a few feet from the statue, he took another look around the room. Circular walls, rising up to a ceiling presumed to continue the circle, all buttressed by those wooden struts. Statue in the middle of the floor, unmentioned by Brian, but fitting with the overall feel of the place. The statue was probably about seven feet tall, made of marble or made to look like it was, and appeared to be of a man, though that was more of an impression based on shoulders and bared arms than anything else, since its face was still turned away from him. Around the base of the statue, roughly equidistant in four directions, were smaller stands, raised just a few inches off the ground. They resembled the top layer of a wooden raft, just a few boards bound together with rope or twine, but Zachary didn't doubt they were the plates mentioned in the limerick outside.

"There's no countdown," Liz said, her voice soft.

"And," Matt added, "there's none of the things Brian said would be usable to hold down the other sets of plates. No loose boards, or small boulders."

"Maybe they're inside the rooms," Eddie offered, coming up behind them. Zachary didn't know what happened to him and Tory when they were separated, but something seemed to have given the boy a little more confidence. He was still short and lean, hair a messy mop of lank strands hanging into his eyes. But his back was straighter, his stride more sure. He walked around the statue, carefully avoiding the boards on the floor, to stand in front of it.

"Who do you think it is?" Tory asked, moving to stand beside the young man.

"Hard to tell. There's no inscription."

Zachary watched the rest of his companions make their way to the center of the room. Big Rich and Li'l Bit still had charge of Zippy, though they were carrying him now more than helping him. The skinny black man's head lolled about on his shoulders. Bright blood was once again dripping from the wound on his side. Moving him hadn't been the safest thing to do, but they certainly couldn't have left him to die in the previous room.

Brian walked like a man seeing a dream come to life. Even under these circumstances, it must be a hell of a feeling to see something made this large, this grand, that once started out as an artist's conception. He moved in little circles, working his way across the ground to the center of the room, head turning ceaselessly, trying to see everything.

"Could it be Zeus?" Matt asked, and Zachary saw that the tall accountant had moved around to the front of the statue.

"No, I don't think so," Eddie replied. "Zeus is usually depicted with a flowing beard, and something that either resembles lightning, or is supposed to actually be a lightning bolt."

"I dunno," Matt said. "Those guns for arms sure look like he could bring some thunder."

Eddie chuckled, which was probably all Matt had been going for. The kid needed to laugh.

"Brian," Zack said as the engineer came close. He waited for the shorter man to look at him. "No announcements so far."

"I know. They may start when we activate the first plate."

"Speaking of that, there's also none of the debris you said would be lying around."

Brian shrugged, which didn't help ease Zack's nerves. "I don't know what to tell you," the engineer said. "Just like with the long passage before. Things might have been changed. And I had absolutely no input into this room." He lowered his voice slightly. "Considering what I told you about it, that's probably a good thing. If they knew that I found out what I did, they might not have used this room at all."

Zachary nodded. "Okay then, so which platform should we activate?"

Brian took a look at the four platforms surrounding the statue. "The way I remember the room described, it really shouldn't matter which one we activate first, since it's more about how the room is being monitored and managed, electronically, than it is about any set release mechanisms."

"Okay," Matt said. "So how about I kick things off and go step on this one over here?" He pointed to a spot to the left of the statue, in the direction its head was turned.

"That one's as good as any," Brian agreed.

"We ready then?" Matt asked.

When no one argued, Matt took a step in that direction.

At that same moment, Li'l Bit said, "Crap!" and Big Rich muttered, "Wait!" as Zippy sagged between them. Matt completed his step, his right foot coming down on the far platform as Zippy slipped between the two other men, his arms and legs completely limp. He folded to the floor soundlessly, landing on the platform closest to Zachary and Brian, which put him directly in line with Matt's platform, just behind the statue's right hip.

"Five minutes until room lockdown."

A chorus of loud, grating noises reached them, and Zachary pivoted first right, then left, noting two sections of wall...opening. The circular sides didn't slide up or down. Rather, there were cunningly disguised doors worked into the sides of the chamber. At the activation of their platforms, these doors slid aside, although they moved slowly. Zachary was certain the rumbling noises were more a sound effect piped through speakers in the wall than any actual noise caused by the doors. The doors were not in line with the platforms that Matt stood on and Zippy lay on, but rather were crosswise, so that if it could be said Matt stood on the front left corner and Zippy lay on the back right, the doors were front right and back left.

Above even the amplified noise of rock sliding across rock came a very different collection of sounds: hoots, shouts, and guttural vocalizations that sounded primal but familiar, the combination enough to send shivers racing up his spine.

The openings widened, and now forms came rushing through. They were men, two from each doorway, but moving in a manner that argued against conscious drive and intent, appearing more instinctual, like animals suddenly thrust into a bipedal stance and propelled forward. They were the source of the strange noises, and Zachary understood. Like the four drug-crazed men who had attacked them in the previous room, these were completely devoid of reasoning, out of touch with even their humanity, and were rushing forward to attack.

"What the absolute hell?" Matt shouted.

"Freakers! Stay on the platform!" Brian yelled back at him. "You stepped on it, you have to stay there until we can lock down the plates inside the rooms!"

Zachary moved to place himself between the statue and the two men rushing from the left. Elizabeth moved up beside him. He stopped Brian with a look. "Stay near Zippy," he said to the engineer. "Protect him."

Brian nodded.

Zachary wasn't sure how the others were arrayed, though he heard Big Rich call, "Don't worry, we can handle these two."

"Hells yeah," Li'l Bit chimed in.

Then it didn't matter, as the first man reached out for him.

Like the foursome in their separate trial room, these men were thin to the point of emaciation, covered in weeping sores and pus-oozing abscesses from what were probably infected drug injection sites. Long, stringy, greasy hair covered their heads, running into and merging with equally filthy scraggly mats of facial hair. The smell coming off them was almost enough of an assault to the senses to make fighting impossible, and Zachary clenched his teeth and held his breath.

THE DUNGEON

The man ran with arms wind milling wildly, or swiping viciously from side to side, as though he ran through a cloud of stinging insects and wanted to sweep them away.

Whatever he saw or felt in his drug-fogged state, Zachary could never know. He waited, trying to time the man's approach, and launched a punch straight at the attacker's face, hoping to use the man's own momentum as extra impetus. Amazingly, the man arrested his movement in time to bring a right arm across his face, pushing Zack's fist out wide, then immediately closed the remaining distance, both grimy hands reaching for the cop's neck.

Zachary was pushed back a step before he could get his feet planted. The ferocity of the attack surprised him. The previous four, though they'd attacked, hadn't been anywhere near as aggressive or cunning. He heard a scream from Liz, cries and shouts from the others behind him, but his main focus was on the man whose hands were around his throat, seeking to cut off his air.

The strength in the crazed man's grip was astounding. Zack tried bringing his arms up, around, and down atop the elbows of his attacker, but that did nothing to dislodge the grip. His forearms flashed with pain from the impact, like he'd slammed them against steel bars. In retaliation, the druggie pulled, bending his elbows, and slammed Zachary in the face with his own forehead.

Lights flashed behind his eyes. Pain blossomed in his head. He tried to cry out and couldn't force a sound past the restriction around his throat. He felt himself pushed back and knew he was going to be head-butted again.

Desperate, he wove his right arm over the left arm of his attacker, then down, bringing his right hand under the man's right arm, with his hand just outside the man's elbow. Feeling himself pulled, he put all of his energy into a left-handed swing, not at the attacker, but at his own right hand. His hands met, and with a solid snapping sound, the attacker's right elbow shattered. The force of the blow, pushing across the druggie's body, forced the second hand off his throat and caused the man to pivot to his left.

Already moving forward, growling through the pain in his head and gasping for air, Zachary wrapped his arms around the man's upper body, pinning both arms to the sides. With the man's body turned ninety degrees, he couldn't use his head as a weapon, but he tried. As Zack lifted and pushed, twisted and carried, the crazed druggie tried repeatedly to turn his head to the right, broken, rotten teeth gnashing, hoping to catch hold of some part of Zachary. The broken arm didn't seem to be hindering his efforts at all. His body writhed in Zack's grip. Not a word of protest or grunt of pain escaped him, just long, keening exhalations that might have been words, or nothing more than misfires from a brain fried like the egg on those long-ago television commercials.

The overripe stench threatened to gag him, but Zachary couldn't allow his grip to loosen. Foot by foot and yard by yard, he pushed the man-animal back into the room he'd emerged from. Coming to the narrow doorway, what now appeared a natural opening in the rock wall, he saw a dimly lit space no more than four or five feet square. The smell coming out of the space was a concentrated version of the nausea-inducing reek of the thing in his arms. Clearly these two had been locked inside for some time.

A stray thought caused Zachary to wonder why they hadn't attacked each other. Perhaps they'd been kept sedated, and only aroused when the room was opened.

Desperate, arms and legs beginning to shake with the effort of holding the man, Zack scanned the interior of the small room. Nothing struck him as an obvious plate or platform. Perhaps the entire floor counted, and all he would need to do would be to get the man inside the room. Before he could do that, though, he needed to see what the others were doing.

Altering his angle of approach, he pushed the man-thing to the side of the opening, mentally preparing himself for his next maneuver. With no idea how much time had elapsed—but reassured that he hadn't heard another announcement—he used his greater weight to press the man against the wall, leaning in. He felt several hard buffets against the top of his head, as the man redoubled his efforts to try to bite with the side of his mouth. Taking a deep breath, he eased off his pressure, leaned back into his legs, then drove forward and upward, letting the top of his head meet the side of the man's face, feeling the force of its head connecting with the rock wall all the way down into his shoulders. Quickly, before the thing could react, he repeated the move, once, then again.

After the third blow, he withdrew his arms and quickly spun the man fully away from him. The man still fought, but weakly, stunned by the blows to the head. Zachary reached up, getting one thick arm around the man's neck, catching the chin in the bend of his elbow. Using his left arm as both leverage and guidance, he squeezed the man's neck on both sides, trying to keep pressure with forearm and upper arm, wanting to render the man unconscious without killing him. Regardless of what drugs were coursing through the man's body, the brain would shut down once it was deprived of oxygen for any period of time.

The sleeper hold worked, and Zachary was rewarded with the sudden weight of the unconscious man sliding face first down the wall. Quickly, unsure how much time he might have before the thing woke up again, he turned and scanned the room.

CHAPTER 26

Eddie

"What the absolute hell?" Matt shouted, turning to his right, looking in the direction of the loudest noises.

Eddie turned too, the howls and moans drawing his testicles tight, almost making him want to duck back into his shell, just cower down and let the grown-ups handle things.

"Stay on the platform!" Brian yelled from behind them. "You stepped on it, you have to stay there until we can lock down the plates inside the rooms!"

"Five minutes until room lockdown."

"It's like DJ said," Tory whispered. "Some of them had to be hauled down here, poked and prodded by those electric rods, remember?"

Eddie remembered.

"I guess this is what he meant," she finished.

Zachary called out something behind them, and Big Rich responded, "Don't worry, we can handle these two."

"Hells yeah," Li'l Bit chimed in.

A grunt from the cop and a scream from the tall redhead sounded behind them. Big Rich, tall and broad-shouldered, and Li'l Bit, much shorter but no less muscled, moved forward.

"Eddie," Brian called.

Looking back at the engineer, crouched protectively over Zippy, Eddie saw the older man waving to him. He watched as the tall policeman took a staggering blow to the face, then was almost choked. Part of him wanted to go help, but the cop retaliated with a brilliant hold-break that snapped his attacker's arm.

Then he was pushing the strange, raving, screaming man backward, and Eddie caught site of Elizabeth fighting another of the men. Suddenly, his mind was back in his Tae Kwon Do studio and he was thirteen years old. The teacher that day had arrayed his four best students, all black belts, in a circle around him. Their uniforms were almost invisible under layers of padding, chest plates, shin guards, elbow pads, forearm guards, and thick, foam helmets. The teacher, a small, Korean man about the same height as Li'l Bit, though much leaner, stood unprotected in the middle of them. The lesson was about recognizing that sometimes, no matter how well-trained you are, your opponent will be beyond control, when chaos overpowers technique and reason, and your only option is to run.

With a shouted word, his teacher went into a frenzy, lunging this way, punching that, throwing his body at his students, rather than just crisp and concise arm and leg attacks. The four black belts staggered back, immediately overwhelmed, and when one faltered, the teacher struck harder, attacking in unconventional ways at unconventional targets.

The fight between Elizabeth and the crazy man resembled that fight, only to Eddie it seemed more a matter of trying to place a bet on which of the two was the craziest.

The man never had a chance.

Screaming, shouting, swinging, Elizabeth drove him back every time he advanced. Neither seemed to feel any pain. When the man tried to grab her hair, she bit his wrist. When he reached for her, she let him grab her loose-flying shirt, then promptly broke his wrist.

THE DUNGEON

When he started to fall, she kicked him in the face, the neck, the chest, until finally he rolled onto the ground, motionless. Then she stood over him, hands clenched tightly at her sides, breathing hard, watching to see if he moved again.

"Eddie, please," Brian said, and Eddie realized the older man must have been calling him for several seconds. "I need your help here."

There were other sounds as well. Big Rich had apparently made quick work of one of the men and was now working the second one back, back against the wall, near the far opening, with Li'l Bit coming in at the sides, helping keep the druggie distracted, the two of them an effective back-and-forth for a foe who couldn't remain focused on one target.

Eddie turned and knelt by Brian, his eyes going to Zippy who—

"He's dead, Eddie," Brian confirmed. "When he fell onto the platform, I think that was when, well, it happened."

Strangely, the engineer's eyes were wet with tears.

"Zachary," Matt shouted suddenly, "they got him to the door. I'm going to count to three. On three, push your guy inside, and I'll jump off."

"You need to help me move him aside," Brian said, his voice catching.

Mutely, Eddie nodded. He didn't understand why the older man was crying; he certainly hadn't seemed the type to be so affected by a stranger's death, not in the short time they'd known each other. It might just be the shock of being near a dead person. Some people couldn't handle it.

Eddie didn't have that luxury.

"One."

"Grab his shoulders, Eddie. I'll get his legs."

Eddie moved to get his hands under Zippy's back, curling his fingers into the loose spaces in the skinny man's armpits.

"Two."

"Four minutes."

"Damn it, woman!" Matt swore. "Stop doing that!"

"I'm ready!" Big Rich called.

"We are too," Elizabeth said. Eddie risked a glance to the side, saw the tall redhead now helping the police officer maneuver the unconscious man to the opening of the door.

"Three!" Matt shouted.

Eddie pushed against the ground, lifting Zippy's upper half off the platform. Brian stood as well, the dead man's lower legs gathered under his arms. The engineer indicated with his head that they should move to his left. Eddie complied. They shuffled a few steps sideways, then laid the dead man back on the ground as gently as they could.

"Both doors are closed," Matt announced, stepping away from the plates and joining Eddie and Brian.

"Is he?" Tory asked softly, joining them.

Brian nodded.

"Damn, that's a shame," Li'l Bit said. "He seemed like a good guy for a crackhead."

Big Rich turned a glare on the shorter man. "What? Dat's a compliment, where I come from."

Zachary and Elizabeth moved back to join them. The cop looked like he'd taken quite a beating, while the redhead looked cool. After seeing her fight, Eddie decided she was the most dangerous person in the room. Anyone who could act that cool after just beating someone into the ground was either a special kind of brave or a special kind of crazy.

Whichever it was, he was glad she was on their side.

THE DUNGEON

"We don't have much time," Zachary said. "Tory, go step on another platform."

"Either one?" she asked.

"Shouldn't matter," Brian said.

Shrugging, Tory turned and faced the nearest platform, more or less in line with the statue's right hip, and directly in line with the hole in the wall Richard and Li'l Bit just closed. She was holding the knife she'd picked up, the one Goob had threatened him with.

"Here goes," she announced, and stepped easily onto its surface.

The fake sound of tumbling rocks came pouring out of the hidden speakers, making Eddie smile. There was only so much realism you could pack into something like this, he decided, then at some point, it all began to seem fake.

"Here we go again," Big Rich said, as three running, writhing forms burst out of the far right corner of the room, their wordless screams rising and falling over one another as they approached.

Everyone, including Brian, moved to intercept the trio, stopping them before they had bridged half the distance to the platforms. Big Rich, Li'l Bit, and the cop fought to secure holds on the men as the others helped push and direct them back to the smaller room.

"A quick word about Zippy Brown," the voice of Mike Callahan said, before being interrupted by the **"*Three minutes*"** notification.

"Oh, stow it, asshole!" Eddie heard someone, maybe Brian, say.

"Like Richard before him, Zippy volunteered, an easy way to get out of prison, where he was facing several more years for Possession with Intent to Distribute."

"Like he understood any of it," Big Rich said. "You used him!"

"He wasn't the brightest of those who chose to join our show, but no one can doubt his bravery. He's the only reason you're still alive, right, Brian?"

"Don't you listen to that crap," Matt said, looking at Brian.

Working together, the seven pushed and maneuvered the three crazy men back into the small room.

"Now!" Matt called out.

Tory must have stepped off the platform, because the door began to slide shut. It didn't seal instantly, like the metal door that snagged the cop's shirt sleeve back in the first room, so the crazy men inside had a few seconds to try getting out again. But Big Rich stopped them, using his large frame to keep any of them from escaping.

"Last door has to be over there," Brian said, pointing across the room.

"Okay," Zachary said. "Let's head over there. Tory, get ready to step on the last platform."

The seven moved quickly around the statue and to the last section of wall, now in line with the platform Zippy died upon. Even knowing that a piece of this round wall would soon open didn't make it any easier to see where it would be.

They lined up roughly shoulder to shoulder, with Eddie down on the right end near Brian. He didn't need to be asked to watch out for the older man. One look at his sweaty face, the way he kept opening and closing his fists, told Eddie all he needed to know. This was a man who was ready to be brave, ready to fight for something, but who was absolutely scared to death about doing it. He would probably get hurt just trying to be helpful, and Eddie figured the man who helped build some of this stuff was probably their best bet on figuring out how to escape it.

THE DUNGEON

"Go ahead, Tory!" Zachary yelled over his shoulder, and Eddie felt himself tense. Though he wasn't confrontational by nature, he had loved sparring in Tae Kwon Do. It wasn't about trying to hurt anyone. It wasn't even about winning, though that felt good. It was more the excitement of pitting skill against skill, trying to spot your opponent's weakness while hoping your own weren't too obvious. It was learning, from each match, how to improve yourself. It was wholly separate from the excitement he felt when he broke a thicker board, or did it with a new kick, or one of a hundred other milestones he'd achieved while in class. As much as he tried to avoid it, he liked the feeling of surging life and adrenaline that filled him when he fought.

And here came the grinding, rumbling noises again, which meant Tory had stepped on the final platform. If what Brian said was true, activating the plate inside this room would open the final door. But they probably weren't going to take it. Instead, there might be another way, another escape, on the southern wall, whichever way that was.

Something was wrong.

It wasn't just in the movement of the door, which wasn't opening side to side, but rather coming up from the ground like a garage door. It wasn't just in the size of the opening, which seemed almost like both sides of a double garage opening simultaneously rather than the three- or four-foot width of the previous doors. It also wasn't just the near-deafening chorus of shouts, whoops, screeches, and screams that reached them as the soundproofed barrier was lifted.

It was all of that plus the multitude of shuffling, lurching, booted and bare feet that Eddie could see under the lifting door. It was the multi-hued, rag-garbed legs, some short, some long, some thick, some thin, that moved frantically, jiving left, juking right, never standing still long enough to get an accurate count of the number of bodies those legs must be attached to. It was the overwhelming smell of rotting teeth, dirty bodies, and feces-stained clothing that rushed out with the sounds.

"Holy shit!" Li'l Bit exclaimed.

CHAPTER 27

DeShaun

As the milling throng of drug-crazed people began to duck under the rising door, filling the room with their stench and their screams, Li'l Bit took a step back. There was no way he wanted to be the first dude to get caught up in that mess.

"We just need to get one Freaker trapped in there!" the big-brained engineer dude yelled. "Just one, then Tory can close the door."

"Eddie," the cop yelled, "watch out for Tory. There's too many for us to—"

And then the words stopped, and the fighting started.

Li'l Bit wasn't a big man, hence the nickname. He was strong, but so were all the other guys where he grew up. He was gay, which would have made him worth about half of nothing if his childhood friends ever found out. But he wasn't a coward. And there wasn't ever going to be a man who could call him one. So when engineer man said they needed one dude down on the ground in the room, that's what Li'l Bit seized on.

As the horde flooded out of the room, arms swinging and teeth gnashing, stinking up the place with their full-on white funk, Li'l Bit picked out a scrawny target in the center of the line, tucked his shoulders, and charged. He didn't want to be first, but if being first meant getting out of here faster, that's what he'd be.

Back when he was younger and not quite sure what he was or why he always felt different, his friends tried to get him to join the football team. "You just the right size," they said, so he put on the pads and went to the tryouts. He played tailback for the rest of junior high, hung out with the team, worked out with the team, and started to feel as though he'd finally found a place he belonged. His height was an advantage, and even though girls were starting to be of interest to his teammates and were definitely showing some interest in him, they weren't the focal point of every aspect of a player's life outside of football.

Fast forward to Clinton High School, and it became immediately apparent that he wasn't going to fit in. By then he'd started to notice his fellows on the team more than the cheerleaders. He avoided the showers after practice, anything to prevent a physical reaction from being apparent. Even before he knew what being homosexual meant, he'd known being homosexual was bad. For all that society pushed to continue the fight against racism, no one ever thought to push against the African American community for their callous and blatant aggression toward homosexuality. The mainstream press and all those pandering politicians loved to preach about the evils of the old, white Republicans, all the while ignoring the fact that the black communities are some of the most sexually intolerant places in the country, because it didn't fit with their agenda or their drive to earn the black vote.

So DeShaun quit the team, tightened up his bad boy mannerisms, and hid in the closet.

None of that stopped him feeling an absurd smile break out over his face as he rushed forward, shoulders lowered, and crashed into the midsection of the

THE DUNGEON

skinny white boy just coming under the garage door. He felt the flailing hands slapping at his back as his ducked and thrust, angling his shoulder up under the man's ribcage, pumping his legs, lifting the lighter man, and pushing him back into the room, driving for that extra yard or two, as his coach would have said.

He got his hands up as he slowed his charge, using his momentum and the strength in his arms to throw the dude back against the far wall of the hidden room, blowing out the air he'd been holding.

Taking in a breath almost made him dizzy; the stink in this enclosed place was suffocating. Eyes darting back and forth as he backed away, watching to make sure the guy didn't come right back at him, DeShaun saw dark, slippery stains on floors and walls, some with tinges of blood, others like greasy smears of brown. The crazy bastards had pissed, shit, and bled all over the place.

Still backing up, he wiped his hands on his pants, feeling a desperate desire to make sure none of that nasty had clung to him.

He hadn't felt so freaked out since the last time a spider landed on him.

Still backing up, clearing the garage door, he shouted, "Yo, get off the platform! I got one cornered!"

"Thank God," someone said, and almost immediately the garage door began descending.

Li'l Bit watched the skinny dude inside the room, who was slowly regaining his feet. Maybe this sad sack of a white boy wasn't quite as messed up as the others, or maybe he'd rung his bell pretty good slamming him back against the wall like that, but whatever the case, the skinny dope-head didn't seem too eager to rush back out, not with Li'l Bit standing guard, waiting for him.

"Two minutes."

"It don't matter, you crazy computer bitch!" Li'l Bit yelled. "We beat your damn timer!"

He turned as the sliding door came to a halt against the floor, just as the sound of another door opening started up. It seemed to be coming from his right, somewhere up in line with the chest of the statue.

The room behind him was a chaotic melee, crazy hopped up freaks running everywhere, attacking each other as often as one of his group. Some of them had actually started climbing the wooden struts along the walls, like wannabe Spidermen trying out for the next comic book movie. Even as he watched, a tall man whose pants were so worn out in the seat you could see his scrawny butt cheeks flexing through the weave, like the winner of the Least Sexy Assless Chaps contest in a Gay Pride Parade from Hell, slipped off a set of crossbeams and fell ten or twelve feet to the floor, landing almost on top of a second nut job whose only goal a moment before had been trying to jump up and grab the leg of the one climbing above him.

The rest of his gang were grouped up near the back of the statue, with Big Rich and the cop laying out some serious punishment to anything that came near them. That crazy, skinny lady wasn't no joke either. She didn't seem to have much in the way of training or technique, but the way she lit into those herky-jerky bastards said she wasn't a chick to be messed with. He didn't know who was crazier, but at least she hadn't tried to kill him.

"There!" the engineer dude said, pointing toward the new door. Li'l Bit looked where he pointed and saw another of those hidden doors, invisible when they were closed, sliding up. It wasn't anywhere near as big as the garage door had been, which might not be a bad thing. Every one of those crazy dudes suddenly stopped running, or swinging, or whatever they'd been doing. Almost like an army obeying a call to form up ranks, they all started ambling, sprinting, or, in some cases, limping, toward the new door.

"If that's north," Matt said, "then south is that way." He pointed to DeShaun's left.

"That's where it'll be," Brian agreed.

More of the crazy things were converging on the new door, as the group of seven left the base of the statue and headed to the only section of the circular room that still looked smooth and rounded. Jogging to catch up, Li'l Bit joined them.

"So what's the deal with this southern wall?" he asked. He'd been helping take care of Zippy when Brian explained it the first time, and with the injured man zoning in and out of consciousness, he hadn't caught all of the details.

"It's not a real wall," Big Rich said.

"Like the others aren't?" DeShaun asked. "I mean, they have doors and all."

"No, like it's just plasterboard and paint," Brian said. "I can't go into all of it right now, but this…thing…this game show…it's all just smoke and mirrors."

They had reached the broad, curving wall. Big Rich pushed his big hands against the surface, fingers splayed out, and started pushing. Matt and the policeman came up a few feet to either side, also probing, testing.

"There's so much more here than a big company trying to get bigger by pulling homeless off the street, or making a few people with mental health problems disappear," Brian said.

"Like what?" Li'l Bit asked.

"This…this place. This set." The engineer spread his arms, turning a slow circle like he wanted the whole room to be part of his explanation. "It's just a part, the smallest part. It touches the real labyrinth, for one thing."

"Is that what's on the other side of this wall?" Zachary asked.

Brian nodded. Then, realizing the cop hadn't been watching him, answered verbally.

Three loud thuds sounded as Big Rich hammered the wall with his fists. "Sounds pretty solid."

The cop banged on his section of the wall, and it sounded the same.

The accountant's hands drummed up a very different tone, and immediately the big tight end moved to his right. When Big Rich swung the next time, DeShaun thought he could see the entire section of wall shiver.

"I'll be damned," Big Rich said. "There's definitely something behind this."

"Can you break through it?" Brian asked.

"Yeah, but I ain't using my fists," Rich answered. "Y'all stand back."

"Listen," Brian said. "It's not just the labyrinth, it's what's beyond it. Magellan Enterprises isn't after the labyrinth. They don't want cleaner cities. Hell, they're not even trying to gain political influence."

"Huh, I thought that was *all* this was about," the little blond woman said.

Big Rich walked a dozen steps back, lowered his shoulders, and took two or three quick breaths.

Then all hell broke loose.

CHAPTER 28

Zachary

Gunshots sounded from behind them, a long rattling chain, without syncopation, shots over shots, multiple guns firing at once. The sounds were somehow muffled but also distinct. You could tell it was gunfire, but it seemed to be coming from behind a wall.

Or from down a tunnel at the other end of the room.

"The hell?" Matt shouted.

"Are they shooting at us?" Eddie asked.

"I ain't waiting to give 'em a target," Big Rich said and charged forward.

"Those poor people," Tory said softly, and Zachary understood. The crazed men who'd charged off through the new door as soon as it opened had just met a very violent end.

Just then the large tight end struck the wall where the knocks had sounded hollow. Shoulder leading, eyes squeezed shut, he plowed through brown-painted drywall like it was cardboard stretched between two poles, with the others following close behind. Matt paused a moment to push a few stubborn bits of drywall aside, clearing the entire panel, leaving an almost surgically cut rectangular-but-curved opening in the wall of the circular room.

"Move, quickly," Brian hissed, turning his head back and forth, trying to watch the room and the open door at the other end.

Zachary could feel his anxiety, like a tickle between his shoulder blades. It felt like being out in the open, knowing there was a sniper up on the roof, and wondering if you'd be able to feel the red dot on your back before the bullet tore through you.

The gunfire sounded again, less muffled, almost in the room behind them, but when he turned to look, the room remained empty.

Still, it was enough of a motivator to push everyone through the opening.

"Holy crap," Matt muttered.

Zachary followed Brian through the hole in wall, noticing the light brightening around him.

He entered a small, square room, lit by bright fluorescents that made his eyes sting after spending the better part of the past hour running through the diffuse, dim light of the dungeon, almost running into Brian. The others were grouped up in the center of the room, looking around. The white light illuminated shelves along the left wall, with what looked like white miner's helmets lined up in neat, orderly rows. There was a row of hooks lining the wall to the right. Drawstring-topped leather backpacks, like wash leather purses made large, hung from the hooks. The straps appeared as though they should crisscross in the front. Odd shapes made bulges in the leather sides. Whoever those packs were meant for, they were stuffed full.

Across from the hole yawned another opening, this one of dank, dark stone, that ran off through the southern wall. The light from the small room barely penetrated into the new corridor. He could see perhaps five feet into the tunnel before the light died or the tunnel curved. All Zachary could tell, from that one glimpse, was that the floor seemed to be angling down.

"Hurry, everyone," Brian said. "Grab a bag and a helmet and start down the tunnel."

"Uh, brothers don't do holes like dat," Li'l Bit said.

A few scattered shots rang out, sharp cracks that made the small, tattooed man flinch.

"This brother would rather be down there than up here," Big Rich said, snagging a helmet off a shelf and reaching a long arm out for a backpack. "How do you turn these things on?" he asked, thick fingers fumbling over the surface of the helmet. Zack noticed a blue icon embossed on the sides of the helmets, two triangles inverted over each other. He'd seen the logo before while investigating the disappearance of the homeless people in Virginia Beach.

"Like this," Brian said, grabbing a second helmet. With a yank, he pulled the yellow headlamp off a clip on the front of the helmet. "This is a miner's light. It's battery-powered, has a bunch of different settings, but the main thing to know right now is you press one of these black buttons on the front of the light and you have light." The plastic, rectangular headlamp featured a half-inch black circle on each side. Brian pushed one, and the light came on. Quickly, he clipped the light back onto the helmet in his hands and handed it to Li'l Bit.

"I still don't like this," the shorter man said, but he accepted the helmet, then took a backpack from Rich. "Thanks," he muttered.

Without waiting any longer, Big Rich headed into the tunnel. Li'l Bit followed behind.

"What's down there, anyway?" Matt asked.

"Does it matter?" Brian hissed. "You heard those guns. We don't have much time before they come in here after us."

As if to accentuate his point, another barrage of gunfire filled the room behind them. Sharp twangs and pings marked the sound of slugs ricocheting off the floor, walls, and ceilings, though none struck inside the room.

Moving more quickly now, Zachary handed helmets to Tory, Eddie, and Elizabeth. All three had snagged backpacks, though only Eddie took a moment to shrug into his, before heading into the passage.

"Wait for us at the first crossing!" Brian called after them.

Then it was only Matt, Brian, and himself still in the small room. Seeing both the cop and the accountant with helmets on their heads, Brian turned to pull at something on the wall near the passage.

"What're you—" Matt began, but then Brian pulled a panel away from the wall, revealing a decent-sized circuit board covered in chips, test points, a maze of solder runs, and a dozen other red, blue, and black parts that Zachary didn't recognize.

"Just come on out of there. You've got nowhere to go."

The voice sounded from the room behind them, amplified and booming.

"Shit!" Matt hissed. "They're here."

"Just go," Brian said.

Matt ducked into the corridor, though he needn't have bothered. The ceiling was more than tall enough for Big Rich to walk upright.

Standing at the edge of the tunnel, one foot in the brightly lit room full of equipment, and one on the hard stone, Zachary said, "You're not coming with us, are you?"

THE DUNGEON

Brian's shoulder's sagged for a moment and then firmed as he straightened them.

"There's a kill switch here," he said. "Kind of a firewall, to prevent, I don't know, something from going into the tunnel."

"Or maybe from coming out of it," Zack finished.

Brian nodded. "It doesn't matter. I can drop it and disable it, give you guys a pretty decent head start."

"You've got three seconds before we unload in there."

"Show me what to push and I'll—"

"You'll what?" Brian said. "*You* can get them through the labyrinth, keep them together, keep them safe."

"3!"

"I—" Zachary began, but there was no more time to argue. Aside from grabbing the technician and throwing him into the tunnel, there was nothing he could do. "Thank you," he said instead, and stepped fully into a world of earth and stone.

CHAPTER 29

Brian

Zachary moved off into the corridor, and before he could second guess himself, Brian pushed the red button he'd been assured would be behind the panel. A steel door slid smoothly down from the ceiling, completely blocking the entrance to the rough rock passage that led down into the earth.

"2!"

"It's okay," he said into the silence following the shouted number. "They're gone."

A young man wearing a flak jacket over a Magellan Enterprises security uniform, all buzz cut, utility belt, and bulging arms, came fast into the room, AR-15 held at the ready. He swept the room with the rifle, face pressed against the stock, so head and gun moved as one. Brian couldn't resist a thrill of sudden fear when the bore of the barrel swept over him. He made no sudden moves, waiting.

"It's clear," the young man said.

Two other security officer stepped in behind him, shouldering rifles as they came, white Magellan logo visible on their right shoulders.

"We'll need an accounting of what they took," a fourth man said, coming in last. He stood about five-eight, with short, salt-and-pepper hair. Thick-framed glasses covered brown eyes that looked intelligent, while small lines at the outsides gave the impression of a jovial man, prone to laughter. His face widened into a smile at the sight of Brian, still kneeling by the control panel. A bright yellow megaphone hung from a shoulder strap, bumping his hip as he walked. Unlike the security personnel, he wore a white buttoned-up shirt and khaki slacks. A navy blue tie hung low around his neck; he'd loosened the knot and opened his collar. The bright lights of the staging room brought out the color of the man's skin, a slight tan tint that was present regardless of the season.

"They each took a pack and a hat," Brian said. "Seven total."

"Thank God you're okay, Brian," he said, extending his hand, helping the engineer to his feet.

"I almost wasn't," Brian said, taking the hand and rising. "Can't believe I froze like that in front of the panther."

"You spent so much time practicing that room, I thought you could run it in your sleep," the man said.

Brian chuckled. "Guess I got a little stage fright, Dan."

Daniel King laughed, and the sound was as honest and refreshing as the face of the man who made it. After what seemed like an eternity in the dungeon, Brian began to relax.

"Fire the blank," Daniel told the first security guard.

"Cover your ears," Buzz-Cut said, pulling a pistol from his right hip holster.

The report was deafening in the closed space. Brian winced despite having his hands over his ears.

Lowering his hands, Dan went on as if nothing had happened, though Brian knew it was forced. The blank shot was meant to convince the others, if they were hunkering down near the steel door, to go on into the labyrinth. No reason to hang around up here. "That stuff you were telling them, about your blood pressure medicine, is that true?" Dan asked.

Brian nodded. "I've looked it up at least a dozen times, found out there's all kinds of other medicines I could be taking, but Dr. Ramirez won't change it."

"It works?"

"Haven't had a blood pressure over one-forty since I started it, so yeah. I'm a little scared to check it right now, though."

"Well, that's good then, and understandable."

The two men took a last look around the small staging area, before heading back out into The Octagon Room.

Brian shivered, remembering the men who'd attacked them.

"I didn't know there were going to be any Freakers in the dungeon with us."

Dan's face contracted for a moment, his eyes tightening in concern. "Walt wouldn't let it go," he said. "He said that Ian pushed for their inclusion, even after we warned him we had an engineer running it to look for bugs. We know the Freakers are aggressive, but would they be aggressive enough to thrill the viewers?" He took a deep breath. "Look, they put them in at the last moment. I still had time to get you out, but it would've meant losing the whole group." He stopped and laid a strong hand on Brian's shoulder. "I'm sorry I didn't tell you, give you the chance to back out."

Brian suppressed a flare of anger. His life was in danger anyway. Hell, his whole world was in danger, everything he knew. Stacked against that, what were a few screaming crazy men? "It wouldn't have mattered if you did. Someone had to go through this with them, and I would still have been the only logical choice. They needed to be told about the wall."

"We might have been able to avoid if it wasn't the first run with the high rollers. To keep them happy, we had to up the stakes. I figured between you and me, we'd make sure you got the Cat Room."

"What did they see at the end?"

Dan smiled. "They saw what our guys wanted them to see. The bunch of you got thrashed by the Freaker explosion from the final door. Then we opened the exit door and blew them all away."

"How many actually died?"

"Not as many as you'd think, Brian. And you really shouldn't be worrying about it. You just survived something no one is supposed to survive. I'd say that's enough for one day. You go asking too many questions, and they'll really think you're out to screw the company."

"Well," Brian said softly, "we are."

Dan fell silent, waiting as the security detail jogged past them, heading into the open door at the northern end of the room. "We are, but you know as well I do that there's only so much we can do from this end."

"That's why I had to get as many into that tunnel as I could," Brian said, "I know. I don't have to like it, though. They deserve better. Hell, they at least deserved a heads-up."

"You didn't, did you?"

"Of course not, Dan. We've both seen the predictions."

As they drew near the center of the room, standing just to the right of the old statue of King Minos, Dan stopped. Brian halted next to him. Turning to look at the engineer, Dan said, "Look, we just have to be careful a little while longer. Eric made a royal screw up of the data upload on the cop, just like we planned. As long as someone picks up the trail, we should have an official investigation coming our way. That's our way out."

"And even if that fails," Brian added, "getting Zachary and Elizabeth into the labyrinth should destabilize that end of the operation."

"As long as Walt and Ian don't find that disk."

"They won't," Brian said.

Dan searched his eyes for moment, then nodded. "Good, you're learning."

"What's that supposed to mean?"

"This is the first time we've talked that you didn't try to convince me to take the disk for safekeeping."

Brian laughed.

"Okay, let's clear on out of here before anyone gets suspicious."

Starting back toward the northern wall, Dan addressed one of the waiting security guards. "Get a cleaning detail down here to reset everything. Mr. Magellan wants to run another ten through the dungeon tonight."

"No escapees this time, sir?" the guard asked.

Dan shook his head. "No, but let's get the door to the labyrinth ready to open. He wants that next batch of Freakers to work their way through."

Brian repressed another shudder. The drug cocktail they injected into most of their subjects rendered them wildly aggressive, a pure de-evolution to just their primal, animalistic instincts. The regression was temporary, thankfully, a necessary step toward the drug's ultimate goal, to remove personality, individualism, and motivation. After a frantic period of functioning at the level of survival instinct, which lasted anywhere from forty-eight to seventy-two hours, the person lapsed into near catatonia, what the Magellan insiders were calling the Power Save mode. About twenty-five percent would never reset and would be allowed to die. The others came out awake, but no longer truly aware, docile and easily controlled.

They called them Freakers when they were in the hyper-aggressive state. After they reset, they were Thralls. The discovery of this creation of a new slave race is what sent Brian looking for a way out. No, he had to stop thinking about them as slaves; these people were far worse off. They had no memory of freedom, no dreams of freedom, and no desire to be free. The would never conspire and were incapable of revolt. They ate, they slept, and they worked.

Learning about the drugs and their intended use opened a door for Brian. The scales fell off his eyes, as his wife liked to say, reciting the story of Saul. Carefully, discreetly, using every research trick he'd ever learned, he dug deeper. Learning that the company he worked for was turning criminals, homeless people, and the mentally unstable into thralls wasn't enough; he needed to know why. Maybe some part of him was hoping for a silver lining. Many and more are the things that had been done throughout history that appeared evil, with no point of reference to show the goal behind it. And sometimes it wasn't the people that were bad, but the information they worked from. He told himself he would still work to undermine the company, but he'd be more careful to protect the people within it if he could only understand why.

What he discovered seemed impossible. It all had to do with the labyrinth, what it really was. More than a dungeon for a king's enemies, more than a home for a monster, it was a gateway.

Finding out about the disk brought him to the attention of Dan and a handful of others, all equally upset by the direction of the company, all ready to do something to bring it down from within. Dan *was* Greek, though only Brian and a handful of others knew it. Because of his heritage, he had a vested interest in making sure the company failed in its current pursuits.

Following Dan into the hallway, Brian muttered a short prayer. He hoped Zachary was up to doing his part on the other side.

INTERLUDE

Michael

"Look, Jackson, I don't know how many more times you need to hear this, but it's the last time I'm gonna say it. Forget about Pavese. He was a goddamn sicko! I don't know how the hell he got into police work or why IA never caught on, but it's over. He's gone. Now you need to own that knowledge and get to work. Make sure none of his stink sticks to you."

Captain Alex Cross stood behind his utilitarian wood desk, plate glass windows behind him showing a depressing view of a rainy Virginia Beach morning. His hands were fisted and planted on the desk's surface. Veins stood out on the backs of his hands, thick ropes that seemed to run up his long shirt sleeves and continue uninterrupted up both sides of his neck. Detective Mike Jackson had never seen the man look so angry or so offended.

None of it made any sense. When he'd left for vacation a week ago, Zachary Pavese, friend and fellow detective, had been eyeballs deep in a boring paper chase trying to figure out if someone was preying on homeless people. It was just the sort of human-interest case the guy was always looking for. Forget chasing drug dealers on the strip or working a homicide around Lynnhaven, Pavese took the longer view. He was good at it too. Whether busting a loan shark ring that took advantage of the young sailors and Marines at NAS Oceana and Dam Neck or apprehending a sex trafficker who rented out young girls by the hour in an off-oceanfront flop house hotel, Pavese got it done, with every *I* dotted and every *T* crossed.

To come back this morning and find that not only was Zack gone but he'd been stripped of everything, thrown out like yesterday's garbage, it stunk. The captain wouldn't give any details, but what he alluded to just wasn't possible. It didn't fit the man that Mike had worked with the past five years. It simply could not be true.

The large manila file folder on the captain's desk, held closed by a fat rubber band, bulged with documents. On its cover, underneath the neatly printed label with Zachary Pavese's name, was a large, red FBI. The captain pointed at the folder several times while telling him some of the alleged doings of his friend. Well, if the FBI was involved, he could find out.

Mike Jackson turned away from the captain's desk. The office was small, and a single step brought him to the glass door that led back out to the hubbub of the station's heart, orderly rows of desks, officers talking, keyboards clacking, phones ringing. He pushed open the door, but a word from the captain caused him to turn just after stepping through.

"And, Jackson?"

"Yes, Captain?"

"While you're checking your six on this, don't go picking up his last case. Damn waste of money and manpower, even if it was only one man."

Jackson let the door swing shut. The glass on this side was reflective. He didn't like what was written on his face. A couple of inches shorter and about forty pounds lighter than Zachary, Mike was more comfortable in the shoes of a plainclothes detective. He kept his brown hair a medium length, scissor cut and tousled. Whenever he went to SportsClips, he joked that he liked it short, but his wife liked it messy. Now, however, he felt the weight of his brows pulling down and saw shadows under his green eyes that weren't there when he came to work that morning.

"Yo, Jackson! How was Disney?" one of the other detectives called out to him, pulling him away from the door.

Mike forced a smile as he turned, heading for his desk, "Kids loved it," he said, which seemed to satisfy the other officer. Quickly, before anyone else could interrupt him, he strode to his workspace, sat in his chair, and powered up his desktop.

What had the captain said? He didn't know how Zachary had even been able to become a police officer?

That more than implied a criminal history. It screamed of background information so damning that his friend probably should never have been allowed to fill out an application, much less be accepted to the academy.

What could possibly be so bad that the captain would seem personally insulted? What skeletons had been unearthed while he was sweating with the crowds and trying not to lose his children in Disney World?

His desktop loaded, Mike spent several moments looking at the icons on his blue screen. How should he go about looking into Zachary's supposed crimes? Assuming this was all still new information, it likely wouldn't be in the department's database yet. Even if it was, if it was tied to a new investigation, it wouldn't be accessible to anyone but the captain and those involved.

He was a goddamn sicko.

On a whim, Mike opened a regular web browser. In the search bar, he typed in Zachary Pavese.

The first three links were for people who shared the same name but were obviously not the man he was looking for: a social media profile of a mountain climber in Oregon, a business website for a dentist in Massachusetts, and an obituary for an eighty-year-old who had died two years before.

The fourth post appeared to be an excerpt from a book, one of those half-fiction memoirs written by soldiers returning from one conflict or another.

Zachary Pavese, necrophiliac police officer, grave robber.

What the hell?

Wondering if he was about to hit the station firewall for suspicious websites, Mike clicked the link to read the excerpt.

> *...got my first real taste of crazy before we ever shipped overseas.*
>
> *We had finished our PT, and the sergeant said anyone who wanted to could go off-base as long as we were back by oh-dark-thirty, which means half past midnight. So me and Dave, Pickles and Tiny, we all headed to Peabody's. We left the Preacher behind because, you know, teetotaler and all that. We took Pickles's car and drove out of Story and down a few blocks to this little parking area where guys with military stickers on their car don't have to pay to park.*
>
> *We pull up next to a van and get out. It's one of those sex-freak, kid-stealer kinds of vans, white, got no windows except in the front, looks like a box with the doors on the back that open in the middle. It's a typical Virginia*

THE DUNGEON

Beach night. You can hear the traffic from Pacific Avenue, some bass coming out of cruisers, and every now and then a pulse of music from one band or another, as people open doors and go into the clubs. But over that noise, we could hear the springs singing under that van. Squeak, squeak. It's doing a little rocking, but not too much. We can hear a dude just a panting and a puffing inside. No chick noises, and that's important.

Now, we ain't quiet, you know. Four young studs out for a night before heading over to the desert, where the dudes'll gut you for looking at a chick's eyes, well, we was a little loud. And pulling up next to some brother getting his groove on right next to us, well, that was some funny shit. Pickles said something, real loud, about how he didn't know dogs made that much noise when they humped, and we all laughed, and the van stopped bouncing.

Next thing we know, the cab opens, and out steps this big ol' cop in his patrol uniform, had to be six feet tall. The nameplate on his chest says Pavese. He introduces himself as Zachary, in this kind of soft, mellow way. When Tiny tells this story later, he says the dude talked like an undertaker, which is extra creepy, all things considering. So this Zachary asks us to keep it down, cause there's someone sleepin' in the van. Then he just turns and walks away. We watched him get into a Virginia Beach patrol car that was parked on the side of the road just outside the parking lot and drive off.

So you're picturing this, right? Four dudes in their greens, high on life but nothing else, and a chick snoozing in a van after getting tagged by a cop. So hell yeah, we opened the back of that baby for a peek.

I wish we hadn't.

As soon as we opened her up, the smell hit us like a ton of dead shit. I've seen guys get themselves blown up, guts spilling everywhere, and never smelled nothing as bad as the inside of that van. There was a chick in there, at least, we thought it was a chick, all splayed out on a gray tarp, like the cop wanted to make sure nothing got into the upholstery. Most of her was ate up with rot and decomp, no idea how long she'd been dead, but definitely longer than a minute. Her dress was all hiked up to her hips, and she still had on the high-heeled shoes she'd been buried in.

That's the thing I can't forget, no matter what else I've seen. That cop, Zachary Pavese, was doing a dead chick in the back of a van, and she still had on those heels.

Hastily, Mike closed the window with the story fragment, but not before noting the timestamp on it. It was from a book published in 2012, and the author claimed to have entered the Army in 2007. He grabbed a small notepad and a pen and wrote down the date. He hadn't known Zachary that far back; they didn't meet until 2012, when Mike transferred from Norfolk to take a position as a detective in Virginia Beach. But what he knew of Zack's history certainly fit the timeline. In 2007, Zack would have been on the force as a patrolman, somewhere between his first and second year.

On the notepad, he scribbled the name of the book, the author, and painstakingly wrote out the full web address that provided the link.

Troubled, he looked to the next link, which appeared to be a news article from 1999, involving a collection of high school seniors who were all seen at a party and who all remembered interacting with another student, a young girl, who was the major focus of the story. Apparently she'd gone missing either during or just after the party, and still had not been found. The article was the third or fourth in a series regarding this missing student, one Jessica Quillin, and Zachary was named as one of the students present at the party and questioned afterward by police. From the list of names, it seemed most of the senior class had made an appearance.

So why did that story bother him almost as much as the first one?

He drew a line under his first set of notes on the notepad and wrote down the name of the girl, as well as the dateline and byline from the news article. Then he closed the web browser and opened the database. In the Query bar, he typed Jessica Quillin.

As soon as the case number appeared, with the CLOSED caption, it clicked. Three years ago, Zachary got it into his head to chase down a series of missing persons from the past ten years or so, because he said he'd found a pattern. Ever since his divorce, he'd do things like this, grab a bunch of old cases to study over the weekend like any normal guy would grab a couple of movies to rent. Most of the time he'd just bring them back on Monday, and nothing would come of it. But every once in a while, his hunch would turn into something.

He found the link. A particularly wealthy neighborhood around a golf course, big houses, rich kids. And a caretaker who knew which families might have kids at home, throwing parties, while their parents looked the other way. The caretaker had his own little space, and he would take the drunken girls there, rape them, and kill them.

It had already stopped by the time Zack caught the guy. The dude was getting old. He'd denied it for as long as he could, until the DNA samples started coming back. Mike remembered that part perfectly, this little man with his perfect dentures, looking at the judge and saying, "It's like magic, you can almost see them again."

Mike tried to open the file and found it locked. The little window that opened said the case was "pending review."

He typed in David Cowan, the name of the sex trafficker Zack arrested the previous year.

Pending review.

He tried four other cases and found them all locked, all pending review.

Finally, Mike thought, *Screw this*, and typed in Zachary Pavese in the query box. *If the captain doesn't want me looking, he shouldn't have told me to watch my ass. How can I make sure I'm clean if I don't look to see what they have against Zack?*

A chronological list appeared, dating back to 2005, the year Zack entered the police academy. There were several entries for every year, marking notable events, such as graduation from the academy, promotions from junior patrolman to corporal, then the move to detective, initially in Homicide. There were numerous citations, which Mike expected, some of which he'd had a hand in earning, one he'd helped write, for valor, for meritorious service, for sheer persistence (in the case of the high school girl serial kidnapper, rapist, and killer.) But dotted in and among those entries in Zack's service log were numerous other notations.

Dating almost back to the day he joined the force, Zachary had apparently faced dozens of accusations from the public and from other law enforcement members. Excessive use of force, improper handling of evidence, suspected theft of evidence, one instance of administrative leave for public drunkenness, two reports by division lieutenants for making threats against another officer, placed on probation for striking a fellow officer—the list seemed endless. Every move within the force, from beat cop to Homicide to Special Investigations, seemed to correlate to an infraction or personnel dispute, that insinuated Zack was moved not as a reward, but to separate him from other officers with whom he could no longer work.

There was even an official request logged from Christina Pavese, Zachary's ex-wife, which implored the department to prevent Zachary from making any further contact with her. Her reasons for this request weren't included in the document. Mike included all of these instances in his notes.

At the end of the list were a series of final notations.
Investigation opened: Bribery.
Investigation opened: Police brutality.
Investigation opened: Sexual assault.
Investigation opened: Kidnapping.
Investigation opened: Manslaughter, murder.

Investigation opened: Wrongful arrest, falsifying evidence.

Investigation reopened: Jessica Quillin.

Investigation reopened: Martina Kedrick.

Investigation reopened: Catherine Grace.

Investigation reopened: Wendy Flood.

Investigation reopened: Shannon McMahon.

All of the newest entries dated from that morning, probably opened by the captain and probably driven by that overflowing FBI folder on his desk.

And it all stank.

Mike didn't believe a word of it. It was too pat, too perfect. Nothing in his experience with Zachary Pavese the man, and alongside Zachary Pavese the police officer, could make him believe any of this. He knew the details behind Zack's divorce, knew there was no bad blood between him and his ex-wife. He'd watched as his friend took the backseat in most investigations, how he'd let other officers do the public work, the interrogations, the press conferences, all while he plugged away in the office, typing out his thoughts, finding the needle that proved the haystack.

And at the end, when his friend was apparently nowhere to be found, unable to defend himself, they were reopening the serial killer case, opening investigations into Zachary himself that seemed perfectly set up to exonerate the caretaker and somehow tie all of the deaths to him, like he was one of those cops who got off on being able to hide his own crimes, like that guy out in California.

This didn't just stink. It reeked.

Before he could change his mind, Mike reached for his desk phone. He had a friend working in the bureau. He'd never used that friendship to influence an investigation, had never tried to get more information than he should have access to, both because he didn't want to jeopardize his friend any more than he wanted to open himself to a successful wrongful arrest appeal.

He dialed the bureau switchboard and asked to be transferred. He could have called Lawson directly, but a little anonymity couldn't hurt, especially if the call logs were checked.

"Special Agent Bechtol."

"Law? It's me."

"Hey, Bad Boy."

"I got a situation here could use a little deeper dive than I can handle with my equipment."

"'Sup?"

"Zachary Pavese." He spelled out both names.

"Have we met?"

"Think so. Look, a lot of jetsam just showed up on his beach. No hint of a storm. I'm wondering how long it's been there."

"I'll take a look. Text you later," Lawson said.

"Thanks. Appreciate it."

"It'll be good to see you."

"You too."

That set in motion, Mike replaced the handset in its cradle. All he could do now was wait.

He looked to his right, at the tidy workspace where Zachary should be sitting, slumped over on his left elbow while he moused around his computer screen, digging into files like a prospector panned for gold, hoping for a glint that might mean payday.

Don't go picking up his last case.

Inside the center drawer of that desk, Mike knew, would be Zachary's latest case notes, neatly printed in block letters. There would be a separate page for every name he encountered in his investigation, just as there would eventually be a document file on his computer that exactly matched his handwritten notes. Stacked on the side of the desk were several thin folders, each with a name on the side. Those would be the official Missing Persons reports that someone had filed, some family member who wanted to find a father or an uncle.

    Mike rose from his chair and went to Zachary's desk.

PART 2
THE LABYRINTH

CHAPTER 30

Zachary

Just a few feet away from the sliding steel door that separated them from their pursuers, the passage began a gentle right turn. It also adopted a noticeable descent, the floor canting away at perhaps a five-degree angle. Not enough to be treacherous, but enough to force everyone to move slowly and keep a hand on the wall. The rightward bend continued, and every few feet there would be a step or two in the floor of the tunnel. The ceiling remained high enough for the tallest to walk unbent, but the walls narrowed to just under five feet apart. Illuminated by the lights on their helmets, the walls shone dull brown and gray, with an occasional flare as the light flicked across an area of moisture, or else touched some hidden piece of quartz within the stone.

Around and down, and after five minutes of walking, Li'l Bit began complaining that the front of his legs were starting to ache. Zachary could feel it as well, a tightness in the front of his legs from the constant downward slope. Every time he picked up his feet, the pressure relented, only to return as he placed it down, feet angled down, always down.

"Shin splints," Eddie said softly. "If we can get to a flat place, I can show you how to stretch them out."

The air grew warmer as they moved, still curving right, still angling down, with more of those rough-hewn steps breaking the monotony. Zachary became aware of greater moisture on the walls, cool against his skin, a contrast to the heaviness of the air around them. The passage looked and felt natural, but of course it wasn't. If this was the fabled labyrinth of Greek mythology, it was designed and carved by men, which meant danger.

Ten minutes farther along, the walls maintained their separation, the ground maintained its pitch, and Big Rich muttered a complaint about how his shirt was starting to stick to his back.

"How you think us short boys feel?" Li'l Bit said. "Our noses be right at your armpit level."

The comment drew a laugh from everyone, but the laughter ran away up and down the tunnel. The oppressive, humid air swallowed the sound. Not a hint of an echo returned to them. Likewise, Zachary was aware of every scuff of boot on stone, dull sounds that seemed to point out their position accusingly. He wasn't breathing hard yet, but he was acutely aware of how loud his breathing sounded.

When he'd dashed into the corridor, leaving Brian behind, he'd barely entered the first turn before he ran into the other six, grouped up and waiting for him.

"Where's Brian?" Eddie asked, but the others had known, or sensed, why the engineer hadn't come with him. Tory looked down. Li'l Bit muttered something about how this sucked. Only Elizabeth met his eyes, and it was the first time he'd seen anything in her face that wasn't anger or fear. Her eyes showed a keen understanding of how he felt, guilt that he had to leave a man behind, relief that he was still alive, and more guilt at the sense of relief.

She laid a comforting hand on his shoulder, which gave him the strength to tell them Brian stayed behind to make sure they got away.

THE DUNGEON

The sound of a single gunshot reached them as they got the backpacks and MSA helmets on correctly.

"Son of a bitch!" Matt swore.

Tears shone bright and ready in Tory's eyes. "They...they killed him."

Zachary swallowed his own feelings. "He helped us. He's still helping us, by giving us a chance. Maybe they'll leave his family alone now." Cinching the straps on his backpack, which was a good bit heavier than he'd thought it would be, he turned on his headlight and led the way down.

That was fifteen or twenty minutes ago, it was hard to be sure of time in the tunnel. Then the tunnel straightened out, and he could feel his spirits rise. Almost immediately it began curving again, now bearing to the left, and still it angled down.

"How far down do you think it goes?" Eddie asked a few minutes later.

"It's not as steep as it seems," Tory replied. "It just wears on you. I'd say we're probably no more than two hundred feet down from where we started, even though we've walked what seems like a mile."

"That can't be right," Li'l Bit argued.

"It's pretty accurate, I'd guess," Matt said flatly. "At a steep ten percent grade, you go a mile forward for every five hundred twenty-eight feet down. This is closer to a four or five percent grade, so we're somewhere between two hundred and two hundred fifty feet under where we started."

"How you figure that so fast?"

"There's five thousand, two hundred eighty feet in a mile, so ten percent of that is five hundred twenty-eight," Tory answered, then smiled up at Matt who, amazingly, returned the smile.

"Oh, that makes sense then," Li'l Bit said, then went back to complaining about his legs.

The sloped floor abruptly came to an end, and a long series of those hacked-off steps appeared.

"Looks like we weren't going down fast enough," Eddie offered.

Encouraged by the change, the seven started down.

"Be careful," Tory called, "the steps aren't all even."

Zachary took point, wanting to be the first to face… whatever might be down here to face. As the minutes wore on and new aches settled deep into his hips and thighs, he started wishing for something to fight, anything but the sight of more steps below him, and solid rock all around him.

Behind him each step began to come with its own set of sound effects, as first Li'l Bit, then even stoic Big Rich began to complain about the work of going down, always down. He felt a pain settle into the back of his neck, the result of keeping his head craned forward, letting the light of his miner's helmet guide the way. The big tight end probably had it worse, he thought, dreading what those extra four or five inches of height would mean in navigating these steps.

The air became still thicker, if that was possible. Zachary considered himself in fairly good shape, but he found himself breathing a little faster as the stairs continued. The air wasn't unnaturally humid or suffocating, but it did have a weight to it that required just a little more effort to draw in. It felt like summer along the Gulf Coast without the oppressive heat. There was enough moisture in the air to be noticeable as such, which was very different from the conditioned air most Americans lived in year-round.

Then he noticed a haze in the air around him. Like two liquids combining in a petri dish to form a powder during a chemistry experiment, the moisture in the air seemed to coalesce, first as a barely discernible wispy waviness, then thickening around his feet. With each step, he moved down into a thickening whiteness, like a cloud had been dragged inside by some Greek god and parked in the stairwell.

"Is that...fog?" Elizabeth said from right behind him, and her voice, soft and full of wonder, made him wish, just for an instant, that they were alone in the stairwell, alone to experience this marvel of weather, which a part of him could appreciate for its beauty. He didn't know if it was a confluence of cold air seeping down from the air-conditioned spaces above meeting the more temperate, possibly stale and stagnant, air of the millennia-old structure below them, or if some other phenomenon was at work, and it didn't matter. He continued boldly into the mist, because they couldn't go back.

More voices rose behind him, hushed and reverent. Whatever they thought of the work of getting here, for a moment, at least, complaints were forgotten as the inner child expressed his or her wonder.

The mist felt cool as it crept up his body, small goosebumps breaking out on his arms as he fully entered the indoor cloud. He almost took in a deep breath, like he was going underwater, then chided himself as acting silly. When his head went under, and his vision became limited to no more than a foot around him, his breathing didn't change, which made sense, when he stopped to think about it. He'd been in fog before, which was the same thing. He'd just never experienced stepping *down* into fog. The beam from his headlamp became almost more annoyance than assistance, as the light lanced out and was immediately reflected and refracted, so that it seemed his head must be surrounded by a brilliant nimbus of radiance. He couldn't see his breath when he exhaled; it wasn't quite cold enough for that, but he could see the effect his breathing had on the cloud around him, eddies and swirls moving away from his mouth, dancing in the light from his headlamp.

Another forty or fifty steps, and the mist began to thin. His light illuminated a greater area around him. He noticed it first as just being able to see the walls again, then his feet below him. Looking down no longer felt like he was blinding himself with reflected light. And just as suddenly as it began, he was through. Stopping a dozen or so steps below the cloud, he looked up, his light flashing past Elizabeth's face to grace the underbelly of the white cloud hanging suspended in the air above him.

Feet shuffled and the rest came close to his level, until only Big Rich stood near the bottom of the cloud. Zachary watched as the tall black man reached up, extending his hand into the cloud. He waved it back and forth a few times, then brought it out. When he looked back down at them, a wide smile graced his young face.

"I've always wanted to do that," he said softly, "you know, to touch a cloud."

"What did it feel like?" Tory asked.

"A little like magic," he said after a moment.

Zachary smiled, preparing to turn around and resume his descent. He caught Elizabeth's eyes as he turned his head and felt his smile widen slightly, meeting hers. She took an extra step downward, coming to rest on the stair next to him. Still smiling, feeling a little goofy, he let her take his left hand in her right as he began moving again.

"Told you," Big Rich's voice carried down to them.

Li'l Bit snickered.

Zachary felt his cheeks burning, but he decided to ignore it.

They stepped down hand in hand, another fifteen or twenty steps, then both staggered forward as the

THE DUNGEON

steps came to an end, and the walls they had been using for balance disappeared.

Zachary moved further away from the stairs, sliding his feet, each step tentative. After climbing down stairs for so long, his legs didn't seem to remember how to handle flat ground. And it was flat. For as far as his headlamp would penetrate, he saw nothing but rocky ground. Looking right, he thought he could make out a rock wall at the very edge of vision. To the left and straight ahead was nothing but darkness, pushed back but not defeated by the combination of his light and the others gathering behind him, ready to spring back into place as soon as someone turned their heads.

"Oh, thank God that's over," Matt said, shrugging out of his backpack and sinking to the ground.

"My legs! My poor little legs," Li'l Bit said.

The air felt lighter, now that they had passed through the cloud barrier. Lighter and cooler. Trying to ignore the sounds of his companions setting down their bags, Zachary listened.

The darkness beyond the light of their headlamps seemed to flow around him as he turned and looked. There were sounds, but almost inaudible. A very faint tinkling, which came from somewhere off to the left, might have been water falling, but could just as easily be mice or rats squeaking, or maybe bats chittering to each other. There were small cracking sounds, random and very sporadic, which came from close by and far away, small rocks moved by minute vibrations in the earth.

"Man, come check this stuff out!" Eddie exclaimed.

An...eck...out echoed back at them in waves, the loudest from right and left, with a slower, lower volume return coming from ahead.

Zachary turned to see his fellows taking a rest, headlamps pointed into their open leather bags.

A much brighter light flared into existence as Matt discovered a handheld flashlight in his bag.

"Are these those military meals, what do you call them?" Big Rich asked, holding up a fistful of slender beige packages with Bridgford stamped on the outside.

"MREs," Tory said, holding up one as well. "Meals Ready to Eat."

"Looks like we got maybe ten each," Big Rich said. He looked up at Zachary. "We should probably save them, though."

Li'l Bit stopped himself just before he could open one. "I guess you right, big man. Not like it's a good time to eat, or anything."

"See if everyone has those lights like Matt does," Zachary said, turning back to them. "They'll probably clip onto the harness of your backpacks." Hastily he shrugged out of his backpack. Kneeling on the ground, he unlaced the top.

The others continued to exclaim about their findings. Eddie seemed particularly entranced by the prospect of camping out with such exotic food. Zachary fought a smile at the wonder in his voice. This wasn't a field trip, but it wouldn't do any good for him to get upset at them. They'd been through a lot in just a short hour or two; let them have a moment to relax.

Besides the yellow-jacketed handheld flashlight, something called a Nightstick, with several different power settings, he found a double handful of the MREs, a small Ziploc baggie with six AAA batteries inside, a small cellophane-wrapped bundle of wooden matches, another baggie with five or six fluorescent chalk sticks, a handful of glow sticks, a bottle of iodine tablets, an old-fashioned compass in a small, hinged, wooden box, a coil of half-inch nylon rope, which he

THE DUNGEON

paid out and estimated at approximately fifty feet, and a small, white box with a red cross on the cover. Under the first aid kit and accounting for probably half the weight of the backpack, were two quart-sized canteens filled with water. Opening the first aid kit, he saw a small collection of Band-Aids, gauze, triple antibiotic ointment, a tiny bottle of betadine, scissors, a small bottle of acetaminophen, a small bottle of ibuprofen, a bottle of Augmentin, a small 5-0 suturing kit with a 13mm curved needle, and a roll of clear tape.

"Matt," he called, "come over here a second, let me see your arm."

"It's nothing," the tall man said, but he gathered up everything and put it back in the knapsack.

Rolling up his sleeve, he showed his right arm to the cop. "See, not bleeding, doesn't even really hurt anymore."

"This was caused by a cat, right?" Elizabeth asked, gently rotating Matt's arm so the scratches were illuminated.

"Yeah, a big ass cat."

"Doesn't look too bad," Zachary said, "but we should clean it. Cat scratches have a nasty habit of getting infected."

Matt protested but allowed Elizabeth and Zachary to brush it with betadine and coat it with antibiotic ointment. As he rolled his sleeve back down, Zachary replaced everything in his bag, keeping out only the Nightstick and one of the canteens of water. Taking off the miner's helmet, he unclipped the headlamp and looked at the back.

"Okay," he announced, putting the lamp back on the helmet and the helmet back on his head, "looks like the headlamps take three triple A batteries, and we have six spares each. These handhelds are a lot brighter, but I think they're the rechargeable kind."

"So let's save those, got ya," Richard said. "I suppose we need to get up and get moving too."

"Damn, man, my legs just stopped hurtin'," Li'l Bit said.

"If they come after us right now, we're done for," Zachary said. "We need to lose ourselves in the labyrinth, if we're not already in it, to at least give ourselves a chance."

"A chance for what?" Tory asked.

"I don't know," Zachary said honestly. "But as long as I'm alive, I'm not just gonna sit here and wait for them to catch me. Who knows what time might have done to this place? There could be other ways out of here. I think Brian got us down here thinking just that, that there's a way to escape."

"Actually," Eddie said, moving into the light from Zachary's helmet, "I'm sure there is."

CHAPTER 31

Eddie

By stepping up and saying something, Eddie put himself in the spotlight. It wasn't like when Zachary pushed and cajoled him for help back up in the tile room. It felt better, for one, to be willing to speak up, instead of being forced to. It felt good to know that he had information that might help himself and his companions. (He wasn't ready to call them friends yet, except maybe for Ms. Tory.)

And they were listening! That was the crazy thing that brought the smile to his face even as he brushed the long hair back out of his eyes. Who would have thought that Eddie Artios, perennial bookworm, would one day be asked to recite years of gathered information to a bunch of grown men and women, one of them a police officer?

When he woke up in that first room, surrounded by strangers, all he could think of was hiding. Not literally, of course, because that wasn't an option. That announcer made it quite clear what would happen to anyone left behind. Fear kept him in his shell, as the events unfolded around him. Until Zachary put him front and center.

Since then, little by little, he'd felt less like ducking back into that quiet corner in his head where he was always safe, no matter what happened to his body. When Ms. Tory was threatened by those men, when Eddie stepped up and fought for her, that was the moment when he decided he didn't need that little hidey-hole anymore. He might be small, but he was still a man. And a man did what a man had to do, as his father used to say.

The adventurer in him was awake now, no longer afraid, but eager to explore this underground cavern, excited by the prospect of seeing the places he'd only read about or imagined.

He used to tell his mom, whenever she asked why he read so much ancient history, that it was hard-wired into him. "Our last name is Artios, after all." She would smile and say that may be true, but they were no more Greek than any other American family; all they had was a name passed down from ancestors who migrated to the country centuries before.

It was his last name that prompted Mr. Bland, his second-grade teacher, to suggest that he read *The Lightning Thief* by Rick Riordan. That was the gateway, the plug that opened the dam. From that moment on, his every minute was spent with his nose in a book about the ancient Greeks. If there was nothing new to read from his favorite author, he researched the names, places, and stories used in the books to provide historical or mythological reference.

Take the labyrinth, for example. In myth, it was built by Daedalus in order to house the half-man, half-bull creature known as the Minotaur, the supposed offspring of an encounter between a white bull and the wife of King Minos. Of course, there was a god involved, because even the Greeks didn't think that a woman and a bull could create a child without divine intervention.

Setting aside the more spectacular aspects of the story, there was a lot of fact built into the myth, which Eddie loved, as it lent credibility to the story, allowing for the suspension of disbelief. If part of it was true, why couldn't it all be true?

There was a palace at Knossos, on the island of Crete. It was excavated by a British archaeologist named Sir Arthur Evans between 1900 and 1903, after the retreat of the Ottoman Empire from the region. While no evidence of a separate or underground labyrinth was found, the team of diggers uncovered a vast complex of rooms within the five-acre grounds, over a thousand all told, which led many to speculate that the palace itself might be the labyrinth. They found ceramics tying the location in time to the reign of King Minos, but also were able to identify a second, much older, civilization, which Sir Evans attributed to the Minoans, dating back eight or nine thousand years to the 7th millennium BCE. Whether the warren of rooms in the palace was supposed to have belonged to the Greeks or the Minoans was unclear, though pictorial evidence in the form of bull motifs, particularly that of a young man jumping over a bull, led Evans to believe the location was more appropriately a Minoan structure, owing to the belief that the bull was sacred to the Minoan religion.

Later archaeologists were skeptical of Evan's assertions that the palace was also the labyrinth, and explored other promising nearby sites, like the Skotino Cave and the tunnels of Gortyn. Until the very recent discovery by Ian Magellan and his crew of diggers, the Gortyn tunnel complex was considered the most likely site of the real labyrinth of Daedalus, despite it being located almost twenty miles away from Knossos.

Eddie had already been an orphan for a few years when the discovery of the labyrinth by Magellan Enterprises was made and had to content himself with sparse news updates in the buried Arts and Sciences sections of local newspapers whenever he had a chance to visit a library. He'd dearly wanted to watch a documentary film which reportedly showed actual footage from inside the labyrinth, but his foster family at the time only had one television and it was a football night. Despite his wealth of knowledge in the history and mythology surrounding the structure, he was woefully ignorant of anything that happened after its discovery. He knew nothing about Ian Magellan or his company, other than that they were responsible for the find.

Add to that what he had learned today, that Magellan was behind this "ultra reality" show, with him as an unwilling participant and where his life and death had no more value than the money that might change hands as faceless people wagered for and against his survival. Any man or company capable of such blatant disregard for the value of life probably hid a lot of other bad things, despite the high praise they received by politicians and reporters as conservators of human history.

Regardless of the circumstances, Eddie felt better than he had in years. He felt alive, in touch with other people, really *in* the moment, more than he had since that awful car accident. The darkness all around them didn't frighten him. It wasn't an evil blackness from which something monstrous might leap out at them. It was the paper around a present, a thin covering under which he might find something miraculous.

As the group of seven moved away from the stairwell, keeping the wall to their right, his was the beam of light that jerked left, right, up, and down, as he strove to see, to memorize, to experience the wonder of the cavern around them. While the short black guy grumbled and complained about his legs and about how "a brother didn't have the skinny ass feet that fit these boots," Eddie marveled at the tight-packed rock

THE DUNGEON

and earthen floor, which retained enough moisture to glisten in the glare of their headlamps.

Perhaps fifteen or twenty yards out into the cavern, conversation became muted, as a sound reached their ears, something normal but seemingly out of place in this underground area.

"Sounds like water," Tory ventured, "but smells a little like a swamp."

Eddie agreed. Somehow naming the sound made him aware of the smell, what he had at first assumed was just a dankness in the subterranean air. Moving forward more slowly, Eddie flipped his Nightstick on low, illuminating the ground ahead just far enough to see the leading edge of what might be a small underground lake or river. His light wasn't strong enough to see all the way across, but it looked to end to the right, as the ground went up a small rise, which should allow them to skirt the pool if they went that way and stuck to the wall. He appeared to be standing near the widest part of the water, as it seemed to narrow to the left, though the river continued farther than his light would penetrate.

As he got closer, the smell became stronger. Not worse exactly, certainly nothing like a swamp or bog, just a more *there* smell, a clean smell that spoke of grass and summer rain, fish in the deep and frogs in the shallows.

"Careful now," Zachary said.

Eddie moved ahead, noting dark shapes out in the water, lighter-than-black shadows against the unrelieved darkness behind them, rising up and out of the water.

"Just for a second," he murmured, then he flicked the switch that powered his flashlight up to its highest setting. Light exploded out into the darkness, turning the surface of the water to an unbroken sea of black reflection. What was barely discernible before came into greater clarity with the brighter light. A column rose out of the water in front of him. It topped out at perhaps five or six feet above the water, though the top looked calved, like the side of an iceberg after a melt. With the low light, it wasn't possible to tell how it was carved, though a noticeable tapering gave the impression of a Corinthian design. More importantly, the column wasn't alone. There were at least two or three others that he could see to the left, marching away with the water.

Someone whistled behind him, but Eddie was too excited to look to see who it was.

Turning his light back down to its lower setting, he turned right, following the water's edge as it worked toward the wall.

"That way's east," Matt said. Good, someone had thought to keep a compass out. Eddie felt a small twinge of guilt that it hadn't been him.

The accountant's voice continued in a low monologue as Eddie followed the water. It wasn't like being at an outdoor lake. There was no beach, no gradual downslope of sand and increasing depth of water. It was dry ground, or it was lake, the line between so sharp it had to be manmade. "So we were facing north when we came out of the stairs. North got us to this lake, which runs to the west. Right now, we're working east to try to get around the lake and continue north."

"You planning to write a travel guide?" Big Rich asked.

"No, just helps me make a mental picture," the accountant answered.

"Li'l man looks excited," Li'l Bit said.

"You missed a good bit after you disappeared," Tory said. "As surprising at it seems, he knows a good bit about this stuff."

"Saved our asses once," the big man confirmed, which made Eddie feel proud all over again.

The water ended a good ten or fifteen feet before the wall, giving them plenty of room to move north. Every few steps, Eddie would lift his flashlight high, shining it out over the water, watching as they came abreast of the first column. From this point, he noticed a second column, farther ahead of them, lined up with the first. After a few more steps, he switched his high beam on again and confirmed it.

"There's two rows of columns, starting here," he said.

"So? Does that mean anything?" the police officer asked.

"I'm not sure yet," Eddie answered, and he wasn't sure, but he had a pretty good idea what those columns indicated.

Despite that the ground was a little higher here, the walking was still easy. There were no boulders to clamber over or go around, no fissures in the earth to grab at the feet and trip the unwary. There weren't even any small stones to slide away or roll down the slight incline and drop into the still water. It was like some cave-dwelling caretaker came through and swept the floor every night, picking up the litter from the previous days' tourists.

Another fifteen or twenty feet north and the lake ended, so Eddie led the group back to the west, now keeping the water and the columns on his left. They followed the lake long enough to count a total of twelve columns in two rows of six, standing tall in the water, though all showed signs of aging. The tallest was perhaps ten feet high and obviously tapering at the top in the Corinthian style, which made them age appropriate for the purported time of Grecian occupation of the island, no later than 400 BCE. They were certainly much newer than the Minoan civilization supposedly discovered by Sir Arthur Evans.

Their way westward came to an end at another wall of rock, which ran from water's edge as far to the north as they could see, even after turning up a couple of the flashlights to their highest setting.

Heading that direction once again, the group moved farther away from the stairs, only now their passage was hampered by the detritus of a collapsed civilization: broken pieces of ornate columns like boulders strewn across the path, great square pedestals made of stone, sometimes with worked and sculpted feet still attached but more often empty, the great masterpieces they once supported now so much more debris upon the ground. Eddie tried to look at everything as they passed it, meandering left and right, bending down low to look upon the carved likenesses of ancient myths and monsters, warriors, kings, and gods. Stone swords ten feet long lay across the ground, often broken along their length from whatever event knocked them from the hands of their holders, forcing the group to follow a zigzag path as they continued north, guided by Matt's compass.

Then there was no farther they could go.

Ahead of them lay a tangled mess of crumbled stone, tumbled rock, and tons of earth. It spanned the cavern from east wall to west wall, an impenetrable mass of centuries-old devastation. The ruins rose up to the ceiling, with some carved pillars seeming to extend up and *into* the rock.

And suddenly, something clicked for Eddie.

It was one of those feelings you get when you know something doesn't fit, but you don't know what it is or even how to put the feeling into words. It had always bothered him, on some level, that Arthur Evans had found evidence of Minoan architecture, but only the barest hints of Grecian pottery, when, by rights, there should have been much more to the Greek aspect since it dominated the area as much as a thousand years after the Minoan civilization was destroyed by volcano and tsunami.

What if this collapsed and destroyed mess was the hidden clue? Located somewhere just far enough away from the Minoan palace, this very Greek palace of stone might have been the home of King Minos, his wife, Pasiphae, and their daughter, Ariadne. This could be where Daedalus built the cow for Pasiphae and the labyrinth for the monstrous Minotaur. Crete was known for earthquakes, so what if all of this was swallowed sometime before Sir Evans made his discovery of the aboveground palace?

What if?

"Well, that's it for this way," Matt said. The lights were turning away as the others turned around. "I saw a way to the west along the far end of the water."

"Which way's west?" Li'l Bit asked.

"To the right," Rich answered.

"Our right now or our right when we were coming this way?"

Tory laughed. "That would be to our right now."

Eddie looked for a moment longer on the crumbled structure. He wanted to explore, to look closer at the ruins, find some answers.

"Come on, son," the police officer said, not unkindly. "We can't get out that way, and right now that's the most important thing."

Eddie took one last look before turning away and hurrying to catch up with the group.

What if?

CHAPTER 32

Matt

Back around the lake and to the southern end, Matt listened as Eddie explained his theory on where they were. More accurately, on what this area once might have been. Strange, but the kid sounded disappointed. Maybe he'd been hoping to see an intact statue or some Olympic rings on top of one of the columns, something that screamed "I am Greek!" but all he'd gotten were shattered piles of marble and a broken-down building. That still seemed pretty cool to Matt, but then he'd grown up listening to his history buff father talk breathlessly about the importance of the discovery of new potsherds on some godforsaken plateau in Utah and how carbon dating would prove that native civilizations had been on the North American continent far longer than anyone ever realized. That man's hobby was so boring it made Matt feel like a rebel when he started taking business and accounting classes.

Retracing their steps back toward the stairway made Matt uneasy. Looking around at the others, he could tell they were feeling it too. Big Rich—don't call him Richard—held his arms close to his body, almost a guarding posture, and his hands were fisted more often than not. Tory seemed to be unconsciously placing herself within the moving triangle of himself, the cop, and Big Rich. Even Li'l Bit felt it; his chatter, which sometimes reminded Matt of an exuberant child, fell silent. Only the kid seemed nonplussed, ranging ahead of the group, rather than huddling within it. He was fully out of his shell when talking about the possibility that this was King Minos's real palace, swallowed by an earthquake and literally buried beneath the feet of the historians and archaeologists who made their names discovering the older ruins left standing above.

As an amateur armchair archaeologist and ardent subscriber to *National Geographic*, *Archaeology Magazine*, *Dig Magazine*, and *3rd Stone*, which ended its twenty-year run in 2003, Matt Absher's father would be over the moon at just seeing a fragment of one of these statues, with an attached carbon dating certifying its authenticity. To have a chance to walk among standing columns and feel the history littered in the bones of this marble and stone graveyard would be the highlight of his life.

For perhaps the first time since he allowed greed and an overbearing pride in his own intellect to take him down the path of the white-collar criminal, Matt felt sorry. It wasn't the angry, self-deprecating type of regret that translated to *I'm sorry I got caught*. It was a true grief that his own actions had led him to this point. Watching the others in their wariness, and Eddie in his very different kind of sorrow, Matt wished only that he could see his father again, to tell him what he'd seen and try to share some of the wonder of this place with the man who'd done his best to raise him right, and who deserved a better son.

They had come back around the edges of the pool and were now following the water west, with the broken pillars to their right. Somewhere in the darkness to their left was the stairway back up to the dungeon set. As they continued west, he felt a need to keep turning his head in that direction, unable to shake the feeling that danger was coming, hiding in the pitch blackness beyond the reach of his headlamp, waiting for the moment to strike. Other beams turned that way more often than any other, as Big Rich and the cop continually searched the area, apparently feeling what he did.

"You hear that?" Zachary asked, stopping, and Matt realized there was a sound, a noise that both fit and seemed wildly out of place in the stillness of this place.

"Sounds like running water," Eddie said.

Tory's headlamp suddenly flared in Matt's face as she turned to look up at him. "If there's water coming down, there might be a way to climb up."

"It's coming from this way." Eddie had moved out in front of them again, though not so far that he was out of the range of their lights. Hurrying, they caught up to him fifteen feet or so ahead, still following the course of the water.

"The wall's closing in," Li'l Bit observed, and Matt saw it was true. When they first came down the stairs, there were walls to the east and west. They'd followed the eastern wall as they worked their way north to the ruined palace. Now they were marching toward the western wall, which was coming north to meet them. If it ended at the lake they would have no choice but to brave the water and hope it wasn't too deep. That was the only thing to worry about with the water, he told himself, ignoring the possibilities a lifetime of watching horror movies tried to insert into his thoughts.

But the wall stopped a few feet shy of the water's edge, turning west itself, offering a pathway for them to follow. To their right, the pillars continued their steady line, their bases hidden underwater, so that it was impossible to tell how tall they really were or have any guess as to how deep the water ran.

The sound of running water was louder now that the wall was only a few feet to their left. It still wasn't anything he'd associate with a strong flow, more like a trickle. Two or three of them kept their headlamps pointed out at the water, now that there was nothing to see to the left but gray and brown stone rising to the high ceiling.

It was Li'l Bit who first noticed the ripples on the water. "Somethin's out there!" he hissed, moving as close to the wall as he could.

There wasn't, at least as far as Matt could tell. There were some ripples in the water, but they were regular and were flowing toward them from the west, almost like a current was being generated.

"It's coming from here," Eddie said. How had he gotten so far ahead of them? He was only visible because of his headlamp, a moving circle of light that looked up and down, left and right, like a searchlight strapped to an amusement park ride. "There's another rock wall here, with some water running down it. I think the water is what made this lake."

A few moments later, they had all gathered around the young man. There was indeed a wall barring their way, but unlike the walls that framed the cavern, or the one on their left, this one was a tumbled and jumbled mass of earth and rock, boulders and pieces of worked stone, probably another casualty of whatever destructive event brought the palace and all its associated landscaping underground. A thin trickle of water flowed over the rocks, originating somewhere high above them.

"It's cold," Eddie noted, holding his hand to the rocks over the waters.

"No telling how far down we are or where that water's coming from," Zachary said.

"Well, Crete is an island," Eddie offered. Before anyone could stop him, he brought his wet hand to his mouth. "It's not salty, though."

"Heh, dude's got balls," Li'l Bit said, drawing Matt's attention. The shorter man started to lean back against the wall on their left, but then fell onto his bottom with a decidedly unmanly shriek.

"Looks like that's where we need to go now," Matt said, trying not to laugh. The wall there, which had been pacing the waterway, suddenly opened up, allowing a path to the south.

"We could see what's on the other side of the water here," Eddie offered, and his handheld light cut on, arcing over the water and illuminating another mountain of debris on the north side. "Or not," he said, cutting off the flashlight.

As a group, the seven turned into the new passage, no more than three- or four-feet wide, forcing them to proceed single file. Big Rich took the lead, but almost immediately stumbled.

Something metallic clanged and banged across the stone floor.

"The hell was that?" Zachary asked, moving forward to offer a steadying hand to the larger man.

"Dunno, but it hurt like hell when I kicked it."

Both the cop and the football player turned on their Nightsticks, flooding the passageway with light.

Eddie gasped, and Matt heard Li'l Bit say, "Well, shut mah mouth," but all he could do was stare.

The narrow passage was littered with bones and metal objects, what looked like some kind of sword blades, along with several sizes of metal disks.

"Are those shields?" Eddie asked, squeezing around the two larger men. His flashlight flared to life again, darting from one item to the next, muted reflections bouncing back at them. And suddenly everyone was talking at once.

"How many are there?"

"What happened to them?"

"How long do you think they've been there?"

And then Zachary was holding up a hand, holding them back, while he moved up to look at the skeletons. They were scattered about the passageway, some whole and some just rib cages and leg bones and other parts he didn't know the names for. As Zachary's light swept from wall to wall, then up the passage, Matt saw other bones and metal objects, sword blades lying every which way, shields turned upside down and right side up, some with shapes and symbols embossed on them, others plain. There were other pieces of metal as well, strange rings of smaller blades attached to each other, almost like skirts. All of the metal had a greenish tint to it.

"Is that rust?" Li'l Bit asked. "Yo, big guy, you best check make sure you didn't cut your leg. Might need a tet'nus shot."

"It's not rust," Eddie said, "cause that's bronze, not iron."

"That's right," Matt blurted. "Bronze gets that green fuzz, and it keeps it from degrading."

Zachary lifted one of the large disks, peered under it with his light, then let it fall back to the ground with another clang.

"There aren't any straps. The leather must have rotted away." His light moved over to one of the blades. "No handles or hilts on the swords either."

"They're called *xiphos*," Eddie said.

"I thought those were called *spatha*, or *gladius*," Tory said.

Eddie shook his head. "That's what the Romans used. We know those better because of the movies."

"Yummy Russel Crowe," Elizabeth said.

Tory added, "Amen."

"Are we not...entertained?" Li'l Bit shouted in a passable imitation of Maximus.

"There's more," Zachary said. His flashlight now focused on the skeletons on the ground. "See how some of these skeletons are torn apart?" He focused on a leg bone, bending down to pick it up.

"Eew, dat can't be sanitary."

"Watch," he said. His right hand tightened around the knobby end of the bone, the part that Matt was pretty sure fit into the hip. He squeezed, and the bone crumbled in his fist, the rest of the femur falling back to the ground. He opened his hand, letting the light from the Nightstick illuminate his palm. White bone dust, some as fine as powder, fell from his hand and through the light from the flash.

"Okay," Elizabeth said. "Now we know for sure that those bones are old and you have really strong hands."

Zachary smiled, but still pointed his light down the passage. "Look," he said.

Matt looked. In several places where the skeletons weren't intact, there were parts of bones that looked smashed, some at the ends, where the knobby joints would be, but some were crushed along their lengths, even in the middle of long bones. Zachary moved his light from the bones to the floor, where splotches of white showed against the dark stone.

"Are those footprints?" Big Rich asked.

Zachary nodded. "There are several different sizes, and they're erratic. I think some of those crazy guys have been down here, and not too long ago."

Matt moved up to Zachary's side. "Sure wish we could use some of those—what did he call them? *Xiphos*?"

Zachary used the toe of his boot to push one of the blades across the ground. "Be my guest, but if you cut your hand on that thing, tetanus might be the least of your problems."

"No, thanks."

THE DUNGEON

"Come on then, let's keep moving."

The seven moved more carefully now, wary of stepping on bones or blades, headlamps more than sufficient to illuminate both walls and the floor. For the first time since stumbling out of the stairway, Matt didn't feel like he was straining to see, squinting just the right amount to keep his eyes from being overwhelmed by the glare from his forehead. The close quarters also made it so that it was easier to catch someone else's beam right in the face, so it wasn't perfect, just an improvement.

As they moved down the passage, Zachary continued to point out other signs of recent activity, while Eddie gushed enthusiastically about one artifact or another.

"See that skirt of bronze? That's called a linothorax, though I'm not sure if that's the real Greek word for it, but it's really rare to see one made of bronze. He must have been someone important. Most people couldn't afford to waste metal on that."

"Then what were they made of?" Tory asked.

"Usually rabbit skins, I think, or some other kind of boiled leather."

"Must not have been very good protection," Big Rich said.

"Oh no, they were," Eddie said. "I read about some college professor, I think he was from Wisconsin, who had his class recreate some, and it was strong enough to stop an arrow. It was also much lighter weight than something made with bronze, which was probably just as important to a soldier."

"I'll keep my Kevlar, thanks," Zachary quipped.

Though strewn about with corpses and discarded bits of armor, swords, and shields, the passage wasn't long, running no more a hundred feet, before ending in another gray wall, similar to the wall on the left, and the other cavern walls they'd seen since descending the stairs.

The wall on the right was very different, at least for the last thirty or so feet. What began as more evidence of collapse, a rock pile that only resembled a wall, had changed. It became straighter, neater, more like the worked stone of a building than like anything occurring in nature, or from the effects of nature. The wall appeared a washed-out white or faded gray in the splash from the headlamps.

"That's a real wall," Elizabeth said, running one slim hand over the surface. "It's smoother, kind of soft, not like brick. Is this another building?"

"Not quite a building," Eddie said. He was ahead of them again, standing at the end of the passageway, turned to the right and sweeping his headlamp around.

"What is it?" Tory asked. "Another dead end?"

Then Matt came to the end of the passage and turned right. The worked wall on the western side turned here as well, and while the southern wall retained much of its look of natural rock, it was easy to see, at least for the few feet illuminated by their lights, that the worked wall had been designed to flow alongside the natural one. The ground became more a floor at the point where the new passage began, no longer uneven. It appeared to be worked of the same material as the wall.

"Look at that," Eddie said, pointing at the wall.

Where the wall turned west, there was a bowl, or something like one, attached at shoulder height. A small, open trench, also of bronze, ran away from the bowl, following the wall. The trench, or gutter, originated about halfway up the side of the bowl, and seemed to be connected to it. Moving closer, letting his light shine into the bowl, Matt was surprised to see a murky liquid inside. A strange smell rose up at

THE DUNGEON

him, though not unpleasant. Oddly enough, it evoked memories of school, that smell of opening a box of new crayons.

"I think this is oil," Matt said.

"I bet it is," Eddie said, "and those metal runners are a way for the oil to move from one lamp to another."

"So we might have light?" the redhead asked.

"If we want to risk it," Zachary said.

"What's to risk?" Big Rich said.

"What if...like...the whole place is filled with oil fumes," Li'l Bit suggested, "and if we light a match... boom...we all go up like torches."

"That's ridiculous," Rich said, shaking off his backpack and looking inside. "Oil doesn't have fumes like that, not like gasoline." His big hands rummaged in the leather bag for a few moments, then pulled out one of the small, wrapped packages of matches. "Guess these are the strike-anywhere kind," he muttered.

"Here, let me," Elizabeth offered after watching the big man fumble with the small package for a few seconds. She gave the cellophane a few plucks with her fingers and pulled a match free.

"Do it," Eddie said, his face awash with excitement.

Matt noticed that everyone was gathered around now, watching expectantly.

Elizabeth struck the match against the gray stone wall. The flare of its lighting was almost blinding in its intensity, so much brighter than their headlamps that Matt was forced to look away.

"Here goes," the redhead said, reaching over the lip of the bowl and dropping the match inside.

There came a low whump, almost like the sound of a grunt when someone gets sucker-punched in the gut and the air explodes out of them. Then light, the soft orange glow of a flame burning in the bowl.

"Look!" Eddie said, and they looked. The light, the flame, flowed out and away from the bowl, racing along the line of the gutter, until it ignited a second bowl, perhaps fifteen feet away. On the floor near that second bowl was a body, a dark stain around it testifying to a bloody manner of death. The light continued following the passage, then it disappeared.

"Did it die out?" Matt asked.

Eddie edged to the left, not moving too far away from the group. Matt could understand. There was a big difference between the skeletons of people who'd been dead for maybe centuries and a corpse fresh enough that its blood still looked a little red.

"I think it turned a corner," the younger man said. He leaned further left, almost against the southern wall, straining to see. "Yeah, it definitely turned, like there's more than one way to go, cause this tunnel continues straight too."

"I don't think we can call this a tunnel anymore," Liz said. "I think we've found the original labyrinth."

"Well, whatever it is, we can't just stand here," Big Rich said. "Let's see where this leads."

The light from the bowl-shaped lamp seemed to be giving off a little more illumination, as well as a decent amount of acrid smoke, as more of the oil got hot enough to burn. Hesitantly, Matt reached up and powered off his headlamp, noticing a few of the others doing the same. With the additional lamp not too far ahead, there was now sufficient light to see by. As they approached the corpse, the orange light turned the mess of blood almost black, but it still glistened wetly. Strangely, it appeared as though a good bit of the blood had run into small holes in the ground.

"Be careful," Zachary said. "This guy, whoever he was, died right there. See the holes? I think this is a trap."

THE DUNGEON

"Didn't that announcer guy say their version of the labyrinth recreated a lot of the original traps?" Tory asked.

"I already seen one of them spike traps," Li'l Bit said. "Lookit those holes, all up his legs and his...um... you know. I bet he stepped on one."

"The holes only cover an area a few feet square," the cop said. "We should be able to jump over it."

"Look at the guy, though," Big Rich said. "He's dressed like one of those things that jumped us upstairs."

"So we have a good idea what's been down here before us," Zachary said. "And what left those prints back there."

"You think there's more?" Elizabeth asked.

"I don't know, but there were certainly more than one set of footprints."

"So where are the others?" Tory asked.

It was one of those questions you weren't supposed to ask, Matt thought. Even as he began a joking reply, something about how the people in horror movies always asked the silly question right before the monster popped out, or before one of their friends' bodies came swinging down out of a tree, the line of fire that represented the gutter system reappeared in front of them, now clearly outlining a doorway or side passage.

The fire lit another lamp, then raced on ahead, flaring inside another bowl, before again seeming to turn a corner to the right.

With the lighting of the last lamp, several things happened at once.

A low humming began, though it was coarse, like old machinery waking, gears grinding. Almost immediately after came the sound of stone grating on stone. Another noise, both more and less human, rose in volume from somewhere further inside, a keening, like a wail of agony, which grew in volume as the noise of the moving stone grew.

"The wall's closing behind us!" Eddie shouted.

Matt looked and saw a wall rising from the floor behind them, blocking the way back out into the natural rock area. Already it was three feet off the ground and rising fast.

Maybe if they'd turned back at exactly that moment and made a run for it, they could have gotten over it before it was too high to reach up and grab.

Maybe.

But another sound came, a crash like thunder that shook the floor beneath their feet, which immediately turned into a deeper grumbling.

At the end of the passage, where the gutter fire took its second turn, a large boulder had fallen into the tunnel.

And it was rolling toward them.

Chapter 33

DeShaun

"Oh, hell no! Not this again!" Li'l Bit said. He looked back at the wall behind them, already high enough that he would have a hard time pulling himself over the top. He turned back to the boulder, and got ready to try his video game parkour run over the top again. Hell, it worked the first time.

But this time he wasn't alone.

"Quick," the cop said, waving his arm in that classic *you-all-go-first-because-I'm-the-cop-and-cops-go-last* move, "jump over the body and duck into the side corridor."

And Li'l Bit decided that was a much better idea.

No one questioned, and no one hesitated. The tall, skinny accountant went first, jumping much farther than he probably needed to, and swung into the passage. Next went the homely woman and the skinny kid, who wasn't so bad for a white boy, followed by the tall girl and Big Rich.

The boulder was just rumbling its way down the passage, coming right for them, but this time there wasn't no other wall coming up behind. It looked too simple, too easy. They had plenty of warning and plenty of time to duck in the side passage. It didn't make sense, not to someone as naturally suspicious of white man evil as he was.

Then it hit him, of course it looked simple. It was supposed to. The wall behind shuts, the boulder rolls, and you just saunter your happy ass forward and BAM, death by something sharp up in your business. They'd finally gotten a bit of luck, that's all. There was already a dead guy there showing them that they needed to jump.

Feeling a little better, Li'l Bit made the jump, landing a good five feet in front of the boulder, and made to turn into the side passage. Then he tripped and fell forward, landing on his hands and knees, only whatever he'd tripped over had a hold of his right ankle, and then it was pulled, and his right knee slid out from under him.

"Jesus!" someone said, maybe the cop, maybe the accountant, but then the cop landed next to him and instead of just leaving his nasty ass to die, the guy spun around, grabbed both of his hands, and started pulling him toward the opening in the wall.

The boulder rumbled closer, three feet away now, and Li'l Bit looked back at his feet, wondering what he'd tripped on, and it was the guy, the dead guy, only he can't have been all the way dead because his hand was locked around his ankle and he'd got his face up off the floor, staring at him.

"Oh shit, oh shit, the dead guy's got me!" Li'l Bit shouted, for once not caring if he sounded girly, too grossed out and scared to care. "Get it off me!"

He might have shouted something else, but then the cop was pulling, and the boulder rolled closer and Li'l Bit could feel himself sliding across the floor and he tried kicking, scraping at his right leg with his left boot, like trying to scratch an itch under a pair of jeans, only this was no itch it was a *damn dead guy* and then Big Rich reached around the cop, got his big hands on Li'l Bit's upper arms, and *heaved* back.

THE DUNGEON

Li'l Bit felt himself drawn into the air, into the side passage, where he collided with the cop who staggered back and into Big Rich, and then all three of them crashed to the ground as the boulder rolled by outside.

There were hands, more hands grabbing at him, trying to help him up. Shaking, he accepted the help.

"You okay?" Tory asked, and the real concern in her voice almost made him lose it.

Instead he focused on standing, testing out his ankle, making sure he wasn't hurt.

"Damn thing stole my boot!" he muttered, and then he laughed because it was okay, he was okay, even if he had to hobble in one boot.

"So, uh, Li'l Bit," Big Rich said, "who's Tony?"

"Say what?" Li'l Bit asked, and just like that, he remembered what he shouted when the cop pulled him.

"You screamed out Tony," Elizabeth said, "we all heard you. I mean, you could have shouted anything, about your little bit getting dragged across the floor, a cry to Jesus, maybe one last shout out to momma with love, but you screamed Tony."

Li'l Bit looked down at the floor, at his missing shoe, anywhere but at the redhead, who wasn't glaring down at him, even though she was tall enough to do it. Her voice was gentle.

"Look, it makes a lot of sense," she continued, "though I won't insult you and say I knew it all along. You hide it well."

"Hide what?" Eddie asked.

"It's his thing," Elizabeth said.

The cop started talking again, and all Li'l Bit had to do was keep quiet, just let it ride.

"His name was Tony, and he was"—he paused a beat, long enough to consider three or four easy lies, things he could build a credible story with if he chose to—"he was my first boyfriend."

His voice caught. He could still remember Tony's face, how he talked, how he smelled. "We were in college...I...he made me a better person, brought me out of myself." He saw a tear fall onto his right sock.

He could feel someone moving close to him, in that way everyone can feel their personal space being invaded. His voice caught again, some part of him wanting the words to stop. But he'd already said the hardest part, had already admitted being gay. The rest should be easy.

He closed his eyes to his tears, to the movement he could see in his peripheral vision. "He was so good and kind that at first I didn't really want anything to do with him, you know? I'm sure that's happened to some of you. I used to think *there's no way a white boy could be so nice to a black man.* Some of that was just the old me, coming from the streets of Clinton. A lot of old anger in that town. Most of us have Mawmaws and Pops that remember what it was like to have to sit at the back of the bus. But a good bit of it was just how I saw myself, so different from everyone else that it must be me who was bad, something wrong with me. It took a lot of time and patience for Tony to make me believe that it was okay, being gay, and that I deserved to be loved.

"Funny, but in the end, it was his drive for both of us to come out of the closet, to show the school who we were, that made everything go wrong. I thought, *can't we jus' be happy like dis? No one needs to know that don't already.*"

He stopped himself, recognizing the street accent that crept back into his voice.

"It...we had a fight, a whispering kind of fight, because we were climbing the stairs up to his dorm

THE DUNGEON

room. It had been going on for a good while, the whole way across the campus from the library, and I could feel myself shutting down, going back to my old way of talking, from when I talked the talk just to keep the other brothers from kicking my ass.

"I don't remember what I said, at the end, but he came up to hug me and I just...I just—"

The look of surprise on Tony's face, that's what he'd always remember, how surprised he looked as he fell down the stairs, and how that look just stuck there, when his head hit a step, then kind of slipped off the edge and down to the next, a stuttering slip and twist that broke his neck and killed him.

"Shh, it's okay," Elizabeth said, and it was her, of course it was her, the one he'd thought was crazy, who put her arms around him and held him. No one had held him like that since Tony, and only his momma had ever put her arms around him before that. It wasn't crazy he'd seen in her before, but more a feeling of like calling to like. No one who didn't understand this pain could know exactly how to offer comfort through it.

"He fell down the stairs," he said. He had to finish it, had to get the rest of the story out. "He died, and I might as well have died then too. The police...they called it a crime of passion, involuntary manslaughter, but his mom...his mom said there was no way her boy was gay, and certainly no way he'd be dating some ghetto-ass nigger like me.

"She pressed charges, said I assaulted and killed him, and the jury agreed." He looked up at the silent faces of the six gathered around him. He expected to see judgment, condemnation. Not only was he black, but he was also gay, and a murderer. "It was an accident," he said, and then the dam broke, and the tears he'd been holding back for almost two years, ever since it happened, finally broke loose. A gut-wrenching sob escaped him, and he turned and buried his face in the redhead's shirt. Two hours ago, he'd thought she was crazy. Two hours ago, these people were all strangers to him.

"Man, that's harsh," the tall accountant said.

"I'm sorry that happened to you," the cop said.

Then there was a new hand on his shoulder, a large, strong, black hand, and Big Rich said, "It don't matter what team you play for, you're still a brother to me."

Chapter 34

Richard

While Li'l Bit got himself together, Big Rich scoped out the area. The new passage ran parallel to the previous one, east and west, though he could see turns to the north in both directions, if that accountant's compass could be believed. In the previous passage where the boulder had rolled, all that was left of the dead but not dead guy was a red spot on the floor. The little man's boot was still there, but it looked like the leather sole had been crushed by the rolling rock and wouldn't be usable again.

He made a mental note to remember that the original passage still looked like there was more to it, a continuation running west with at least one more turn, or side passage. This new passage, with flickering firelight-filled trenches and bowl-shaped lamps on either side, was more interesting. The view to the west was short, only a few feet and then a turn to the right, but the passage extended further to the east. With no real thought to what he was doing, he took a few long strides in that direction.

"I'm just gonna take a quick look around," he said to no one in particular.

"Use the chalk," the cop said.

Although Big Rich wasn't the type to smack his forehead when someone else said or thought of something that he should have, he felt like it right then. Of course, the chalk.

"Theseus used a magic yarn," Eddie said, stepping up beside him, a piece of fluorescent green chalk in his hand. "Of course, that's if you believe in magic."

Taking the offered chalk, Big Rich started forward again. Noticing that Eddie wasn't following, he said, "You're coming with me, right? I want to know more about this magic yarn. Plus, I saw you in that big room. You got some killer moves."

Eddie smiled up at him, which reminded him of so many other kids who'd looked up at him over the years.

Big Rich wasn't proud of many things he'd done in his life. He'd gladly take most of them back if he could. He wasn't a crackhead like Zippy, or even someone who accidentally killed someone like Li'l Bit, but he was a disappointment all the same. Especially to his mom.

When it became clear that he was more than good at football, that he had a natural gift for the game, an intuitive feel for the ebb and flow of the offense, his mom started working more, extra shifts, a second job, just to make sure that her Big Rich had every opportunity she could give him. She didn't make it to most of his high school games, but she cut out every picture of him that made the local paper, whether it was catching a touchdown or throwing a key block to free up a runner. She switched shifts to be there with him when college coaches wanted an in-home interview. The last time he could remember her smiling was when they realized that he'd have a full ride to whichever of three major college football programs they chose.

Those were the good times. Younger players looked up at the senior tight end who drew more cheers from the crowd than the quarterback. It didn't hurt that he was good academically as well. He wasn't chess team material, but he took his share of honor's classes (paid for by his mom) and played a few parts in the drama club after football season. Like Zachary, even though he was big, he didn't dismiss people who were smaller than him. His momma raised him to understand that it was God's gift to him that he was big and healthy and able to play football. It was up to him to always try to be worthy of that gift, and the biggest part of that was being kind to everyone and being extra kind to people smaller and weaker.

Then came the injury, the tackle that started his free fall from college bound to prison inmate. It shouldn't have been as bad as it was, not after catching a pass at the ten-yard line and going in for a touchdown. But he'd felt the pressure of that linebacker on his right, so he moved the ball to his left arm, tucked in tight at the elbow, to prevent it being stripped. He crossed the goal line, and a split-second later three hundred pounds of flying muscle hit him high on the right side. He fell onto his left side, ball still held securely, and felt something pop in his left shoulder.

It was an anterior shoulder dislocation, identified on X-ray and easily reduced in the emergency room where he was taken for treatment. It was a bad injury, a season-ender, but not a career-killer, as long as he followed the doctor's advice and didn't play for the remainder of the year. An arrangement was made for a follow-up visit with an orthopedist, and a prescription for pain medicine was provided.

The medication made him feel a little dizzy, but it took away the pain in his shoulder to such an extent that he downplayed the severity of his injury. Instead of staying out of football for the remainder of the season, he only missed one week. He took double-doses of the pain medication before each workout and before the next game. He took a couple of hits in the first half, but nothing that taxed his shoulder too badly, and was able to shake that pain off with another two pills at halftime.

His shoulder dislocated again during the second half, and again he was rushed to the emergency department, where another X-ray and a follow-up CAT scan were performed. The damage to his shoulder from the initial injury was worse than originally thought. There had been an avulsion of the anterior-inferior glenohumeral ligaments, a fracture that results from a ligament pulling away from its attachment to a bone and taking a piece of the bone with it. He needed surgery to stabilize the joint, or else his shoulder would continue to slip. Even after surgery, the odds of returning to football were slim.

This time the school's athletic director was contacted directly, and that was the end of Rich's football career. The pain in his shoulder was nothing compared to the loss of his dreams, but both were helped by medication. The next four or five months went by in a haze of hydrocodone and oxycodone. He could remember going in for the surgery, but not much beyond that. He participated in a rehabilitation program, but more and more he felt that only the pills were enabling him to function.

Before he finished his senior year, he'd progressed from legal medication to pills bought on the street from strangers. He graduated, but it was a close thing. He dropped out of the honors' classes and barely squeaked out a C average in everything else. The college scholarships were gone, and his mother didn't know how to handle the depressed man he became.

It was only a matter of time before the little five milligram pills became ten, and when those weren't enough, one of his suppliers turned him on to heroin.

THE DUNGEON

Big Rich wasn't comforted when others in his court-mandated drug abuse program described similar tales of progression from prescription pain medication to illegal drugs. Neither their sympathy nor their empathy could erase the memory of the look on his mother's face when he was arrested. Nothing they said could ease the guilt he felt for the pain he'd caused her.

He was high on heroin when he showed up for his third meeting, and that marked the end of his probation.

Going to prison was bad. Going cold turkey was worse. The medical staff kept assuring him that opioid withdrawal wasn't serious or life-threatening, but his memories of those ten days were a constant reminder of what drugs can do to the body. His memory of his mother's anguish were worse, haunting him, pushing him through the chills, the nausea, and the wracking body aches. When the man from Magellan came and offered him a chance to win his freedom, he signed eagerly. Their promises were petty: participate in this show and never have to worry about finding drugs again. He wasn't doing it for a pill-bottle payout. He was doing it to get out and to get started redeeming himself in his mother's eyes.

He and Eddie moved east until the corridor turned north. After a couple of steps, it turned right, heading back toward the eastern wall. There were no side passages or other openings that he could see, just a straight path defined by those smoothly worked gray walls.

"So about that yarn," Rich said.

"Oh yeah, well, it all comes back to that riddle we had in the room with the floor tiles."

"Uh-huh."

"You see, Pasiphae was the queen who gave birth to the Minotaur, right? Well, one of her other children was Ariadne, this beautiful princess who fell in love with Theseus when he came to kill the Minotaur."

The passage turned right again, now heading south, and still there were no side passages or tunnels.

"So Ariadne offered to help Theseus if he would agree to take her away from Crete when he left."

After only a few steps, the passage turned right again, now heading back to the west. Though he didn't have the best head for navigation, Rich was fairly certain this was just a brief spiral, and they were about to come to a dead end.

"She gave him a spool of yarn to unwind as he progressed through the labyrinth, so that he could find his way back out after killing the Minotaur."

Another short turn to the right, then another, and they were facing a blank wall, a dead end.

"Crazy," Big Rich said. "So how big was this ball of yarn?"

"That's where the myth comes from," Eddie said. "It either had to be a humongous ball of yarn, or else it had some kind of magic that let it never run out, because Theseus supposedly spent a long time wandering through the labyrinth before running into the Minotaur."

"Did he keep his promise?" Rich asked.

"He did," Eddie said, smiling, "he took Ariadne with him, and they stopped for a night on the beach of Naxos. That's where the myth kind of gets muddled."

"What do you mean?"

"No matter how you look at it, he left her there and returned to Athens. Some of the stories say he was just a tool, that he never meant to marry her or anything, but there are others who say he was put under a spell by Dionysus, who wanted Ariadne for himself."

THE DUNGEON

"Too bad he didn't leave some of that yarn for us, 'cause it looks like this way is a no-go," Big Rich said, turning back.

The floor rumbled, deep vibrations that he could feel in his shoes. A few shouts reached them, muffled by the intervening walls, but clearly coming from their friends. Eddie and Big Rich looked at one another, and immediately began racing back the way they'd come.

Two quick lefts and they were heading back to the east, anticipating another turn left, to the north, which would then turn left again, working a circle around the dead end and back toward the others. They made the turn to the north, but then Big Rich stopped, confused.

This should be a short leg, ten or fifteen steps, before turning back to the left.

Something had changed. Now, it looked like the passage continued for a long ways to the north, but there was an opening to the left. It didn't seem to be exactly where it should be, but at least it was there.

"Eddie, quick, grab your compass," Big Rich said.

While the younger man dug in his knapsack for the wooden compass box, Big Rich backed up to the turn that led to the dead end. Assuming the corridors all had roughly the same width, then the passage back to the left, back to their companions, should be only fifteen feet, give or take, north of the corner he stood in. Instead, the new passage looked to be perhaps as much as eight feet beyond where it should be.

Feeling a brief surge of panic, more from confusion than from any real fright—after all, how can you get lost when there are no side passages—he moved up past Eddie again, turning to look down the western hallway. It appeared to take a turn to the left—south—after the right distance, but now it also sported an opening on the north side.

"The walls changed on us," he said softly.

"I think you're right," Eddie said, holding up the compass. "We're still going north, but I know we didn't come down that long hallway."

"Okay," Rich said, thinking fast, "the worst thing we could do is start running around like rats in a maze."

"Even though that's kind of what we are?" Eddie said.

"Even though, right. Let's step into this passage on the left, just in case the walls move again. That way at least we'll be on the right side of the wall."

"Okay," Eddie said, slinging his backpack onto his shoulders again.

Together, the two stepped into the new passage, gray walls, fiery lamps, a dogleg left and a passage north.

"Now what?" the younger man asked.

"Now we call and hope they can answer."

Chapter 35

Elizabeth

Elizabeth Ott knew about keeping secrets. Hell, no one but her even knew that it was an argument that precipitated her father's death. So when Li'l Bit shouted out another man's name, it all made sense to her: the brash attitude, the hyper-sexual comments, it was a smokescreen to hide behind. It made her sad, to think that in this day and age of an almost-aggressive acceptance of homosexuality that there were still people deathly afraid to admit the truth, made to feel bad for something they had no control over.

Having spent the latter half of her life in and out of mental institutions, Liz had heard her share of sob stories, of people who stole because Daddy didn't understand them, or who did drugs because Mommy didn't like their life choices. Li'l Bit should almost be an inspiration to those, a young man who was truly persecuted, but who found a way to escape. Until it caught up to him, that is.

Holding him, letting him sob into her shoulder, Liz felt like she was letting something go as well, though she wasn't quite sure how to put a name to it. For those few moments, it felt almost as though the past fifteen years hadn't happened, that she was once again the bright, young, sixteen-year-old who loved to read, who had a complete family that loved and supported one another. In this moment, she was the family Li'l

Bit had been missing, she was the provider of support and encouragement that is a part of the human equation, one set of parenthetical addends that make up the sum total of the man or woman.

It was amazing, she thought, the feeling of completeness it brought to be able to offer something as simple as a hug to someone who needed it. For someone like her, someone who had desperately tried to avoid conflict and entanglement because they did nothing but cause problems, it felt almost like coming home, completing a circle back to the happier times in her life, before the infamous interview exposed so many of the problems in her parents' marriage.

It brought forth questions as well. Was her deliberate refusal to connect one of the reasons her illness plagued her so badly? Could having someone to share her hopes and fears with have made any difference in her progression?

Then the floor shook, and people were shouting, and she let go of Li'l Bit and rose to her feet just in time to see the impossible. The floor outside their little side passage, the floor of the corridor they had left, it *tilted*, that was the only way to describe it. It tilted down to the right, and immediately came more vibrations and rumbling noises as the boulder they had narrowly escaped a few moments before suddenly came rolling back, flashing by the doorway, returning to the eastern side of the corridor. She listened as the rumbling receded, but never heard the crash of it striking a wall.

Carefully, Liz edged to the opening that led back to the initial passage. The bloody mess where the man had lain, the one who'd grabbed Li'l Bit, was still there. Moving off to the left were more bloody patches, which gave her a mental image of the body flattened and adhering to the boulder, leaving bloody footprints

THE DUNGEON

every time it completed a revolution. As far as the lights reached, the way was clear. It even appeared as though the wall, which had closed off their escape route from the boulder, had now opened again.

Either the dungeon reset itself or someone triggered another change.

Turning her head to the right, she traced the line of fire to its next branching but couldn't see much of the passage beyond that. She couldn't see the boulder at all, but some of that was from her unwillingness to step out into the corridor.

"Big Rich and Eddie haven't come back," Tory said. Li'l Bit was on his feet, using his dirty white poet shirt to dry his eyes. Neither Zachary nor Matt were paying him any attention, but it had an intentional look to it, like they were trying not to look at him, probably to give him time to compose himself.

Zachary moved off to the right, in the direction the other two had gone. He came back just a few seconds later. "Something else must have changed. After that first turn is nothing but a dead end."

"What do you mean?" Tory asked.

"I mean they're not there, and there's nowhere they could have gone."

"Of course they're there," the shorter woman argued. "You must have just missed a turn."

"Go look for yourself," the cop snapped, but then his face mellowed, his frustration evaporating. It was painfully obvious to Liz that Zachary was not a man given to outbursts of temper. He almost looked embarrassed that he'd snapped at all. "I'm sorry, that was uncalled for," he said. "It looks like a dead end now."

If Tory was upset about what Zachary said, it didn't show. Her face was all worry for Eddie, Liz was sure. It was almost as if the older woman had adopted the younger man, perhaps as a surrogate for a lost child of her own. Despite Zachary's apology and explanation, Tory still jogged up and around the corner. She was gone for several long moments, then came back running.

"They're still over there, somewhere," she gasped. "I can hear them."

"Seriously?" Matt asked, darting into the same passage. "Big Rich. Eddie. Can you hear me?"

Liz looked up and met Zachary's eyes. "Let's go look around this way," he said, indicating the northern exit from the hall. "I know it's another corridor running parallel to this one. Maybe it meets up with where they are now."

She nodded, and they stepped out to the north. To the left was a very short hallway ending in a wall. To the right looked like a carbon copy of the previous hall. A short stint east, followed by a jog to the north.

"Don't wander off too far," Li'l Bit called from behind them.

"Just stay there," Zachary shouted back. "I've got my chalk, and I want you to make sure Tory and Matt know where we've gone."

"You got it."

Liz wasn't quite sure how she felt moving off alone with Zachary. She wasn't sure how she felt about him, or if she should feel anything. He was attractive, in that rugged kind of way. Broad shoulders, strong hands, a strong face that didn't betray much of what he was thinking. But the way he talked and acted, not tough at all. And he seemed to know about her, about her illness, though how he'd figured it out, she couldn't begin to tell.

They took a few steps to the left turn, which Zachary marked with the green chalk. "He sounds different," she said.

THE DUNGEON

"He sounds like who he's supposed to be, I think," he replied. They took two steps to where the corridor jogged to the east again, and Zachary marked that too. "That happened when you went to him. You helped him, Elizabeth."

"Call me Liz," she said, and that was just stupid. Why would she say something so stupid?

"Okay, Liz. And please call me Zack, unless you like saying Zachary. I mean, I don't mean like you like saying my name or anything." He trailed off, and she looked up to see the sweetest, most confused look she'd ever seen on a man's face. She wanted to laugh but managed to hold that impulse inside.

"I like Zack," she said after a moment, and took his hand.

Pounding footsteps brought her heart racing into her chest, but it wasn't Li'l Bit or Matt or Tory coming up from behind them.

"Yo! Damn, that was crazy!" Big Rich said, running toward them from the east, meeting them at the point in the corridor where another passage opened off to the north.

"What happened?" Zack asked.

"We followed that other passage around a few turns to a dead end," Eddie said. "But just when we turned around, all that shaking happened. Did you guys feel that too?"

Liz nodded. "The floor tilted outside, and the boulder rolled back where it came from."

"Seriously?" Eddie asked, his blue eyes wide. "I mean, some of the myths say that the labyrinth could change itself, but I didn't think any of that was possible."

"Brian would know," Zack said softly, reminding Liz of the small man who helped them get out of the dungeon.

"Well, it changed something," Big Rich said. "It closed off the way we went to get down to the dead end, but it opened up this passage so we could get back."

"It opened up a way north too," Eddie said, holding up his compass. "I can't tell how far it goes, but maybe we should check it out."

"Why is north so important?" Matt said, coming up behind them. Both Tory and Li'l Bit were with him. "The original passage was heading west. We only got off it to avoid the boulder."

Tory moved over to be near Eddie, though he didn't seem to notice. "North will take us back behind that palace we saw. Maybe the way out is on the other side."

Matt didn't look convinced. "I can see where you'd think that, but doesn't it make more sense to try to get beyond the boulder trap? Maybe its whole purpose was to throw us off the most direct path."

"Dat...I mean that kind of makes sense," Li'l Bit offered.

Now it was Eddie who looked confused, his young brow furrowing as he thought. "So it's like a videogame, I guess."

"I'm not sure I follow," Matt said.

Eddie flushed, perhaps thinking his reference was a bit childish. But he went ahead with his explanation. "In a lot of games, like *Uncharted*, where you explore tombs and dungeons, there's always something good beyond the traps. Sometimes you need to get past them just to progress, but other times there's...um... well...treasure."

"Treasure like what?" Rich asked.

Now Eddie looked truly embarrassed. "Well, like a special coin, or a figurine."

"I don't think we'll find any of those down here," Matt said. "But I still think we'd do better checking out that direction."

Zack had stayed out of the discussion until now. "I like Matt's idea better for one reason. We already know there's at least one trap, the boulder."

"I just remembered something," Li'l Bit interjected, fumbling at his pants pockets. He pulled out a handful of dark, round objects, maybe stones. "I found these when we got separated. I used them to see where the traps were." He pantomimed rolling one of the stones.

"That's an idea too," Zack said. "I don't know how well they'll work down here, but it's certainly worth a try."

"Why wouldn't they work down here?" Li'l Bit asked.

"Up there, the traps were designed by modern engineers recreating ancient technology. With all the hidden lights and climate control, and the motion sensors that knew when we entered a room, it makes sense that similar technology would be used for their traps. Down here, it might take more weight than a pebble to set them off."

Seeing the look of disappointment on the shorter man's face, Zack added, "But like I said, it's a good idea and we'll give it a try."

Liz walked to the end of the hallway, where Big Rich and Eddie had come from, and took a peek. The hallway indeed ran north and south, with the southern end turning right after a short distance. Presumably, that's where the two found the dead end. To the north, the hall looked like it ran a good distance without any noticeable deviation.

It's probably lined with traps, she thought, but just as she was about to turn around and offer her agreement with Matt's plan to return to the first corridor, she saw something, way down at the northern end of the hall. It was hard to tell with the way the lighting worked. Those fire runners and burning oil lamps gave decent illumination at head height but left a lot of shadows at ground level. It looked like something was there, on the ground, some deeper mass of shadows that couldn't be explained away by distance and lighting.

"I *thought* I saw something," Eddie said, once Liz told them what she'd seen.

"If there's something there, we should probably check it out," Zachary said. "Okay, Li'l Bit, see if you can keep one of those pebbles in the center of the hallway."

"Um...if it's okay, I think I'd rather be called DeShaun. Li'l Bit was my...you know."

"All right then, DeShaun, if you would do the honors."

"Gladly," the shorter man said, stepping out into the north-south corridor. "Here goes nothing."

CHAPTER 36

Eddie

Eddie watched avidly as DeShaun rolled the pebble down the hallway, waiting to see something cool happen. The pebble skittered and bounced as much as rolled, but maintained a more or less straight course, at least until it rolled out of sight, disappearing into the shadows. No spikes shot out from the wall, no pits opened up in the middle of the floor. Nothing.

And then they heard it, a low sound, like a cross between a sigh and a moan.

"Did you hear that?" Big Rich said.

"We heard that before," Eddie said, "when the walls shifted and the floor shook."

"I can hear it," Mr. Zachary said, "but as far as I can remember, we didn't hear anything like that when you guys went missing."

"Nada," Matt confirmed.

The moan repeated, a slow exhalation, then it stopped, perhaps long enough for someone to draw in a breath, then repeated at the same low pitch and volume.

"What if someone's hurt down there?" Ms. Elizabeth asked.

The cop nodded. "Could be, but it also begs the question what hurt him. Was it a trap that got him, or is it some device making the noise to lure us into a trap?"

The tall black guy spoke up. "I get what you're saying. We can't afford to ignore it, but we also can't all go traipsing down there."

"Exactly," Zachary said. He took a deep breath, like he was psyching himself up. "So I'll go take a look."

Eddie wanted to go too, but he was also afraid of going. The things DeShaun had described sounded awfully scary, but also exciting, like being in a real-life *Tomb Raider* game, dodging spikes and jumping boulders, all while a wall closed in behind you.

Ms. Elizabeth reached out and grabbed the cop's hand, just for a moment, as he squeezed past everyone out into the hall.

"Get ready to run, just in case," he said, then he flipped on his Nightstick flashlight and moved up the corridor. To Eddie, he looked like a movie cop, not walking boldly down the hallway, but instead sticking as close to the right-hand wall as he could. It meant he had to walk a little hunched over, which also added to the cop-stalking impression, because he needed to keep his head below the height of the oil trench.

Once he was about halfway down the hallway, his flashlight pointed at the end, it became clear that the object they'd seen was a body, someone slumped against the wall.

"It's another one of those crazy people," Zachary reported in a forced whisper, just loud enough to reach them. "He's…I don't know…sleeping or something. I'm going closer."

Eddie felt the tension building around them. Most of it seemed to be coming from the tall redhead, whose face and body language radiated worry almost like a baseboard heater putting off hot air. Though she stood behind him, her hands were clenched on his shoulders, like she was going to stop him from running out into the hallway. She was tall enough to look over him, but not tall enough to look over Big Rich, so she leaned to the right, which was almost enough to make Eddie feel a little off-balance.

"Be careful," she hissed back at the cop. It sounded loud to Eddie, like an explosion of sound in his right ear, but he wasn't about to shrug or shift position. Something told him that her holding onto him was really a way for her to prevent herself from going after the cop.

Another sound reached them, a burst of a higher pitched noise, like the wordless cries of the crazy druggies from the Octagon room. It didn't sound too close, but sound might travel weirdly in these walled in corridors. It startled them, however, and both Ms. Tory and DeShaun let out a couple of swear words. Everyone except him and Ms. Elizabeth turned to look back the way they'd come. A second cry seemed to answer the first. It sounded like a second person, though it was hard to be sure. There was just enough difference in pitch and timbre that it might be a different person.

"It's coming from that other side passage," Matt said, pointing at the opening in the north wall of the hallway.

The first voice sounded again, followed a few moments later by the second, only now the cries were fainter, as if the two people were moving away from them.

Mr. Zachary was coming back down the hallway, again hugging the right side. Eddie didn't blame him. If you already knew one side was safe, why risk the other one?

The pressure on Eddie's shoulders lifted as the cop drew closer. He turned to look up at the redhead and saw a smile on her face that made it beautiful, something he wouldn't have thought possible when he first met her, with her lean features and dark eyes.

"What's down there?" she asked softly.

"It's another—" Zachary began, but was interrupted by an immediate *shhh*ing from both Matt and Tory. He looked a question at them, and Tory said, "We think there are more of those druggies that way." She pointed at the northern opening.

"At least two," Matt whispered. "We heard their…I don't know…their calls."

"Okay," Zachary said. "Well, there's another one at the end of the hall. The clothes are different though, not all ratty and dirty. I mean, they *are* dirty, but no more than you'd expect after a day of running through tunnels."

"Is he going to follow us?" Big Rich asked, stepping past the cop and peering up the hallway.

Zachary shook his head. "No, I don't think so. There might be something wrong with him. He's propped up against the far wall like he just backed up to it and slid down. He's breathing and his eyes are open, but other than that, you'd have a hard time convincing me that he's capable of chasing anyone."

"Is he dying?" Ms. Tory asked.

"No, well, I don't know. He looks catatonic."

Big Rich shook himself, backing away. "I used to… well…before I went to jail, I used to do heroin. That high can knock you out, like, you don't move, not even as much as a sleeper does in the bed."

Zachary was nodding. "I've taken guys like that to the hospital before. One of them almost lost a leg because he slept so long in a bad position that it cut off circulation. I didn't think of that, but it does seem to fit."

"So maybe all of the creepy druggy dudes just pass out after a while?" Eddie asked.

"It's probably too early to generalize like that," Zachary said, "but it's a nice thing to hope for."

THE DUNGEON

The call and response of the two voices came again, louder this time, and Eddie was surprised at how fast Zachary moved. One second he was at the edge of the long north-south hallway, and in an eye blink he'd moved through the group, putting himself closest to the apparent source of the sounds, the opening in the northern wall of the passage.

"Big Rich," Zachary whispered, waving his arm.

"Oh, the hell with it," the big man said. "If Li'l Bit can step his game up to DeShaun, you guys can just call me Richard or Rich."

"What about—" DeShaun started to say, but the larger man glared at him.

"I'm still not gonna be a Dick, got it?"

DeShaun smiled, and Eddie was glad to see his good nature reasserting itself.

"Okay, Rich," Zachary said, smiling, "we're gonna move up nice and slow. The passage dead-ends to the left, so we'll turn right. The rest of you stay behind us but try not to fall too far behind."

"You figure with our size, we can keep anything from getting through us?" Rich asked.

"I hope so," Zachary said. "I want to make sure we aren't leaving something bad that might come up behind us later."

They moved through the north opening, Eddie as close behind the two taller man as he could get, though still behind Elizabeth, who stayed as close to the cop as a shadow. The flickering light of the oil lamps kept the passage illuminated, but he wished there weren't so many shadows up by the high ceiling. He didn't like how his imagination kept painting images of giant spiders crouching up there where walls met ceiling, all fat bodies, hairy legs, and glistening fangs, or some other thing capable of climbing vertical surfaces, ready to jump down on them when they least expected it.

Through the arch and to the left was a short bit of hallway and a dead end, just like Zachary reported. To the right was a stretch about fifteen feet long, then a turn to the left, which meant north. Eddie dutifully marked an arrow on the wall, indicating their direction of travel, though it felt silly given there was only one way to go. Still, his and Rich's back trail had changed once, so anything was possible. Even if the gray stone wasn't so obviously worked, this entire construct would scream of human design, if for no other reason than because all of the walls were straight, all of the angles exactly ninety degrees. It made keeping track of direction fairly easy, even for a city boy like him.

As they moved north, they heard the sounds again, and though they were clearer, they didn't seem to be any closer. In his mind, Eddie pictured it as there were fewer walls between them and the noisemakers, which explained the increased clarity, though not necessarily why the volume waxed and waned.

Zachary stopped at the end of the northern leg, then eased his head out to look around the corner. He must not have seen anything, because he quickly got them moving again, around the left turn, now heading west.

This hallway appeared to be almost as long as the first corridor, where Elizabeth discovered the burning oil lamps. It was too long to see its entire length, but what he could see consisted of a continuous wall on the north side and what might be an opening on the south. Carefully, the group of seven eased down the hallway, covering twenty feet before the cries repeated. They were definitely louder now and sounded almost as though they were right on the other side of the southern wall. There was a strange quality to the sounds. They didn't seem as violent. Eddie thought that a good description. They still sounded like a noise made more by instinct that sought to convey an emotion, rather than intelligible speech, as though the speakers had been reduced to the communicative ability of pre-historic man. But whereas their previous encounters with the crazed men had demonstrated a frenetic energy, an urgency to commit acts of destruction, these sounded almost lost, forlorn.

Zachary and Rich eased along the southern wall, creeping up to the opening. Once there, the two tall men leaned far enough to be able to see the neighboring corridor. The moan sounded again, so close now, followed immediately by its near-echo, and both men jumped back. Eddie tensed, expecting to have to run or fight, but nothing happened. No one came out of the doorway. A few moments of silence passed before the cop and the tight end repeated their lean and look. This time when the cries rang out, neither man moved, though Eddie and a few others flinched.

Then Big Rich was backing away, and Zachary was waving them to come up, come closer, but be quiet. Curious but cautious, Eddie moved up to the doorway, peering diagonally into the next corridor, his view of the western running part. A form shuffled into view, it's back to them, moving west. It was one of the crazy people, but like Zachary had said, the clothing was different. It wore leather pants, just like them, the bottoms tucked into boots. Instead of a white linen shirt, it wore just the leather vest, bare arms hanging limply at its sides. The head tilted up, and one of those lost, lonely wails sounded. As the cry faded, its head came back down, and it continued to the end of the corridor before turning left and moving out of sight. At the same time the first was turning, a second figure, similarly dressed, shuffled past the opening, apparently following the same track as the first. When he sent out his cry, it was obviously the second voice they had heard, eerily similar in cadence but different in pitch. Then he too shuffled on his way.

Eddie couldn't explain why, but seeing the two men made him feel sad. They looked like lost animals, stuck in a maze they didn't have the intelligence to figure out, wearing themselves down past the point of exhaustion. It reminded him of something a fellow shelter-sleeper once said, about how the machinery of commerce does something similar, trapping people in circular fields, working them at the same tasks over and over, day after day, until they're nothing more than rats trapped in a cage and their only form of escape is to jump on the wheel and run, run, run, until they fall over exhausted. Eddie wasn't sure that was exactly how the world worked; his father had seemed to love his job, but he couldn't banish the comparison from his thoughts.

Then Zachary was pulling him away from the door, back the way they'd come. They retraced their steps around several corners until they were back in the hallway immediately adjacent to the initial passage, where the boulder presumably lay waiting. Not until they were several hallways away, the cries of the endlessly circling insane barely audible, did anyone speak.

"We could probably sneak past them," DeShaun said.

"We might, but it would be risky," the cop answered. "They're pretty evenly spaced apart."

"Still worth a thought," Tory offered.

"I want to try Matt's way first," Elizabeth said. She was holding hands with Mr. Zachary again, Eddie noted. "I can't explain why, but something about it makes sense. Why else would you have a way for the boulder to reset, except to make that the most dangerous way to go?"

"Maybe too dangerous," Tory said.

THE DUNGEON

Rich shook his head, looking at the shorter woman. "I'm with them on this. Those dudes are way unpredictable. But if this doesn't pan out, we know where to try next."

Tory looked at him for a moment, then sighed and said, "I'll make it unanimous then, the boulder passage first."

With that settled, Zachary moved to the opening in the south wall, Nightstick in hand. He flashed it left, then right, looking for long seconds before pulling back into the corridor. While Big Rich went to look second, Zachary reported, "The wall back at the entrance is gone. It might only come up to keep the boulder from rolling out of the labyrinth."

"Or to squish you if you aren't fast enough to get out of the way," DeShaun interjected.

"Or both," Zachary continued. "Either way, the boulder is all the way back to the right, as far as I can tell."

"That would be west," Matt said.

"It's definitely farther than the next opening and we know it doesn't move that fast, so I'm thinking we can make that next opening before it rolls our way."

"If it even moves again," Eddie said.

"What do you mean?" Zachary asked.

"What if it only moves when someone trips a plate near the entrance?"

"Or when someone light the lamps?" Elizabeth added, pointing to herself.

"Then what would we assume reset it?" Matt asked.

"It could be on some kind of old-fashioned timer," Eddie said. "I've read about timers that were gear-based or used some kind of water drain, even candles. What if lighting the lamps started something like that, a candle timer, and when it burned down or burned through something, the rock came back?"

"It's not a bad idea," Matt said.

"Wouldn't that mean someone would have to replace the candle?" DeShaun asked. "I mean, you know, supposing it used a candle."

"Either way," Zachary said, "it might mean that the boulder won't move again. It's certainly something to hope for."

"Okay," Rich said. "So we doing this, or we just gonna keep talking about it?"

Slowly, carefully, the seven crept out into the hallway. Nothing had changed, really, but everything seemed different. Knowing that there was a massive hunk of rock that might start rolling at you at any moment added to Eddie's sense of adventure, so that everything looked sharper, every sound seemed louder.

Zachary took the lead again, with Rich right behind him, both hugging the north wall, almost sliding along it with their backs to it, like it was a foot-wide ledge over a canyon a mile deep. Zachary kept his light pointed at the floor almost as much as ahead, watching for inconsistencies in the rock that might indicate another trip plate, or for the small holes that spoke of a spike trap.

But nothing happened. In less than a minute, they reached the second opening. The boulder was now clearly visible without the aid of any artificial light, resting against the western wall, not quite large enough to disguise a final turn in the passage, which looked to continue north past the boulder.

Zachary ducked his head through the opening and shone his light around. "Nothing in there," he reported. "A dead end both ways."

"So how do we get around the boulder, then?" Matt asked.

THE DUNGEON

"Yo, you little people might be able to squeeze around it," Rich said, "but me and Zack are probably too big."

"The pebbles," DeShaun said. "I knew I saved these shooters for a reason, not just 'cause they remind me of my sister's rabbit."

Before anyone could ask about either his sister or her rabbit, he pulled one of the round rocks from his pocket. "This my last one. You want me to throw it at the opening?"

Matt nodded, and DeShaun pulled his arm back. "Everybody get in the doorway," he said.

"Wait," Eddie cried, reaching out to stop DeShaun before he could let it fly.

"What is it?" Zachary said.

"Yeah, what the hell?"

Eddie thought fast. Something was wrong with the idea of throwing it at the entrance. "We don't know what set the boulder moving the first time," he said, working through the idea as he spoke. "It seemed to come with those flames followed the trenches, but we were all standing around the lamp. Maybe one of us tripped something, but maybe we didn't."

"Okay, so why not try to throw a stone out there?" Elizabeth asked.

"Because the boulder is what we want to test, right?" Eddie said. "Look, it'll be tight, but I'm sure we can squeeze everyone past it. And even if we can't, once some of us get behind it, we might be able to push it out of the way. The problem is, what if it starts moving while we're trying to slip past?"

"So what do you want me to do?" DeShaun asked.

"I think you should throw that stone at the boulder as hard as you can, see if the impact causes anything to happen."

DeShaun looked up at Zachary and Rich. The cop shrugged. "I'm open to the idea. Heck, if it doesn't do anything, it won't be a problem to go pick up the rock and try again in the other direction."

"All right, then," DeShaun said, pivoting to face the boulder. He stepped out into the middle of the corridor and went into a long windup, looking left and right like he was checking the status of runners in a comical parody of a baseball pitcher. Then he left fly.

With the combined light of the oil lamps and Zachary's Nightstick, it was easy to follow the rock through the air. It struck the boulder with a completely unremarkable *plunk* sound that seemed anticlimactic, bounced back a couple of feet, then landed on the floor.

"Well, that was—" Matt started to say, but then the rumbling started up, the floor shaking, tilting.

"Get inside!" Tory yelled, pulling on his shirt sleeve.

DeShaun scooted up to him, pushing him even as Tory was pulling. Then they were all inside the short corridor, watching the narrow opening as the boulder rolled slowly past.

"Quick, let's get around it," Zachary said, moving back out into the passage even as the boulder crashed into a wall.

The crash happened too soon, Eddie thought, even as Tory went from pulling to pushing, forcing him out into the hallway. He looked left and saw the boulder only a few feet away, having come to rest against a new wall. The new wall lay between the two side passages, making Eddie's thoughts swirl. There was more to the design of this major corridor than just one trap. It was setup in such a way that it not only taunted them to try to get past the boulder. It pushed them that way, like they were being herded.

THE DUNGEON

Zachary, Elizabeth, and Matt were already halfway to the final turn, sidestepping along the wall at high speed, but the floor started vibrating again, the air filling with the grinding of stone on stone, or of old, rusted gears rotating, shifting the slope of the floor. Eddie could *feel* the angle changing, and even as he took his first steps toward the end of the hall, he heard the awful sound of the boulder beginning to roll again, this time right back at them.

He ran full out, passing Tory and DeShaun, yelling, "It's coming back! Run!" They picked up their pace as well, running after him, and even the first three were abandoning their safe slide along the wall as the boulder rumbled after them.

Eddie made the turn first, followed immediately by DeShaun. Looking back, he saw the others clear the turn as well, saw a look of shock and horror spring to life in Elizabeth's face.

"Eddie, no!" she yelled.

And he turned around and saw the pit yawning under him, saw that there was nothing for his outstretched foot to land on and he tried to push off with his trailing leg, desperately tried to jump, but it was too late, and he was falling, and now he could see the spikes at the bottom.

CHAPTER 37

Brian

It felt weird to be back in the offices of Magellan Enterprises, freshly showered and wearing modern clothing, which in this instance consisted of a T-shirt emblazoned with the company logo, plain navy blue sweat pants, and a pair of his own sneakers, retrieved from the company locker room near the racquetball court. So much had changed for him since waking up in the dungeon, and yet much was still the same.

Even though he wore no fetters, he was still a prisoner. Not in a physical sense, of course. His circle of coconspirators had done everything they needed to in order to keep his "almost whistle-blowing" from reaching the ears of Ian Magellan or any of the project heads. A good part of their ongoing research involved trying to determine how much Mr. Magellan actually knew, how much involvement he had. Like any large corporation, there was a hierarchy of officers and department heads, numerous disparate interests with their own power structures, each one controlled by its own board of directors who designated an "ambassador" to be their representative in the governing body of Magellan Global. Sitting above all of this was the visionary, Ian. So while Ian was suspect because he was at the top of the food chain, it was unlikely anyone outside of the Greece power structure had any idea what had been discovered here, or what direction the current project had taken. Brian wondered how much Magellan himself really knew and how much was false information, fed both by the Greek resistance, and by those who fought to advance the party.

When he first discovered that Magellan was creating thralls for the express purpose of working them as mining slaves, he'd been appalled. When further digging led him to the conclusion that everything was tied to gaining political influence in two time periods, he'd been filled with outrage and a nagging sense of guilt. Here he was, happily collecting a generous paycheck from a company out to recreate the modern world in a very different manner than history dictated and were on the cusp of doing so by means of kidnapping and coercion, using hacked databases to blacklist prominent opponents, or even potential troublemakers, innocents like that detective, Zachary Pavese.

He shuddered to think what might have happened to him or his family had Daniel King not interceded before he could go public with what he'd discovered.

Such a small thing, to be worth so much, he thought, picturing the tiny USB jump drive he'd hidden deep in the soil of a potted plant. Only a small fraction of its data capacity was in use, as it held only three files. One was a .jpg of a bronze disk, roughly a foot in diameter, upon which were etched letters and words both recognizable and unintelligible. The words ran in circles around the circumference of the disk, starting at the outer edge and winding their way around and around, always moving closer to the center, much in the way music used to be recorded on vinyl records. Whether you read modern English or Ancient Greek didn't matter, the words were the same, translations of each other that told the history behind the creation of the disk.

The disk was part of a jumble of similar items, ancient shields and blades collected during the third or fourth descent into the labyrinth, that were delivered in a large crate to his team of engineers. While some items were selected for curating, Magellan's main interest had not been the furtherance of archaeological knowledge. The sheer volume of artifacts meant that some could be used for decoration, or to allow the engineers the opportunity to copy designs, or to attempt to reverse-engineer an item's creation to better understand its construction. It was sheer luck that Brian was the one to flip over a large shield to find the smaller disk lodged by time and corrosion to the underside.

The words he'd discovered were impossible, of course. How could something that seemed so old have an inscription written in English?

That discovery set him on his path. He sent a small section of the disk, shaved by a microtome, for analysis and dating. He then spent ten or twelve hours digging through the facility's extensive database of Greek translations, painstakingly recreating, word by word, the inscription on the disk, which only confirmed his suspicion: the same message written in two languages.

The other two files on the jump drive were a printed transcript of the words and its dating verification, performed with voltammetric curvature analysis, as carbon-dating doesn't apply to metallic objects. That had come as a surprise to the engineer, who liked to believe he was abreast of most technological advances, even if he didn't work with them directly. It did make sense, once he read the research, why carbon dating was only appropriate for things that had once been alive, like bones, or which contained elements of previously living material. The development of voltammetric analysis by Spanish and Portuguese scientists measured the current peaks of tenorite and cuprite, two preferential products of corrosion found on copper-containing material. The results of the technology had been verified by comparing the dated metallic products found in situ with organic objects dated by traditional carbon analysis.

The disk and its inscriptions were at least three thousand years old, placing the date of creation at or around 1,200 BCE. The existence of this disk, if it became public, would shock every major scientific community, drawing massive scrutiny from all governments and governmental agencies down upon Magellan Enterprises and its Greek operations. There would be learned talking heads denouncing the relic as a fraud simply because their entire belief systems were threatened. How could something three thousand years old possibly have modern English inscriptions? There would even be attempts to sabotage Magellan's Greek operations in an attempt to destroy the evidence before it could be certified.

People hate what they don't understand. Even worse, people seek to destroy that which threatens them, and this disk would certainly threaten long-held beliefs about everything from ancient civilizations to the spread of man from the cradle of life, long-believed to be in Africa.

Worse still, the sky-watchers and *I was butt-probed* alien conspiracy theorists would clamor and shout that this was rock-solid proof of some form of alien intervention and would use that to buttress their points that aliens still hold influence today.

While the disk and its confirmed dating were enough to convince Brian of the reality of the danger posed by Magellan Enterprises and its desire to utilize its miraculous discovery to further the ambitions of the men in power directing the company's course, it took the transcription to get him to agree to join forces with Daniel King in his effort to undermine the company's efforts. Logic dictated his presence shouldn't be necessary, unless one followed the logic that he had been meant to discover the disk and tie its incredible contents to the names of the people slated for the first live dungeon run. By that same token, it might be logical to assume his presence was necessary to ensure the disk's creators survived to create it. Those were Daniel's arguments, and they were enough to firm Brian's resolve whenever his fear threatened to overwhelm him.

He promised Mr. King he would get as many of them through the southern exit and into the labyrinth as he could, but two of them were of paramount importance.

It was up to Daniel and his team of special effects wizards to make sure the higher-ups believed them dead, with his creative use of video editing, and up to Brian to continue to play the part of loyal employee, while still working to gather evidence. Eventually, if the computer nerds did their job right, there would come an investigation, and he needed to be in a position to help.

For the moment, playing his part meant appearing to be in a state of psychological shock, after having witnessed such a display of violence in the Octagon Room. Only the timely arrival of the security forces had saved him from sharing everyone else's fate. He relied on his knowledge of the parts of the labyrinth they'd explored and the creative engineering behind the traps to keep himself at a peak state of anxiety, in case anyone chose to debrief him.

Any actions he took might still undermine the effectiveness of their campaign of resistance. A well-armed security detail could be dispatched into the depths to find and eliminate Zachary, Elizabeth, and the others before they could affect any change. Even if those security people could never return, the loss would be considered minimal compared to the potential gain.

Even now, suspecting nothing, the leadership threatened to screw everything up through their impulsive actions. There was no need to send another batch of ten through the dungeon, except to further promote this "reality" game show. They could just as easily decide to inject another hundred subjects and send them through the back door into the labyrinth, but that wouldn't satisfy the need to realize every dollar or euro possible.

It was all a tangled mess, Brian thought, folding his hands on the office desk and cradling his forehead. And it wasn't soon to be over, if what Daniel said was true. Eventually the authorities were going to come, looking for the lost policeman, maybe tying together other breadcrumbs the hackers left to show the way. Brian needed to keep himself above suspicion, needed to be free to interact with them when they came. He needed to get that jump drive into the right hands or, failing that, to make sure copies of the dating analysis and transcript were somehow seen or seized.

Once it became known that Zachary Pavese and Elizabeth Ott's names were listed on the ancient disk as contributors to the fall of Magellan Enterprises' bid to rewrite history, his job would be done.

Only then would he be free to leave.

CHAPTER 38

Elizabeth

She came around the corner fast, almost stepping on DeShaun's heels, trying to get clear of the rolling boulder and trying *not* to be so slow that the men behind her, one in particular, were unable to get to safety. Eddie was only a few feet ahead, looking back at her, at all of them, when she saw a piece of floor just disappear. It was there one second, and gone the next, flipping down on silent hinges. Eddie didn't see it, was running right for it.

"Eddie, no!" she yelled, but it wasn't soon enough. Even though time seemed to slow to a crawl, it would not be soon enough.

She could see it, could understand the cunning mechanism that rigged the boulder to roll one way, then another, the mastermind who predicted victims running full out to beat the boulder back to the corner, setting one of those pressure plates, but placing the piece of flooring it activated just far enough ahead to catch a man with a running stride.

The floor seemed to open into darkness, but there was something gleaming inside of it.

And as the scream left her throat, she saw the young man whip his head around, suddenly acutely aware of the danger.

But it was too late. His running stride meant that his leading foot would fall squarely in the middle of that open space. Nothing he did could change it.

She felt herself shoved aside as the boy started to pitch forward, no amount of screaming or wishing or praying able to change the inevitable. Shifted toward the wall, she was able to see around the broad back of Zachary.

She saw DeShaun lunging, reaching.

She heard a yell like one of those Karate masters letting out all of his air as he blasts through a concrete block with his head, but it was DeShaun's voice.

And then DeShaun was gone, and Eddie was clinging desperately to the lip of the opening on the far side.

The boulder rolled to a slow stop behind them, settling into its previous spot as gently as a car being parallel-parked by a nervous septuagenarian.

"He saved him," Zachary said, and the shock and grief in his voice was real and honest.

"Are you okay?" Tory called, but Liz could see that the boy was all right, was already climbing up over the lip on the far side of the hole in the ground, only six or seven feet away. The boy was all right, but what about the man?

Moving up beside Zack, she was surprised again when he turned to face her, like he knew she was there, and wrapped his arms around her. "Don't look," he said.

But she had to. She needed to see.

Gently she pulled away from him, moving to his side, and peered down into the pit.

It was another of those openings filled with spikes, the tops of which were perhaps six feet below the level of the floor. She couldn't be sure how long the spikes were, maybe only two or three feet, but their length was irrelevant in relation to their deadly effect.

DeShaun was face down, pierced in half a dozen places, arms outstretched in a grotesque parody of a Superman pose. Blood-washed spikes protruded half a foot out the back of his white shirt, through the leather of his leggings. The fall had dislodged his backpack. That was one of the details that grabbed at her. His hardhat was still on his head, and none of the spikes had penetrated his pack.

"He pushed me!" Eddie said, gasping. "He pushed me enough so that I could grab the other side."

DeShaun's wasn't the only body impaled on the spikes. There were two others, dressed alike in what appeared to be grays and browns. It was hard to be sure because of their postures, but they might have been more of those Freakers. The other two had been dead long enough that more than just blood oozed out of their bodies; the smell of decay rose thick and cloying, a miasma that set both Eddie and Tory to coughing and gagging.

"God, that's awful!" Matt said, looking down.

Eddie was crying now, sitting down with his back against one of the walls. Liz and Tory shared a look, a wordless exchange that asked, *You going, or am I?* Then both took a two-step running leap, clearing the hole. They knelt beside Eddie, holding him, comforting him.

"I can't believe he's gone," the young man said, breath hitching in and out, a combination of grief and relief, mixed with a liberal sense of shock at how close he'd come to death. He looked up from between them and said, "He saved me."

"I know, sweetie," Tory said. "I saw him. He was a hero."

THE DUNGEON

As she held the sobbing young man, Elizabeth felt an odd sense of something, not quite family, but certainly stronger than any connection she'd felt in a very long time. She looked up in time to see first Rich, then Matt, then finally Zachary make the leap across the hole in the ground. As the cop landed, almost as an afterthought, the hole closed, the piece of flooring swinging back up into place as smoothly as it had fallen away.

"Damn them," she said, feeling the hot sting of tears in her eyes.

The big former football player stood where he'd landed, facing back toward the boulder, head down. Liz wasn't sure if he was praying or just saying goodbye.

"Dude had it rough," he said, his voice low and husky. "As my momma used to say, 'He hoed a hard row and still had a way to go. But he did it with a smile.'"

"Amen to that," Matt whispered.

Then Big Rich turned and reached out a big hand to Zachary. Zack took the hand, gripping it firmly.

"You promise me, Mr. Policeman, if we get out of this, the people that did this to us, they gonna pay."

"My way or your way," Zack answered, and it wasn't a question.

"Exactly," Rich replied. "Your way or my way."

Then Zack was offering her a hand up, helping her to her feet, while Rich and Matt helped Tory and Eddie up. The kid still looked shaken, which she could understand, but then he took a deep breath, like he was sucking his courage back in. "I'm okay," he said. He looked around at them, eyes flashing from one person to another, like he was counting them.

That's right, Liz thought, *just six of us left.*

"We should keep moving," Zachary said.

"I'm not sure I can just yet," Tory whispered. "So much has happened, so much. I just...maybe I just need a little break. Wouldn't you like a little break, Eddie?"

"A break," Zachary said, tasting the word. "We could all use a little rest, but not here."

"I'm worried that boulder might decide to come this way," Matt said. "Let's at least get a little away from here."

"I...okay, that'll do," Tory said.

The hallway looked like every other one in the labyrinth: gray stone walls illuminated by burning oil lamps that gave off a scent like rotten crayons, gray stone floor that might or might not try to kill them again, and high above, so high that even a tall man like Rich holding a smaller man on his shoulders wouldn't have a chance of reaching the top, was the cavern ceiling, brown and earthy, a natural color. But it was short, only running north for a few feet before it turned right.

The right turn immediately became a left, then another right and a left, as they followed a zigzag course that seemed to go a little farther north with each turn. They made a final turn to the right, now facing east, and saw a corridor that continued in that direction far beyond the light of even the Nightsticks on their brightest setting.

Near at hand, a side passage opened to the north, and Liz could just make out another opening on the north wall farther on. There were no rumblings, no vibrations in the floors, no pits, and no spikes.

"Shall we check this first passage?" Matt asked.

"Sure, but let's mark where we turned, in case we get turned around, or in case the walls change again," the cop said, drawing an arrow on the ground that showed the direction they'd come from, as well as the path they'd chosen to follow.

THE DUNGEON

The northern passage quickly became another set of east and west zigzags, until they came to a three-way intersection. A quick look to the right showed a dead end, while a few steps left led to another couple of turns and another dead end, facing north.

"This seems like a good place," Rich said, setting down his bag and folding his long legs under him, leaning back against one of the walls.

Without another word, the remaining five found spots on the floor, Eddie and Matt already digging into their packs to find something to eat.

Zack chose to sit next to her, which brought a smile. Closing her eyes, she leaned over and rested her head on his shoulder.

In the silence, which only lasted long enough for Eddie to begin exclaiming over the food choices he'd found, Liz came to a realization.

She hadn't heard a thought that wasn't her own since coming down here.

CHAPTER 39

Matt

As soon as Matt sat down, he felt weariness seep into him, spreading from feet he hadn't realized were hurting up legs that had done more running, jumping, and stair-climbing in the past three hours than in the past three years combined. Just shrugging off the backpack and swinging it around to his lap seemed almost more than he could handle.

Still, he wasn't going to complain. Three days ago, he was facing twenty years in a Federal corrections facility in Allenwood, Pennsylvania. Two days ago, he listened to a sales pitch, decided what the hell, and signed a paper. Yesterday—God, was it only yesterday?—he was transported in handcuffs from his temporary lodgings in New York to a private airfield. He remembered them taking the handcuffs off after a businessman signed papers transferring custody from the Corrections Office, then they were airborne and he was offered a drink. The next thing he remembered was waking up surrounded by nine strangers.

Somehow, over just a few hours, he'd learned to like some of them, and he actually held a measure of respect for both the cop and the high school football-player-turned-heroin-junkie.

As he pulled out a Bridgford Honey BBQ Beef Sandwich MRE, tore off the wrapper, and took a tentative bite, he reflected more on the ones they'd lost than the five who rested near him. The first guy, the pedophile, according to Mike Callahan, was no loss to anyone. But everyone else had made an impact. First, Zippy, a guy whose brain was probably just one or two hits off a crack pipe from being totally fried, had figured out a complex mathematical pattern and not only ran through it perfectly, but was also able to instinctively deduce a way to loop a segment of the pattern as he dodged, weaved, and waited for the exit door to open. He wasn't a bad guy, just someone swept up into the not-so-gentle arms of Mother Justice while she sought out the real criminals. And at the end of the day, when someone else's life was in danger, he'd placed himself in harm's way.

Matt found himself nodding as he took a second bite of the crust-like pouch of food. This was actually pretty tasty.

Then there was Brian, an egghead like himself, more concerned with facts and figures than people and personalities, who stumbled upon a truth that shook him out of his academic shell and prompted a need to do something important, to expose the lies behind the company he worked for. Matt wasn't sure he could empathize with that need. For most of his ten years with the accounting firm, he'd been the one behind the scenes finding ways to siphon off a little extra here and there for himself. It was another egghead, one with federal credentials, who'd figured out his little scam and gotten him arrested and convicted. So maybe Brian, as a whistle-blower, wouldn't normally figure high on Matt's Christmas card list, except that he'd sacrificed himself to make it possible for them to escape.

Which brought him to Li'l Bit, or DeShaun, as he'd asked to be called. Being one of the last around the corner, he had only heard Elizabeth's shout and hadn't seen little Eddie about to fall. But he'd seen DeShaun's final heroic moment, launching himself straight at the skinny boy and pushing. The only sound he'd made had been a grunt of effort.

Matt wasn't sure how he'd felt about the man, especially after he'd admitted his homosexuality. Matt had no illusions about himself; he barely tolerated the idea of homosexuality. God forbid he should have to work with one, or sleep near someone like that. He knew his mind-set wasn't politically correct, and considering his larceny, it certainly wasn't based on some *God-says-it's- bad* mentality, it was just the way he felt.

In the end, he decided it didn't matter. He would remember DeShaun as a man who sacrificed himself to save someone else. There wouldn't be an asterisk attached to it, like what many of the sportscasters were predicting would happen during baseball's Steroid-Gate. No matter how he'd lived or how he'd wound up running the dungeon with them, he'd died a hero.

Having finished his sandwich, Matt dug back into his knapsack for one of his two canteens. Conscientious of the fact that they hadn't seen any water at all since entering the labyrinth proper, he took only a few small sips, enough to quench the thirst brought on by the sandwich. Replacing everything in the knapsack, he left the canteen on top and clipped his own Nightstick on one of the leather straps running over his shoulders.

"Pretty good, huh?" Eddie asked him, smiling around his own pastry. When he pulled it away, he left a small blue stain around his lips, like he was eating some form of pie or cobbler. *Must be nice to be so young*, he thought.

Matt pulled off his hardhat, rubbing a hand over his hair to rearrange the short whorls in an effort to make his hair stop aching. Sighing, he leaned his head back against the gray stone wall, holding the hard hat in his lap. Zachary and Elizabeth had their heads together near the back of the dead end. They were both eating, talking softly between bites.

Tory sat between him and the couple, across the hall from Eddie, like she didn't want to let him out of her sight. There was something motherly about the way the older woman acted around Eddie. Maybe she was a mother, he didn't know. Her eyes were red-rimmed, like she'd just stopped crying. Whether she was crying for DeShaun's loss or was still reacting to the near loss of Eddie, he couldn't tell.

The way Elizabeth had moved to comfort Eddie also surprised him. He hadn't taken her for the motherly type. Then again, he hadn't exactly taken her for the type to attach herself to the cop either, so perhaps his character-judgment skills were much worse than he'd always assumed. She definitely seemed...softer... or something, like she'd decided to lower a few layers of her defensive shields. That must have happened when they got separated. It hadn't stopped her from fighting like a wildcat when those crazy men attacked them, so soft or hard, he was glad to have her around.

Which left Rich, sitting off a little ways from everyone else, close to the turn that led back to the main passage, like he was placing himself as the first barrier should anyone come looking for them. He'd also eaten an MRE, and now sat with his back against the wall. His eyes were open, staring across at the opposite wall, but probably not actually looking at it. It was one of those faraway stares, that kind that means lost in memory. Whether he was regretting the choices that led him here, worrying about his family, or just thinking about the things they'd already experienced, Matt didn't know. Rich was another solid one, like Elizabeth and Zachary, someone you could depend on. Matt hoped they thought the same about him.

He lay his head back against the wall and thought about closing his eyes for a moment...then he was being shaken.

"Wake up," Zack hissed at him.

Matt started, his hands jerked, sending his hardhat into a short, clattering roll on the floor. "What?" he asked.

"Shhh. Quiet," the redhead hissed.

Matt realized everyone was up but him, eyes darting nervously, hands shaking as they tried to hastily tie backpacks closed and sling them over their shoulders.

"Just listen," Rich said softly, which for him meant a low growl.

Matt reached for his hardhat, slipped it onto his head. He'd retied his knapsack before falling asleep, so it was a quick matter to slip his arms into the straps and shrug it up into position. Aside from the sounds the people around him were making, the whisper of leather on linen, the occasional scuff of boot on stone, he didn't hear anything.

"What was it?" he asked softly.

"A sound, a rumble," the cop answered. "Felt it in the ground, like one of the traps going off."

"You think someone came down here after us?" Matt asked.

"That, or some more of those crazy people still wandering around. Either way, we've rested long enough."

As quietly as they could, the group retraced their steps north and east, then wended through the S-curve until they came back to the fluorescent chalk markings Zachary made on the ground.

"Hug the wall," the cop said. "And hold hands. Maybe we can avoid falling into anymore pits that way."

Matt yawned but reached out to take Eddie's hand with his right, and Tory's with his left. He was next to last in line. Cautiously but steadily, the group moved east along the long passage, hugging the south wall. He remembered seeing openings on the north side, so it made sense to stick to the side away from them. "How long was I asleep?" he asked.

"No way to know for sure," Elizabeth whispered back at him from her place just in front of Eddie. "We dug through the bags again, but nothing in them tells time."

"I fell asleep too," Eddie said.

Then he heard it. They all did. High-pitched shrieks and screeches, long moaning wails that fell just at the cusp of hearing, far enough away that they were safe for the moment, but definitely more noise than anything they'd heard since coming into the labyrinth. And though faint, the voices rose and fell over one another, with varying pitch and duration. All remaining vestiges of sleep fell away from him as his heart began to race.

"Jesus, sounds like a lot of them," Tory said from behind him.

"All the more reason to keep moving," Rich said from the front.

"Hold a sec," Elizabeth said. "Let me go check out that opening."

Matt realized they had sidled up to the first break in the north wall. Moving quickly, Elizabeth darted forward. The cop reached out a hand like he wanted to stop her or go with her, but then he let it fall. He did take a step away from their wall, a man obviously torn with concern, his body almost quivering with the need to protect. Then Elizabeth was back, rejoining the line, and they continued heading east.

"Nothing in there but a couple of quick turns and another dead end," the redhead reported.

Echoing off the ceiling, the cries of ancient tunnel-dwelling monsters, or those created by the slow frying of brain cells, reached them again. The walls shook, vibrations felt through their backpacks, making Matt's jaw ache with the effort of holding it closed, teeth pressed together. It was that or feel them chatter. He spent more time looking along their back trail, every moment expecting to see one or more of those hopped-up crazy people come tearing into view, racing to attack, voices raised like wolves on the trail of prey.

But the hallway behind remained clear.

They approached a second opening to the north, what appeared to be a large room, except there was a row of something like looked like large teeth separating their side from the far side.

"What the hell?" he whispered, letting go of Eddie and Tory's hands and stepping away from the wall.

As he crossed the threshold into the room, he noted that the burning oil ran off to the left and the right, defining the east and west margins of the room, but did not run across the barrier.

Reaching for his Nightstick, still clipped to one of the leather straps of his backpack, he pulled it away with a click. Turning it on, he played the light over the barrier. What he'd initially thought of as teeth appeared to be a strange arrangement of stalactites and stalagmites, natural brown rock formations extending down from the ceiling and up from the ground, respectively, growing in such a way that they had slid between one another, like a huge, fanged maw almost completely closed. There was enough space between them that he could make out another arch directly across from the one he'd entered and what appeared to be another hallway paralleling their own.

THE DUNGEON

"Weird," he muttered, backing away from the toothy wall and rejoining the other five.

As they began moving again, aiming for what looked like a left turn, he described what he'd seen to the others.

"I wish I'd gone and looked," Eddie said. He sounded excited, thought Matt, but it could also just be his adrenaline pumping. Fear and excitement could be close cousins when all you had to go on was a breathy way of talking. "I'll bet it was a trap," he went on. "Like, those teeth can come apart and then snap shut when someone walks through them."

Definitely excitement, Matt corrected himself.

This time it was the floor that rumbled, a long, slow series of vibrations. The screams sounded again.

"I think that was the boulder," Zachary said.

Matt silently agreed. He didn't know if the screaming had to do with someone getting squashed by the rock, or stepping on the spikes in the first corridor, or perhaps falling into the pit trap on the crossing corridor, and it really didn't matter. What mattered was that the screams were louder, and it sounded like there were more of them.

Then they reached the left turn. Matt took one last glance back down the hall and saw nothing. Sidling along the walls they moved north, then turned left, then north again, and right. Four more twists completed a double S-curve that now had them heading west, back the way they'd come. The northern wall still ran high above their heads, but he could see the dark brown of the natural cavern surface coming down to meet it.

"We're at the northern edge of the labyrinth," Eddie whispered.

"Does that mean anything?" Matt asked.

"I don't know. The stories are very vague about how long Theseus wandered in the labyrinth until he found the Minotaur. And they don't really give any directions." He shrugged. "So it might not mean anything with regards to that."

"Weren't you wanting to find the northern edge?" Tory asked gently.

"Yeah, because I thought it might lead us behind that broken-down palace we saw." His smooth brow furrowed. "But I don't think we've gone anywhere near far enough north since we got into the labyrinth. A lot of east and west, but probably not far enough to be near the palace."

The moans and groans came again, much louder this time.

"They have to be past the traps by now," Rich said, and he sounded nervous.

"I think you're right," Elizabeth said.

"Any chance they could have gotten ahead of us?" Matt asked nervously.

"Maybe, I don't know," the cop answered. "We never fully checked out the area where we saw those two wandering."

"I think we've done gone past that spot," Rich said.

"Maybe, but I don't really want to assume anything," Zach said.

And then they reached a short turn left, heading south, which immediately zigged back to the west, and there was an opening in the south wall. Still sliding along the gray stone, unwilling to risk themselves in the middle of the corridor, they paused in front of the opening. Looking through the arch, Matt could see a square room, with some kind of discoloration in the middle of the floor. Directly across from them was another arch, with another corridor running east and west outside of it.

THE DUNGEON

He closed his eyes, mentally trying to piece together the puzzle in front of him. Picturing the turns they'd taken, the distance they'd traveled, he said, "I think that's the room with the teeth in the middle. But they're gone."

Just then, another scream sounded, this one seeming to come from across the square room. Immediately after, a form darted past the opening. In the brief glimpse, Matt saw flapping flayed rags and long, unkempt hair.

"If that's the teeth room, he'll be catching up behind us soon," Zack said.

Perhaps the Freaker heard their voices or registered their presence in his peripheral vision even as he ran past the doorway, because suddenly he was back, swinging into the room and bracing strong arms in the doorway. From that distance, looking at each other across the room, Matt couldn't smell the crazed man, but his mind began preparing him to deal with his stench, nonetheless. Wide and wild eyes seemed to roll crazily as the man-thing moved his head left and right, up and down, almost as though he'd lost control of his extraocular muscles and had to move his head to focus his vision.

"Shit! Here he comes!" Elizabeth said, stepping away from the wall. Both Matt and Zack stepped up beside her, ready to meet the crazy man's charge.

The ragged man lunged toward them, propelling himself with his arms, crossing a quarter of the distance in one step. His next step brought him to the discolored, bisecting line in the floor, where Matt was certain the stalagmites had been when they passed this room from the other side.

The man never made a third step. As fast as thought, the stalactites shot down from the ceiling, the stalagmites rose up from the ground, and the crazy man's body was torn in two, shredded at the waist, so that his torso dropped on their side of the dividing line, while his legs twitched feebly once or twice on the other.

Tory screamed, startling Matt, but it was nowhere near as disturbing as the calls that answered her, six, ten, maybe a dozen other voices rising from the halls across from them.

"We need to keep moving," Zachary said, and no one argued.

A few more steps west led them to a short jog north, then back to the east, north, then west, another S-curve with longer horizontal lines.

"What if this is a dead end?" Rich asked as they turned west, once again seeming to be tracing the far northern wall of the labyrinth.

Ahead of them, the oil lamps and burning trenches of firelight came together along the top of the wall facing them, and Matt had a few seconds to wonder if Rich hadn't just jinxed them, that they actually were racing toward a dead end, with nowhere to go, trapped by the vagaries of this damned maze and the crazy Freakers rushing up from behind them.

"It's a door," Elizabeth said, and Matt saw that it was. In the middle of the wall was one of those wood-slatted, iron-bound doors, so familiar to them from the dungeon above.

"Wow! It looks really old," Eddie said, moving up to it.

"So help me, if I hear that computer voice say something, I'm gonna scream," Tory said.

"Door probably won't even open," Rich said.

Eddie pushed on it, and it opened.

CHAPTER 40

Tory

Tory regretted screaming, acutely aware that her sudden explosion of noise might be the very thing that drew more of those crazy men after them. She regretted it, but she hadn't been able to stop it. Considering all that they'd been through so far, she thought she'd held it together pretty well. But the sheer, brutal suddenness of that man's death had caught her completely by surprise. It was scary enough when he came rushing toward them, but she hadn't been worried then, not with the cop and the big football player, and even the redhead, all ready to protect her and Eddie. But then came the teeth—she didn't care if they were technically stalactites and stalagmites, they looked like teeth, and that's how she was going to think of them—fast as lightning, slamming together, cutting the man in half, showering the room on both sides with blood and viscera.

She was slightly amazed that she hadn't puked.

But that was behind them, and now, before them, was this room.

It was smaller than the room with the—*don't think about the teeth*—rock formations meeting in the middle, more of a square, maybe fifteen feet on a side. Aside from the door they'd come through, there was another door directly across the way. None of the oil lamps ran into it, so they'd powered up their headlamps again, the combined light of six low-power flashlights more than enough to illuminate the space.

Truth be told, there wasn't much to see. The walls continued the bland gray motif, and there wasn't any furniture to speak of. There were no tables, no chairs, no bookshelves with rotting, ancient scrolls waited to be discovered. The only things of interest were a large, discolored area in the center of the room, roughly rectangular, maybe eight feet by five or six feet, and what appeared to be a large tusk, like from a rhinoceros or—

"It's a bull's horn," Eddie said, almost reverently, squatting down beside the curved, pointed piece of bone. It was only about six inches long but had obviously been broken through some trauma. The non-pointed end was ragged and uneven, much wider than the tip. It was easy to imagine it much longer, much wider, when it had been attached.

"You can't possibly know that for sure," Rich said, moving toward where Eddie knelt.

"It makes sense, though, doesn't it?" the younger man said. "Look at that dark area." He pointed at the darker stone in the center. "Doesn't it look like a rectangle to you? Maybe once that piece of floor was covered with straw or whatever people slept on back then. It's all decayed now, but it left a stain."

"So why would one of his horns be here then?" Rich asked.

"Maybe it got chopped off in the fight with Theseus," Eddie reasoned. "Many versions of the story say that Theseus came upon the Minotaur while he slept. Several even make it a point to say that if he hadn't, he wouldn't have been able to kill the beast."

"So you're saying that the Minotaur was killed right here in this room?" Tory asked, awed in spite of the fact that she didn't really believe any of the Greek myths.

Eddie nodded.

More screams sounded outside the room, and now it was clear that the noises were only coming from the east side.

"They haven't caught up to us yet," Zack said from his place by the eastern door, back braced against it to keep it from opening, "but they're coming closer."

"Okay then," Rich said, "let's keep moving."

As they moved to the west side of the room, Rich already pulling the door open, Tory noticed that no one was willing to step on the dark-stained area. Maybe she wasn't the only one not buying the idea that it was discolored because it once held a sleeping pallet. To her, it looked about the same color as the rocks had in the teeth room, and she had no intention of being impaled because she stepped in the wrong place.

"If the horn's here, where's the rest of his body?" Matt asked.

Eddie shrugged, fiddling with the straps of his backpack as he moved to join them by the door. "I don't know," he said, finally managing to get his pack on his back. "The stories say Theseus came upon the Minotaur sleeping, and they fought. There's no real description of the fight itself or how long it took. Then it says Theseus slew the Minotaur, cut off his head, and followed his unwound yarn back to the entrance."

Tory squeezed up behind them as they moved out of the room. Somehow, even though the oil lamps had not run into the sleeping den, they continued beyond it. A long wail sounded behind them, low enough in volume that she wasn't yet worried about someone leaping out and grabbing them. More interesting was a new sound, a rhythmic clicking and swishing.

"Is it just me, or does that sound like a huge metronome?" Matt asked.

"I don't know what it is," Zachary answered, "but I suppose we're going to find out soon enough."

Taking the lead, the cop led them west, still hugging a wall, though there hadn't been any sign of a trap since the pit. And the jaws, she amended. Can't forget the jaws.

Even though there hadn't been any traps that directly threatened them since the…place where DeShaun died, they still hugged the wall, moving fast but not nearly as fast as they could if they just ran.

The corridor turned right, heading north, and—

"Holy shit!" Matt cried. "No way! No effing way!"

The corridor moved north and the ceiling lowered, no longer ten or twelve feet high, now maybe just a little taller than Rich. The walls changed, gray, worked stone giving way to a dark, reddish brown rock, a much more natural tunnel that seemed to wind a little, small shifts left and right, but generally running fairly straight. The oil lamps stopped where the tunnel began, but enough light remained to show Tory what it was that had Matt suddenly cursing like a sailor.

"Sorry, Eddie," the accountant said. "Just surprised."

"It's okay, it's really cool!" Eddie replied.

Cool was not how Tory described it. Horrifying, terrifying, impossible. Those words made more sense.

The passage ahead was lined with great double-bladed axes, or maybe sickles—she wasn't that up on her ancient Greek weaponry—that swung back and forth from their handles like pendulums.

"Now we know what that sound is," Zack said.

How the hell can he sound so calm? Tory wondered.

There appeared to be four or five of the swinging blades, each one two or three feet beyond the one before. It was hard to be sure.

THE DUNGEON

"Okay," Zachary said, "Rich, if you'll go first, secure the area, I'll stay back here and hold the rear. I'll keep my Nightstick held up high and pointed your way. You do the same back at us. Let's give everyone as much light as we can."

"On it," the big man said.

There was a bloom of light as Zachary turned on his flashlight, and now Tory could clearly see the death trap that lay before them. Six blades, not four or five, swinging left and right, some moving faster than others, none of them in sync. Each time the heavy blades swung across the corridor they created the swooshing sound. The space between them didn't look equal either, but she couldn't be sure without getting closer. And she wasn't sure she wanted to do that.

Rich had no such qualms. He walked up to the first blade, watched it swing pass once, twice, then darted through as the blade cleared the passage, moving right. Matt and Eddie cheered, but Tory just held her breath. Rich seemed to take only one step before he was up near the second blade. Again he waited, rocking forward and back at the waist, timing the swing, then stepped through.

"Get ready, Eddie," Zachary said. "As soon as he's through, you're going next."

"Right on," Eddie said. Tory closed her eyes, unable to watch any more. She knew they had to do this, knew that it was positively crazy that here, now, at this time, would come something that she couldn't face. She couldn't let her fear infect anyone else. A few more cheers sounded.

"All right," Rich called. "I'm through." Tory opened her eyes as a second flashlight flared to life, shining back along the corridor, aimed high so as not to blind them. "Remember to allow room for your backpacks when you go through. Don't stop too soon," he added.

"You might want to try carrying it in front," Zachary suggested, but Eddie was already moving. Tory held her breath, not daring to blink, as he stepped through one, then the second, then, amazingly, the next three seemingly without stopping. He paused just a moment before clearing the sixth.

"Eddie's through," Rich called.

"Elizabeth?" Zachary said.

"No way, I'm going when you go."

"Okay then, Matt."

"Man, I've wanted to do something like this ever since I watched Indiana Jones," the accountant said. Like Eddie, he actually seemed to be having fun. The long-legged man made a few fast steps, and just like that, he was through.

"Okay, Tory, you're up," Elizabeth said.

Tory swallowed hard, trying to force her fear down. She couldn't understand why this was affecting her so badly. None of the other traps had, but those all had the potential to be instantaneous. This would all depend on her timing. What if she wasn't fast enough?

"Go on, Tory," Zachary said gently. "It's not difficult. Just wait till one passes and move through it."

"Come on, Ms. Tory!" Eddie called.

Just step through. She could do this.

Firming her resolve—she would do it, she needed to stay near Eddie, look after him—she stepped up to the first swinging blade. Idly, she wondered what force kept it moving. It certainly didn't seem to be slowing down, just swinging back and forth, back and forth, an eternity of motion trapped in a dingy tunnel under the island of Crete.

Behind her came another set of those inhuman screams, and they were close, much closer than they'd been.

"You need to go now!" Elizabeth said, and Tory swallowed again, watched, felt her air stirred by the air of the blade's passing, and took a long step forward.

She'd done it! She'd gotten past the first one!

She stepped up to the second axe blade, which seemed a little smaller, swinging a little higher and maybe a little faster, and tried to time its back and forth. Did it take longer to go right, or left?

The screams again, and this time one of them was Elizabeth's voice!

She stopped, turning, and saw the redhead and the cop straining, trying to hold the door shut as an unknown number of those crazy things tried to push it open.

"Come on!" Eddie urged.

She turned back around, watched for a second, and jumped through.

Two down, four to go.

"Ms. Tory, listen to me," Rich said, and his voice was so soft, so mellow. "Step up to the next blade... that's it, now close your eyes."

"What?" she asked.

"The next three have to be done in succession," he said, and she looked and saw that he was right. Separated by only a foot, they swung left to right in almost perfect unison, except that the closest axe was always a little ahead of the second closest, which was ahead of the third.

"Close your eyes, and when I say go, you run forward."

"What about the last one?" she asked, but even as she asked it, she could see there were several feet of rock after the fifth blade and before the sixth, a pure mile of space when compared to the space between blades three and five.

"You move when I say move and stop when I say stop, okay?" Rich said.

"I...okay."

"And no looking back. You let Ms. Liz and Mr. Zachary handle their business, and you and me, we'll handle ours."

She nodded, not trusting herself to speak. If her heart had ever raced before, now it was hammering, a drumroll that she could feel pulsing in her neck, in her temples.

"Get ready," he said.

He won't let me die, she thought. *He's too good a man for that.* She tried to steady herself, bracing one foot behind the other. She closed her eyes. She could still hear the struggle behind her as the cop and the redhead tried to hold back what might be a horde of crazy people, could still feel the passing of the blades in front of her. She waited, anticipating the order to move based on the air coming off the passing axe, so when he said, "Go," she was ready. She stepped forward once, twice, three steps, then four, and finally five, and his soft voice said, "Stop."

Tory opened her eyes, seeing the kind face of the tall black man just a few feet in front of her, only the sixth blade separating them.

The final blade was different, only swinging from left to right.

How is that possible? she wondered idly.

"It's swinging a full circle," Eddie said, and that made sense, like the pirate ship rides in the amusement park, that might start off like a pendulum, but eventually worked up to a full three hundred sixty degree vertical turn, often stopping in the midpoint, holding people upside down just long enough for all their pocket change to fall to the ground under the ride.

THE DUNGEON

She watched and waited for a second and stepped through just as she heard Zachary and Elizabeth screaming behind them to move, get moving, run.

She started to turn to look, but Rich grabbed her by the arm and kept her facing north. Eddie grabbed her other arm and started to run, pulling her. Her choice was clear. Go with Eddie or stay and help.

She went with Eddie.

CHAPTER 41

Zachary

"She's almost through," Elizabeth said, but all Zack could do was grunt. She was facing out, away from the door, keeping tabs on Tory as she navigated the swinging axes. He was facing forward, hands against the door at the midline near the jamb, forearms locked, back locked, legs braced and straining. The pounding on the other side of the wood vibrated into him, shaking every muscle. The inhuman screeches and screams drove a spear into his head, hardly muted at all by the wooden barrier.

"How long between swings?" he asked. He shouted the words, really, wanting to make sure he was heard over the din from the other side.

"Only about three seconds," Liz said.

"Okay, so we'll have to cut this close. Go as soon as you can and shout when you're past the second axe. But don't stop."

"You can't expect me to leave you," she shouted back. "I—"

Whatever else she started to say ended up in a grunt, as a renewed surge against the door inched it open, pushing them back. *Give me shoes with some tread*, he thought desperately, digging in with the toes of his boots, trying to hold the door a moment longer.

A nasty, dirty hand managed to slip through the narrow gap, broken fingernails raking the air. The door vibrated, another inarticulate cry of rage, or need, or want, sending shivers up his spine. God, the person making that noise must have their mouth pressed into the gap. Then Elizabeth leaned away and slammed herself backward, once, then again, and he pushed, and somehow, they managed to close it again.

"Now! Go now!" he shouted.

He looked over at her, saw those big, brown eyes looking back at him, and knew what she wanted to say, what maybe she had tried to say, before the door came open. She smiled at him, nodded, then ran off. Had he ever thought her face too narrow, her lips too thin, to be beautiful?

No. He couldn't waste energy thinking about her like that. He needed to give her time, maybe only a few seconds, but even that might be enough for them to get away. He counted two, then three Mississippis, felt another brief surge at the door, which somehow he held on against, then he heard her shout, "I'm through. Come on!"

There's no way I can get ahead of them, he thought. But he had to try. He held on against one more surge, and as he felt it subside, he pushed off from the door, twisting, already breaking into a run.

Three seconds, she'd said. That's how long it took the first axe to go from one side to the other, then start back. He watched it as he ran, stuttered his steps as he came, heard the door burst open behind him but he was already at the first axe and it had just swept past going to left to right and he raced through, never breaking stride.

The screams of the Freakers filled the tunnel, but he couldn't turn to look, because he was at the second axe. He paused for a split second, then darted through. At the far end, the bright light that showed where Rich waited had been joined by a second light, much brighter, arcing through the dark tunnel. It wasn't aimed at the axes, or at him, however. It appeared to be directed at the things behind him, perhaps trying to blind them.

He risked a quick glance back just as the first Freaker raced at the axe. The beam of light flashed into its face and it stopped, hands going up to its eyes, trying to block the light. It managed to get its arms up just as the swinging axe came back across, striking it somewhere low on the torso, sending its broken body flying sideways, where it collided with the side of the tunnel. The axe never slowed, continuing its arc, driven by some unknown and unknowable mechanism that never allowed it to lose momentum, never allowed it to alter its speed or trajectory.

Seeing more forms coming behind the first, herky-jerky in their spastic movements but somehow able to anticipate and navigate the swinging blades, Zack spun back around and raced up to the third axe, with the fourth and fifth lined up immediately behind. He watched through one pass, and was about to lunge, when a shouted "Look out!" by Liz had him spinning, barely avoiding the reaching talons of another crazy man.

Years of practice and training kicked in, and he reached up with both hands, securing a hold on the Freaker's left wrist and upper arm. Ducking, turning left, he used the man's own momentum to pull him over his back, flipping him over and to the ground just as the threesome of blades started their next pass.

Unhurt, not even appearing stunned, the man tried to rise to his knees. The first blade decapitated him. His body collapsed, but even flat on his stomach, the following blades crossed low enough that the second one scored him across his back, while the third nearly took his feet off at the Achilles' tendons.

THE DUNGEON

Zachary closed his eyes as the blades did their work, feeling the initial spray of hot arterial blood paint his face and shirt. Opening them, he saw the spray had become a river, pouring out of the man's neck. He looked up and saw Liz still moving her Nightstick back and forth, trying to distract the men behind him.

The blades swept back across, further cutting the dead man, and Zachary raced forward, clearing the three blades.

One more to go.

"They're still coming, man," Rich said. "I see five, no, six, already out of the room, coming fast."

Another scream sounded, though this one had a gurgling quality to it, like someone trying to speak with a mouthful of water or blood.

"Five now," Liz said. "The second one pushed the first one into one of the blades."

Zack had to trust their word. He tried to tune out the incoherent wails that filled the narrow tunnel with sound, concentrating on the last blade, which always passed in the same direction. He lunged through as it came by, and immediately the other two joined him in racing north, no longer worried about hugging one wall or the other, just trying to put some distance between themselves and the pursuing horde.

"Where do you think they all came from?" Rich asked.

"Above, I guess," he said, trying not to think too hard about what it might mean. Had they managed to reopen the steel door that Brian closed? And why send these things first? Why not an armed contingent of security personnel? It was obvious they had access to firearms.

"There has to be something we're missing," Liz said. "Something about this place that's so bad, they wouldn't send security after us."

Zachary was surprised at her near echo of his thoughts but appreciated her ability to grasp the situation.

"These traps are dangerous," Rich said, thinking.

They came to a sharp right turn, which opened up into a small circular room, no more than five feet in any direction. Eddie, Tory, and Matt waited for them, anxiously darting looks back at them, then to the east.

"Look out there, man," Matt said.

"We don't have much time to look," Rich said. "Those things are right behind us."

Zachary went to look, Elizabeth at his side.

To the east, the small room fed through a very short tunnel, then opened up into a large, circular arena. From the ground level, where they were, they could see rows of concentric circular seating areas, rising in tiers, up and up, almost too far for their Nightsticks to reach. There was something wrong with the benches, though it was hard to tell for certain what it was. To Zachary, they didn't all seem to run the right direction, as though there were perpendicular segments, ninety-degree angles at the ends of some of the rows, which didn't make sense. If you thought of this as an arena, or as any other kind of spectator locations, you'd want all the seating to face toward the center.

"Look out there," Liz breathed. "Is that a giant hole?"

The center. Where one might expect a raised stage, or pulpit, or some kind of scoring mechanism or goal, there was nothing, just a deep blackness that seemed to draw the light from their Nightsticks, sucking it in and giving nothing back.

"Shit! Here they come!" Rich shouted from behind them, and suddenly everyone was rushing past, out the tunnel and into the circular area.

Zachary turned back in time to see Rich deal a devastating kick to a crazy man, knocking him back and down, causing two or three others to trip over him. Rich turned and raced for the exit. Zachary and Elizabeth turned too, hurrying out into the open area.

"Make for the high ground," he yelled. "Look for an exit."

The floor of the arena was more brown rock, and he could see some of the tiered areas looked to be made of the same, though cut and carved in gentle slopes that should allow for easy climbing. Only the first level of seats would require a jump and scramble, as they were about four feet off the floor.

The room or cavern was absolutely huge, the full scope unable to be appreciated from the side room where they'd gathered. Even with five Nightsticks shining around, jerking beams moving up and down as arms pumped and legs churned, it was impossible to fully grasp the entirety of the area. Only Tory, running desperately to keep up with Eddie, did not have a light, though the light of her headlamp still served to provide some illumination.

Entering from one side as they had, everyone immediately cut to the right, cutting a wide berth around the deep darkness in the center of the arena floor, angling for the four-foot wall that would give them access to the higher tiers. Fussing with his handheld light, Zachary switched it to full power and aimed it across the floor. Though he couldn't be certain, it appeared as though the retaining wall went all the way around, with only the opening they'd come through as an egress point. Hopefully, there was another way out in the upper levels.

Loud moans, wails, screams, and wordless cries echoed from behind them. Zachary risked a look back and saw at least a dozen, perhaps more, of the frenzied men chasing them. There might be women as well, but so far he hadn't seen any. In the dark cavern, he knew those in his group were easily followed targets for the Freakers, who probably couldn't see anything but them, with those bright flares in hand, but the idea of dousing their lights was quickly discarded. They needed to be able to see to get away.

As first Matt, then Rich and Eddie reached the nearest side, quickly scrambling up, a new explosion of sound reached them, a resounding crash and boom that shook the cavern floor, making Zack stumble. He turned his flashlight to the left, seeking the source of the sound, which continued beyond the initial crash, a resonant rumbling like thunder. His eyes widened when he saw a large, round…something…rolling and bouncing along the upper tiers far across the arena.

Then Tory reached the wall, jumped and had just managed to pull herself up, when another crash sounded, this time coming from far up to the right. The rumble and shaking dislodged her, and she slipped back to the ground.

"There's another one," Liz said, panting slightly.

They caught up with Tory, who had managed to gain access to the first tier of seating on her second try. She immediately turned to the side, short legs pumping as she sought higher ground, while Zack and Liz jumped and clambered up.

The men chasing them were a little farther behind, but still coming fast. It might have something to do with their collective inability to fully commit to chasing them, rather than any advantage they had in speed. Even now, with darkness all around and the only light being carried by their targets, the crazed men still swung their arms wildly, flailing really, which kept them from maximizing their speed.

THE DUNGEON

As Zack and Liz gained their feet, another series of crashes and booms rattled the arena. The vibrations were near continuous, making the flooring feel less than stable. Taking a look around, Zack could now understand why he'd thought the seating was strange. Those weren't benches rising off the floor, they were concrete runners, and this wasn't an arena. It was a massive, real-life marble maze game, like one of those handheld children's toys where the player tries to guide a marble along a series of plastic routes in order to get it into one or multiple holes, depending upon the rules of the game. The flooring up here had a slight slant to it, all canted toward the center. The reason some of the runners were set perpendicular to the concentric rings was perhaps to provide a momentary shelter to people trapped within the maze, or perhaps just to better guide the rolling boulders along a predetermined path.

"Zachary, come on!" Elizabeth yelled at him, obviously surprised to find that he'd stopped, that he was shining his light all around.

He knew he couldn't stand still for long; the leading crazy men would be climbing up after them any second, but he needed to understand.

There were four massive boulders in play. He didn't know where they'd dropped from and couldn't begin to understand the mechanism by which they'd been released or how they might be returned for reuse. After seeing the boulder in the first passageway roll first one way, then another, the trap resetting several times, he no longer had any doubts as to what was possible within the labyrinth. Whether god-inspired or not, the mythical engineer, Daedalus, had certainly earned his reputation as a mastermind.

The boulders had begun at the top tier, but were following the slope, guided by the concrete runners, and would soon be falling into the lower tiers. The nearest boulder, almost directly to the right of where they'd come in, was following a route that paralleled Tory's frantic running, and might soon intersect her path if she couldn't get ahead of it.

Elizabeth was beside him again, reaching for him, grabbing his arm, and he let her lead him, staying on the lower tier, running near the edge of the wall, heading for the far end of the arena.

"Tory, come on!" Eddie called from ahead of them.

"You got two of them behind you," Matt yelled, though Zack couldn't tell who he was yelling at. He was almost halfway across the length of the arena, at least thirty yards ahead of them.

Zack risked a glance behind them, seeing that two of the Freakers had indeed made the lower tier and were coming after them. He glanced right and up, saw a boulder dropping from one tier to the next, but it was being guided away from them. Still watching, he looked ahead along its path and saw—

"Tory, jump down!" he yelled.

The shorter woman was a good ways behind them, having spent more time climbing than focusing on lateral motion. He didn't know what she could see or how much she could see. She'd never unpacked a Nightstick and was relying solely on the lesser light of her headlamp. Despite the calls and cries of the Freakers, she had to be able to hear the boulders and must have looked up and seen them. Even with her lesser light, she had to be able to see them.

But it appeared that she couldn't. The boulder which had been pacing her reached an opening in its runners and dropped to the second tier. Tory had remained on the third tier and was making her way toward them, but the boulder was ahead of her, already coming to another break and dropping, maybe fifteen feet in front, and rolling back toward her.

"Tory!" Eddie screamed again, and she must have looked up, must have seen the boulder coming at her, because she jumped down a tier, maybe halfway back to the lowest level. Rather, she tried to jump down a level. Her leading foot didn't quite get high enough, and she tumbled, one second spotlighted by Zack's Nightstick, the next a falling, rolling shadow that he tried desperately to find again.

The boulder kept rolling, passing where she had been, then continuing on. Scanning around, looking for her, Zachary noticed that each of the boulders seemed to be consigned to a specific quarter of the arena. The next closest boulder was between them and the far end, still only at the second or third tier from the top, currently rolling away from them. The other two were across the sunken center, likewise winding their way left and right, occasionally dropping to a lower segment.

Scrambling, Elizabeth took off, rushing back and up, heading for Tory. Behind them, the two crazy men, apparently focusing on the closest moving target, had stopped coming for Zachary and were instead climbing also.

"Shit!" Zachary swore, beginning to move as well, climbing, running, angling to try to cut off the two Freakers before they could converge on the women. Far ahead of them, the boulder dropped another tier, continued moving away for a few feet, but then came up against one of the ninety degree stops, which it struck, rebounded from, and began rolling the other direction.

There must be other variations in the flooring, slight changes in elevation, that enabled such large, moving objects to reverse direction once their inertia was absorbed by a barrier.

"More are climbing up!" Rich shouted, his deep voice audible even over the rumbling and screaming.

Zack risked a look over his shoulder, confirming what the big man said. At least five or six of the ragged men were scrambling up to the lowest tier, coming over the lip at various points between where they'd begun, and the midway point. His look also showed the other three men rushing back toward them. Matt had gotten the farthest, and he was waving his Nightstick frantically.

Zack couldn't wait to see what the accountant wanted. Jumping another riser, he aimed for the midpoint between the two men who chased the redhead, closing fast. They were almost at Elizabeth, who he was able to track because of the flashlight in her hands. A dimmer glow on the ground might be Tory, but he only had eyes for Liz.

Putting on a burst of speed, he climbed over one more riser and crashed between the two crazies, stretching his arms out, trying to tackle both. But either he misjudged the distance between them—understandable given the lighting—or the lead man put on a sudden burst of speed, for he only felt contact with his right arm. Even as he found himself suddenly grappling a skinny frame with far more strength than should be possible, he tried to call out a warning.

A sudden scream made him pivot, literally picking up and carrying his opponent in a half-circle, to see Elizabeth swinging, each fist striking somewhere on the man facing her. And there was Tory, struggling to her feet, backpedaling from the confrontation. The scream wasn't one of fury, however, but of warning. Even as Liz screamed again, driving a foot into the midsection of the man facing her, forcing him backward over a riser, where he landed head first and did not rise, the oncoming boulder struck Tory from behind, launching her forward and sideways, so that she tumbled down several risers, coming to rest near one of the lower tiers.

Screaming himself, Zachary pushed with everything he had, driving the filthy man up a foot or two, then wrenching him around and tossing him to roll down the sloped tiers. He immediately began running for where he'd seen Tory fall, and he could see Liz coming down as well, running recklessly, jumping risers and downed Freakers alike, but another one that had just gained the lowest riser lunged for Tory, apparently attracted to her still-glowing headlamp. Before anyone could reach her, the crazed man fell upon her, covering her face with his.

Zack didn't even know if she was still alive. She never screamed at the new insult, didn't make a sound. He saw again the hit, how she'd been thrown by the impact. What would that do to a human body, to be struck by something so massive, hit so hard that the body is thrown, rather than simply run over.

The others caught up as well, Richard holding back Eddie, who screamed Tory's name again and tried to get to her. Matt surged forward, joining Zachary in reaching down, grabbing hold of whatever part of the man they could, wrenching him off of her.

In the brief flashes of light from the swinging Nightsticks, seen in glimpses as he and Matt wrestled the struggling man back and away, finally pushing him over the wall and down to the floor, Zack saw blood, a nose both broken and bitten. Most tellingly, her head lay cocked at an unnatural angle relative to the neck.

Another thud sounded, the boulder nearest them falling another level, now only two tiers above them.

"Eddie, we gotta move," Rich said, the big man using his great size to force the young man back.

Liz was sobbing openly, wanting to reach down to help the other woman, but Zachary and Matt were there, gently forcing her back.

"She's gone," Zack said, "her neck's broken."

"The exit's at the top over at the other end," Matt gasped.

"That rock's getting closer, and more of those guys are coming," Rich said over Eddie's cries.

Somehow, they got Liz moving again, pushing her along the lower level. Rich lowered a shoulder into the midsection of the next Freaker that came too close, easily throwing him backward and to the ground. Moving, climbing, unsure how many were still behind them, the five moved away from the body of their friend, got above the second boulder, and raced for the questionable safety of the exit tunnel.

Chapter 42

Elizabeth

She couldn't believe it. Tory was gone. Just like that, and not even from one of those lunatics that were chasing them, just another victim of this twisted, crazy maze. Even now, running across the huge, bowl-shaped arena, with more and more of the psychos climbing up after them, she wasn't sure if any of them were going to survive.

They could fight, like they'd done before, if the odds were better. But there had to be twenty or thirty of them back there now. That they were as likely to grab onto each other as focus on catching them was probably the only reason they were still alive.

Climbing the tiers, avoiding the last huge boulder, which finally crashed down to the center of the arena, apparently landing on a few of the Freakers, she did her best to will the tears from her eyes. She needed to be able to see, needed to be able to think.

Thankfully, that latter was easier now. She was alone inside her own mind for the first time since she was a teenager. Alone, but not alone. She was forging friendships with the people around her, maybe something more, something surprising, with the gentle policeman who ran near her. And this damned place, those damned people, were intent on taking it away.

"Up here." Matt panted, climbing the last riser, every one of them just one misstep away from sharing

Tory's fate. One trip, one stumble, and those things would be on them, clawing, biting. She growled away her fear, summoning up the anger she used to use to focus her thoughts through the distracting voices. Now it gave her strength, helped her to banish the fears and worries and concentrate on just running, keep moving, jump that riser, one foot at a time, one after the other.

Rich and Eddie were at the opening, a near identical match to the short tunnel that led them into the arena from the other side. Everyone had their Nightsticks in hand, bright streaks of light washing out the walls closing around them, so everything looked gray and dingy, almost like stepping into a black and white movie.

They moved through the short tunnel and were back in a corridor, gray stone, designed and shaped by man, running off to the left and right, oil lamps and trenchers lining the walls, burning with a flickering firelight.

They were back in the labyrinth.

It was so unexpected, so absolutely *unfair* that she felt like screaming. Not that she would even be able to hear herself with those crazy people chasing them, ragged voices echoing behind them, but quickly growing louder.

"Which way?" Eddie asked, breathless.

"We don't have time to play it safe," Rich said.

"Those things are going to stay after us as long as they can see us," Matt added, "so we need to move."

Zachary looked at her, a quick glance that told her more than words could. He was afraid of making a bad choice. But as far as she could see, there weren't really any good choices. "Right," she said, nodding at him.

"Right," he agreed, and they turned right.

"I wish we knew which way we were going," Matt mumbled.

"'Cause that would help, how?" Rich asked.

No pits opened beneath them, and there was a left turn coming up. Maybe they could get around it before the first of the men chasing them made the turn into the corridor and saw them.

"I remember something about mazes," Eddie said, but before he could continue his thought, the corridor behind them filled with the sounds of stamping feet and hoarse cries. So much for her hope that they could lose them at the first turn.

"If you pick a wall," Eddie said, continuing his previous thought, "and stick with it, even if you hit dead ends, you'll eventually get all the way through the maze."

They reached the end and turned and found themselves facing another immediate left turn, which became a right turn that offered another immediate right or a second choice, a right just a few feet past the first. Without a thought, Zachary and Elizabeth took the first right, then a left, and there, in front of them, was another of those pits with metal spikes. For once, with no boulder behind them, with everyone focused, there was no hesitation and no delay. Almost without breaking stride, the five of them hurdled the pit and kept moving.

Past the pit the tunnel ran straight for about fifty feet, with only a single doorway opening to the left.

"That whole right wall thing might be true," Rich said, "but if we hit a dead end, we're gonna be backtracking through a lot of pissed off crazy people."

"Then let's hope we don't hit a dead end," Matt said.

More screams behind them, more yells. Elizabeth risked a look back just in time to see the lead runner round the corner behind them. He gave a louder scream, almost the baying of a hound as it picked up the scent of its prey, or like one of those infected viral freaks in *28 Days Later*. She remembered being scared to death by the way those monsters moved in that movie. Go see a movie about a zombie apocalypse? Sure. What's scary about a bunch of dead guys shambling, shuffling, arms outstretched in classic Romero style? But not those zombies. They ran, jumped, actually seemed to hunt for the survivors, and that freaked out a younger Lizzy so much that she slept with a light on in her bedroom closet for weeks afterward.

The runner screamed again, and two more crazies showed up behind him, not stopping. They shoved, and the first one fell forward into the pit, his scream cut suddenly short. The two cleared the trap, jumping over the fallen Freaker, voices raised as they continued the pursuit.

Liz was beginning to feel the strain of the non-stop fear, the constant running. She wasn't accustomed to such sustained activity. Her legs ached, and each breath came hot and harsh. But she'd seen what one of those things did to Tory's face. If adrenaline and fear suddenly became insufficient to sustain her, then anger would. She had plenty of practice with that.

Ahead was the left-sided doorway, and immediately beyond it a left turn. A brief glance in passing through the door showed what looked like a short passage, dead ends on both sides, and then they turned left, and ahead was another long straightaway. Matt dropped back from his position near the front of the group, his attention focused on something in his hands. Then he put on a burst of speed to catch back up with them.

"North," he gasped. "We're going north now."

Still running, Liz had a moment to wonder at something. Something had changed, but she couldn't define it, didn't remember when it had happened. It was like waking up in a hot bedroom, soaked in sweat.

THE DUNGEON

You don't know when the heat came on or why it got too hot. But even that wasn't quite right, because in that example, at least you knew what had changed, even if you didn't know when.

"Is it just me," Rich said, puffing, "or does everything look a little…cleaner?"

"I was thinking newer," Eddie said, and *he* didn't even sound winded.

"Newer," Zachary agreed, puffing like she was, and why that should make her feel better, she didn't know. "Cleaner. Fires brighter. Less smoke."

She supposed that was what she'd noticed. This whole area felt different, less old, like the weight of ages wasn't bearing down on them, turning the oil rancid, the stones darker. Even the spikes in the pit trap had less a look of great age, not gleaming, but certainly brighter than what they'd seen in other parts of the labyrinth. The air was also cleaner. Part of that was because the oil didn't give off so much smoke, but not all. It actually smelled fresher, newer.

Another dozen pounding steps, the five of them grouped up, hands linked almost in a wedge formation, a term barely remembered from an armchair-quarterback boyfriend complaining about some football rule change that made the iconic formation illegal. Yet here they were, charging north, praying that the floor wouldn't open up beneath them, that spikes wouldn't shoot out of the wall, or that another boulder wouldn't drop on their heads, sucking air so loudly that it almost drowned out the sounds made by their pursuers.

She risked a glimpse over her shoulder, saw that two or three of those things had made the turn into their hallway. She had no idea how many more were behind them.

"They're still...back...there." She gasped, whipping her head to face forward. The long hallway was coming to an end, another left turn up ahead.

"Good," Matt said. "I'd hate...to think...we lost them." He tried on a smile. It looked ghastly, but it still almost got a laugh out of her.

Then they turned left, and fifteen feet later, left again. Then came a right, and another right.

"Another S," Rich said.

"Heading...west...now." Matt panted.

"Not for long," Eddie pointed out. A break in the left-hand wall showed a large room, square, with a brown stripe running along its center. She didn't want to remember seeing one of those crazy people torn apart by rock teeth, as floor and ceiling, stalagmite and stalactite, came together, but she couldn't banish the image either.

Then they turned right again.

"I smell—" Eddie said.

Another right.

"Flowers?"

A quick left.

They dashed through an opening into a small room. There were stone tables to either side, what looked like bookshelves to the right behind the table, except that the shelves were actually small squares, almost like the sections in a wine rack, but not tilted in diamond formations. Some of the sections had scrolls in them, or what looked like scrolls, rolls of parchment of some kind, maybe blueprints. Others held small items, pieces of rock, carved figurines. The table on the left had some kind of paper spread out over it, images too faded by time to truly comprehend covering its surface. Maybe it had been a map, or a portrait.

Then they were through the room, out the far side, and the walls were no longer worked walls made by hand, no longer gray, shaped stone but just a deep brown stone the color of earth. The ceiling lowered again, like it had before they reached the swinging axes, but no axes were present here. Just a stone tunnel illuminated by their lights; the burning oil lamps ended with the room. And it was sloped, none too gently either. Their way forward became a staggering lurch upward as the tunnel climbed and curved.

North became east became southeast and it straightened out but still canted up.

"There's light!" Rich almost shouted, and Liz realized he was right. There was light up ahead, filling the tunnel.

"That's sunlight!" Eddie yelled, and suddenly they were moving faster, their aches and pains forgotten in a renewed burst of energy. Their hands dropped from one another, but still they moved together, climbing, breathing the sweet air, leaving the darkness behind.

There was one final, gentle half-turn to the left, and then they were pushing through green.

"What the hell?" Rich asked, as Eddie's mad dash forward left him fending off rebounding branches.

"Bushes?" Zachary asked, letting his shoulder lead, clearing a path for her through the sudden thickness of slapping branches and scratching leaves.

Liz didn't care. There was sky and sun above.

"Oh, wow," she heard Eddie mutter, and then they broke through the bushes and into the open.

CHAPTER 43

Zachary

Zachary burst through the bushes, still leading Elizabeth by the hand. Eddie, Matt, and Rich were a step ahead of him. Not expecting them to have stopped, he ran into Rich's broad back.

"Oh, wow," Eddie said, but Zack couldn't immediately see why they'd stopped or what Eddie was reacting to.

The feral screaming of their crazed pursuers echoed out of the tunnel behind them, galvanizing Zack to shove past Rich, Liz quick-stepping up to his right side.

The bushes behind them were a hedgerow that lined one side of a massive open courtyard. Starting in front of them and running off to the right was a gigantic reflecting pool, maybe as long as the one that separated the National Monument and the Lincoln Memorial in Washington DC, bordered by a foot-high marble balustrade. Each newel post appeared different, and though he was too far away to be sure, they looked to be carved in fantastic shapes. More fantastic and unbelievable, the pool featured marble statues standing whole and complete upon marble plinths. The plinths marched two by two the length of the pool, identical except for the statues adorning them, which seemed to be larger than life representations of the various gods of ancient Greek mythology. Poseidon and Zeus were the closest, recognizable by trident and lightning bolt, respectively. The others were farther away, faces he didn't recognize, names he didn't know, holding strange objects like an owl or a red-crested Spartan helmet.

To the left stood what could only be the broken-down palace they'd seen below ground, but rebuilt and renewed, a massive construction of limestone and marble, columns and porticoes, terracotta roofing and wooden doors and shutters.

None of these features, not palace or statues, neither the brilliant green of the grass beneath their feet nor the vibrant colors of the multitudes of flowers displayed in carefully tended beds around the balustrade, not even the cobalt blue sky above or the blazing sun almost directly overhead, had the immediacy of the dozen or so men arrayed before them.

They were a strange and threatening display of abstract creative anachronism. Garbed alike in helmets that covered the head but left the face exposed except for a thin bar that extended down from the center of the forehead over the nose, breastplates that matched the helmets for the dull sheen of bronze but were intricately fashioned to resemble the torso of a well-muscled man, and skirts fashioned of what appeared to be multiple blades pointing down, hanging almost to the knees, though they had the color of leather rather than metal, they almost captured the appearance of an ancient Greek military force. Almost, because each man also had what appeared to be a very modern Bluetooth earpiece covering the right ear. Almost, because though they were armored similarly, the clothing they wore under the armor differed as much as did their skin tones and facial structure. Two were Black, one was clearly Asian, and the rest were a hodgepodge of Caucasian varieties. Only one had the olive complexion commonly associated with Greek heritage. One wore jeans under his man-skirt, and one had what looked like board shorts hanging past the knee. Two wore sweat pants, one with the characteristic Nike swoop on navy blue, while the other's had Under Armour emblazoned in white on the side of each burgundy leg. Their footwear was equally diverse, with tennis shoes, hiking boots, and black leather combat boots in equal measure.

Only the man with the olive skin seemed to be fully in character with his dress, bare legs under the skirt, with feet covered by leather sandals secured by a leather thong wrapped in an intricate pattern around his lower legs, the image only slightly despoiled by his Bluetooth earpiece.

Whatever picture they strove to present was ruined entirely by the very black, deadly sleek, and undoubtedly modern weapons they held, some form of tactical assault rifle with a barrel over barrel style that usually meant grenade launcher and assault rifle or shotgun and assault rifle, though neither barrel appeared to have a bore large enough to fire any particularly large caliber round. A few of the men carried their weapons on their shoulders, or pointed at the ground, while only two were pointed at them, initially.

As the maddened cries echoed out of the tunnel a second time, much louder, more of the rifles came up to the ready, and the man with the Greek coloring said, "Come on, get behind us. Move."

He and Liz shared a brief look, deciding on the instant that being behind the men with the guns, no matter how they were dressed, was better than being between them and the frenzied horde coming up from behind. Eddie, Matt, and Rich didn't even hesitate that half-second, already scrambling to the sides, curving in an arc that would allow them to avoid being in the line of fire while still clearly showing they were complying with the man's instructions. Whether friends or foes, none of them had the capability to fight such well-armed men, and it would serve them best to follow orders, at least for now.

Scooting right as the other three circled left, Liz and Zachary got behind the armed force.

"Who are you, people?" Matt asked.

Instead of answering, the apparent leader addressed his men, "Remember, no more than two tags on any given target. If there's a third, I want it out immediately."

All of the rifles were at the ready now, stocks braced at the shoulder, a dozen men with heads tilted, sighting along their barrels, watching the hedgerow. Zachary remembered several times in his career when he'd been a part of a similar setup, hunkered down behind a patrol car with his pistol braced across the hood, hoping to be the one to bring down the perp, yet also worried that his might be the bullet that took a life. He clearly recalled being lectured by the academy instructors that if he ever lost that worry, it was time to retire.

The next round of screams was louder and clearer, no longer bouncing off stone walls but outside with them. The six-foot-tall bushes rustled and swayed, torn left and right by flailing arms. Zachary saw brief flashes of dark color behind the thrashing limbs, brown leather against green.

Then one burst through, and a second two feet to the side of the first. A third appeared and, for one brief moment, it was almost a recreation of the tableau from just a minute prior, when his group came upon the waiting men. But these were not normal men acting with rational thought, weighing consequences before acting. These were almost-pitiable men, driven past the point of insanity either by their own addictions or through the merciless actions of others. Zachary could see the pain in their faces, now that he had a moment to look, the tears in their clothing that made them look ragged, but which lined up with new, fresh lacerations and abrasions on the skin underneath.

"What are they?" Eddie breathed.

More rustling in the bushes, more screams, more bodies breaking through.

"Take them," the leader said.

Soft sounds came from the rifles, puffs of compressed air released in rapid succession, like a shootout in a paintball game. Some of the Freakers jerked, especially if they were struck in a shoulder or arm, but most just grunted from a chest impact. A few started forward, grimy hands outstretched, beseeching or eager to rend, it made no difference. Looking more closely, Zachary saw small darts appearing on their bodies as they jerked, tiny blue feathers spread out on the tails to aid flight. Some of the men managed a single step before collapsing to the ground, most dropped where they stood. More screams arose, and a second wave emerged, larger than the first.

"Jesus," Matt swore.

"We woulda been dead no matter what." Rich breathed.

The line of shooters in their strange, mismatched Greek garb took aim and fired again, all cool professionalism. Clearly this was a practiced exercise. The second group collapsed, often half-burying others beneath them.

A third group emerged, only three this time, and they too were put down.

The leader cocked his head to the right, finger reaching up to put pressure on his earpiece, listening to something. "All right, men," he said, "there's nothing else moving down there. Call the working party and help transport these men to recovery."

Something in the way he talked spoke of a sadness, as if he either was tired of this duty or didn't like the necessity of doing it.

Separately or in small groups, the gathered men shouldered their rifles and moved off. One of them, the Asian man, spoke briefly while tapping his ear. Others began dragging bodies off of each other, rolling them on the ground so that they were face up, removing darts and pocketing them in small satchels slung low on the hip.

Seeing his men attending to their duties, the leader turned to face them. Reaching up, he removed his helmet to reveal soft brown eyes, and a spill of dark hair liberally streaked with gray. His features were Mediterranean, long face, narrow nose, full lips.

"First things first," he said, "are any of you hurt?"

"Matt got scratched by a mountain lion," Eddie piped up.

"It's nothing," the accountant said, his face more closed than Zachary had seen before. He didn't trust the man yet. None of them did.

"Maybe, but we'll get it looked at. Cats are nasty." He took a moment to look them over, and Zachary was acutely aware of how bad they must look, dirty, haggard.

Unaware of any tension, or ignoring it, Eddie goggled at their surroundings. "I swear that's the same palace we saw underground, but that doesn't make any sense." He turned left, scanning the statues. "And look, there's Zeus and Poseidon, and Athena and Ares."

"You'll find twenty statues in total, if you want to go look," the man said. "King Minos owed much to Poseidon, but he didn't want to offend any of the gods."

Eddie looked a question to Zachary, silently asking permission. It said a lot that the man was willing to let one of them wander off. Maybe he could be trusted, or maybe the whole area was a lot more secure than it seemed. Still, it couldn't hurt to let the young man exercise his curiosity. He nodded, and Eddie moved away.

Strangely, the man suddenly seemed less confident, almost embarrassed, or perhaps remorseful.

"Look," he said, "there's no easy way to do this, so let me try to get through it."

Liz took his hand, holding it tightly. Matt and Rich edged closer to his other side. It was a clear statement. They may have started as strangers, but circumstance and experience had brought them together. Now, they stood as one.

"Good, that's good," he muttered. Then he seemed to collect himself. His back straightened, and he cleared his throat. "First of all, my name is Roman King. I work for Magellan Enterprises, as do all the other men here. But we're working to bring it down," he added hastily, no doubt seeing the sudden tension in Zachary's shoulders, probably in everyone else as well. "Damn, this is harder than I'd thought it would be."

He looked to his left, at the palace, perhaps seeking inspiration. "When most people come here, they already know what to expect. Except for the Freakers, of course."

"Brian called them that too," Matt interjected.

"Ah, yes, Brian. Looks like he did his job."

"You mean he got himself killed," Rich growled.

For the first time, Roman smiled. "No, Dan wouldn't let that happen. But you were supposed to think it did."

"I knew we shouldn't have trusted him," Liz snapped. "His whole story stunk."

THE DUNGEON

Roman held up his hands, trying to calm them. He eyes hardened though, a look of determination.

"You should thank him. He volunteered to make sure you got through the dungeon alive. And my brother, Daniel, put himself in the crosshairs to help. I—" He sighed. "This isn't going anything like I'd hoped."

He looked at them again, sizing them up. Then he focused on Liz. "Since you're the only woman here, can I ask if your name is Elizabeth Ott?"

"It is." She released Zachary's hand, stood up straighter. "But why would you need to ask? I'm sure your people have been watching us the whole time."

He seemed to relax a little at her answer. "And you, sir," he said to Rich, "what's your name?"

Rich looked over at Zachary. "You think he's screwing with us?" he asked.

Zachary shook his head, not taking his eyes off Roman. "No," he answered slowly, "but maybe he's seeing if we'll screw with him."

Roman said, "Ah, to hell with it." He looked at Zachary. "The young man called the other guy 'Matt,' so that must make you Zachary. Zachary Pavese, police detective?"

"It does," Zachary answered.

"Good, that's good."

"I'm Richard Cranston," Rich said.

"Okay then. Here goes." He took a deep breath. "You're here because we need your help to bring down Magellan from this side, while my brother and Brian work on their end to do the same."

"What do you mean, 'here?'" Liz asked. "We're just outside the labyrinth."

Roman smiled. "Look around, Ms. Ott. Listen. Feel the air. Do you notice anything?"

Zachary took the advice too. Aside from the softly murmured conversations of the men arranging the unconscious Freakers, there were no other sounds. Well, there was a soft trilling as of birds, far enough away that it was barely audible, and a low rustle as a gentle breeze stirred the leaves of the trees and bushes. The air was remarkably clear, the sky above a deep blue, marred only by a few high, thin clouds. He could smell the grass beneath his feet, and faintly, carried on the breeze like a memory of a memory, the briny scent of the ocean.

"There's just us," she said.

Rich gasped. "There's no cars, no planes, no sounds of—"

"It's like a deserted island would be," Matt said. "Nothing that stinks of civilization, just"—he sniffed—"clean air and ocean."

Roman was smiling. "Did you know that the island of Crete is the most populous Greek island, with more than six hundred thousand permanent residents? In 2017, more than twenty-eight million tourists spent time in Greece, making it the world-record holder as a tourist destination. More than five million came to Crete alone." He looked at them.

Eddie came running up, eyes shining. "Guys, you have got to come see this."

"And what's your name?" Roman asked.

"I'm Eddie…Eddie Ortios."

"A fine Greek name," Roman answered. "Tell them, what did you see?"

Eddie smiled. "It's like we've come out in the world's biggest medieval fair! Go look through the gates at the other side of the lake. There are people dressed in robes, guys in armor, people carrying jugs of water, even some boys running around with just loincloths on."

"How many cars did you see, Eddie?" Roman asked.

"None, no trucks either. I...I don't think the roads are wide enough for anything like that."

Roman laughed. "A problem which will continue to plague Greece for the next three thousand years."

Matt put it together first. "No, but...that's not possible." He ran down the hill, exhaustion forgotten, long legs eating ground as he raced down the long side of the reflecting pool.

"Mr. King...Roman...what are you saying?" Zachary asked, and felt a sudden painful squeeze on his hand.

"Time is a funny thing, Zachary. We've been grinding our gears here, trying to delay everything Magellan wants us to do, because we believe things should be left as they are. Then you got involved, investigating the homeless disappearances. Magellan makes plans to stop you, and my brother sends me a message, telling me to expect you, and you, Ms. Ott, as well. He had a message you see, that the two of you left, explaining why you did what you did, why you destroyed"—he opened his arms, indicating the palace, the bushes, the statues—"everything here."

"But we haven't," Zachary began.

Liz squeezed his hand again. "We will, though," she said.

Roman smiled again. "Let me be the first to welcome you to the island of Crete—"

"When?" Liz asked.

Roman's smile widened. "It's 1255 BCE, we think."

Epilogue

Michael

5118341128.

The text flashed on Detective Michael Jackson's cell phone. He didn't recognize the number that sent it, and it didn't matter. Lawson had come through.

Calling his friend by the nickname "Law" had been the key. He'd responded by calling Michael "Bad Boy," a joke from their childhood, where Michael got teased for every sensationalist paparazzi report about Michael Jackson, the singer and alleged little kid diddler. As his mother used to say, "I don't know if he's guilty or not, but when there's that much smoke, something's gotta be on fire." They never offered an apology for his name. Their Jackson family predated the signing of the Declaration of Independence, and his father was Michael Jackson before the name became synonymous with pop music. They were not, however, a New England WASP family of juniors or the thirds. Every Michael had a different middle name, and most of them ended up being known by (or yelled at) primarily by that name.

So now this text, from a strange number. It didn't matter if Lawson borrowed a friend's phone or used a burner. He'd sent the code that meant it came from him and told him where to meet.

05-11-83.

Their birthday. Both Michael and Lawson were born at the Norfolk General Hospital, moms rushed in by panting, panicking dads doing that hiss-hiss-puff-puff breathing. Their waters broke early, and both were attended by the same young doctor. Their fathers met in the waiting room, two anxious men pacing, alternating between joy at the birth of their firstborns and fear at becoming fathers. Their mothers were introduced while the babies rested in the nursery. Their families had not met previously, even though they lived in the same neighborhood, shopped at the same stores.

Michael and Lawson grew up as close as brothers. In a time where men changed jobs at the whim of the economy and families were uprooted to seek better opportunities in different cities, somehow the Jacksons and the Bechtols stayed solvent and stable. They attended high school together, went to parties together, and even shared a hotel suite with their prom dates. They chose different in-state colleges but got together almost every weekend. Michael pursued criminal law courses at Old Dominion University, while Lawson majored in cybercrime investigation at Norfolk State University, a growing field back in 2001 and 2002.

Though their passions within the realm of law enforcement differed, their goal to serve never did.

411-2-8.

Lawson had information for him and wanted to meet at their middle location, a place called the Sportsman's Grill in Williamsburg. That meant his friend was probably working in Quantico but felt he could make it to the restaurant by eight.

The text came through at three in the afternoon and gave a welcome break from the rough slog through the case files of the missing homeless persons. True to his expectations, Zachary's notes were meticulous and methodical. Clear lines of inquiry led from one "last seen" location to another. There were transcribed interviews with pastors and food service volunteers at various soup kitchens, restaurant workers who remembered giving a plate of leftovers to "this lady or that man" after closing, even the residents of a four-story apartment building that overlooked the parking lot of a Goodwill store.

"In the mornings," one woman was quoted as saying, "that parking lot would have ten, maybe a dozen, men hanging around. Some days there'd be a few trucks come by, and maybe they picked up some of the guys."

"What kind of trucks?" Zachary asked.

"Oh, you know, ladders on the sides, maybe a trailer behind them with yard equipment. Those men are doing God's work, Officer, offering productive labor to them that want to work. I'm not telling no tales on what companies they worked for."

"Did you notice anything else?"

"Well, one day it wasn't a truck, but a big old white van come by, real fancy-looking. It picked up every guy in the lot. I don't know who they worked for, but I think it was those guys' lucky day."

"Why's that, ma'am?"

"Well, the next morning weren't no one out there looking for work. The van came by again, but there wasn't no one to pick up, so it went on about its business."

"Did you ever see the van again?"

"Yes, sir. A bunch more. After a few days, maybe a week, more guys would start to show up in the lot, looking for work, as it were, and that van just kept checking, just coming around every day, and whenever there were people there, it would pick them all up and give them jobs. Now look out there."

"I don't see anyone, ma'am."

"You sure don't. Ain't been a homeless guy in that Goodwill lot for almost a month now."

Observations like this had eerie echoes in some of Zachary's other recorded interviews, with food kitchen managers observing that the homeless population seemed to be shrinking. One kitchen went so far as to project they wouldn't have a shortage of food come winter, as happened almost every year.

"It's weird, Detective. Our contributions haven't increased; if anything, we're a little short of where we were last year at this time. But we're using less, which means we're feeding fewer people."

It became clear, as Michael pushed through the notes, that Zachary's investigation had long since stopped being about a few specific missing people and had morphed into something much larger. He began trying to track the company responsible for the mysterious white vans, which he confirmed in multiple locations.

How the hell could the captain call this investigation a waste of manpower?

Even if nothing bad was happening, which seemed unlikely, it bore investigating, if only to satisfy the citizens who asked for the investigations to be opened. The argument would be between the missing homeless people's right to privacy, if they didn't want to be found, and the rights of their family members to a measure of justice, especially when their only desire centered around finding out if their dad, brother, aunt, or uncle was alive and safe.

The captain ignored Michael for the rest of the day, which suited him fine. He didn't have any pressing cases at the moment. Having just returned from vacation, he was expected to take a day or two to reacquaint himself with the particulars of any ongoing casework, to be available as a fresh set of eyes if another detective requested a consultation, or to pick up a new case if one presented itself. Several did, but rather than raise his hand to take them, Michael hunkered down. No one else said anything either. It felt like he'd walked into a roast session, where he was the subject, only no one was letting him in on it yet. He had no idea what the others knew, or thought, about Zachary's sudden change of circumstance, but their silence screamed. A good many of them would assume he was a part of it, until it was proven otherwise.

As the hours dragged on, the almost palpable sense of oppression grew stronger, until Michael felt like shouting at everyone in the room to just shut up and quit talking about him. And wouldn't that set people to talking, if he lost his cool like that?

Instead, he buried himself deeper in Zack's notes, with one eye to the little digital display in the bottom right corner of the computer screen. As soon as it showed five, he powered everything down, grabbed his notes, and headed for his car.

Once clear of the parking lot, he pointed his car northwest, and tried to lose himself in the slow and go crawl of commuters making their way to Norfolk, Portsmouth, and Hampton. Only after he'd left the city did he call Savannah, his wife, to let her know he would be eating out with Lawson.

"Give him my love," she said.

Assuring her he would, he hung up and tried to enjoy the drive to historic Williamsburg.

Unfortunately, it was still dreary and overcast, and the Monday afternoon rush hour traffic didn't allow for any relaxation. Attentive drivers could tell his was a police sedan, even without the telltale light bar on top or grille on the front, so there were always some people willing to leave the left lane and allow him to pass. Just as frequent, however, were those who never learned to watch the cars around them, or who had long since lost the ability to do more than clench the steering wheel in a death grip and try not to go over fifty, and those stymied his progress as much as they did everyone else's.

A part of him wanted to activate his siren, to turn on the bubble light on his dashboard, but he resisted the impulse. As anxious as he was to meet with Lawson, to learn...something...he didn't need to get there any earlier than he already would. Even with the traffic, he pulled into the parking lot of the Sportsman's Grill at a quarter to seven, more than an hour ahead of his scheduled meeting.

Sitting behind the wheel as the sun went down, the humid outside air drawing a battle line of condensation on his windows as it fought the car's air conditioning, Michael forced himself back into Zachary's notebook. Maybe he was grasping at straws. Maybe Zachary really had played him for a fool all these years. But if he wasn't, if he was innocent, then maybe the reason for this sudden disappearance and thick line of smear paint was this case. It was all he had to go on. Zachary never had more than one project at a time.

Reading through the fourth or fifth interview with a self-avowed, off-the-grid, homeless person, a collection of stream of consciousness rantings interspersed with vitriol at the entire societal system that schemed to reduce the average human to nothing more than thralls of an ancient alien overlord, Michael came across a drawing. In any other man's notes, it might have constituted a doodling, just an idle run off of mental energy while other parts of the brain were involved in deeper thinking. It was a perfect layover of two isosceles triangles, one tip up and one tip down, with an open eye in the center.

Though he couldn't place it at the moment, Michael knew he'd seen that image before.

"No words on the sides, Officer, my life on it. I seen three of them vans so far, pickin' up guys lef' and right. And they all had that sign on it. Do you think it means something?"

"Like a corporate logo?" Zachary asked.

"O' course you would think that, good li'l union lapdog like you. Does it mean something in their language, you think?"

"Whose language?"

"Why, the aliens what sent 'em, of course. They's the only ones what go around abductin' people."

A sudden pounding on the driver's window almost made Michael drop the notebook. Looking out through the fogged glass, he spotted the brown eyes and light mocha face of Lawson Bechtol, bending in to look at him, a large smile on his generous lips and the sound of his deep laugh coming through. Closing the book, Mike killed the engine, grabbed the keys and his notes, and climbed out of the car.

Though Lawson was closer to Zachary's height than Michael's, the larger man never let his friends feel small. He bent his knees just a little while giving his friend a hug, clapping him on the back.

"Just back from Disney and already sneaking off to meet me? What will Savannah say?" he joked.

"She sends her love," Mike answered. "Thanks for doing this."

"No worries, bro. Let's get inside before the sky opens up again."

Despite its reputation as one of the better places to eat in Williamsburg, the Grille wasn't crowded on a Monday evening. At their request, Lawson and Michael were seated in a booth near the kitchen. A twenty-dollar bill given to the hostess, and a second to their wait-

THE DUNGEON

ress, ensured no one would be seated next to them for at least an hour. They each ordered a tall draught beer and waited until the drinks arrived to start talking.

Lawson took a long pull on his beer, watching Mike over the rim of the glass, before setting it down. He removed a small spiral-bound memo book from the hip pocket of his slacks, flipped it open, and said, "Okay, what did Zack get himself into?"

"Thank God," Mike muttered.

"What? You didn't think I'd believe this crap about him, did you?"

"I had no idea. I'm not sure what I believe," Mike admitted.

"Well, you should trust your gut more. I've been telling you that since high school."

Mike nodded, took a pull of his beer, and immediately felt better, like he'd passed through a dark cloud of doubt and suspicion and only now could begin to feel the sun shine on his face again.

"So what makes you a believer?" he asked.

Lawson held up one his large hands and started ticking off fingers. "First, you're you. Even when you don't listen to your gut, your gut is one of the best judges of people I've ever met. You like Zack. You liked working with him. And what's more, you respected him enough to introduce him to me, and I know you don't bring just any old stray out with me.

"Second—and if you tell anyone else this, I'll deny it to my dying breath—I've made a habit of checking into any new partners you tell me about." The counting fingers turned to a pat of placation as Mike started to protest. "I know you never asked it of me, but you're my bro, even if I got all of the looks. There's some other guy out there supposed to be watching your back? Well, I check to make sure he hasn't ever let anyone else down, know what I mean?"

Mike nodded. "I'd probably do the same, if our jobs were reversed."

"Damn right you would," Lawson said. "If you let me get killed because you didn't run a quick background on my partner, I'd haunt you so bad Sam and Dean couldn't save you."

Mike chuckled.

The fingers went back to ticking. "Third, when you asked me to look up his name today, I found all kinds of crap that I can promise you wasn't there when I looked before. Not just the story by the drunk Army guys, but the black marks on his service record. Hell, even that weird tie-in to the dead high school girls. Zack went to Bayside High School, not Kellam; he wouldn't have been at those parties."

Michael exhaled. "Okay, so this is a smear campaign. But why?"

Lawson spread his hands. "I might have something for you there, but first let's deal with the smear part. This isn't a campaign. This is a brutal blitzkrieg assault on your friend." He smiled again. "But that's where they screwed up."

"What do you mean?"

"I'm talking about the long game here. In data terms. What you put on the Internet today is there now. In twenty-four or forty-eight hours, depending upon the server, it'll be archived. Still retrievable, but not necessarily front and center. Gotta keep the space open, you know."

Mike nodded.

"Take another forty-eight hours, call it a data half-life, and those recent archives are archived again. You follow?"

"I'm not sure."

"Let's put it this way then. When I ran the initial background check on Zachary, it created a point in the data stream where his data was accessed. It put a bookmark in the archive. When I went back to look at that search again, it was the same as when I last saw it. None of the negative marks, none of the incendiary mentions of his name, were present five years ago, not even the administrative warnings for brutality and drunkenness, even though those charges supposedly happened before I looked him up."

Mike looked up. "Can you use that to prove these are false charges?"

"Man, I won't even have to do that."

"You won't?"

"Nope." Lawson took another long pull of his beer, smiling as his friend waited for him to reveal what he knew.

"You're enjoying this a bit too much," Mike observed dryly.

"All right. You win. Remember what I said first about data half-lives, how it gets archived, then archived again?"

"Yes."

"It's a very general thing that basically backs up copyright requests, licenses, that sort of thing, in case there ever comes a time when a doctor is charged with practicing without a license, for example. We can look back at a point in time and see, even if there's no paper documentation, if there was an existing license for a person. In copyright law, it lets us pinpoint when a copyright was applied for, even if it's a difference of minutes, in order to determine who did something first. You follow?"

"Okay, but I don't see how something this general could help Zachary. All of those charges would be localized to law enforcement," Mike said.

"This is their big mistake. Whoever wants to destroy Zachary went so far as to create an entry in a book."

"Yeah, I wrote down the title, *From Slum to Soldier*."

"The copyright on that book is 2012, but here's the thing. The book didn't exist in 2012. It didn't even exist forty-eight hours ago, in our most recent archive."

"Wait," Mike said, "you're serious?"

"Yup. And given the likelihood that it's just a planted nugget on the Internet, one more search item guaranteed to pop up on Google for anyone interested in looking up our boy Zack, I ran a query through the copyright office. Turns out they have no record of a request for a copyright on any work by that name. Neither do they have a digital or physical copy of the body of the work, which is a requirement to prove originality and authorship."

"So it's all fraudulent."

Lawson nodded, finishing his beer. "Okay, so here's where you offer to pay for the rest of the evening."

"I'm listening."

"I had a pretty dull day planned, you know, the glamorous life of cyber crook catching. There's been a lot of rumbling about this international corporation spending more money than they should have access to, so I've been tasked with running a little hide and seek in their finances, see if everything's on the up and up. Routine stuff. So I programmed a mole and set it to digging, and while it did its thing, I retrofitted a different data mining program to see if I could unscrew poor Zachary.

"I made a hard copy back up of the clean archives, so they can't be manipulated, then loaded that data in as a clean boot. I set my program to seek out and erase any entries into Zachary's history that were inputted more than ninety days after their effective date. I also set it to log all such erroneous entries and made a database searchable by entry type, be it commendation or administrative action, date of entry, and host gateway address where the entry was placed."

Mike made a motion with his hand, swishing it in the air over his head.

Lawson laughed. "Yeah yeah, I know, too much inside baseball."

"Baseball, I understand."

"Here's the two-part takeaway, then. First, every one of those negative entries you saw in Zachary's record met the criteria of erroneous as I had programmed it, meaning all of them were inputted more than ninety days after their supposed date of occurrence. As such, every one of them has been removed from the FBI files, and those changes should push out to local law enforcement at the next archive cycle, which is tonight at midnight.

"Naturally, I have copies of all of it, so that if it should turn out something needs to be in his record, we can put it back."

Mike glared for a second, then let it go. He couldn't be mad at Lawson for that. Despite his belief in Zachary, he wouldn't be much of a law enforcement officer if he didn't try to maintain at least a modicum of objectivity.

"So Zachary will be cleared? Tomorrow?"

Lawson nodded. "Electronically, at least. But you still don't know where he is or how to find him. And you haven't heard the second thing my program discovered.

"There were over two dozen negative remarks on his record, spanning over ten years. Yet all of them were uploaded within seconds of each other, basically pushed into his record in much the same manner that

I'm pushing the corrections. It was a data dump, a mass file upload that occurred at midnight this morning."

"But there was already a fat FBI file on the captain's desk when I got in," Mike said.

"I wasn't aware of that, but it makes sense. This was a coordinated effort. A bunch of people had to be involved to give this kind of access to an outside computer. Though it pains me to say it, at least one of them had to be FBI."

"Wait. Outside computer?"

"Yeah, from a set of gateways that all originated from a foreign IP. You'll want to get me another beer for this next part."

Mike signaled the waitress and ordered the drinks. As she returned, he asked for ten more minutes before they'd be ready to order dinner.

"Mmm, that's good stuff," Lawson said. "Okay, remember me saying my top priority today was sniffing around a multinational, looking for funny accounts, since they've been spending a lot of money lately?"

"You said more than they should be able to."

"Exactly. So imagine my surprise when I get this list of addresses from my reverse dataminer and it matches the host address of the company I'm investigating."

"Wait. You're saying the company with the big pockets is the same one that tried to set up Zack?"

"Bingo."

Remembering the doodle in the notepad, Mike opened the notebook on the table.

"Is this their logo, by any chance?"

Lawson whistled.

"Who's the company?" Mike asked.

"Have you ever heard of Magellan Enterprises?"

THE DUNGEON

To Be Continued.

Don't miss Rob Horner's first novel, *Brightness*, a supernatural thriller, available on Amazon.com in paperback and Kindle formats.

A desperate father is terrified when his oldest daughter begins seeing things no one else can see. As the hallucinations take on more clarity, he discovers there are greater forces in the world than modern science can explain. With his family in danger, Michael Richards must accept the destiny chosen for his children, and protect them at all costs from dark forces intent upon destroying them.

Author's Note

A lot of work goes into a title like this, finding the facts that make the fiction all the more believable. The descriptions of the Minoan palace at Knossos wouldn't be possible without the actual fieldwork of Sir Arthur Evans, who in 1900 began digging holes in a hill on Crete. Months later, he'd uncovered a large portion of what he thought was the Palace of Minos, though he discovered relics that seemed to predate even the Greek myths he'd hoped to confirm or disprove. In *Minotaur: Sir Arthur Evans and the Archaeology of the Minoan Myth*, Joseph MacGillivray provides not only a biography of this great archaeologist, but also gives an excellent view into the political and military concerns during the time of Evan's discovery.

Though the labyrinthine complex of the palace at Knossos remains the top contender for the title of Home to the Labyrinth, there are two other contenders. The Labyrinthos Caves at Gortyn and another cave complex at Skotino on the Greek mainland still draw exploration and comparison, while amateur and professional archaeologists alike look for something to tie the past and present together. I've taken the liberty of placing the labyrinth at Evans' site—well, below it, actually—but this is purely artistic license, and shouldn't be taken as confirmation of any kind.

Finally, coming into this book, I thought everything was carbon-dated. If you wanted to know how old something was, you had it carbon-dated. It never occurred to me to actually look at those words and realize that something would need to have a carbon base for it to be carbon-data-able, which means this wouldn't work for metallic objects. After a little research, I came across numerous articles describing methods of dating leaded bronze objects using voltammetry, a science which develops rates of decay for signals through metallic objects to determine the length of corrosion time. First proposed in 2017 by Spanish and Portuguese scientists, the method has been confirmed to be accurate by comparing metallic objects found alongside other objects dated with the traditional carbon method.

With the book stuff out of the way, please allow me to offer thanks once again to my wife and children, who put up with a lot of nights where I'm either "half-there," clattering away on my laptop, or sequestered in my office. Their belief and love drive me and are the biggest blessing any man can know this side of heaven. Thank you to Covenant Books for the tireless efforts of their staff, notably Sheree Pruett in acquisitions, and my amazing liaison, Tina Collins, who kept me on target and on deadline. Thanks to you, dear reader, for coming with me into this story and for meeting this colorful cast of characters, some of whom have grown on me just as much as they have on you, even those who left us all too soon. We'll see most of them again in the conclusion to this story, and one or two may pop up in a future work.

Last but certainly not least, a thank you to God above, from whom all things are possible, even this crazy dream of becoming a writer.

ABOUT THE AUTHOR

Rob Horner is a Virginia Beach native and former Navy Avionics Technician who spent twenty years working with electronics before finding his calling in medicine. Now a nurse practitioner in a busy urgent care clinic in Hickory, North Carolina, he splits his time between work, writing, and family. He is blessed with a loving wife, two sons, and three beautiful daughters. He and his family live in Lenoir, North Carolina, along with a cat, a rabbit, a guinea pig, three dogs, two horses, and seven chickens. His social media activities include Facebook, Twitter, where he can be found @RobHorner8, via e-mail at fansofrobhorner@gmail.com, or on his blog at https://Rob-Horner.com.

Printed in June 2019
by Rotomail Italia S.p.A., Vignate (MI) - Italy